29
Gk

GATE OF HIS ENEMIES

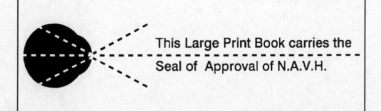

This Large Print Book carries the
Seal of Approval of N.A.V.H.

GATE OF HIS ENEMIES

1840-1861 THE ROCKLIN FAMILY AT THE DAWN OF THE WAR BETWEEN THE STATES

GILBERT MORRIS

THORNDIKE PRESS

A part of Gale, Cengage Learning

Detroit • New York • San Francisco • New Haven, Conn • Waterville, Maine • London

Copyright © 1992 by Gilbert Morris.
Scripture quotations are taken from the King James Version of the Bible.
Thorndike Press, a part of Gale, Cengage Learning.

LIBRARY OF CONGRESS CATALOGING-IN-PUBLICATION DATA

Morris, Gilbert.
    Gate of His Enemies, 1840–1861 : The Rocklin Family at the Dawn of the War Between the States : By Gilbert Morris. — Large Print edition.
        pages cm. — (The Appomattox saga ; #2) (Thorndike Press Large Print Christian Historical Fiction)
    ISBN 978-1-4104-6338-8 (hardcover) — ISBN 1-4104-6338-9 (hardcover)
    1. United States—History—Civil War, 1861–1865—Fiction. 2. Large type books. I. Title.
PS3563.O8742G3 2014
813'.54—dc23   2013033796

Published in 2014 by arrangement with Barbour Publishing, Inc.

Printed in Mexico
1 2 3 4 5 6 7 18 17 16 15 14

GENEALOGY OF THE ROCKLIN FAMILY

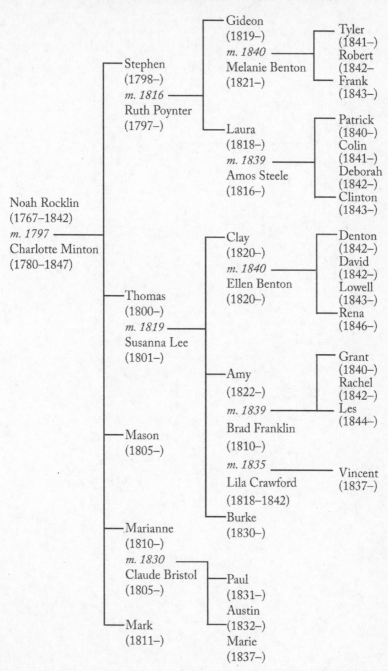

Noah Rocklin
(1767–1842)
m. 1797
Charlotte Minton
(1780–1847)

Stephen
(1798–)
m. 1816
Ruth Poynter
(1797–)

Gideon
(1819–)
m. 1840
Melanie Benton
(1821–)

Tyler
(1841–)
Robert
(1842–
Frank
(1843–)

Laura
(1818–)
m. 1839
Amos Steele
(1816–)

Patrick
(1840–)
Colin
(1841–)
Deborah
(1842–)
Clinton
(1843–)

Thomas
(1800–)
m. 1819
Susanna Lee
(1801–)

Clay
(1820–)
m. 1840
Ellen Benton
(1820–)

Denton
(1842–)
David
(1842–)
Lowell
(1843–)
Rena
(1846–)

Amy
(1822–)
m. 1839
Brad Franklin
(1810–)

Grant
(1840–)
Rachel
(1842–)
Les
(1844–)

m. 1835
Lila Crawford
(1818–1842)

Vincent
(1837–)

Burke
(1830–)

Mason
(1805–)

Marianne
(1810–)
m. 1830
Claude Bristol
(1805–)

Paul
(1831–)
Austin
(1832–)
Marie
(1837–)

Mark
(1811–)

Genealogy of the Yancy Family

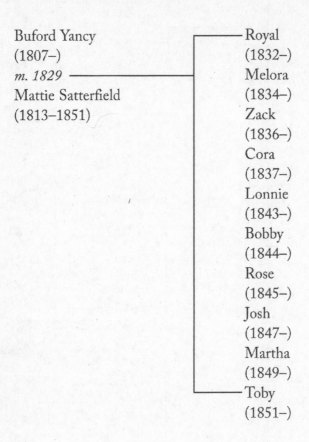

Buford Yancy
(1807–)
m. 1829
Mattie Satterfield
(1813–1851)

Royal
(1832–)
Melora
(1834–)
Zack
(1836–)
Cora
(1837–)
Lonnie
(1843–)
Bobby
(1844–)
Rose
(1845–)
Josh
(1847–)
Martha
(1849–)
Toby
(1851–)

■ ■ ■ ■

PART ONE:
WASHINGTON

■ ■ ■ ■

CHAPTER 1
MR. PRESIDENT

Washington was dark as Deborah Steele walked slowly down the street that led to her home. The clock in the belfry of the Congregational church her father pastored sounded out nine times, but the voice of the bronze bell seemed muffled by the darkness and the fog that enveloped the city like a thick mantle.

Deborah was tired. The news of the fall of Fort Sumter in South Carolina had brought a heaviness to her — as it had to Washington and the North. Some of her fellow abolitionists were celebrating the event, rejoicing that at last a blow could be struck that would set the slaves free. Most felt it would be an easy matter: Send a few of our fine Northern troops down and teach the Rebels a lesson! Won't take thirty days — then we'll have a land free from the awful bondage of slavery!

Somehow Deborah had sensed that the war would not be like that, and a heaviness

9

had quenched her lively spirit. Though the April night was not cold, the dampness of the air and the thick canopy of fog sent a shudder through her. Finally she reached the walk that led to her home and paused for a moment, gazing into the darkness, remembering.

It wasn't that long ago, only a few nights, that she had come home on a night very much like this one — and a man had moved toward her out of the shadows, calling her name.

Deborah remembered how the sudden appearance of the man had sent a startling fear through her. Washington, since the fall of Sumter, had been filled with crowds drinking and celebrating the beginning of the war. Deborah knew there had been several nasty incidents.

"Who are you? What do you want?" she had demanded. The reply had astounded her.

"It's me, Deborah — Dent Rocklin!"

As she relived that moment, Deborah closed her eyes, feeling once again the shock that had rolled over her. Dent had moved toward her, telling her that he'd had to come, had to talk with her. Even in the murky darkness broken by a pale yellow gleam from the streetlamp, she had been

10

able to see the tension in his lean face. He was the best-looking man she had ever known — tall, lean, with the blackest hair possible and strongly formed features.

That night, though, he had looked worn and tired. She had wanted so much to reach out to him . . . but had known she must not.

Deborah moved restlessly. She did not want to remember any more. Passing a trembling hand over her eyes, she wished things could have been different. But it had seemed, from their very first meeting, as though Deborah and Denton had been destined to fall in love.

She remembered vividly every detail of her visit with her uncle Gideon's family, of her time in Richmond and at Gracefield, the Rocklin family home just outside of that city. She clearly recalled how startled she had been by the powerful attraction that had sparked between Dent and herself. Even the fact that Dent was a fiery advocate of slavery and secession while she had been active as an abolitionist hadn't weakened that attraction. There had been some violent arguments between them, and finally, to avoid the strong feelings that Dent was creating in her own heart, Deborah had fled back to her home in Washington.

In a scene that could still tear her to pieces, she had said, "You'll forget me, Dent — and I'll have to forget you!"

She had left then and come home. Once back with her family, surrounded by all that was familiar and safe, she had been sure that was the end of her encounter with Dent Rocklin.

Then, a few nights ago, he had shown up, right here by the gate in front of her home.

She had scolded him, telling him he should not have come.

"I know that," he had said wearily. Looking at him, Deborah had noted that he was changed somehow. He had lost his light-hearted air. Then he had spoken the words that struck her heart a fierce blow. "Deborah, I'm in the Confederate Army."

Deborah breathed deeply, struggling with the tears that suddenly threatened to overcome her. The Confederate Army. Dent was in the Confederate Army. How could she love a man who would be fighting to destroy everything she believed in?

She had sent Dent away that night, but not before he had grasped her arms and leaned down, his eyes fierce. She could still hear his words ringing in her ears.

"Now you can tell me it'll never work. Tell me I'll probably get my head blown off. Your family would never agree. My family would never agree. Then tell me I'll be fighting against your brothers. Give me a dozen reasons why we can't be together. Go on!"

Trembling in his grasp, Deborah had answered, "It's all true! Everything you say is true!"

"I know it is, Deborah. But I know one thing more. Something you've overlooked."

"What —"

And then he had pulled her close and kissed her, cutting off her words — and filling her with the same stirring that had shaken her back in Virginia. Despite herself, Deborah had responded to Dent's caress.

When he had finally lifted his head, he had held her close, whispering, "That's what you've forgotten, Deborah!"

Everything within her had longed to say, "I love you, Dent! We'll make it somehow!"

But she could not. The obstacles were too overwhelming. There was more than just their love at stake. There was her family — parents, brothers, and all the others — and all that she had worked for, including the freedom of the slaves.

She had told him that, told him she could never turn her back on her family, told him that there were all kinds of love . . . and sometimes one kind of love works against another.

She had known Dent had wanted to take her in his arms again, but he had not. Instead he spoke to her simply with a great determination.

"Deborah, I love you. And I know you love me. I've got to go, but this isn't the end. When the war is over, I'll come for you."

He had whirled and walked away, pausing a few feet away, almost hidden in the shadows, to say, "Don't forget me, Deborah. After it's over, I'll be coming for you!"

Then he had disappeared, swallowed up by the shadows. Deborah now stood peering into the thick grayness where he had disappeared and struggling with the emotions sweeping over her. Then a break in the sky allowed the full moon to appear. It poured down a silver bar of light . . . until a ragged cloud racing across the sky closed it off, and the darkness moved across the land as Deborah turned slowly and walked into the house.

"Amos, I'm worried about Deborah."

The Reverend Amos Steele looked at his wife over his coffee cup, startled by the abruptness of her statement. He was a tall man with a pair of piercing hazel eyes, which he fixed on his wife, Laura. "Why, what's wrong with her? Is she ill?"

Laura Steele gave him an impatient look. She was a small woman of forty-three, still well formed and in almost every way the opposite of her husband. Her round face and dark blue eyes concealed a streak of humor, and she was quick in both emotion and action.

"Amos Steele," she said with a trace of asperity, "if you'd get your head out of your theology book and look around at the world, you'd be —"

She paused so abruptly that he looked at her with surprise. "I'd be what?" he asked. Then he sighed and put his cup down. "Well, you might as well say it, Laura. I'd be a better father. And a better husband, too, I expect."

Laura jumped to her feet and ran around the table. Throwing her arms around him, she cried out, "No! That's not what I meant! You've been a good father and a fine husband!"

But Steele, shaking his head, put his arm around her and said, "I know I get too caught up in my work, Laura. But I'm not so blind that I don't know what you mean about Deborah." He rose and walked to the window, staring out at the pale sunshine that was tinging the fog with a trace of

15

color. Without turning to look at his wife, he said, "She's in love with Denton Rocklin."

Laura came to stand beside him, slightly surprised at his quickness. She knew him for a man who got so deeply involved in the work at hand that he forgot to eat. And for ten years the work at hand had been the abolitionist movement. Laura believed in the movement, too, and had worked at her husband's side, but she was aware that he had sacrificed much for the cause. Now she said in a voice edged with worry, "Yes, she is. Or she thinks she is, and that can be just as bad."

"Denton's a fine young man," Amos said slowly, "but —"

He didn't finish. He had no need to. Laura had been a Rocklin before she and Amos had married, and that family had divided into two branches. Thomas Rocklin, Denton's grandfather, had founded a dynasty at Gracefield Plantation outside Richmond. Thomas's older brother, Stephen, had left the South and founded the Rocklin Ironworks. Laura, Stephen's only daughter, along with her brother, Major Gideon Rocklin, formed the Northern branch of the Rocklin family. Stephen and Thomas had their differences, like any brothers, but these

16

were minor compared to those that the clouds of a civil war had brought in the past few years.

The worst situation that had faced Laura and Amos was the attraction of their daughter, Deborah, to Dent Rocklin. When Deborah had accompanied her uncle Gideon and his family to Gracefield, nothing had been further from her parents' minds than a love affair between their daughter and a staunch Southern firebrand. But it had happened. They had not spoken of it much, as though leaving the thing alone would cause it to go away. But unfortunately, it was still very much alive.

"It would be tragic for both of them," Amos said heavily. He was a stern man — or at least was possessed of a stern manner — and he knew a great deal. But the one thing he had not known was how to get close to his children. Now that they were all grown, or almost so, the minister felt a gnawing regret that he had not done more with them. He turned and put his arms around Laura in a gesture that surprised her.

"With God all things are possible," he said quietly. "We'll trust Him to bring Deborah — and Denton, too — through this thing." Stepping back, he said, "I have some papers to take to Gideon. I thought it would be good if Deborah went along." He hesitated, then added, "We could talk, perhaps."

"That would be very good, Amos," Laura said and smiled. "Perhaps you'll get to see the new president. He stays very close to Gideon's commanding officer, General Scott."

"He's very busy, Gideon says. Sucked dry by office seekers." Amos shook his head, adding, "Mr. Lincoln's got a heavy load to bear. We must hold him up in prayer." Then he kissed Laura on the cheek and smiled. "You've held this family together, my dear. Don't think for a moment that I don't know that." Then, embarrassed by the scene, he gave a halflaugh and left the room. "We'll be back for dinner early," he said over his shoulder.

When Amos found Deborah, he noted how tired she looked. But she was ready enough to accept his invitation. The main thoroughfare of the city was four miles long and one hundred sixty feet wide. The Capitol, with its unfinished dome topped by a huge crane and encircled by scaffolding, blocked the straight line of Pennsylvania Avenue, which led eastward from the expanding Treasury Building and the Executive Mansion, as the White House was called.

Deborah thought of the gracious streets of Richmond as she and her father drove past the Center Market at Ninth Street, a place that was taboo for the elite because the brothels and gambling houses there operated more or less openly. As Amos drove, he kept well away from sections such as Swampoodle, Negro Hill, and the alley domains that were inhabited by rabble-rousers, thieves, and cutthroats. Fortunately they did not have to pass the iron bridges that linked the two sections of the city. He couldn't avoid, however, passing along the Old City Canal, a fetid bayou filled with floating dead cats and all kinds of putridity and reeking with pestilential odors. Cattle, swine, sheep, and geese ran at large everywhere. Only two short sewers served the entire city, and often they were so clogged that their contents backed up into cellars and stores on the Avenue.

Steele drove into the open area beside the Executive Mansion, got down, secured the team, then helped Deborah down. "General Scott has a temporary office here so that he can be close to President Lincoln," he said as they walked down the broad sidewalk. "That's the War Department over there."

He motioned toward a square building off to their left. "But Gideon says the president wants to know everything that's going on in the military."

He led her up the steps of the two-story building, past the massive columns of the semicircular portico. They were met by a sergeant wearing the flamboyant dress of a Zouave. As he inspected Steele's pass, the father and daughter took in the soldier's scarlet pants held up by a crimson tasseled cord, the short, richly embroidered vest, and the tasseled fez that perched on the man's head. After he had allowed them entrance into the mansion, Deborah said, "He looked more like a music hall entertainer than a soldier, Father."

"I think so, too, and so does your uncle Gideon," Steele agreed. "He's one of Commander Hawkins's Zouaves from the Ninth New York Infantry Regiment — or so Gideon told me. He says lots of outfits have gone wild over the French uniforms." He led her down several halls, up a long stairway, and finally to a door marked MILITARY ADJUTANT.

"This is General Scott's office," Amos said. "I hope Gideon is here."

The two of them entered, and a corporal sitting at a desk covered with papers asked for their pass. Then he rose, saying, "Major Rocklin is meeting with his new commanding officer, Mr. Steele, but I think he'd want to see you." He disappeared into one of the doors leading to an office, then came back at once, saying, "Go right in, Mr. Steele. And you, too, ma'am."

Deborah stepped into the room, which was much plainer than she had expected. There was only a desk, four chairs, and a walnut bookcase against one wall. Two officers, one of whom was her uncle, were standing by a large map on the wall. Gideon came to Deborah at once, holding out his hands. "Well now, this is fine! My favorite niece!"

Deborah had always idolized her uncle Gideon. He was an intensely masculine man, strongly built and straight as a ramrod. A heavy-duty man with big hands and legs, Gideon was well able to overwhelm any soldier under his command. He was a fine soldier, decorated for courage in Mexico. But what was more important to Deborah was the fact that he had always been partial to his niece, spoiling her whenever he got the chance.

Taking his hands, she swiftly reached forward and kissed his cheek. "You owe me a visit." She smiled impudently. "Don't

21

think you can get out of taking me to the next review with a little old compliment!"

"You'll have your own way, of course," Major Rocklin responded, smiling fondly. "You always do." Then he turned toward the tall officer. "I'd like you to meet my new commanding officer, Colonel Laurence Bradford. Colonel Bradford, this is my brother-in-law, Rev. Amos Steele, and his daughter, Deborah."

"I have heard of your work, Rev. Steele. It's a pleasure to meet you." Bradford shook hands with the minister, then bowed to Deborah, a smile on his lips. "And you, too, Miss Steele."

Deborah put out her hand impulsively, and he took it at once, his long fingers closing around it firmly. He was, she thought, no more than thirty-five, which was young for his rank. He had a sharp, aquiline face, with a pair of large brown eyes overshadowed by heavy brows. He was not tall, but his erect posture made him seem so. As he released her hand, he said, "Your uncle is a godsend, Miss Steele. I asked General Scott to give me a man who knew everything about the army, who was patient with new commanding officers, and who would keep me from any fatal blunders. I didn't request that he have an attractive niece, but happily,

Major Rocklin meets all the requirements, even that one."

"Colonel Bradford has been commissioned to raise a new regiment," Rocklin said, nodding. "I might add he is doing so out of his own pocket."

"Actually, I'm just a dowdy businessman," Bradford said with a shrug. "But I want to do my part in this war that's coming up."

"Most commendable of you, sir!" Amos Steele said warmly. "I am certain that God will bless your efforts and your battalion."

"Father may not like it so well," Gideon said with a sudden grin. "Colonel Bradford and I are going to his plant to make an appeal for volunteers to serve with the new unit. He'll hit the ceiling when we entice some of his best workers away."

"Do you think they'll volunteer?" Deborah asked. "Leaving a settled job for a chance to get killed isn't very prudent, is it?"

"It doesn't seem to work that way, Miss Steele," Colonel Bradford said. "Most men are sick of their jobs anyway, and the chance to put on a uniform and play soldier — well, a lot of them like the idea. They'll only enlist for three months, you know. They can go to summer camp and let all the pretty girls fuss over them. Most of the men we've recruited so far are worried that the thing won't last long enough for them to see any action."

"They don't have to worry about that," Rocklin said soberly. "It won't be like that at all."

Colonel Bradford laughed and winked confidentially at Steele and Deborah. "The major is the best soldier General Scott could find, but he's also the gloomiest! Come now, Rocklin, you know what the South is like. Some of your people are there, you've told me. Now how can a mob of half-civilized mountain rubes be made into a trained army?"

"Ask my niece," Rocklin said at once. He was taking very seriously the instructions of his commanding general that Colonel Bradford was to be humored.

"He's worth thousands, Rocklin," Scott had growled. "Gave an enormous sum to President Lincoln's campaign fund. Now he wants to play soldier. Well, sir, he's paying well for the experience — but you keep him from getting our people killed!"

Gideon Rocklin fully understood politics of this sort and had gotten on well with the new colonel.

"So, Miss Rocklin," Bradford said, fixing his large eyes on Deborah, "did you see any of the South's military?"

"No, not really." The subject was painful to Deborah, so she added only, "But they're a very determined people, Colonel. Don't underestimate them."

"Certainly not," Bradford said, smiling. "Not with Major Rocklin to keep me from doing so."

"When will your regiment be ready, Colonel?" Amos asked.

"Very soon. If we can get a good response at Mr. Rocklin's factory and a few other places, we'll have a full complement by next week." An idea came to him, and he turned to face Deborah. "Miss Steele, I must call upon you as a patriot for a very important military service!"

"Sir?"

"Next Friday, you really must come to the rally at your grandfather's factory."

"Oh, Colonel, I couldn't!"

"Maybe you should, Deborah," Major Rocklin interjected. "The only man who spoils you worse than I do is my father. I'll need all the support I can get if we take his best men away. Come along and soothe him for us."

"Father? Do you approve?"

"Certainly! And, gentlemen, if you'll pardon my pride, I must point out that my daughter has been a most effective speaker at our abolition rallies. You might let her give a patriotic speech and see what happens."

"Excellent!" Colonel Bradford cried, slapping his hands together with pleasure. "It's settled, then. Now if we can —"

He was interrupted as the door burst open, and the corporal on duty scurried in, excitement making his eyes large. "Sir! It's General Scott — and the president is with him!"

"Well, show them in, Corporal!" Colonel Bradford snapped at once. As the corporal disappeared, he said, "Well, Major, perhaps our little talks with the general weren't all wasted, eh?"

The door opened and Deborah recognized the two men at once. General Scott was an old man, worn from his service to his country. He had been a hero of the War of 1812 and again during the Mexican War, but time had marked him, and now he was a huge whale of a man, weighing more than three hundred pounds. His face was lined and flushed with the effort of movement.

But it was the other man who drew the gaze of everyone: Abraham Lincoln, president of the United States. He was very tall, Deborah saw, and as awkward as rumor and a hostile press had stated. But he was not ugly. His face was homely as a plowed field, but there was such strength in the cadaverous cheeks and such compassion in the deep-set brown eyes that Deborah could not think of him as ugly.

"General Scott, this is Rev. Amos Steele and his daughter, Deborah." When Scott rumbled his greeting, Gideon said, "Mr. Steele, Miss Steele, the president."

Deborah put out her hand and found it swallowed in the huge hand of the president. He held it gently, his warm eyes seeking hers, then said, "Major Rocklin, you'd better have a guard for this young lady. She's much too pretty to be wandering around our rough soldiers unchaperoned."

"I'll do that myself, Mr. President," Colonel Bradford said at once. "Miss Steele has just come back from Richmond, I understand. She's going to attend our rally next Friday."

"You've been in Richmond?" Lincoln picked up on Bradford's statement. "A fine city. What was it like, Miss Steele?"

Deborah was so flustered she could hardly think. The lean face of the president was turned on her, and she knew that he was not making idle conversation. "It's a very disturbed city, Mr. President. People are . . .

well, they're not what they were when I was there a few years ago. It's like a fever."

"Yes, that's it," Lincoln agreed, nodding. "It's here in Washington, too. Good people, but they've lost their balance." Then he shook off the gloom that had come to his gaunt face, saying, "Tell your grandfather I will be expecting a great many rifles from him, Miss Steele. He's a fine man, strong for the Union."

"Yes, sir, I'll tell him."

Tactfully Gideon said, "Well, Mr. Steele, thanks for stopping by."

"Oh — yes!" Amos said hastily. He pulled a sheaf of papers from his inner pocket and thrust them at Gid. "Here are the papers you agreed to look over, Gideon. Now we'll be going."

"I'll be by to pick you up for the rally next Friday, Miss Steele," Colonel Bradford said quickly. "Will two o'clock be convenient?"

He was, Deborah realized, a clever man. He had caught her in a position that would have made a refusal awkward, even unpatriotic.

"Two will be fine, Colonel." She nodded, then added with a glint of humor in her eyes, "I suppose it will be all right if I bring my mother along?"

"Why — ah, yes —" Bradford stumbled over the words, and when the pair left, Lincoln gave the new officer a knowing grin.

"You were outmaneuvered that time, Colonel. You'll have to study up on your tactics."

"I propose to do so, Mr. President!"

As Amos and Deborah left the building, Deborah said thoughtfully, "He's had considerable success with women, the colonel."

"How could you know that?" Steele asked, giving her a startled glance.

"I just know it, Father."

Steele studied her, a baffled look on his face. "Well, are you going to the rally, knowing that?"

"Oh yes. He's Uncle Gideon's commanding officer. I have to be nice to him. Besides, perhaps I really can be of help."

"Help in getting men to volunteer?"

"Yes."

"And what if you do convince a man to volunteer — and he gets killed?"

She did not answer, and he said quietly, "I'm sorry, Deborah. I shouldn't have said that." They didn't speak again until they were in the carriage, and then Steele said, "This isn't going to be just a soldiers' war, Deborah. All of us are going to be touched by it."

They drove by the Washington Monument, which was just a stubby base. Suddenly, for no reason she could think of, Deborah said, "I'll bet George Washington would have hated all of this!"

CHAPTER 2
DEBORAH'S RECRUIT

Will Kojak's shack was squeezed between two other shabby frame buildings that were no better than his own. Living cheek-to-jowl with the Sullivans and the Millers created tensions that grated on his temper, but the battered three-room house he rented was so frail that it was kept from falling only by his neighbors' shacks. Every time he paid the monthly rent of ten dollars, he cursed the landlord's representative harshly, vowing that he'd move if improvements weren't made. But they never were, and he never did.

The landlord, a wealthy politician named Jennings, attended a large downtown church and kept himself and his family well away from the Swampoodle district. This section lay on the south side of Pennsylvania Avenue and was composed of slums, brothels, gambling clubs of the worst sort, and a scattering of small, grubby shops and businesses. On the north side of the Avenue were the dwellings of the respectable people of Washington, along with the offices of government.

Pennsylvania Avenue itself was a massive Sahara of dust during the dry seasons and a river of mud and filth during the wet days. It served not only as a street, but as a metaphysical line, as well — for those who lived on the south side in the Swampoodle district were as isolated from the well-to-do segment of Washington's populace as if they lived on the moon. They might cross the Avenue to attend the presidential inauguration — as they had done by the thousands a few weeks earlier — but they turned back to their side of the Avenue when such things were over.

A thin, pale light outlined the city at dawn on Friday, April 19, 1861, just as Noel Kojak, Will's eldest son, appeared at the door of the house. The boy paused and admired the symmetrical rise of the skyline. He had come to get wood for the cookstove, but it was typical of Noel to momentarily forget his task in admiring something he considered beautiful. There was nothing in his appearance to attract attention, for he was no more than average height, and his features, though regular, were not handsome. His short nose and high cheekbones evidenced the European roots of his family, but the steady gray eyes and shock of light brown hair came from other roots.

Old Red, the rooster kept in a small pen in the backyard, broke the silence of the morning with a shrill clarion cry, and the suddenness of it shook Noel from his rapt attitude. Walking over to a pile of wood, he picked up an ax and, with quick, economical movements, split the cylinders of beech into small wedge-shaped slices. It was a task he liked, for with each sharp blow of the ax, the short lengths of beech fell as splinterless as a cloven rock. Noel didn't stop when he had enough for the first fire, but cut enough to last the day. He knew that his mother would have to chop the wood if he didn't, and to help her any way he could was as natural to him as his habit of staring at things that seemed unusual or beautiful.

Piling his arms high with wood, he went back into the house and deposited the load in the wood box. Quickly he built a small fire. When it was blazing nicely, he picked up a book and began to read by the dim light filtering through the single window that broke the wall on the east side.

At once he was lost, unaware of anything except the words on the page. He had that sort of mind, one that gave him the ability to lose himself in books. Noel had never heard of Coleridge's words about enjoying literature, that one must cultivate "the willing suspension of disbelief," yet he was adept in applying the principle. In an instant, he could leave the shabby world of reality in which he was trapped, entering instead the world of the imagination. When he read Sir Walter Scott's romances, he was in a world of romance and color, far away from the grubbiness of Washington with its dust and mud and poverty.

The fire crackled, but Noel did not look up. If he had, he would have seen a bare room with rough planks adorned only with a few cheap prints. He would have seen Sarah, his seventeen-year-old sister, asleep on a shabby horsehair couch, and fifteen-year-old Grace swathed in a dirty blanket along one wall. The stove occupied a space on one wall, and a table and an assortment of patched-up and rickety chairs took up most of the space. There were two doors on the back wall, one leading to a small room where Noel slept with four brothers, and the other leading to his parents' bedroom. There was no grace or comfort in the place, but Noel's family seemed not to miss those things. Noel had realized that he himself was aware of the shabbiness of life in Swampoodle only because he had caught a glimpse of other things in the world of literature.

A woman came into the room, pausing to look at the young man. Though she was only in her late thirties, her brown hair was streaked with gray, and her brown eyes had the look that chronically ill people sometimes have. Too many children and too little comfort had worn her down, though there were still faint traces of beauty in her worn face. She was thin and slightly stooped, but as she spoke there was no evidence of discontent.

"What a nice fire!" she exclaimed; then she moved over to pat the shoulder of the boy, who lifted his head, startled. "You don't know how nice it is to get up with a fire already made, Noel," she said. For one moment she stood there, her worn hand on his sturdy shoulder, looking down on him fondly. There was a special bond between these two — always had been since he was a small child. Except for six-year-old Joel, her other children, for the most part, were not demonstrative. Anna Kojak received little thanks and few gestures of affection.

Then, as if embarrassed by the scene, the woman laughed, saying, "Better get breakfast. It's late." As she began to prepare the meal, the two of them talked quietly. He spoke of the book he had been reading, and she listened, smiling as his face grew animated with excitement. The smell of the food began to fill the room, and one by one the sleepers awoke. "Better go get your brothers, Noel," Anna said.

Noel said, "All right, Mother," then rose and went into the small room, where he found Joel awake and staring at him with enormous eyes made larger by the thinness of his face. "Breakfast, Joel," Noel said, ruffling his fine brown hair. As the boy arose and pulled on his ragged clothes, Noel spoke to Peter and Holmes, ages sixteen and eleven. They occupied a double bunk bed and came tumbling out with sleepy protests. Ignoring them, Noel turned to the large bed where Bing lay, his face up, his mouth open, snoring loudly.

"Breakfast, Bing," Noel said loudly, but Bing only snorted, flopped over, and buried his face in the thin pillow. "Come on, boy," Noel said, pulling at his brother's thick shoulder. "Got to get moving. We're going to have to hurry to get to work on time."

"Lemme alone!" Bing thrashed about, striking at Noel's hand. When the older boy kept at him, he said angrily, "All right, all right! I'm awake." He shook his head, which brought a streak of pain that pulled a groan out of him, then swung his feet to the floor. "Bring me a cuppa coffee, will you, Noel? I've got the granddaddy of all hangovers!"

Noel said, "Sure," then went to the kitchen and poured a cup of black coffee into a chipped mug. Taking it back, he handed it to Bing, who took it with an unsteady hand. Moving slowly, he swallowed the black liquid carefully, keeping his eyes shut. Noel watched to be sure his brother was awake. At nineteen, Bing was the most handsome one of the family. He was tall and muscular, with a shock of wavy black hair and a pair of large brown eyes set in a well-shaped head. "Better get to the table before it's all gone," Noel warned, then left the room.

When he got back, his father came stumbling in, his eyes red, a tremor in his hands. He had been with Bing at the taverns until early morning and was in a surly mood. He slumped down at the table and grasped the coffee that Anna put before him, saying nothing to anyone. Nor did anyone speak to him, for he had a terrible temper when he'd been drinking.

"Sit down and eat while it's hot," Anna said, and then as they found their places and waited, she bowed her head and said a brief blessing in a hurried voice. When she finished, Will Kojak stared at her with a hard look in his dark eyes, half inclined to belittle her. But his head hurt too much to bother, so he began stuffing the scrambled eggs into his mouth.

The rest of the family ate hungrily, for there was never enough. Sarah was a dark-haired girl, already shapely and giving evidence of real beauty. She began begging her parents to let her go to a dance that was being held, but Anna said sharply, "No, you're too young, and I know what sort of men will be there." Sarah slammed her knife down, her dark eyes bright with anger, but one sharp word from her father brought her to a sullen silence.

Grace, at fifteen, could have almost passed for a boy. She kept her dark auburn hair cut short and wore the cast-off clothing of her older brothers. Now she stuck her tongue out at Sarah, her dark eyes sparkling as she taunted, "Now poor old Jimmy Sullivan won't have a girl, will he?"

"Keep your mouth shut!" Will Kojak said harshly, then looked at Anna. "Any more eggs?"

"Just a little," Anna said, and she gave him what was left in the bowl. Noel looked at her sharply, knowing that she had given her own breakfast to his father.

Will had just finished wolfing them down when Bing came in and sat down. He complained when his mother gave him two pieces of bread and some gravy, but his father said, "Get to the table if you want to eat."

"Wouldn't do any good." Bing dipped the bread into the gravy, put half of the piece of bread into his mouth, then said, "Guess we'll get something to eat at the rally today."

"What's a rally, Bing?" Joel asked, his head barely clearing the table.

Bing grinned at him despite his headache. "It's a meeting where the bigwigs try to get dunces like me to go into the army."

"You're going to b–be a soldier?" Pete asked, his mouth open with surprise. He was a thin, gawky boy, so plain and awkward that his father often said he was worthless. He stuttered slightly, which embarrassed him so much that he usually kept quiet. Many thought he was slow of mind, but actually he was rather bright.

"No, stupid, I'm not going to b–be a soldier," Bing mocked him. "I'm not dumb enough for that. I can make more in one fight than a soldier makes in six months." Bing, whose real name was Michael, had been a street fighter since he was twelve.

Then he had been taken up by a sharp operator, and before long he'd had four professional fights and won three of them. His purses weren't enough to live on, but he was certain that day would come.

Anna stared at him, then asked her husband, "Will, do you think many of the men will volunteer?"

"Yeah, I guess so. Dumb dogs!"

"Why are they dumb?" Sarah demanded. "Ain't we got to go down and whip the Rebels?"

"What do I care what they do down South?" Kojak snapped. "Let 'em own all the slaves they want to. Most of them live better than we do." The thought seemed to anger him, and he was off on one of his tirades. "Look at this swill we have to eat. Down there they got fresh vegetables and plenty of meat. Just work a few hours in a cotton field and then it's back to a nice warm cabin. I say let Abe Lincoln go down and get himself killed if he's got such a bleedin' heart for the poor old slaves!"

He raved on, then got to his feet, saying, "Come on. We ain't gonna fight in no war, but there'll be plenty of food and maybe a little whiskey at that rally!"

As he put on his hat, Anna came up to him and asked nervously, "Will, I need a little money to buy some food —"

He pushed her away so roughly that she stumbled and would have fallen if Noel had not caught her. A sudden flare of anger showed in Noel's eyes, and seeing it, his father scowled. "You gonna do anything about it?"

Noel hesitated, then shrugged. "No," he said quietly, but after his father and Bing left, he reached into his pocket and found a few coins. Slipping them into his mother's hand, he said, "Today's payday, Mother. I'll have more when I come home tonight."

She blinked back the tears, saying, "You never have a penny to spend on yourself, son."

He smiled easily, looking very young, then kissed her. "When I'm rich, I'll buy you the prettiest blue dress in Washington," he said, then turned and left the room.

The three Kojak men joined the other men who were trudging along the dusty street, all headed toward the factory section. Bing and his father spoke of the fun they'd had the night before, but Noel kept silent. His mind was far away, reliving what he'd read before breakfast.

"You're looking lovely today, Miss Steele . . . or may I call you Deborah?"

Colonel Laurence Bradford looked with frank admiration at his passenger. He was accomplished in the art of charming women, and as soon as he had handed Deborah into a carriage driven by a smartly dressed sergeant, he had begun his campaign. He studied the young woman as a soldier might study the terrain and measure the strengths and weaknesses of an opposing force. It was an old game with him, the only one — except for making money — that he truly enjoyed.

What he saw sitting next to him was a young woman of nineteen who was dressed in a deep blue crinoline dress trimmed with pink satin ribbons. She had a heart-shaped face and a pair of eyes such as he had never seen before. Large, almond-shaped, and shaded by thick lashes, they were a beautiful violet color. Her lips were red and shapely, and her complexion was smooth and beautifully set off by thick blond hair. A beauty!

Bradford had become satiated with the professional and slightly worn beauties of the stage. Now, as he glanced at Deborah Steele, he saw her as a refreshing change — as well as a challenge to his masculine pride.

"Why, yes, and I'll call you Colonel Bradford," Deborah answered him with a smile.

She was aware of the man's charm, and equally aware that he was a man who had captivated many women. She had agreed to come at the urging of her uncle but was now looking forward to the rally. She gave Bradford a steady look as he protested that she should call him Larry, interrupting to say, "You must be very proud of your new life. I know you've been successful in business, but serving in the army is very different."

"Oh, I'm proud of my regiment, Deborah," he said with enthusiasm. "It'll be a refreshing change from business."

"Have you thought much about the danger?" she asked. "Men do get killed in wars, you know."

"You just don't know how tough the world of business is!" he shot back, laughing. "It's worse than any war."

"Oh, not really," she objected. "On the battlefield men are going to be killed. Even officers."

"I fancy I can take care of myself!"

"What about our men?"

"Why, you can't make an omelet without breaking a few eggs, Deborah," he said with a careless wave of his hand. "Some of the boys are going to take a bullet, but that's to be expected."

As he went on, it seemed to Deborah that he took the war too lightly. Still, she did not argue with him.

"There's my grandfather's factory." Deborah pointed out a low brick building with tall smokestacks that belched huge puffs of rich, black smoke. "The rally will be around on the other side, Grandfather said." She directed the colonel down a side street, noting that the large area next to the factory was already swarming with men. Bradford found a place for the buggy, got out, and helped Deborah to the ground.

"There's Grandfather over there with Uncle Gideon," she said, and the two of them made their way through the crowd to where the men stood.

"Well, granddaughter, you're all dressed for the occasion." Stephen Rocklin gave Deborah a kiss and smiled at her fondly. He was a thickset man of sixty-two, with a pair of steady gray eyes in a face characterized by blunt heavy features. There was something ponderous about him, not only physically, but in other ways. He was slow to make up his mind, but once his decision was made, nothing could stop him. He had come to Washington from Richmond as a young man, knowing nothing but how to grow cotton. From his first job as a janitor

44

at a small foundry, he had progressed steadily in the business world — and now the Rocklin Ironworks was one of the most profitable factories in the North.

"This is my commanding officer, Colonel Bradford. Sir, this is my father, Mr. Stephen Rocklin," Gideon said.

Bradford took the strong hand that was offered, saying, "An honor, sir! Your son must have told you that I'm the most inept officer in the army, but he's taking good care of me."

Stephen Rocklin studied the officer for a moment, as was his custom, then smiled. "Not at all, Colonel. Gideon is very pleased about your new endeavor. And I congratulate you on your spirit." A shadow fell across his broad face as he added, "I'm afraid it's going to be hard on all of us, this war."

"Oh, I hope for better things, sir!" Bradford smiled confidentially, looking very official in his dress uniform. "All we need are good men — such as some of these fine fellows here." He waved his hand at the crowd milling around in the large open space. "Very generous of you to allow us to make our appeal to them."

"Well, the decision is theirs," Rocklin said. "I understand it's an enlistment for only ninety days. I've told the men that those who enlist can count on having their jobs back when their time is up."

"Splendid!" Bradford exclaimed. "We should have the Rebels properly thrashed long before that time."

Bradford did not catch the look that passed between the two Rocklin men, for he was looking out over the crowd. Deborah, however, saw that both her grandfather and her uncle were skeptical of the officer's judgment. She herself had been reading the writings of Horace Greeley, the powerful owner and editor of the *New York Tribune.* Greeley was totally confident that the Northern military forces would crush the Rebels, and he was already printing large headlines that said "ON TO RICHMOND!"

"Would you like to address the men now, Colonel? Or perhaps you'd rather let them get the eating and drinking out of the way?" Stephen asked.

"Let them eat and drink, by all means," Bradford responded. "They'll be more ready to volunteer on full stomachs. While they're doing that, there's a matter of firearms I'd like to discuss with you, Mr. Rocklin — an idea that I've been toying with."

"Certainly, sir." Stephen went to the

raised platform and called for quiet, and as soon as the talk ceased, he said loudly, "Men, there's plenty of food and refreshments. Eat hearty, and when you've finished, we'll hear a word from Colonel Bradford and my son, Major Rocklin. But now let's enjoy the food. Rev. Stoneman, will you ask the blessing?"

After a tall minister said a prayer, the men moved at once to the long tables laden with sandwiches of all kinds, barbecued beef, fresh pork, and vegetables of all sorts. The men ate and drank, talking at the top of their lungs and enjoying the break from the hard labor of the foundry.

Colonel Bradford took the mill owner off to one side, speaking in an animated fashion, and Deborah's uncle said, "Come along, Deborah. Let's get something to eat."

He led the way to one of the tables, and when the roughly dressed working men saw them approach, they stood back, making a place for them. A short, thickly built man with a pair of sharp dark eyes was serving the men, but he paused long enough to say, "Right here, Major Rocklin. Let me fix you and Miss Steele a plate." This was John Novak, Stephen Rocklin's secretary and second in command. Piling the plates high with food, he smiled fondly at Deborah, whom he knew well from her visits to the foundry. "If you give me another smile like that, Miss Deborah, I may forget myself and be one of the first to enlist as a soldier."

"Why don't you, Mr. Novak?" Deborah dimpled at him. "It would do you good to get away from your dusty old books. And Caroline would marry you if you came home with a chestful of medals!"

Major Rocklin laughed with delight, for John Novak's pursuit of Miss Caroline DeForest was one of the longest-lasting on record. "Better do it, John," he said, taking his plate. "No woman can resist a uniform!"

The men around the table were taking in their conversation, and as soon as Gideon got his food, one of them began to question him. "Think it'll be a hard fight, Major?"

Gideon began to speak, and for a time Deborah stood there awkwardly balancing her plate. It was impossible to eat with a plate in one hand and a glass of tea in another. The men were managing, some of them, by placing the glasses of beer provided for them on the ground and swooping to pick them up to wash the food down from time to time — but that would not do for her.

She moved away from the table, threading her way through the men, but found no place to sit. Most of the men were gathered into small groups, enjoying their food as they talked, but she could not join any of those groups. Finally she saw a lone figure sitting on the low platform that had been built especially for the speakers. It was located on the far end of the open space, far from the tables, and the man looked isolated and somehow a little lonely. Balancing the glass, she walked toward the platform. As she approached, he looked up with a startled glance, then came to his feet.

"Hello," Deborah said with a smile. "I can't seem to manage all this food standing up. May I join you?"

"Oh — yes, miss!" He was, she saw, a young man with a round face and a pair of large gray eyes. He glanced at the seat. "It's a little dusty, I'm afraid. Let me clean it for you." He whipped out a handkerchief that was none too clean and used it to remove most of the dust. "That's about the best I can do, miss."

"Thank you. That's very nice." Deborah sat down, put her glass down, then started to eat, only to notice that the young workingman was still standing, staring at her uneasily. "Oh, do sit down!" she urged. "My name is Miss Steele. What's yours?"

"I'm Noel Kojak." He sat down gingerly,

then picked up his plate and began to eat.

"Have you worked here long, Mr. Kojak?" Deborah asked. She did not see his reaction, nor would she have understood it. In all of his twenty years of life, nobody had ever called Noel *mister,* and he could not believe that this beautiful young woman would do so. He felt more uncomfortable sitting there than he had ever felt in his life! He had never been in the presence of anyone from the upper class, much less in the company of a beautiful and wealthy young woman. He had read about such women, but now that he was in the presence of one, he had the strange feeling that he had stepped out of the real world and into one of the romances he had read.

Belatedly he realized that he had not answered her question. "Oh, I've been working here for eight years, miss."

Deborah turned to look at him more closely. "Why, you must be much older than you look!"

"I'm twenty, ma'am."

"But —" Deborah did some quick arithmetic, then said with some surprise, "You can't have come to work when you were twelve years old, surely!"

"Oh yes, miss! That's what I was, twelve."

Deborah had never spoken with a workingman of Noel Kojak's class before. She had read of some of the abuses of the working class and had been indignant over them. But those were stories; this young man was flesh and blood. Forgetting her food, she stared at him — which made him more nervous than ever. "You were only a child! What could a child do at an ironworks?"

"Oh, there's plenty to do, Miss Steele," Noel replied. "I was a wiper when I first come to Rocklin's. I cleaned the machinery and oiled it."

"Isn't that a little dangerous?"

"Oh, a little, I suppose. Fellow has to watch what he's up to." Noel paused, and a thought came to him, making his face serious. "My best friend, Charlie Mack, he got caught up in a crane when he was only ten. Pulled his arm off right at the shoulder."

A vivid picture of what the young man had just related flashed before Deborah's mind, which caused her to put down her sandwich suddenly. "I see," she said evenly. "So you didn't get to finish school?"

"Finish?" Noel smiled for the first time. "Bless you, miss, I never even got to start!" Then he saw the look of dismay in the strange violet eyes of the girl and said hastily, "But I learned to read and write. My mother taught me. She's a fine scholar, my mother!"

Deborah was intrigued by Noel. She would never have noticed him in a crowd, and without meaning to, she pictured the young workingman with his shabby clothing and hard, calloused hands beside Dent Rocklin. At once she told herself she was a fool. Dent was one of the most handsome men she had ever met, and it was foolish to put this young man who had had no advantages alongside the Southern aristocrat. It was a bad habit she'd fallen into, thinking of Dent too much, and she grew angry with herself. "What do you do at the mill now?" she asked quickly.

Noel was ordinarily a quiet young fellow. He lived a secret life through his books, and no one except his mother had ever shown any interest in hearing about what he did. At first he spoke in monosyllables, but Deborah had learned much from her father on their trips to meetings around the country, and she was very good at drawing people out. Now she began to encourage the young man, and as he got over his hesitancy and began to speak, she found a picture beginning to form in her mind. A picture that, had it been put on a daguerreotype by the photographer Matthew Brady, might have been titled "Portrait of a Poor Working-man."

Noel painted a vivid picture of poverty, of the everlasting battle for enough bread to live on and for keeping some sort of roof overhead. His words showed Deborah the lack of anything more than the bare necessities of life, the starchy diet and the hunger for something sweet and rich to break the monotony. He opened her eyes to long, weary days of standing at a machine and working until dusk, only to plod home to a shack without any conveniences whatsoever. As he talked, she envisioned life without the finer things to which she had become so accustomed, things that she accepted as thoughtlessly as the air she breathed.

It was a disturbing picture, and when Noel's voice trailed off, Deborah did not know how to respond. To gain time she asked, "What do you think about this war, Mr. Kojak?"

"I—I'd like it better if you'd call me Noel, Miss Steele," he said nervously. Then he thought of her question, and his answer surprised her. "Well, I don't know much about it, of course. But I don't think it's right for one man to own another. I guess if it takes a war to stop that . . ."

Deborah stared at him speechlessly. This

was the philosophy she and her family had struggled so to share, yet it was brought down to the simplest statement. This crude young man had said more than all the speeches and books; his simple words had eloquently framed what she believed.

"And you'd risk your life for that cause?"

Noel hesitated. He had never seriously considered going into the army — he bore such a heavy responsibility at home — but the woman's words stirred something in his spirit. An awareness that he had long ago buried began to rise and became a fervent desire to do something that mattered, something with color and life and excitement!

"If it wasn't for my mother, I'd go in a minute," he said, his eyes steady. "She'd — she'd have a hard time without me."

Deborah waited, and he spoke of the hard, bitter life his mother endured. He said nothing about his father, but the girl could guess what the woman's life was like. As he spoke, something came to her — an idea that she tried to ignore but that kept returning. Finally Noel said hopelessly, "I'd enlist right off, but my family would go hungry without my wages."

Deborah hesitated, then suggested carefully, "Noel, if you really want to go, I'd be

glad to help your mother with expenses."
She saw the shock and refusal in his face,
then added quickly, "It's not so much to
do. I have an income, and what I want most
is for men and women to be free. I can't
fight as a soldier, but I'd feel like I was doing my duty if I made it possible for a man
to do so."

Noel was dumbfounded. This conversation was stranger than anything he had ever
read in fiction! He sat there thinking hard
and slowly began to discover that the desire
to enlist had been deep inside of him. He
longed to do something worthwhile, to be a
soldier, to fight for what was right!

"I'll do it, Miss Steele!" he said suddenly,
his lips pressed together firmly. "It's only
for three months, and if you can help my
mother until I get back —"

"Oh, Noel, are you sure?" Deborah asked
at once. "It might seem romantic, but you
could be killed or maimed!"

Such things were far from Noel's mind.
The decision had come so suddenly that he
scarcely believed what was happening, but
he knew that it was going to happen. "I
know, but some have to risk that," he said
simply.

A rush of excitement swept over Deborah,
and she stood up. Noel rose with her, and

55

she put out her hands. As he took them, she felt the hard calluses and the strength of his hands. "I'll pray for you every day, Noel, and I'll write you, too — and you won't have to worry about your family! I'll see after them!"

Noel had never felt anything like Deborah's hands. They were softer than he had known hands could be. As he held them and looked into her violet eyes, he could not speak for a moment. Then he said huskily, "I'll do my best, Miss Steele. I won't let you down, nor the army either!"

They stood there, two people so far apart in birth and breeding and every circumstance that it would have been difficult to picture them ever having anything in common. But somehow Deborah knew that this young man was tied to her from that very moment on!

CHAPTER 3
THE WASHINGTON BLUES

"I think it's about time to make our appeal, Colonel."

The rally had been a tremendous success. At least, the men had eaten and drunk incredible amounts of food and beer, and Gideon felt that it was time to get on with the matter. "Some of them have drunk so much beer they'd volunteer for a trip to the moon," he commented dryly to Bradford.

"All the better, Major," Bradford said cheerfully. He was in excellent spirits, having gotten what he considered to be a good response from Stephen Rocklin. Looking over the milling crowd, he nodded confidently. "Suppose you say a few words first. Being the son of the owner, you should have some influence. Then I'll come on and make the appeal."

"Very well, Colonel." Gideon and Bradford made their way to the platform, where they found Deborah talking with a young worker. "Come on up here, Deborah," Gideon said. "Time to get this thing moving." He helped her up onto the low platform, then turned and held his hands up, calling in his best parade-ground voice, "Attention! Will you all move in toward the platform, please." When the crowd had moved forward and was standing quietly, he said in a more moderate voice that carried easily to the outer edges of the crowd, "Have you enjoyed the refreshment?" When they roared back, "Yes!" he grinned and glanced at his father, who had remained on the ground. "You can thank my father for that, and for the time off from work. Let's give him a round of applause, for Colonel Bradford and I are grateful, as well."

The crowd was feeling expansive, and they lifted a cheer for the owner.

"Fine!" Gideon said, then began his remarks. He spoke simply, reminding the men that the country was facing a crisis and that it would take a sacrifice from all its citizens to meet it. There were no promises. Gideon made it clear that the life of a soldier was not an easy one.

Finally he said, "Men all over the North are rising up to meet this crisis, and none has done so with more honor or spirit than the man I introduce to you now." He sketched Laurence Bradford's career as a successful businessman and politician, then said, "It would have been easy for this man to just sit back and let others do the job, but he did not. He left the profitable world of business and, out of his own pocket, is raising a regiment, the Washington Blues. It gives me great pride to introduce my commanding officer, Colonel Laurence Bradford. Will you give him a warm greeting and listen carefully to what he has to say? I know you will!"

The men burst into hearty applause as the tall officer stepped forward, but quieted down as he began to speak. "Men, the country needs you!" he began, then swept into a passionate appeal. Deborah stood there beside her father, listening carefully. She had heard many fine speakers in the abolitionist movement — from the fiery Lloyd Garrison to the famous black orator Frederick Douglass — so she was a good judge of speakers. Bradford was quite good, she decided. He had been a man of power for a long time and had learned how to move the minds of men. Now he proved that he also knew how to stir their emotions.

He had, she knew, been listening to the opponents of slavery, for he used some of the more graphic examples of the evils of that system. After he gave several classic examples of terrible beatings, of families being torn apart and sold to different owners, of the misuse of black women by white owners, the crowd responded as Bradford expected: They grew angry and restless. Then he began to outline the future of the Washington Blues, and what a rosy picture he painted! Beautiful uniforms, marches in parades, comradeship with other good men, a military life that was colorful and exciting — all these things Colonel Bradford set forth in glowing terms.

Gideon leaned forward and whispered to Deborah, "Sounds sort of like a summer picnic, doesn't it? Makes me want to enlist myself!"

Deborah shushed him quickly, for she was caught up in the colonel's rhetoric. From time to time she let her eyes fall on Noel Kojak, who stood far off to one side of the crowd. He was listening carefully to the speech, his eyes glowing with an inner desire. Deborah thought of their talk, and a feeling of pride came to her that she had been able to do something to help the cause.

Finally Bradford said passionately, "I call upon you to follow the flag of your beloved country. And I promise you, men, that as the flag goes forward against the enemies of our nation, I will be with you! I will be in the first line, and if necessary, I will shed my blood to defend this great nation of ours!" He looked around with flashing eyes, then lifted his voice, crying out, "Are you with me? Will you help me put down this terrible rebellion?"

A shout went up, and at once Bradford said, "Fine! You are heroes! Now my sergeants have a table over there, and the papers are all ready. If you'll go there, you can enlist right now."

The ranks of the workmen broke, and many headed for the table, where the trimly dressed sergeants waited. Bradford turned to say, "Well, it looks as though it went very well, doesn't it, Rocklin?"

"Yes, I think we'll get some good men," Gideon agreed. "I think I'll go over and help the sergeants, if you don't mind."

"Certainly! I'll be here with Deborah if you need me." Bradford waited until Rocklin left, then turned to say, "Well, you didn't get to make your speech, did you?"

"Oh, I didn't really expect to. The men need to hear from soldiers, not from women."

"I disagree," Bradford said as he shook his head. He was still heady with excitement from the speech and put his hand on her

61

arm, saying, "A man needs a woman to fight for, Deborah. That's what it's all about, isn't it? When you strip everything else away, what's left is what men and women feel for each other. Isn't that true?"

"The war is over slavery, Colonel, not love."

"Why, Deborah, don't you think that men and women should be free to love where they will?"

"Why — of course, but —"

"And slaves are not free, are they?"

"Well, no, they're not."

"So the war is about love!" He pressed her arm, adding, "I'm just a businessman turned soldier, Deborah, but what I need most in the world is a woman's love. All men need that, and I think you know it."

Deborah found herself unable to answer. He was, she realized, a clever man, as well as a most attractive one. She smiled faintly but said only, "Love is important, Colonel. All women will admit that." Then because she felt he was in some way pressing her, she said, "Let's go down where the men are signing up, Colonel."

"All right, but only if you stop calling me Colonel." He grinned suddenly, adding, "I feel like an impostor as it is. Men like your uncle have earned their ranks with years of service, and here I come, just a rank impostor. So if you'll call me Larry, I'll feel a little less uneasy."

He seemed so genuine that she agreed. "Very well. Let's go meet some of your new soldiers, Larry!" He took her arm possessively, helped her down to the ground, then led her through the throng across to the tables.

Noel had listened to the speeches intently, and his resolve was strengthened by Colonel Bradford's words. As soon as the call to sign up came, he moved at once from the edge of the crowd toward the tables. He was not the first — both tables were surrounded by men clamoring for attention. He stood there as the sergeants, smiling but firm, said, "All right, we'll have a line, men. Right here, now, and don't worry — we'll get you all into the Washington Blues soon enough!"

Noel moved to take his place in the line forming in front of one of the tables, but as he did so, a hand suddenly grasped his arm. His father's voice rose above the talk of the men: "What the devil do you think you're doing!"

Will Kojak had been drinking freely from the barrels of beer that had been provided. He had told Bing, "We can eat anytime, but this is good beer!" During the speeches, he had stood at the back of the crowd with Bing, scoffing at the words of both officers, laughing at the response when the call to enlist came. Then he had caught sight of Noel in the line, and his anger flared up. "Get yourself out of that line, you young idiot!" he snarled, yanking at Noel so powerfully that the boy was jerked off balance.

Noel pulled himself up, very much aware that his father's voice had drawn the attention of the crowd. His face flushed, and despite himself, there was a tremor in his limbs. He had always been an easygoing boy and, unlike Bing, had never crossed his father. But now he could not give way.

He faced his father and said in a voice that was not quite steady, "This is something I have to do."

"Have to do? What the devil do you have to do with the slaves?" Kojak's anger was always just below the surface, and something about Noel's refusal made it boil over. He had given up trying to force Bing to do anything, for the young man could put him on his back with ease. But Noel had never challenged him. Until now.

Kojak began to curse, and he moved to grab his oldest son by the collar, intending to drag him off bodily.

"Better stop that, Rocklin!" Bradford said quickly. "He's going to destroy the spirit of the recruiting."

Gideon agreed and moved toward the pair but was shouldered aside by his father. Stephen Rocklin had already decided what to do and, heavy as he was, moved quickly to stand beside the father and son. "Kojak," he said quietly, but loudly enough for the crowd to hear. "You've got a right to do as you please. But you won't quench the spirit of any man who wants to fight for his country, not as long as you work for me."

Kojak glared at him, his brutal face blazing with wrath. Deborah was standing to the left of her grandfather and could see the anger burning in Kojak's eyes. Wondering if the man would strike out at his employer, she thought of what Noel had said about his mother and was filled with anger that the woman had suffered mistreatment at her husband's hands. She half hoped Kojak *would* strike out at her grandfather or at least curse and quit his job.

But Will Kojak was aware that jobs were scarce. He struggled with his anger briefly, then said, "Well, a man has to look out for his son, don't he?"

"Your son is old enough to make his own decisions," Stephen Rocklin said. "Now I won't have you disturbing this meeting. Either stay quiet or go back to work. If you can't do either of those, go draw your time."

Kojak said at once, "I'll say no more." Turning on his heel, he stalked away toward the factory.

"All right, men, you can go on with the recruiting," Rocklin said. "And remember, when your enlistment is up, you'll have your place back here at the factory."

Good humor was restored at once, and the sergeants began writing furiously.

"He never was any good," Stephen said to Gideon and Colonel Bradford. "Comes to work with such a hangover he can barely see straight. The boy isn't like him, though, far as I know."

"You saved the day, Mr. Rocklin," Colonel Bradford said warmly. He looked at the long lines, then said, "This may hurt you some. You'll be losing some good men."

"You do the fighting, Colonel Bradford, and we'll take care of things here at home."

"Well said, sir!" Bradford exclaimed. "And we'll do exactly that, won't we, men?"

As he raised his voice so that the crowd could hear, Deborah saw that her uncle's face was a study. She moved closer to him, asking, "What's the matter, Uncle Gid?"

"Why, nothing, Deborah," he answered

quickly, but then added, "Bradford's quite a fellow. Good at motivating men. But he's always been in charge of everything. No soldier is that much in control. There's always someone above him. I'm just wondering if our commanding officer will be able to take orders as well as he gives them."

Deborah stood talking with her uncle, waiting for a chance to speak to Noel. Enlisting was a slow process, but finally he finished, and she caught his eye. He nodded and would have passed, but she said, "Uncle Gideon, I want you to meet someone."

"Oh? Who might that be?" her uncle asked in surprise, but he allowed her to lead him to where the young Kojak was standing.

"This is Noel Kojak, Major Rocklin," Deborah said. "We had lunch together, and he's going to be one of your fine soldiers."

Gideon studied the young man, noting the honest gray eyes and sturdy body. *Better type than his father,* he thought and said with a smile, "Glad to have you in the Washington Blues, Kojak. I know you'll do well."

Noel swallowed, managing to say, "I'll do my best, sir. I don't know much about soldiering, though."

"You'll get good training," Gideon said, then noted that Bradford had come over to stand beside them, a curious look in his eye.

"Colonel Bradford, this is Private Noel Kojak, the newest member of the Washington Blues."

"Glad to have you in the regiment, Private Kojak," Bradford said, then seemed anxious to leave. "Are you ready, Miss Steele?"

"Yes, of course." Deborah paused long enough to say to Noel, "The matter we spoke of, don't worry about it."

"Thank you, miss." Noel nodded, then turned and left.

"Seems to be a nice young man," Gideon remarked.

"Have to keep your eye on him, Rocklin," Bradford said sternly. "Seems to be a little weak, allowing his father to make his decisions and all that. Well, come along, Miss Steele, if you're ready."

On the way back to her home, Bradford asked, "What did you mean by what you said to Kojak?"

"Oh, he was reluctant to enlist because his family would suffer. He comes from a large family, and they depend on his wages to survive. I told him I'd help his mother from time to time until he got home."

He shook his head but smiled at her. "You have a strong mothering instinct, I suspect, Deborah. But you can't be responsible for the family of every soldier I recruit. Most of them are just lazy anyway."

Deborah stared at him. "I don't think that's true of many of them, Larry."

He was a man who was accustomed to women agreeing with him, and Deborah's comment annoyed him. Then he shook off his resentment and grinned. "You're a strong-minded young woman, Deborah. A man would never be bored with you."

He took her home; then at the door he took her hand and kissed it, saying, "Dinner tonight? I insist! You must let me have my way sometimes, Deborah!" She agreed, but as he left and she moved inside the house, her thoughts were more about Noel Kojak than about the colonel.

Noel had gone back to work, but for the rest of the afternoon he had dreaded getting off for the day. He knew that his father had been intimidated by Stephen Rocklin, but he also knew that the anger would be building up in him. Noel tried to brace himself for the explosion that was sure to come.

And come it did, as soon as the three Kojak men began their walk home. Will Kojak began cursing and reviling Noel, keeping on even after they got home. All night long he raved, and the entire family, except for Bing, came in for a share of his abuse.

Noel had wanted to break the news to his mother gently, but there was no chance of that. It was not until after supper, when Bing and his father went off to the tavern to get some liquor, that he had a moment alone with her. The children were all outside seeking relief from the heat of the summer night, and he came to sit beside her after the dishes were done.

"Mother, I wanted to talk to you, to tell you," he said, putting his hand on hers, "but there was no time."

"Is this something you feel is right, Noel?"

"Yes, Mother!"

"Then you must do it." She picked up a worn, black Bible that lay on the battered table, found a verse, then read it. " 'Whatsoever thy hand findeth to do, do it with thy might.' " She closed the Bible, then sat there quietly. "You came to know the Lord Jesus when you were only eleven years old, Noel," she said quietly. "And you've been faithful ever since. I don't think I could have lived if you hadn't stood with me! Now promise me that you'll be faithful while you're in the army. It will be hard, for there'll be many wild young men. Promise me you'll keep yourself free from the sins that soldiers are likely to fall into."

"Why, I promise," Noel said, somewhat

surprised. "A man doesn't have two selves. I mean, if a man is a Christian, he's a Christian when he's away from home just the same as he is at home."

"That's exactly right, Noel!"

He spoke of his absence, then said awkwardly, "Mother, I made a friend today. It will be hard for you to do without my wages, so you'll be getting some help."

"Oh? What's his name, Noel?"

"Well, actually it's a young lady, Mother. Her name is Miss Deborah Steele. She's the granddaughter of Mr. Stephen Rocklin, the factory owner." Noel told her of his meeting with the young woman and of the agreement that had taken place. When he was finished, he said, "She took your address, so you'll be getting some money from time to time." He hesitated, then added carefully, "I suppose it might not be best to tell Pa about this. Just use the money for food and for the things the others need."

"This young woman, Noel, is she a Christian?"

"Why, I don't know, Mother," he said, then added, "But she did say she would pray for me."

Anna Kojak nodded, thinking of the strangeness of it all. "I think she must be, Noel. And I praise God for the way He's worked this all out. When will you leave, son?"

"The day after tomorrow, the sergeant said. Tomorrow will be my last day at the ironworks."

"You'll be back soon, only three months," his mother said. Then she put her hand on his and held on to it possessively. "It's going to be hard to let you go, Noel, but I believe God will bring you back safe. If you should fall in battle, well, you belong to God, so you'll be in a better place!"

They sat there quietly, each of them thinking their own thoughts. Eventually Anna broke the silence.

"I wonder how many mothers in this country are saying good-bye to their sons. And some of them for the last time on this earth."

He had no answer for her. He could only clasp her hand, praying that God would protect her while he was gone.

Chapter 4
A Visit to Camp

All through April, Washington was hot, dusty, loud, and packed with a confederation of frantic seekers of all sorts. The new administration of Abraham Lincoln had drawn office seekers from all over the North, and their continual swarming around the presidential mansion almost drove the tall rail-splitter to flight. They laid wait for him in every conceivable location — not only in the White House, but on the streets as he tried to get some exercise, and even on the Sabbath in St. John's Episcopal Church near the White House, where Lincoln sometimes worshipped.

Some of the men who thronged the city were not friendly to Lincoln, for the presidential campaign had been bitter. Some in the North had become angered during the campaign, but even more bitter were the Southerners in the city who carried their pride and anger over Sumter like a flag —

John Hatcher was one of these angered Southerners. A handsome man, six feet six inches tall, he was with one of his friends from South Carolina when a line of people formed to shake hands with the president. "I'll never shake the hand of old Abe Lincoln," Hatcher said.

His friend responded, "I'll bet you a suit of clothing you will. You can't pass by Mr. Lincoln."

"Agreed!" said the tall and handsome John Hatcher. The two fell in line, Hatcher in the lead, his head erect and determination showing in every line of his face. The retiring president, Mr. Buchanan, took Hatcher's hand and shook it cordially. After receiving Hatcher's name, Buchanan turned to introduce the man to Mr. Lincoln, but the Southerner removed his hand, let it drop to his side, and began to move on without greeting Mr. Lincoln or even looking upon his face. Lincoln grasped the situation instantly and, with a smile, said, "No man who is taller and handsomer than I am can pass by me today without shaking hands with me."

As they left, Hatcher's friend said, "John, I have won the suit of clothes."

"Yes," Hatcher replied, "but who could refuse to shake hands with a man who would leave his position and put his hand in front of you as Mr. Lincoln did?"

"Well, I have won the suit of clothes fairly," replied his friend, "but I won't take the wager, because you surrendered like a courteous Southern gentleman and shook the hand of our new president, as all Americans should do."

Abraham Lincoln took the office of chief executive at the most critical time in the nation's history, and it was with acts such as his encounter with John Hatcher that he began to win the hearts of his people. The nation sensed that grand and awful times were coming. Crowds of young men flooded into Washington to find their part in the coming war. Every hotel was packed, and private homes were invaded by young relatives coming to the capital to get into the cauldron of excitement. Most of them were afraid that the war would be over before they could get in on it, a sentiment that came close to driving Major Gideon Rocklin to despair.

"The young fools!" he said to his brother-in-law, Rev. Amos Steele, as the two of them left the War Department late one afternoon on the last day of April. "They don't have the faintest idea what they're getting into!"

"Do you think it will really be that bad,

sir?" Steele asked cautiously. "I mean, after all, we have the Regular Army on our side. The Rebels have nothing to match it, surely?"

Gideon had picked up his hat, but he paused to stare at Steele. "The Old Army, yes, we have that, Amos. But it's not what people think. Do you have any idea at all how small the Old Army is? No more than sixteen thousand men at most, and scattered all over the continent. And no more than eleven hundred officers of all grades."

Steele was shocked. "I had no idea!"

"And of those officers, many will fight for the South. I got a letter from Captain Winfield Scott Hancock yesterday, from his post in California. They had a supper for a few friends, including General Albert Sidney Johnston, Lewis Armistead, George E. Pickett, Richard B. Garnett, and others — all of whom are leaving to take commissions in the Confederate Army!

"I know for a fact, Amos, that General Scott spoke with Robert E. Lee and asked him to be commander in chief of the Federal Army. And he refused! Said he couldn't take up arms against his native state. The very cream of the crop of West Point officers have gone to the South to fight against us." Jamming his hat down savagely on his head, he growled, "And these young firebrands think we can run down South, fire a few shots, and the Rebels will run for cover. Well, let me tell you, men like these don't run!"

Steele walked quietly to the carriage with his brother-in-law, and it was not until they got almost to his house, where Gideon's family was invited to dinner, that he said, "You know, Gid, I feel guilty about this war."

Amos Steele was a man of the firmest convictions, and his confession caused Gideon to stare at him in surprise. Ever since he had known Steele, the minister had pursued the cause of freeing the slaves unswervingly. At times Gideon had tried to warn him that he was sacrificing his family to his work — but he never pushed the point since he felt that he himself was somewhat guilty of the same offense.

"I've been so determined to see the black people freed," Steele said in a painful manner, "that I never thought what it would cost to bring it about."

"You should have listened to your hero, old John Brown," Rocklin said. "He warned us all that it would take bloodshed for slavery to be eliminated in this nation."

"I know, Gid, but that was something far off, something distant. Now it's here with us — and it's going to be bad."

The two men found out exactly how bad that evening at dinner. The large dining room was filled with Rocklins and Steeles, and the table was covered with food. At first, the meal went well. Gideon sat at one end of the table with his wife, Melanie, at his right, and their three sons — Tyler, Robert, and Frank — ranked on her right. Amos Steele sat at the other end of the table with his wife, Laura, on his right. Beside her, across from the Rocklins, were their three sons — Pat, Colin, and Clinton — along with Deborah.

Melanie Rocklin was wearing a crimson dress of silk, and her hair was as blond as it had been when she had married. She had been the beauty of Richmond society in those days and still was a most attractive woman. Looking at her, Gideon wondered how he had ever managed to get her as his wife. It was Colin Steele, wondering much the same thing, who precipitated the difficulties of the evening.

Colin was a short young man of twenty, not as smart as his brothers, but very likable. He was a brash young fellow, saying whatever came into his mind, and now as he looked at his Aunt Melanie, he blurted out, "Aunt Melanie, I suppose you're glad you didn't marry that Rebel, aren't you?"

A dead silence fell on the table, and Colin flushed. He tried to patch up the damage his remark had wrought by stammering, "I mean — well, after all, if you'd married Cousin Clay when him and Uncle Gid were courting you, why, you'd be down in Richmond about to take a licking from us, wouldn't you?"

Never had Gid Rocklin admired his wife more, for she showed no sign of the agitation she must have felt. Instead she smiled at her nephew, saying, "Colin, Clay Rocklin is a fine man. But there was no man for me but your uncle."

As Melanie spoke, the painful memories of her courtship came back to her. She had been courted by Clay Rocklin, the son of Thomas and Susanna Rocklin, and had fancied herself in love with him. She had thought at one time that she would marry Clay, become mistress of Gracefield Plantation, and reign in Richmond society. Then Gideon had come into her life, and she had fallen in love with him. Never for one moment had she regretted her choice, but she did grieve over the way her marriage to Gid had affected Clay.

As a young man, Clay Rocklin had been strong and handsome, with all the natural gifts one could desire. But he had been completely undisciplined, unable to control his passions. When Melanie had refused him, he had married her cousin Ellen Benton, and they had known nothing but unhappiness together. Clay had tried many things to resolve his restlessness, including joining Gideon's company during the Mexican War — but that, too, had been a failure. Dishonorably discharged from the army, Clay had disappeared without a trace for years. He had returned about two years ago, but from what Gideon and Melanie could discover, he was still not happy with his marriage.

Colin's hapless question reminded the entire family of the situation. It was Pat, the Steeles' twenty-one-year-old son, who suddenly asked, "What will they do, Uncle Gideon? Our family at Gracefield?"

Gideon gave the tall young man a careful glance. Pat had the same intensity as his father, along with the same hazel eyes and sharp features. "They'll do what we'll do, Pat," he said. "Fight for what they think is right." He added heavily, "Clay won't serve in the army. He seems to have mixed feelings about the war. Melanie got a letter from Clay's mother, Susanna, last week."

"She said," Melanie spoke up, "that Clay

was very unpopular, that anyone who questioned the war was being persecuted." She gave Deborah a glance, then added, "What makes it worse is that Clay's son Denton is a lieutenant in the Confederate Army."

At this, everyone at the table stared at Deborah, for they were all aware that she and Dent Rocklin had been in love — or at least that Dent had courted Deborah while she was in Richmond. Deborah's cheeks reddened, but she said only, "Yes, I got a letter from Uncle Clay's daughter, Rena. She's only fifteen, but we grew very close while I visited there."

"I hate to think of it," Laura Steele said. She was Gideon's only sister, and the two were very close. She was a small woman with a wealth of auburn hair and a round face. A thought came to her, and she gave her brother a startled look. "Gid, you might have to fight Denton."

"I hope not." Gid Rocklin's face was sober and his eyes hooded as he looked down. It was something that he knew would become a burning issue in many families. "Even so, I must do my duty."

"Exactly right!" Pat Steele spoke up so loudly that they all turned to look at him. Pat gave his father a direct look. Then, lifting his head in a stubborn gesture, he said,

"I guess this is as good a time as any to let you all know. . . . I joined the Washington Blues this morning."

Amos Steele blinked, caught completely off guard. His lips grew white, and he said sharply, "I don't recall that we talked about your decision."

"Yes, sir, we talked about it," Pat said quietly. "I said I wanted to join the army, and you said I couldn't. That was the whole discussion, sir." He was a handsome young man with a firm will, but it was the first time he had ever directly disobeyed his father.

"We'll talk about it at a more convenient time," Steele said sharply.

"Sir, I'm twenty-one years of age," Pat said stubbornly. "We can discuss the future, but I will be leaving in the morning to take my place with my company."

Tyler Rocklin had observed the clash between his cousin and his uncle silently, but now he gave his parents a steady look, then said, "Father, Mother, I'd planned to talk to you tonight when we got home."

Gid suddenly felt a warning go off in his spirit. He glanced at his son, then at Melanie. Slowly he asked, "Have you joined the army, too, son?"

"No, sir, I haven't. But I want your permission to join the New York Fire Zouaves."

"That's Colonel Ellsworth's unit, isn't it?"

"Yes, sir. He's come to Washington at President Lincoln's request. I want to join his regiment."

Colonel Elmer E. Ellsworth, a favorite of Lincoln's, had been busy for several years organizing his unit. The men were wonderful at close-order drill, and Ellsworth, though he had absolutely no military experience, was a fine organizer. With Lincoln's support, he was becoming a nationally known figure.

Gideon Rocklin was too wise a man to make an issue of the matter. He said only, "Ellsworth's unit might not be the best choice, Tyler. Why don't you come to my office tomorrow and we can see what's available."

Tyler nodded at once, relief washing over his face. "I'd like that very much, sir," he said.

The suddenness of this news had taken both sets of parents unaware, though they had expected that the young men would eventually want to go. After the Rocklins left, Amos went to his study with Pat. Colin said to his sister, "Boy, I'll bet Pat's catching it!"

"I hope not," Deborah said quietly. "Pat's

determined on this thing, and the more anyone tries to change him, the more stubborn he's going to get."

Colin thought about it, then said, "I may enlist myself. I'm twenty, the same age as Tyler. Maybe I will."

"You're too lazy," Deborah said. "Do you think your sergeant will fix your breakfast like Mother and I do?"

Colin grinned at her, then came over and squeezed her till she gasped. "I'll take you along, Deb. I heard that some of the Rebs are taking their black servants along to wait on them while they're in the army. I'll just take you along. You can press my clothes and cook for me."

"You'd like that, wouldn't you?" Deborah tried to pull away from him, but he held to her tightly. "Let me go, you monster!" The two of them wrestled around the dining room, joyfully laughing. Colin was the best-natured of Deborah's brothers, the one with whom she had played as a child. Now she gave him a hug and a kiss. "Don't enlist, Colin," she said, a serious look in her large violet eyes. "I couldn't bear it if anything happened to you!"

"Oh, shoot!" he grumbled, embarrassed by her concern. "No ol' Rebel's going to hurt me!" Then he gave her a curious look.

"What about you and Dent? You still going to let him court you?"

Deborah pulled away from him, her face growing tense. "He won't be thinking about me now, Colin," she said quietly.

Colin stared at her, his large blue eyes considering her. "Bet he will, Deb," he said quietly. "Any man would be a fool to give you up!"

Deborah quickly kissed him, then ran from the room, saying, "Don't you sign up, Colin! You'd be miserable!"

"Come on along, Deborah. You might find yourself a handsome beau to come courting!"

So Pat had said to Deborah on the first day of May 1861. He was getting ready to head for his camp. His excitement and enthusiasm had infected his sister.

"All right, Pat," Deborah said at once, and the two of them had left the house after breakfast. On the way she asked tentatively, "Was your talk with Daddy very bad, Pat?"

He considered the question for a few moments, then shook his head. "You know, Deb, it wasn't all that bad. Oh, he was hurt because I enlisted without talking it over with him, but he seemed all right." He glanced out at the streets, which seemed to be filled already with busy people. Then he said slowly, "I think he feels that he hasn't been a good father to us. He said he wished he'd spent more time with all of us. But I guess it's too late for that."

"No, it isn't," Deborah said at once. "It won't be easy, but you've got to make an effort. All of us do."

"Sure, I'll do that." The two of them had not been close, but now that he was leaving, Pat felt somewhat nervous and spoke with vigor of how wonderful the army was going to be. There was, Deborah sensed, an apprehension in him, and she did her best to encourage him.

As soon as they got to the camp — a large area filled with parade grounds full of drilling men and a small city of Sibley tents in neat rows — they got directions and made their way to regimental headquarters. Inside the large tent, they found that the commanding officer and his adjutant were present, but not in the happiest of moods.

Colonel Bradford's face was flushed when he turned to greet the visitors, and it was obvious that he was not happy. He greeted them with a smile that seemed forced, saying, "Well now, this is a pleasant surprise!" When Pat informed him that he'd come to volunteer, Bradford said, "Well, I'm pleased, of course. Did you recruit this young fellow, Miss Rocklin?"

"No, I can't claim any credit for it, Colonel." Deborah smiled. "It was all his own idea. But I came along to see that you give him the best of treatment."

"Private Steele, you couldn't have picked a better advocate," Bradford said. "What company do you suggest, Major Rocklin?"

"A Company might be the best, Colonel," Gideon said at once. "Captain Frost is pretty hard-nosed, but he's a professional."

The remark, both Pat and Deborah saw, irritated Bradford. He snorted impatiently, saying, "Oh, Major, you've got a fixation on the Regular Army! You don't give the militia and the volunteers a chance. But you'll see what fine fellows we have soon enough."

Gideon started to speak but then seemed to change his mind. "Shall I take Private Steele to his new company?"

"Yes, do that, Major," Bradford said. "I'll take Miss Steele out to see some of the drill."

Gideon said, "Come along, Private," and the two left the tent. Soon Pat was being introduced to Captain Hiram Frost, a hard-bitten individual of forty-five. "Captain Frost will be watching you very closely, Private," Gideon said. "Captain, I know you will make a good soldier out of my nephew."

Frost nodded slightly, then turned to a bull-shouldered soldier who was wearing sergeant's chevrons. "Sergeant Cobb, take Private Steele to the commissary. Get his equipment; then get him settled in. Put him in Lieutenant Monroe's platoon."

"Yes, sir." Frost waited until the pair had left, then asked abruptly, as was his manner, "Well, Major, did you make any headway with the colonel?"

"Afraid not, Captain," Gideon said, shaking his head. He and the captain — who was an ex-lobsterman from Maine turned Indian fighter — had been unhappy with the training of the men. Both of them wanted to see less close-order drill and more marching and firing practice. "I tried to talk to him just now, but he won't hear of it."

The captain rested his weight on one foot and stood there, a heavy shape in the morning sun. There was a ponderous quality about him that made him seem slow of thought, but his friends soon learned that once he did make up his mind, he could act as fast as any man in the army. Now he added, "The men like it, all the exhibitions in the city. It's flashy enough. But the first time one of them drops with a Rebel's minié ball in his gut, all those fancy drills won't help them much."

While the two men were speaking, Bradford was explaining the situation to Deborah. The two of them were walking along the dusty lanes between two large fields, and he pointed out the fine execution of the men as they drilled. "Your uncle and I have had a bit of a disagreement over the training of the men," he had explained. "Now, he knows the army, but I think I know something about what makes men tick. He wants to toughen them up with long forced marches and short rations. Well, that's important, of course. But I know what's equally important, and that's pride." His eyes flashed, and he looked very handsome in his blue uniform.

Finally he smiled, slightly embarrassed, saying, "I expect you think I'm very opinionated, don't you, Deborah?"

Deborah said quickly, "I think you're both right. You need both qualities. I'm sure you'll be able to work it out." She looked around at the men, then up at him. "You must be very proud, Larry. This is a fine thing you're doing."

Bradford was used to the praise of women, but his eyes lit up at her compliment. He would have spoken, but just then a lieutenant came to say, "Sir, the meeting with the staff — ?"

Irritation swept across Bradford's face, but he said, "Oh, blast! Deborah, I've got to speak to my staff. I won't be long. Would you like to go back to my headquarters?"

"No, I'll just watch the drill." She saw that he didn't like to leave her, but when he did turn on his heel and leave the drill ground, she felt more at ease. For a time she watched the lines move across the dry grounds, raising clouds of dust as they performed their intricate maneuvers.

Then as she began to walk slowly down the dusty pathways, a sergeant came toward her. "The colonel said you can get out of the sun if you like, miss," he told her.

"Oh, I'm fine, Sergeant." She hesitated, then asked, "Do you know where A Company is? My brother is with them."

"Come along, miss," he said, his eyes filled with admiration for her. "I'll take you to their area."

He led Deborah through the labyrinth of tents. Finally he stopped. "There's Captain Frost's tent. He'll be glad to help you."

"Thank you, Sergeant." Deborah smiled at the young man, who at once fell in love with her; then she turned and walked toward the tent. She passed along the line of tents and was surprised when one of the soldiers working with a detail called out to her, "Miss Steele — ?"

She turned. Noel Kojak was standing a few feet away, an ax in his hand. At once she exclaimed, "Why, it's you!" She went to him with a smile on her face and, without thinking, held out her hands to him.

Noel blinked with alarm but took her hands, releasing them almost at once, aware that his fellow soldiers were not missing any of the action. "Noel, are you in A Company?"

"Yes, I am, Miss Steele."

She smiled at him, exclaiming with delight, "My brother will be with you. His name is Pat, Noel. You two will have to become friends."

"Yes, I'd like that." Noel was wearing a blue uniform and had a forage cap pulled down almost over his eyes. He was watching her with a pair of warm gray eyes and said at once, "I got word from my mother about the money you sent, Miss Steele. It was such a help, she said."

Deborah said uncomfortably, "Oh, Noel, it was nothing."

"That's not so," he insisted. "It means a lot."

Deborah changed the subject. "How do

you like the army?"

He laughed at that. "It's easier than working in the plant. Good food and not much work."

The two of them stood there talking, Noel forgetting that he was on a work detail, lost in the pleasure of her company. She was wearing a pale blue dress with a white bonnet that framed her heart-shaped face. She was so pretty that he had to remind himself not to stare — but could not seem to help himself. He had thought about her constantly, though he had not said a word about her to anyone in his platoon.

Deborah was enjoying the moment. It pleased her to think that Pat would be in the same company as Noel. She had said little to anyone about what she was doing, but resolved to ask her brother to befriend Noel.

Finally he said, "I'm worried about Ma. She's been sick. I hope it isn't this flu that's got everybody down. Some families are hard hit. Everyone down at the same time."

The two of them were so lost in conversation that neither of them heard the approach of Bradford, who came up to say, "Well, here you are, Miss Steele. I thought you were lost."

"Oh no, Colonel," Deborah said, turning

with a smile. "I came over to meet my brother's captain — and I found an old friend. You must remember Noel Kojak? He was one of the men who worked in my grandfather's factory."

"Yes, of course." Bradford gave Noel a brief nod, then took Deborah's arm. "Come along, I'll introduce you to your brother's officer."

"Thanks again, Miss Steele," Noel called out as the two left. Then he went back to the woodpile.

Manny Zale, a hard-faced man of twenty-seven, was waiting for Noel, a grin on his thick lips. "Hey now, Kojak. I didn't know you moved in such high company. Who's the doll?" When Noel just shook his head, Zale grabbed the younger man by the arm, his hand closing like a vise. "You psalm singer! Don't clam up on me! Who was she?" Zale had been the leader in the small group that made fun of Noel. They were a godless bunch, and when they discovered that Noel prayed and read the Bible, they had delighted in making his life as miserable as they could.

Corporal Buck Riley had been watching what was happening between the two men and said at once, "Zale, if you got enough energy to do all that arguing, I'm glad to hear it. You can cut some more wood after dinner."

Zale turned angrily, but Riley was a tough one himself, so the burly private just muttered, "You won't always have somebody around to baby you, Kojak!"

Noel knew that he was in for a bad time down the road — Manny Zale had a vicious streak and seldom forgot offenses. But as Noel went back to chopping wood, he could think only of a pair of violet eyes.

CHAPTER 5
EPIDEMIC

When Pat and Tyler enlisted in the army, it brought the grim reality of war home to the Rocklins and the Steeles in a way nothing else had. Of course, both families had been caught up in the events of the times — the Steeles in the abolition movement, the Rocklins in the military — but with the departure of the young men, life changed for all of them. For Rev. Amos Steele, his son's absence was a continual reminder that he had failed as a father, at least in his own mind. Steele was an honest man, and when he faced up to the fact that he had neglected his family, he admitted it to his wife, Laura.

"If he dies in battle, Laura," he said in a strained voice, "I'll never know a moment's peace!" She had tried to comfort him, telling him that he had given much to his family. He just brushed her off, saying bitterly, "Don't try to make excuses for me! As a minister of the gospel, I, of all men, should have been a good father. And I will be, Laura, the best I can, but the children are all grown. Pat is twenty-one, Colin is twenty, and Clint is eighteen. And Deborah may be only nineteen, but she is a grown woman."

"It's not too late, Amos," Laura insisted. She came to stand before him, putting her arms around him and lifting her face to kiss him. "You have love in you. You've always been afraid to show it."

"Not to you."

"No, dear," she said with a smile. "Not when we're alone. But even with me you're afraid to show affection in public."

Staring at her, Amos said slowly, "My family was never demonstrative. I don't ever remember seeing my father kiss my mother. Even now none of my brothers and sisters show emotion. I was taught such things were a weakness." Then he shook his head, adding almost angrily, "Well, those who taught me that are wrong! And with God's help, I'll give more of myself to the children from now on!"

"Now don't go falling all over them!" Laura warned, a light of pride in her eyes. She had yearned for years to see this stern husband of hers break out of his rigid mold. "You'll scare them to death."

"Well then, I'll just practice up on you!"

Steele pulled her to him and kissed her so forcibly that she could scarcely catch her breath. When he released her, she laughed at him. "Now remember, I'm an old married woman, Amos!"

"You're a child!" he said, and from that moment — though he wasn't sure just why — he found it easier to be more expressive in his relationships with his children. He spent much of his time with Clinton, taking him fishing, something they both loved. The lad was strong and agile, and Amos loved watching him. By the time the two of them had been together on two trips, he had opened up to his father in a way he never had before.

As welcome as this was, it was a sorrow for Steele, for the thing Clint shared with his father was that he wanted nothing so much as to be a soldier. He had finally come out with this as they were wading a trout stream. The swift water bubbled over their feet, and their creels were full of fish.

"Pa, I want to be a soldier," Clint had said without preamble. It had been on his mind for years, but he had not dared to mention it to anyone.

Steele had restrained the impulse to flatly squash the notion, which was what he would have done not long ago. Instead he laid the fly line down on the water with an expert motion, then, getting no strike, said as easily as he could, "Because of Pat's decision to enlist?"

"No, sir. I've always wanted to be a soldier. Like Uncle Gideon, in the Regular Army."

"It's a hard life, son."

"I know it is, but it's all I want." Clint's square face was set as he added, "I want to go to West Point. For a long time I've wanted to ask you to try to get me an appointment." At that moment, a trout took Clint's fly. For the next few moments he played the fish expertly, his face alive with pleasure. He removed the fish, admiring the red and gold stipples on its sides, then slipped it into the creel at his side and turned to face his father. "Will you do it?"

Amos Steele stood there, everything in him longing to deny the boy's request. He hated the world of the military, or at least what it stood for in its ultimate purpose, which was to destroy an enemy. Yet the past few days had brought changes to him, and he knew that he had no choice. Slowly he nodded. "If it's what you really want, Clint, I'll try to get you an appointment."

Clint Steele stood transfixed for a few moments, staring at his father's face. Then he suddenly splashed through the knee-deep water and threw his arms around his father. Holding on to him tightly, he gasped, "Oh, Pa! Pa!"

Tears rose in Steele's eyes as, for the first time since his son was a child, he held him in his arms. *And it took a war to teach me how much this means!* he thought bitterly. Then he slapped Clinton on the back, saying, "Well, we'll have to tell your mother — and your uncle Gid, too. I expect he'll like it better than she will!"

The two of them went that afternoon to see Gideon, who received the news with less surprise than they had expected. "You've always been fascinated by the army, Clint." He smiled at the boy. "You've read everything there is, I guess, about the service, and sometimes you've pestered me to death with your questions. I thought it might come to this."

"Can you get me into West Point, Uncle Gideon?" Clint asked eagerly.

"Well, that takes a congressional appointment, and I'm just a lowly major. But I'll work on it. You've got a little time to wait." Smiling at Clint, he said, "Maybe you'll change your mind and decide to become an actor."

"Oh no!" Clint said, shocked by the very idea.

Gid laughed, then turned to Amos. "Tell you what, Amos. You bring your whole brood over to our house for supper tonight. Clint can make his big announcement about his plans to become a general to all the family."

"I wish Pat could come," Clint said. "But I guess he can't get away."

"Well now, that's one of the advantages of having an uncle who's a major," Gid said. Then he added with a sly glance at Steele, "But if you'd really like Pat to come, you might have Deborah ask Colonel Bradford. I think he's about ready to do whatever she asks."

"I'd rather you did it, Gideon," Steele said at once. He did not amplify his remark, but the soldier understood.

"Of course, Amos. I'll bring him along."

The Rocklin home was not as large or as expensively furnished as the Steeles' home, for a soldier had to be ready to move at a moment's notice. But the old brownstone, located just off Pennsylvania Avenue, was large and fairly comfortable. After the cramped, miserable quarters that Melanie and Gideon had occupied at Fort Swift in the Dakota Territory, the house seemed a palace!

Melanie and Laura, with some help from Deborah, worked on the meal, running into each other at times in the small kitchen. Meanwhile, the men sat in the parlor and talked. When the pot roast was done, Melanie said, "Well, the food's ready, so let's see if we can sandwich ourselves into the dining room."

They all crowded into the dining room, a cheerful space with yellow wallpaper and a large bay window that admitted a slight breeze and bars of yellow sunlight. The six Steeles and four Rocklins squeezed themselves into place. "We can't eat much, that's for sure," Clint piped up, pinched between Pat and Colin. "All squoze up like this, there's not much room for food!"

"That's right, Clint," Gid said, grinning. "Part of our strategy to live on a lowly soldier's pay! Squeeze 'em in so tight they can't hold much grub!"

"Well, it won't work with me, sir!" Pat said at once. "I've missed home cooking so much, just don't anyone get his hand too close to my plate or he's likely to draw back a stub!"

"Ask the blessing, will you, Amos?" Gid said.

101

"Oh God, we thank Thee for the food, which is Your provision. But we thank Thee even more for each other, for our family. You set the solitary in families, and we ask Your protection on every member of this family." Steele hesitated slightly, then added, "And we ask Your protection and blessing on our family at Gracefield, on the grandparents, the parents, and the young ones there. In Jesus' name, I ask it."

"I'm glad you did that, Amos," Melanie said as they began to fill their plates. "We need to remember Thomas and Susanna. I miss them so much, and now it looks as though we may not see them for a long time."

"Father says Thomas isn't well," Gid remarked, carving the roast with a long knife and laying neat slices on the plates that came to him. "He said that if Clay hadn't come back when he did, Gracefield would have been lost. Clay took all the money he made while he was gone and paid the notes off."

Deborah took a bite of fresh biscuit, then said slowly, "It's strange, isn't it? Clay made all that money in the slave trade and it saved the family home. Now he hates slavery, and everybody there is angry at him because he won't enlist in the army so that slavery can

102

be preserved. It must be hard on him.”

“I’m very proud of Clay,” Gid said warmly. “He started out making such a wreck out of his life, but he’s come back and done all he can to put things right. Not many men can do that, and it’s sad that some people in his world don’t seem to realize it.”

As the meal went on, they talked across the table, enjoying the food and the company. When Amos asked about Tyler, Gideon shrugged. “He likes it very well in the New York Zouaves. Since Virginia seceded, the president sent eight regiments across the Potomac to seize Alexandria and Arlington Heights. Colonel Ellsworth’s Zouaves were part of that force.”

“That’s really the beginning, isn’t it?” Robert asked. At nineteen, he was more like his mother, Melanie, than his father. Always a quiet boy, he had grown up to be a studious young man, thoughtful and curious about everything. “It’s the first invasion of the South, isn’t it, Father?”

“Yes, it is, Rob,” Gideon said, and a sadness touched his dark eyes. “It won’t be the last, though.” Then he shook his head and said with a smile, “Well, what about your announcement, Clint?”

Clint stammered, “Well . . . I’m — I’m

going to be an offic— uh, in the army. Father has agreed, and Uncle Gideon's going to get me an appointment to West Point!"

His announcement brought cries of surprise from everyone. Pat grinned at him, saying, "Well, you son of a gun! I'll be taking orders from my own brother!"

"Not for a while, Pat," Clint said, pleased with the attention. "I can't get into the Point for a while. By the time I get out, the war will be over."

After the meal, they were all drinking coffee when Pat suddenly snapped his fingers. "Hey, I almost forgot! I have a message for you, Deborah — from one of your admirers."

"Must be Colonel Bradford," Amos grunted. "He's been at the house twice."

"No, the colonel doesn't send messages by lowly privates," Pat said, grinning. "But it's right handy having the commanding officer stuck on your sister! Makes you kind of special."

"Bet you wish Captain Frost was in love with Deborah, don't you, Pat?" Gid said with a slight smile. "You'd never have to dig a ditch!"

Deborah sniffed. "Oh, don't be silly! A message from whom, Pat?"

"Noel Kojak. He said to tell you thanks for the help you sent to his mother."

"What's that?" Amos asked, surprised, and Deborah flushed. She explained, "Oh, I encouraged the young man to enlist, so I'm helping his mother a little until his enlistment is up." Wanting to change the subject, she asked, "Is he a good soldier, Pat?"

"Better than I am, for sure!" Pat grinned ruefully. "Matter of fact, he's the best in the platoon. Always up first and keeps his equipment polished and clean. Never makes sick call." He scowled at Deborah, saying, "You might tell him he could make life a little easier on the rest of us if he'd mess up once in a while!"

"The working class makes the best soldiers," Gid said. "They've had hard lives, so soldiering is easy. Spoiled characters, like Pat here, have to get weaned from Mama before they can function as troopers. The same in the South. The farm boys like the army because they have better clothes, more fun, and less work than they've ever had in their lives."

"Well, Noel is in trouble enough with some of the fellas in the platoon," Pat said. "Mostly because he insists on letting his religion show."

"How's that, Pat?" Amos Steele asked at

once, his eyes alert.

"Oh, Noel reads his Bible all the time, it seems like, and every night he gets down on his knees and prays."

"And you don't, Pat?" It was his mother who asked the question, and Pat was embarrassed.

"Well, I can pray just as well in bed, Mother. When a fellow shows too much religion, it makes the men think he's showing off." The conversation bothered Pat, and he changed the subject. "By the way, Deborah, Noel told me something else. He said his family's down with the flu, and he wants you to pray for them."

"Bad epidemic," Gid stated. "We've been blessed, but quite a few of the men have been down, and Father tells me many of his men and their families are in bad shape."

The evening ended soon, but Deborah did not join in much of the talk. On the way home, Clint said, "You're worried about this fellow's family, aren't you, Deb?"

"Yes, I am."

"Well, you'll have to do what he asks," Clint said practically. "You'll have to pray for them."

Deborah did pray that night after she went to bed, but by the time she went to sleep, she knew that prayer wasn't going to be enough. She dropped off to sleep, a plan hatching in her mind. That night it was only a vague notion, but by morning it was fully developed.

The Swampoodle district announced itself to Deborah first by the almost overpowering stench that issued from the hundreds of ramshackle privies behind the crude shanties. It had rained during the night, and the moist air seemed heavy with the rank odor.

The visual impact of the area offended the eyes almost as much as the smell offended the nose. There was no trace of beauty to be found, not anywhere. Line after line of shacks, unpainted and scoured to a leprous gray-brown by wind and weather, met Deborah's gaze. Drying clothes hung from a crisscross of lines and billowed in the breeze, but the clothing had no more color than the shacks. There was no attempt at decoration, no flowers or fresh curtains — all was crude, plain, and depressing.

Deborah drove her buggy down the muddy streets, doing her best to miss the pigs and chickens, most of which were as scrawny and lean as specters, that were crossing in front of her. The children who watched her pass stared at her, eyes large in their thin faces. They seemed to have been born exhausted, too tired to play as children should.

A trio of men leaning against a stark building with the single word SALOON over the door looked up as she approached. Deborah resisted the impulse to whip the horse up, and when one of them leered at her, saying, "Hello, girlie. How about a little drink?" she did not even look at him. The man made a coarse remark as she moved on, her heart beating rapidly, but he did not follow.

A small general store at an intersection drew her attention. She got down, hitched the horse to a rickety rail, then walked to the board sidewalk. Stepping inside, she blinked to adjust her eyes to the gloomy darkness. A single room with an assortment of cans on shelves made of rough lumber, and barrels of pickles and crackers on the floor, met her gaze.

"Help you?" Deborah turned quickly to face a short, fat man who was smoking a cigar. It had burned down so far that the ruby glow seemed to touch his lips. He was sitting on a cane-backed chair and made no move to get up.

"I'm looking for a family named Kojak," she answered.

The man studied her, then removed the cigar and studied it. "Which one?"

"Oh, why, I don't —"

"Three Kojaks I know of around here."

"The one with a son named Noel. He's in the army."

"Yeah, well — that's Will." Replacing the cigar between his lips, the owner drew on it, and in the gloom the glowing end made a vivid period under his stubby nose. "What'cha want with 'em?"

Deborah stared at him, stopped dead still by his abrupt question. "I have something for Mrs. Kojak," she said.

"Down this street five blocks, then go right for two blocks. Ask some of the kids you see where Will Kojak lives."

Deborah said, "Thank you," but as she turned to leave, an idea came to her. "I'd like a few groceries." The man got to his feet quickly, his eyes brightening. His stock was pitifully small, and Deborah cut that by a full quarter before she was through. He found an old box, packed it with tins of canned food, then stuffed fresh vegetables into old newspapers. He had some hard candy, and she took a large sampling of that, as well as some staples of flour, sugar, and coffee.

"Comes to nine dollars and sixty-six

cents," the thickset man said, looking at her fearfully, as if afraid that the price might overwhelm her.

Deborah counted out the money, and he poked it into his vest pocket with aplomb, then said, "Lemme put this in your buggy, ma'am." When the goods were loaded and she got into the buggy, he lifted his hat, saying cheerfully, "Top o' the morning to you, miss!"

Deborah smiled at him. "Thank you," she said, then made her way down the street. As she followed his directions, she thought of how a few dollars had made the man civil. It wasn't just the money, she felt, although she was sure that her order had been a large one for the owner. The sale had brought cheer and hope into the man's countenance, and it somehow shamed her that she had come to think so little of the abundance she'd lived in all her life.

The section she came to was, if possible, even worse than the collections of shanties she had passed already, but she pressed on. A group of children, none over seven or eight, stood watching her listlessly. When she pulled up and asked, "Do you know where Will Kojak lives?" none of them answered. Finally one of them pointed to one of the shacks and piped up, "Right there."

"Thank you." Deborah flicked the reins, and when she reached the house the youngster had indicated, she got down and hitched the horse to a sapling that had somehow survived. As she approached the door, her courage almost failed her. But she lifted her chin and made herself knock on the door. There was no response at first. Then she heard a faint rustling. The door opened slowly, and the interior was so dark that Deborah could see nothing. Uncertainly she said, "Hello? Is anybody here?"

A voice came from somewhere. "Yes. I'm here." She looked down and saw a small boy staring up at her. He was wearing only a tattered shirt, and his eyes were frightened.

"Is your mother here?" Deborah asked.

"She's sick."

"Oh. Well, are any of your brothers and sisters here?"

The boy nodded. "They're all sick."

Deborah stood there nonplussed, for the situation was beyond her. But the boy didn't move, and she had to do something. "Can you ask your mother to come to the door?"

The child disappeared, and Deborah stood there wishing she'd never come. He was gone so long that she was ready to leave, but then he was back. "Mama says you come to her."

Deborah said, "Well, all right." She stepped inside and was almost knocked down by the incredible, fetid odor of unwashed bodies and worse.

I can't do it! she thought desperately, gasping and standing stock still in the dark room. The only illumination came in from two small windows. Deborah struggled with the overpowering stench, longing for a breath of fresh air, but the boy said, "Back this way."

A door led into another room. When Deborah stepped inside, she was able to see, by the light of one small window, a woman lying in the bed that took up most of the space. She was sick, more so than anyone Deborah had ever seen. Her face was shrunken to a skull, and her eyes were dull and lifeless. The hands were little more than bones, and Deborah could see that the woman was in danger of dying.

"Mrs. Kojak . . . ," she said tentatively. The head on the soiled pillow turned, and a faint light came into the woman's eyes. "I'm Deborah Steele, Mrs. Kojak. I think Noel's told you about me."

The shrunken lips moved, but no sound came. Deborah saw a pitcher on the table and filled a chipped cup with tepid water. "Let me help you," she said and reached down to help the woman raise her head. The terrible smell of human waste smote her, and she closed her eyes, trying not to faint. Then with all the resolution she could muster, she opened them and concentrated on the task of holding the glass steady. When Mrs. Kojak had drunk a few swallows, Deborah lowered the woman's head, saying, "Noel sent word that you were sick, but I didn't know how bad." She put the glass down, then asked, "Are all the children sick?"

"Yes." The single word seemed to take all the strength the sick woman had. After a moment she nodded and whispered, "Thank you for coming."

Deborah had never been at such a loss. What little nursing she had done had been with doctors on hand, not to mention clean linen, medicine, and food. She tried to organize her thoughts, but her brain seemed to be paralyzed. She glanced about her, searching for any available supplies.

There's nothing here to do anything with, she thought, almost in a panic. But there was a stubborn streak in Deborah Steele that came down the generations from her grandfather Stephen — or perhaps from his father, Noah Rocklin, who was, according to every report, a tartar. Now in the gloomy room, with every instinct telling her to get out, she felt that inbred stubbornness begin to rise. It swelled until she said suddenly, "Mrs. Kojak, you've got to have help. Do you have any family coming, or are there any neighbors who could help?"

"No."

Deborah was launched into action by that hopeless monosyllable. "Well, I'll do what I can now; then we'll see. First I'm going to get you all cleaned up."

The simple act of bathing Mrs. Kojak was a monumental task, but Deborah did it. There was no hot water, but she found a small basin and filled it with water from the well in back of the house. For soap there was only the coarse, powerful lye soap used for washing clothing in the big black pot outside the back door. Even so, she managed. She found one gown that was not soiled, and when she had put it on the woman, she looked down, saying, "Now I'm going to fix you something to eat."

The cupboard was bare, she discovered when she moved to the kitchen. She was grateful that she had brought some things from the small store. The two girls in the larger room were in need of bathing, but

Deborah thought that food was the number one priority. Finding some small sticks, she managed to get a fire going in the ancient stove and put together a meal of sorts. It was difficult, for there were few cooking vessels. Those that she did find were caked with old food, so that she had to scrub them at the pump. She managed, though, to brew a pot of tea and make a broth out of the stores of rice and tinned chicken.

When it was ready, she said to the two girls who were watching, "I'll feed your mother; then you girls can eat."

She got Mrs. Kojak into a sitting position, and the sick woman ate half a bowl of the broth and two cups of sugared tea. When she was finished and Deborah laid her down, she lifted a hand and caught at Deborah. "God bless you! I've been praying that He'd send someone. Praise His name!"

Suddenly tears rose in Deborah's eyes, and she said, "Try to sleep, Mrs. Kojak. I'll take care of the children."

She left the bedroom and, for the rest of the day, threw herself into a frenzy of work. Mr. Kojak, she discovered by talking with the two girls, had been taken sick first, and he had nearly died. Then as soon as he had recovered and gone back to work, the rest of the family had gone down within three days. "All but Bing," the older girl, Sarah, said. "He left soon as we got sick." Then she cursed her brother with a terrible oath and lay back, bitterness on her face.

Somehow Deborah got them all cleaned and fed, even the two boys. She gathered all the soiled clothing into a pile, the stench of which gagged her when she hauled it out to the backyard. Finding some small sticks, she started a fire under the blackened wash pot, built it up, then filled the pot with water and added lye soap. It took three pots to do enough clothing for the whole family, and she dried them on the single clothesline that ran between a tree and the house. After the clothes were done, she washed the ragged sheets. By that time it was growing dark.

Sarah, the oldest of the girls, seemed to be the fittest of the family. She had come outside to sit on the step and watch while Deborah labored over the washing. When Deborah came inside and was putting the clean bedding down, she followed, watching with wary eyes. As Deborah cooked supper, she asked suddenly, "Who are you?"

"Why, I'm Deborah. A friend of Noel's."

The answer only puzzled the girl, who sat watching silently for a time, then asked, "Why are you doing all this stuff for us?"

Deborah looked up from where she was

116

mixing biscuits. The girl was pale, but she had dark hair and a pair of beautiful dark eyes that made her very attractive. "Because you need help, Sarah." That was no better, Deborah saw, for the girl was still suspicious.

When supper was ready, consisting mostly of biscuits and battered eggs, Deborah sent Sarah to get the two boys to the table. While the four children ate, Deborah took some food to the sick mother. "How do you feel, Mrs. Kojak?" she asked, sitting down and picking up the bowl of broth.

"Better, much better. It feels so good to be clean." She ate the broth — some of it, at least — then sighed. "My stomach's shrunk. But it's so good! How are the children?"

"Sarah seems almost well, and the rest of them feel better."

Anna Kojak watched the young woman with faded eyes as she sipped the tea. She had been almost delirious when the girl had come earlier, but now she felt able to think more clearly. "You don't know what all this means to me, Miss Steele," she said suddenly. "We've been so grateful for the money, but this is different." She hesitated, then said, "You must be a Christian."

"Well, my father's a minister," Deborah

said, nodding. "And I promised Noel I'd look after you while he's gone to the army."

"He's such a fine boy!" Anna's eyes filled with pride as she spoke of Noel. "Never a minute's trouble all his life. And such a dedicated Christian boy, too."

"I like him very much. And my brother Pat says Noel's the best soldier in the company."

"You don't tell me! But I'm not surprised. Noel always was one to work at whatever he put his hand to. His writing, for example."

"You taught him to read and write, he said."

"Oh, I taught him his letters, but I mean his story writing. He done all that himself. Never had a soul to teach him."

"Noel writes stories?" Deborah was surprised. "What kind of stories?"

"Stories about people. He didn't tell you? Well, no, he wouldn't, I suppose." She was growing tired and said, "Look over in that drawer. There's a tablet there with some of them. Take them with you."

"All right." Seeing that the woman was growing sleepy, Deborah found the tablet, looked inside to see it filled with the most beautiful handwriting she'd ever seen, then left the room.

As she gathered her things together, the

door opened and Will Kojak walked into the room. He had seen the buggy outside and could not guess whose it was. Even he, Deborah saw, was not over his sickness. His eyes were still hollow, and he had lost so much weight that his clothing hung on him. Quickly she said, "Hello, Mr. Kojak. Do you remember me? I'm Stephen Rocklin's granddaughter."

He blinked at her, then looked around the room, startled by the changes he saw. "What you doing here?" he demanded.

"I heard that your family was sick, so I came to help out a little." Deborah knew the man had a frightful temper and said nervously, "I've cooked some supper. Why don't you have some eggs while they're hot? I really have to run."

"It's good, Pa," Grace Kojak spoke up. "It's real good!"

Kojak stared at the food on the table, then back at Deborah. "I don't understand this," he said.

"Sit down and eat," Deborah said, then turned to go. But she paused long enough to say, "I thought I'd come back in the morning and help a little more. Would that be all right with you, Mr. Kojak?"

The face of Will Kojak was a study in bewilderment. He had nearly died with the flu and had gone back to work too soon. When he had left that morning, he had half expected to find some of his family dead when he got home. The sight of the clean sheets, the food on the table, and the improved condition of his family seemed to stun him. Biting his lip, he looked around the room, then back at Deborah. For a long moment he studied her; then finally he spoke.

"I guess . . . I guess it'll be all right."

CHAPTER 6
NOEL

Major Gideon Rocklin was confronted with two requests the moment he walked into his office on the morning of May 25. The first was actually a command rather than a request, but it was the easiest of the two to handle. Sergeant Benny Thomas rose as the major entered and said at once, "General Scott wants you in his office for a meeting right away, Major."

"Very well." But just as Rocklin turned to leave the room, he almost ran into his niece, who practically ran through the door. "Oh, Uncle Gideon!" she cried breathlessly. "I have to talk to you."

Gid Rocklin looked down at her, admiring her clear eyes and clean-cut features. "Of course, Deborah," he said, "but you'll have to wait. General Scott wants to see me right away."

"Oh, he can wait for a minute," Deborah said, and her remark brought a burst of laughter from Benny Thomas.

Rocklin gave him a withering glance that wiped the smile from his face; then he himself had to smile. "Well, he *is* the ranking general in the United States Army, but I guess I can keep him waiting for a little while." Not having any daughters of his own, Gid had been partial to Deborah all her life. He delighted in buying her the girlish things she liked and was well pleased with the way she had grown up. "What's the matter?"

Deborah said, "It's Noel's family, Uncle Gid. They're all down with the flu. I did what I could for them yesterday, but they need more help. I want you to give him a pass so we can get them through this illness."

"Noel? Who's Noel?" Rocklin could not place the name, but when Deborah mentioned the young man she'd recruited at the rally, he said, "Oh yes, I remember. But I can't give one of the men a pass because his family is sick, Deborah."

It was true — he couldn't. He knew that.

But somehow he did.

Deborah stood there looking up at him, her lips parted with concern, her voice pleading and insistent, and in the end he walked to his desk, scribbled out a note, then shoved it at her, growling, "There it is; now go on, woman! I've got a war to fight."

"Oh, thank you, Uncle Gid!" she cried ecstatically, throwing her arms around him and kissing him soundly.

She ran out of the office, and Rocklin turned to see Sergeant Thomas grinning broadly. "Not one word out of you, Benny!"

"No, sir, only —"

"Only what?"

"Well, sir, I don't blame you a bit! I guess that young woman could get just about anything from any man when she wants to." He sighed, adding, "I just wished she wanted me to do something, Major!"

"Get on with your work, Sergeant!" Rocklin snapped, but he had to smile as he left the room to meet with the general.

He's right about that, Benny is! Gideon thought. But he was somewhat worried about Deborah — had been since she had fallen in love with Denton Rocklin, his cousin Clay's son. He hoped that was over but wondered what she was doing chasing around after a private in his regiment.

He had to shelve that problem, however, as soon as he stepped into the general's office and saw that the president was there with several members of his cabinet. Gid knew something was terribly wrong.

"Come in, Major Rocklin," General Scott said. "Have you heard the news?"

"News? No, sir. I've just come in."

Lincoln looked haggard, and his dark eyes were hooded with grief. "It's a tragedy for all of us, Major. Colonel Ellsworth is dead!"

Rocklin stared at him. "My son is with his command, sir. Was there an engagement with the Rebels?"

"No, nothing like that," Scott grunted. "He was murdered by a secessionist." Scott quickly gave the details — Ellsworth had led his troops into Alexandria and had seen a Confederate flag flying on a flagpole above the Marshall House. It was obviously a challenge, and Ellsworth, followed by some of his men, went inside the hotel, up to the roof, and cut down the flag. Going back down the stairs in a shadowy hallway, the colonel met the proprietor of the inn, a Virginian named James T. Jackson. Jackson had lifted a shotgun and killed Ellsworth, then was himself killed by one of Ellsworth's Zouaves, who first shot the man, then ran a bayonet through him.

Lincoln, Rocklin saw, was hit hard by the news. Ellsworth had been only twenty-four and had won the affection of the president. Now he was dead — the Union's first casualty. Lincoln moved to the window, staring down silently, and there was a moment's silence in the room.

It was broken by William Seward, the secretary of state — he was a tall man with a wild crop of white hair and a terrible temper. "Now we see what sort of men we are fighting!" he said angrily. "Butchers and murderers! Mr. President, surely now it's clear that we must strike the Rebels!" Lincoln didn't move, and Seward continued to argue for a quick blow that would destroy the fledgling Confederate forces. "One quick blow, drive them back to Richmond; then we can put an end to this thing!"

General Scott stared at Seward — Scott was an old man now, sick and obese. He could no longer mount a horse, and just moving from one place to another tired him . . . but he was still an astute soldier and perhaps the best military mind in the world. Now he grunted angrily and stated flatly, "It cannot be done, sir! Our men are untrained, and you cannot move a military force of untrained men."

Seward argued angrily that the Confederates were also untrained, and the air grew thick as the argument raged. Finally Lincoln turned from his place at the window, saying, "We must see to the burial of our brave young Ellsworth." When Seward tried to press him, a flash of irritation showed in the president's eyes. "I know you think you should be the president instead of me, Mr. Seward, but you are not! Now we will bury our dead; then we will proceed with the war."

Lincoln walked out of the room, followed by the cabinet members. As soon as they were gone, Scott slapped his hand on his huge thigh, growling, "Pack of fools! Especially Seward!"

"He's wrong, sir," Rocklin agreed. "We have good men, but they've never been put under fire. Of course, the Rebs haven't either, so it would be a toss-up as to which bunch would run."

"I won't have the future of this country settled by a toss-up, Major! I've put too much into it to allow such a thing." The two men spoke of what must be done, but as they worked, Gid felt depressed and thought to himself, *We can do all the planning we want, but it'll be Horace Greeley and his newspaper that decide when we'll fight. Him and the politicians like Seward!*

Noel had slipped out of his blankets early, earning a muffled curse from Manny Zale as he stumbled around getting dressed. The round Sibley tent was packed with men.

Supported by an upright center pole, its fifteen occupants slept with their feet toward the center and their heads near the edge, like the spokes of a wagon wheel. The sky was still black, and Noel had to walk carefully to avoid falling over tent stakes as he made his way to the parade ground. It was a vast ghostly plain at this hour, but one of the few places where a man could be sure of solitude. After spending so many miserable hours drilling there, the men hated the sight of it.

It was here that Noel came every morning to think and pray. He had found it almost impossible to find any quiet place other than this, for the army was a noisy organization. Now the best times of his day were these cobwebby times of the early morning, and he walked slowly around the field, enjoying the silence. He prayed and thought, remembering his family and his new friends in the company. There were only two other Christians in his platoon, and they were not too strong. The rest of the group were not bad fellows, Noel believed, just careless and open to temptation. He prayed for the men he knew, and then he gave a special prayer for his mother, who must bear the whole load of the family. He also prayed for his father, who did not know God.

Finally he heard the brassy sound of reveille and went at once back to the camp. The corporals were busy waking up the men, and soon the camp was a beehive of activity. Some commanders allowed their men to answer roll call in any sort of dress, but Colonel Bradford insisted that his men turn out in full dress. Noel joined the sleepy soldiers as Cobb, the first sergeant of A Company, called the roll. Then the men were allowed to return to their tent for thirty minutes. Next came breakfast call, followed by sick call.

At eight o'clock the musicians sounded the call for guard mounting, at which the first sergeant of each company turned out his detail for the next twenty-four hours. Usually that meant digging latrines or chopping wood, but Cobb gave his men a careful look, saying, "All right, this morning you'll fall in at the firing range for target practice."

A cheer went up, and Jim Freeman exclaimed, "About time we got to do some shooting, ain't it, Noel? I joined up to shoot Rebs, not to dig latrines!" Jim, a towheaded, happy-go-lucky young man of eighteen, was usually in trouble for minor infractions such as failing to make his bed. He was a Christian, but not a very dedicated one. Now he chattered like a magpie as the platoon trudged toward the rifle pits. His comments got on Manny Zale's nerves.

"Shut your face, Freeman!" Zale growled. His temper, bad at the best of times, was like a land mine in the morning. He scarcely spoke before noon, unless it was to curse anyone who got in his way. Jim gave Noel a baleful look, then dropped his head to stare at the ground.

It took some time to issue the weapons, but as soon as the men had them, Cobb said, "All right, listen to me. The weapon you're holding is a Springfield rifled musket. It weighs nine and three-quarter pounds, including the bayonet, and fires a .58 slug. By the time I get through with you, you'll be able to get off three shots a minute. Right now, we're going to find out who can shoot."

He took a few minutes to show the men how to load the muskets, then said, "All right, there's the target." He pointed to a log barricade some distance away. A white target about one foot square was affixed to the barricade. Cobb said, "I'll take the first shot." Lifting his rifle, he got off his shot, which clipped the outside edge of the target. "All right, who's next?"

All the men clamored for the chance to shoot, and Cobb said, "Armstrong, take a shot." Armstrong, a short, trim man with a lean jaw, aimed carefully — and missed the whole barricade! A howl of derision went up, and Armstrong stepped back with a red face.

Noel stood back as the others shot, keenly interested in the affair. He had never even held a gun in his hand and was certain that he'd do no better than Tate Armstrong. Several of the men did very well; Manny Zale put his bullet within two inches of dead center. He grinned wolfishly at the others, boasting, "That's the way to plug the Rebs!"

Finally Cobb said, "All right, Kojak, take your shot."

As Noel stepped forward, Zale said, "Why, it won't do no good to let the preacher shoot, Sergeant! He's too good a Christian to kill anybody. Ain't that so, Preacher?"

Cobb said irritably, "Shut up, Manny. Now just squeeze that trigger easy, Kojak."

Feeling very awkward with the eyes of the squad on him, Noel stepped forward and lifted the musket. It was heavier than he had thought, but years of hard work in the foundry had given him a set of formidable hands and forearms. He leveled the piece and held it true on the target. Somehow, though he had never held a rifle, it felt right. He squeezed the trigger, taking the kick of the piece with his shoulder.

"Dead center!" Cobb yelped. He turned to stare at Noel with wide eyes. "You done a lot of shooting, Kojak?"

"No. That was the first time I ever shot a gun."

"Beginner's luck!" Zale snorted.

"We'll see," Cobb said. "Load up and take another shot, Kojak." He watched carefully as Noel loaded the musket. Cobb was aware that his men would, on the whole, be poor shots. He needed a few good men to serve as sharpshooters. Zale was a good shot but a bad soldier. Oh, he was plenty tough, but he was always truculent and in fights.

One thing was certain — they were heading for some serious battles. Cobb and the captain had been concerned about leadership in the ranks. Now, as Noel brought his musket to bear, the first sergeant found himself hoping the young man's shot hadn't been a fluke. Kojak was a model soldier in some respects — always ready to do whatever the sergeant ordered, took good care of his equipment, and got along with the men. He was a Christian, but Cobb was willing to put up with that if he could bring some sort of steadiness to the company.

Noel took his second shot, and this time the slug hit not one inch away from the other. "Hey, that's shootin'!" Jim Freeman yelped, and Sergeant Cobb said with satisfaction, "Good shot, Kojak. You can give the rest of the boys some pointers."

Noel shifted uncomfortably. "I'll have to learn a lot more than I know now before I can do that, Sergeant Cobb." He hated being the center of attention and was glad when practice went on. He got only one more shot, though, for Sergeant Locke from regimental headquarters came up to give a note to Cobb. The sergeant studied it, then called out, "Kojak — fall out of rifle practice." When Noel looked at him in confusion, Cobb held up the note. "Go by the adjutant's and pick up a pass. You got three days' leave."

As Noel left in a daze, Manny Zale glared after him. "What's he get a leave for? He ain't done no more than the rest of us."

"Why don't you go take that up with Major Rocklin, Manny?" Cobb said with a grin. "If you don't like his answer, dress him down." Then he turned to the squad, booming out, "Get that rifle out of the dirt, Freeman!"

Noel hurried to his tent, put on his uniform, then presented himself at regimental headquarters, where a lieutenant gave him a pass, saying sourly, "You'd better be back right on time, Kojak!"

"Yes, sir!" Noel saluted and left the area hurriedly. It was seven miles from the camp to the city, but he managed to catch a ride with a civilian teamster who'd just delivered a wagonload of supplies to the quartermaster.

"Think you boys will be movin' out to stomp the Rebs pretty soon?" the driver asked. He was a cheerful middle-aged man with huge hands that held the reins expertly.

"Guess so," Noel said, then sat there listening for the rest of the trip as the teamster outlined the best strategy for overcoming the Confederacy. When they got to the outskirts of Washington and Noel stepped off, he said, "Git a few o' them Rebs for me, sodjer!"

Noel grinned and thanked the man, then turned to make his way through Negro Hill. As he passed through the area, he tried again to find some explanation for his leave, but nothing came to him.

Passing into the Swampoodle neighborhood, he was greeted several times by acquaintances. More than once he had to stop and give a brief greeting to those who insisted on speaking to him, but finally he arrived at his house. He saw at once the horse and buggy drawn up outside. *Must be the doctor,* he thought, then froze for a moment when he realized it might be the undertaker. Many people had died of the flu, and fear fluttered through him as he hurried forward to enter the house.

As he moved down the walk, the door opened, and a large black woman with a red bandanna around her head came out of the house, pausing to stare at him. She stopped abruptly, staring at him with a pair of careful brown eyes. "What you want?" she asked directly.

"Why — I live here," Noel said, faltering. Then he asked inanely, "Is somebody dead?"

"Daid! I reckon not!" The black face gave him a scornful look. "Whut fo' you talk lak dat?"

At that moment the door opened again, and Noel was astonished to see Deborah Rocklin come sailing out of the house. "Noel!" she cried out, coming to meet him. "I've been waiting for you forever! Now come on and see your mother!"

Noel felt her hands on his as she greeted him, but there was a sense of unreality as he passed through the front door. Deborah was wearing a simple brown dress with a white collar, and the sunlight made her hair seem more golden than it really was. Her eyes were sparkling as she pulled him inside, where he got another shock.

The room he knew so well was gone — or rather, transformed! There was nothing really new in it, except for some dishes he'd never seen before on the shelves and on the table, but it was spotlessly clean. The floor was whitewashed and the walls were clean. The pots and pans were hung neatly on hooks instead of being piled haphazardly on the table. Most striking of all were the yellow curtains that framed the windows.

He stopped, looking around the room, a startled expression on his face. Then he saw Grace and Sarah sitting on a bed with a quilted coverlet on it. "Hi, Noel!" Grace said. "Deborah said you'd come today." Noel went to her, noting how thin she was, but she said at once, "I've been real sick, but I'm fine now!"

He touched her hair, which was, he noted, clean and brushed. Deborah pulled at him impatiently. "You can talk to Grace and Sarah later." She pulled him into the bedroom, and he saw that the same magic had touched his parents' room. It was his mother, though, who caught his eye. She was sitting in bed and was dressed in a white gown, her hair neatly done.

"Noel!" She spoke to him, and he went to

her at once, bending over to kiss her. She clung to him, and he felt the thinness of her trembling body. "Are you all right, son?"

"I'm fine," he said, then straightened up. He turned to look at Deborah, who was watching with a smile from the doorway. "I've been wondering how I got a leave. But I guess I know now."

"She's done everything, Noel!" Anna Kojak said, her eyes fixed on Deborah. "We were about gone. I think I would have died if she hadn't come."

Noel stared at the girl who looked so unlikely to be in such a place as this poor shack. She flushed at his look, then shook her head. "Oh, nonsense! You'd have been fine, Anna!" Then she turned and left the room, saying, "You two visit. Delilah and I have work to do."

Noel sat down beside his mother. "Tell me," he said, and for the next half hour Anna told him how Deborah had arrived and thrown herself into the battle to save them.

"She worked like I never knew a woman of her class could work, Noel! You know how dirty it is taking care of sick people, but she done it all. And the next day she brought a doctor and her family servant, Delilah. And that woman is a saint! She's stayed here and nursed us all night and day. Them women have took care of us like we was their own kin, Noel!"

Noel sat there, his mind numb. He could not grasp what had happened, for it was something outside of his experience. Finally he saw that his mother was getting sleepy. "I'm better, son, but I sleep like a kitten — all the time taking little naps."

She dropped off to sleep, and Noel looked down at her, reaching out to replace a strand of her hair that had come loose. Then he turned and left the room. "Go see your brothers," Deborah commanded from where she sat with Delilah shelling peas. For the next hour Noel talked with his brothers and sisters, finding them all weak but obviously on the mend. He didn't have to pry information out of them about their rescuer, for they could talk of little else.

"She went out and got us all new stuff to sleep in, Noel," Joel piped up, pointing at a red nightshirt with pride. "I told her we just slept in whatever we had, and she went right out and come back with new clothes!"

Finally he went to where the two women were cooking on the ancient stove, saying, "Anything I can do?"

"Why, yes, Noel," Deborah said. "I've got to go buy a few things. You can drive that cantankerous mare of mine and then carry my things to the buggy."

He followed her outside, helped her in, then got in beside her and took the reins. "Go to the general store first," she commanded, and he turned the horse back toward the business district. On the way, she spoke lightly and easily of his family.

"What about Bing, my brother?" he asked.

Deborah hesitated, then said, "He came to the house once. But he's staying with somebody downtown." When he didn't respond, she said, "I had some difficulty with him, Noel. You might as well hear it from me. I thought he behaved badly, leaving the family alone, and I told him so."

"You told Bing that?"

"Yes, and he told me I was a meddlesome woman, and then he —"

She broke off abruptly, and when Noel looked at her, he saw that her face was flushed. "Well, he tried to kiss me — and I hit him with a stick of stove wood!" she finished defiantly.

Noel laughed out loud. "Good for you, Miss Steele! I hope you laid him out!"

"Oh no, nothing like that. It made him so mad he went off, cursing me."

"I'll talk to Bing." Noel sat there silently, then finally said, "Miss Steele, it's — hard for me to say what I feel."

"Oh, Noel, I hate thank-you speeches!" Deborah turned to face him, adding, "You swore an oath to serve your country, didn't you? Well, I made you a promise that I'd help your family while you were doing that. And that's what I've done."

Noel struggled with the things that were inside him, but saw that she was speaking the truth. "All right, I won't say any more, Miss Steele —"

"Noel, my name is Deborah. I think we're friends enough for first names."

They spent more time than was necessary buying the things she'd come for. She made him tell her all about his experiences, and to his amazement he was talking more than he ever had in his life. He found himself telling her about the rifle practice, about his difficulties with Manny Zale, and about his efforts to keep Jim Freeman out of trouble. He was amazed when they arrived at the house. Helping Deborah down, he shook his head, saying ruefully, "Gosh, I don't think I ever talked so much in my whole life!"

"It's been fun, Noel," Deborah said. "I guess all of us wonder what it's really like, being in the army." A thought came to her, and she said, "Before I leave, there's something I want to talk to you about. But not now. You get some wood chopped, and I'll see how Delilah's doing with the cooking."

It was a fine day for Noel. He chopped enough wood to last a week, then spent hours with his brothers and sisters, telling them about the army. Finally his father came home, and Noel was shocked to see how thin and pale he was. "Glad to see you, Pa," he said, going to meet him as he came down the walk. "You've had a hard time."

Will Kojak stared at his son, taking in the neat blue uniform, the tanned face, then nodded. "It ain't been no picnic." He paused, trying to think of some way to ask what had been on his mind for days. Finally he said, "That woman who's been comin' around here — old Rocklin's granddaughter? What's she doin' it all for? Taking care of your ma and the kids and buyin' no end of stuff?"

"Why, she just wants to help. She's done a lot, hasn't she?"

Kojak stared at the ground. He was a rough man, in form and in manners. The sickness had been his first illness, and he had been frightened by it. Always before he had been strong enough to meet whatever came, but the flu had nearly killed him. Now he was feeling his own mortality, and

140

the appearance of the Rocklin girl had confused him greatly. His was not a world that was filled with people who were willing to give. It was a dog-eat-dog existence, and he could not get the girl out of his mind. Now he looked up and asked abruptly, "She want to marry you?"

"Marry me!" Noel stared at his father, shocked at the suggestion. "Land no, Pa! She's a fine lady. That's crazy!"

"I guess so." Kojak shook his head wearily. "She had a row of some kind with Bing. He says she's no good."

"Well, you know Bing, Pa. Come on in. Supper's on the table."

Kojak said little at the table as Delilah moved around efficiently, keeping all the plates full. He watched her cautiously but said nothing. Finally, when the meal was over and Delilah had washed the dishes, it was growing dark.

"I'll drive you part of the way," Noel said. "This is a rough neighborhood."

"All right," Deborah said. "Delilah, I think this is the last night you'll have to stay. I'll take you back home tomorrow."

The night was warm, and Noel insisted on driving Deborah all the way through the worst district. She protested that it was too far for him to walk home, but he only laughed at her. The streets were filled with people out for late walks, but by the time he reached the better neighborhoods and pulled up, the stars were faintly shining.

"Don't get out, Noel," Deborah said. "I want to talk to you about your writing."

"My what?"

"Your stories." Deborah grew serious, her lips firm and her eyes glinting. "Your mother gave me some of them. I hope you don't mind."

"Why, no, Deborah — but they're just stuff I made up for my own pleasure. Can't think why they'd interest anyone else."

Deborah had not been anxious to read the stories. She had not, as a matter of fact, touched the tablets for several days after she had taken them from the drawer. But once Delilah had come and the work was done, she found time one afternoon and took out the tablet, thinking to scan it. She well knew that she would have to comment to Anna on it and wanted to be able to say, "That's nice," or something that would please the woman.

But it had not happened like that. She had begun to read rather carelessly, admiring the fine penmanship but not at all excited about reading what she assumed would be a crude type of amateur fiction. Deborah loved literature and had at one time considered becoming a writer herself, but she quickly discovered that it was one thing to appreciate good writing and quite another to produce it. She was honest enough to see that she did not have the gift and had resigned herself to reading. She read everything, but fiction was her first love, and as she began to read the story titled "No Hope for Emily," she was rather blasé about it.

Almost at once she became aware that this was not an ordinary composition. There was a roughness about it, to be sure. Some misspelled words and some awkwardness of sentence structure. But there was something else that seized her at once.

The story was about a sixteen-year-old girl named Emily who lived in the Swampoodle district. The plot was simple enough: A young girl longed to find a husband and have a good home. But there was such a graphic quality in the description that Deborah entered into the story fully. Noel had caught the essence of the poverty and hardship Deborah had seen during her days in the district. He had brought to life the coarse food, the barren houses, the dirt that never got cleaned up, the grinding labor that wore men and women out by the time they were barely out of their teens. All of this was there, in a simple prose that fixed everything on the page.

And the girl — Emily — was real. Deborah somehow sensed that Noel had known her and had liked her. She was no creature of fiction, for by the time Deborah finished the story, tears were in her eyes. The girl had struggled to keep herself pure, but the world she lived in had been inexorable. She had turned bad, going through the worst of her world, ending her own life in despair at the age of nineteen.

Deborah had read all the stories and now knew that Noel was the most gifted writer she'd ever met.

"Noel, you don't know what you have," she now said earnestly. "I'm no expert, but I've read a lot. God has given you a great gift."

Noel stared at her, for such a thing had never entered his head. "Why, Deborah, you're just being kind. I just write down stories that are in my head. I mean, I just write about things I've seen."

"That's what makes you different," Deborah insisted. "People can learn to write, up to a point. They can learn the techniques, how to make chapters and things like that. But most of us can't put any life into the things we write. Did you know your Emily?"

"Yes. She lived two houses down from us. I — liked her a lot, Deborah. Made me feel so bad when she went the way she did."

"And when you put what you felt in your story, it made me feel the same way!" Deborah said. "That's what great literature is, Noel. Great writers like Dickens and Cooper, they make us *feel.*"

Noel was struck by her remark. "You know, Deborah, I never thought of it until right this minute," he said thoughtfully, his face broken into sharp planes where the yellow glow of a streetlight reflected on it. "But the times I seem to be most alive are when I'm writing about people." Then he laughed shortly, adding, "But I could never be a real writer."

"You *are* a real writer, Noel!" Deborah insisted sharply. In her desire to get through to him, she took his arm and held it tightly. She had the feeling that somehow she was responsible for the young man. He had a talent that the world needed and might never do a thing with it unless someone helped him develop it. "What you've done proves it," she insisted. "You didn't write to make money or to see your name in print. You write because it's what's in you, because you want to share what you think and feel with others."

"Well, I guess the others are Ma and you. Nobody else has seen them."

"But they should see them, Noel." Taking a deep breath, she paused, then said, "Noel, I've been thinking a lot about this. You're going to be a soldier. My uncle thinks this will be a long war, a terrible war. Who's going to write about it, to let the world see it as it really is?"

"Why, the writers, I guess."

"That's right — and where will they be? Cooped up in their study in Boston! They'll never hear a cannon fire or hear a young man gasping his last breath on earth, will they? But you will, Noel! You've got to write about it!"

Noel was stunned by Deborah's intensity. He sat there in disbelief, then finally shook his head. "Even if I could write it, Deborah, who would read it? You have to be somebody big to get a book published. Even I know that!"

Deborah shook his arm, saying fiercely, "Noel Kojak, you are somebody! You're a soldier in the United States Army! You're a young man with a great talent! Don't ever let me hear you say you're a nobody, you hear me!"

Suddenly Noel smiled. "I hear you all right, Deborah — and I guess everybody else on this side of Washington hears you, too. Do you know you're shouting at me?"

"Well, I don't care!" Deborah lowered her voice, then sat there quietly. She had been waiting for the chance to talk with Noel ever since reading the stories, and now she feared she had done it badly. Finally she said, "I know all this is new to you, Noel, but you've got to let me help you. Would you let me take some of your stories to a man who can help? His name is Langdon Devoe. He's a publisher right here in Washington."

"Why, sure, Deborah," Noel said. "What kind of books does he print?"

"Oh, all kinds. He did a lot of publishing for the movement, the abolitionist movement, I mean. He likes me and he knows good writing when he sees it. I'll see him as quick as I can, but you have to promise me something."

Noel stared at her in the glimmering darkness. "I've been wishing there was something I could do for you, Deborah."

She looked at him sharply, hearing something in his voice that hadn't been there before. "Well, Noel, this is for both of us. You write all the time from now on. I know you'll be busy and it'll be hard. But make yourself do it. Write about the drills, the men in your company. The bad ones and the good ones. And make it honest. Don't try to make it literary. There'll be lots of people writing that sort of thing." She thought hard, then added, "Write it like the one about Emily."

"I'll do it," Noel said at once.

She put her hand out, and he took it readily. "It's a bargain, then," Deborah said. "You do the writing, and I'll do the rest."

He found her hand soft and somehow enticing — and he was suddenly totally aware of the beauty of the girl who sat beside him. He became so engrossed with admiring the smooth loveliness of her cheeks and the lustrous darkness of her eyes that he unconsciously held on to her hand.

Deborah, too, was suddenly aware of Noel for the first time as a young man who admired her, and she did not know what to do. She had, at first, thought of him only as an object of pity. Now as she looked into his face, she was aware that this was an unusual young man. There was a clean strength in his even features, in the sweeping jawline that denoted determination and the steady gray eyes that were warm and honest. There was, she understood, no trickery in this young man, and she suddenly felt very close to him.

"I–I'm glad we're going to be good friends, Noel," she said, and when he released her hand, she smiled at him. "I'll see you in the morning."

He got down and looked up at her. "It sure has been a strange time for me, Deborah. When I got up this morning, I never imagined I'd be here with you tonight. I — I know you said not to mention it, but I got to thank you for all you've done for my family." He said no more, but she saw the gratitude in his eyes. Then he ducked his head, and when he lifted it, he grinned. "About me being a writer, I got to say that I'm doing it because of you. Good night, Deborah!"

"Good night, Noel."

He turned and disappeared into the night, but as Deborah Steele watched him go, she had a premonition. She had never had one before, but as she sat there in the buggy, something deep within her seemed to tell her that Noel Kojak would play a big part in her life. It was very real, and as she drove homeward, the impression grew stronger. Finally she looked up into the stars, wondering what it all could mean. But the stars had no answer. They were impressive enough, winking like diamonds in the deep velvet sky, but they had nothing to say.

"We'll see," she said to the mare, who perked her ears, nickered twice, then picked up her hooves and started down the dusty road at a fast pace.

■ ■ ■ ■ ■

PART TWO:
RICHMOND

■ ■ ■ ■ ■

CHAPTER 7
A SMALL ISLAND

The pearly morning light that spilled over the distant treetops pleased Clay Rocklin. He had risen before dawn, saddled his gray gelding, and made his way to the fields where he now sat. The sight of the broad fields that made up Gracefield, his plantation, always filled him with pleasure. Sitting hipshot in the saddle, he achieved a moment's stillness that was uncharacteristic of him.

He was a man of loose, rough, durable parts. Like a machine intended for hard usage, he had no fineness and little smoothness about him. He was one of the Black Rocklins, those of raven hair, olive skin, and dark eyes. His long mouth was expressive when he smiled, and he had the darkest of eyes, sharp and clear.

All of this made a face that, in repose, reflected the mixed elements of sadness and rash temper. A scar shaped like a fishhook was at the left corner of his mouth, the relic of a fistfight he'd had when he was younger and eager to indulge in action. Now, at forty-one, he had better control of himself.

Clay could only remain still for so long, and with an impulsive tug at the reins, he touched the gray with his heels. The large animal responded by throwing himself into an enthusiastic gallop and following the edge of the mile-long field. The soft warmth of May had bathed Virginia, and by the time Clay had circled the edge of the field and made his way through a first-growth thicket of towering water oak, he was beginning to feel the heat. He pulled King to a halt at the edge of a sea of emerald sorghum and removed his light jacket, stuffing it into a saddlebag. Clay's deep chest swelled against the thin white cotton shirt, and his considerable physical strength, gained through years at sea, was evident in his corded wrists and square, powerful hands.

Once again he paused, pleased by the fields. It had been his idea to plant sorghum. His father, Thomas, was adamantly certain that planting anything except cotton was a waste of good land. Clay was equally certain that planting only cotton was a sure way to ruin. He had seen the mountains of cotton bales on the docks and was sure the market was headed for a glut. Already the rumor was rife that the new president of the Confederacy favored an embargo against Britain. The hope was that the refusal to send cotton to England would draw the British into giving aid to the new nation being birthed in the South.

When Clay had first heard his brother-in-law Brad Franklin state this, he had stared at the man, saying, "Brad, we're not the only country that grows cotton. Besides, England's got a good supply in their warehouses. What we'd better do is ship every bale we've got to England right now, because you can bet the first thing the Federals will do is blockade our coasts. Then what will you do with your cotton . . . sell it to the Yankees?"

Brad had only laughed at him, saying, "Cotton is king, Clay. You'll see!"

Ever since planting had begun, Clay had carried on the same battle with his father, the older man resisting every innovation his son tried to make. Clay had kept his temper for the most part, for he had no desire to anger his father. Actually, Gracefield belonged to Clay more than to Thomas Rocklin. Clay had returned two years ago after a long exile from his family, just in time to save the great plantation from financial ruin.

It had been difficult for him to return.

The reason was perhaps natural, for Clay had abandoned his wife and children after a wild and misspent youth, leaving them at Gracefield to be provided for. As he sat now atop his horse and watched the sea of green shoots waving in the breeze, he thought of his youthful, rash love for Melanie Benton, who was now married to his cousin Gideon. Quickly he shook that off, for it was painful to think how he had allowed his raw passions for the beautiful young girl to drive him into ruin — and into an imprudent marriage to a woman he did not love. Saving Gracefield meant coming back to face all that he had run from . . . and that had been most difficult indeed.

Clay also struggled with guilt over the fact that he had made his small fortune in a dirty business: slave running. And it was that ill-made fortune that he had used to reestablish the plantation. Even now, two years after he had sold his share of the ship, he awoke at night crying out in fear and disgust at the thought of the terrible suffering the black men and women — and children — had undergone in the passage from Africa to the States. He still felt dirty and unclean at times. Though he knew he was forgiven by God, he wondered if the shame he felt would ever go away completely.

As the sun rose over the oaks surrounding the fields, Clay turned King's head north and made his way slowly around the field. He was in no rush to get home for breakfast, so he let the horse pick his way slowly through fields still damp with dew. He passed a line of slaves, led by Highboy, headed for the fields. Highboy greeted him cheerfully as always: "Hi, Marse Clay!"

"Hello, Highboy. Better take care of that twenty acres over by the pond today." Highboy gave him an indignant look, whereupon Clay smiled suddenly, his teeth making a white slash across his tanned face. "But you know that better than I do," he said, knowing it to be true. The tall son of Box and Carrie knew every blade of grass on the Gracefield earth. "See you later, Highboy," Clay said, touching his heels to the horse. The gray responded at once, breaking into an easy run. Clay let him go, enjoying the motion of the animal. As they covered the ground, the man's eyes moved constantly over the fields, missing nothing.

Finally he rounded a cornfield and took a barely discernible trail through a small forest of loblolly pine, pulling the horse to a walk as he emerged into the wide clearing where the Rocklin mansion sat. The sight of the house always stirred Clay; the long years of alienation at sea had whetted his love for the place. Smoke was rising from the kitchen chimney, and though he knew that Dorrie would have breakfast waiting, Clay sat there for a moment, savoring the silence and peace of the morning.

Gracefield had been built by an Englishman who had incorporated in his creation more than a few of the characteristics of the fine homes of England. The house was an imposing Greek Revival plantation home, and it glittered white in the morning sun as Clay sat there admiring it. It was a two-story house with a steep roof adorned by three gables on each side. The most striking feature was the line of rising smooth columns, which ran across the front and down both sides, enclosing the structure within the imposing white shafts. The ground behind the house held the outbuildings. Large grape arbors flanked the main house on both sides. The front lawn was a flat carpet of rich green broken by a sweeping U-shaped driveway filled with oyster shells.

As Clay moved out of the grove and toward the house, he thought suddenly how similar Gracefield was to an island. The plantation, surrounded by others like it — as well as by hills, fields, and streams —

was almost self-sustaining. Almost all the food the Rocklins ate was grown in their own fields, and up until recently, communication with the outside world had been tenuous. Riding down the sweeping driveway, Clay remembered how as a boy he had thought that Gracefield was all the world. Longingly he thought, *I wish it was! There are worse things than being marooned on a desert island.*

He dismounted and tossed the reins to Moses, Dorrie and Zander's oldest son. The boy grinned at him, saying, "You better git in to brekfuss, Marse Clay, 'fore Dorrie have her a fit."

Clay grinned at Moses. Dorrie had been a house slave at Gracefield since she was six and was more or less the general of the mansion, second only to Susanna, Clay's mother, in power and authority. And she did not look with favor on anyone who flaunted her well-orchestrated schedules, even "Master Clay," who had always been a favorite with the dark woman.

Clay fished in his pocket and found a piece of hard candy wrapped in paper. Tossing it to the boy, he said, "Walk King for me, Moses, then let him graze in the meadow." He left the boy sucking ecstatically on the candy and entered the house by the front door. Two of the house slaves, both young girls, were polishing the heart-pine floor, and he spoke to them as he passed by the massive stairway that led to the second floor. The family was gathered in the dining room, already eating as he entered.

"Whar you been?" Dorrie demanded, staring at him out of a pair of sharp brown eyes. "You sit down and eat 'fore them eggs freeze!"

"Sorry, Dorrie," Clay said contritely, taking his place across from his mother, just to the right of his father, who sat at the head of the table. "Good morning," he said, taking the plate of eggs his mother handed him. "Sorry to be late." He filled his plate with grits, eggs, ham, and biscuits, then said, "The sorghum looks good. We'll be eating our own syrup next fall."

"How do you make it, Father?" It was typical that David would ask, for he was the one of Clay's sons with the sort of mind that had to know things. Dent, his twin, had never shown any interest in the workings of the plantation, nor had Lowell, the youngest boy. David, however, had put his nose into a book as soon as he could read and had poked into every nook and cranny of the place, insatiably curious about everything. At nineteen, he was the best student in his college, and Clay had to smile as he answered, "Don't know, David. We'll have to go over to the Payson place. They've got a sorghum mill over there. I guess you can draw a plan of the thing."

"Yes, sir." David nodded, brightening at once. "Then Box and me will make it."

"Don't see any need of such a thing, Clay." Thomas Rocklin was shoving his food around on his plate. Clay glanced at his father and noted how ill he looked as he added, "We don't eat much of the stuff, and we can buy what we need from Payson. We could get five bales of cotton off that land."

"Why, Grandfather," Rena said, "We can't pour cotton over our pancakes!" She was the only daughter of Clay and Ellen and, at the age of fifteen, was caught in that awkward period between childhood and womanhood. She had deep blue eyes, dark brown hair, and a sweet expression.

Thomas stared at her, snorted, and said almost harshly, "You can't make cloth out of sorghum, either, miss! And England wants cotton, not syrup!"

Clay said quickly, "We'll have a good cotton crop, sir. But the land needs a rest from too much cotton."

Denton put his fork down with a violent gesture. He was wearing his new uniform of ash gray with polished leather and straps. "This is no time to worry about such things. We're in a war!" Denton and David were identical twins, but few people ever mistook one for the other. Both were fine-looking young men, but there was a fiery manner about Dent that his brother lacked. Some of that raw impatience came out now as Dent stared across the table at his father. "When we've whipped the Yankees, it'll be time to worry about rotating crops."

"Right, my boy!" Thomas Rocklin gave an approving thump to the table. He was a tall, thin shape at the table, and as his wife, Susanna, looked at him, she thought how much he had been like Denton as a young man — rash and impulsive. He had lost that ramrod-straight posture of his youth and was now bent. His once-black hair was tinged with silver, and his shoulders were thin. Yet despite the ill health that had plagued him for the last year, he was still handsome. For all his good looks and powerful personality, though, Thomas Rocklin had been a poor husband. But Susanna had remained true to him.

Susanna Rocklin was the driving force of Gracefield, inside the house at least. She was an attractive woman of sixty, her auburn hair darker than when she was younger, but still glossy and full. She had a pair of even, greenish eyes, which were now fixed on Clay.

He's done so well since he came back! she thought. But it would not do to say so in front of Thomas, for her husband still harbored a black streak of anger toward his son. He had never forgiven Clay for what he felt was rank disloyalty to the Rocklin family. His feelings had smoldered over the years, and when Clay had finally returned, it had taken much persuasion from Susanna to get him to let Clay stay.

Suddenly Susanna looked at Ellen, Clay's wife, and a startling thought flashed across her mind as she studied the woman's face: *She hates Clay. She never loved him — but now it's worse.*

As if she had sensed Susanna's thoughts, Ellen Rocklin turned and looked across the table at her mother-in-law. At nineteen Ellen had been a lush beauty, but there had been something predatory about her even then. It had come as a shock to Thomas and Susanna when Clay had brought her home from Washington to announce their engagement. Something had happened there, Susanna had always known, but neither Clay nor Ellen ever spoke of it. One thing Susanna knew for certain — it had something

163

to do with Melanie Rocklin.

Susanna remembered how Clay had been wildly in love with Melanie and how devastated he was when Melanie had chosen Gideon, the son of Stephen Rocklin, Thomas's older brother. Somehow, in the midst of that devastation, Clay and Ellen had come together. Susanna had worried that the marriage was a mistake . . . and there was little even now, so many years later, to prove that worry wrong.

Clay and Ellen's marriage had been stormy enough before Clay had abandoned them all. Now that he was back, it was different. Not better, just different. Clay did not even stay in the big house but kept his quarters in the summerhouse. Ellen stayed in Richmond most of the time, coming back to Gracefield when her funds ran low. They shared none of the closeness of man and wife, as Susanna — and everyone else — knew.

"Clay, I need to talk to you," Ellen said, breaking into Susanna's train of thought. Susanna watched as the woman rose and left the table. Clay, after giving his wife a strange look, rose and followed her. She went into the library, then turned at once and said, "Clay, I've got to have some money."

Clay gave her an even look but shook his head firmly. "There isn't any right now, Ellen. I told you when I gave you your allowance it would have to do you."

She stared at him, the anger in her eyes plain to see. "You've got to give it to me!" She was forty now and still attractive. There was a certain quality in her lips and figure that caught men's attention. She had begun to use too much makeup and wore clothes that were too young for her, yet men were drawn to her. She had worked hard keeping her figure and her reputation, though the latter was more difficult. Still, she had entrance into some of Virginia's plushest homes.

But nothing could change the one overriding factor in her life: her hatred of her husband. That hatred was based on two things, two things for which she had never forgiven Clay — for loving Melanie Benton and for abandoning her. She always insisted that it was his abandonment of the children that was the basis of her anger, but it was not; Ellen was a woman who had to possess things, and Clay had refused to let her own him. She knew that his flight was as much from her as from his hopeless love for his cousin's wife.

"You love to make me beg, don't you,

Clay!" she cried, her voice rising. "If it were your precious Melanie, you'd hand out the money fast enough!"

Clay stood there, his heart cold and barren as polar ice. Whatever he had felt for Ellen had died long ago. She had tricked him into marriage, and it had been wrong from the start. He had hoped that the children would make it bearable, but finally he had gone over the edge and fled his home. Now he half wished that he had never returned, but he kept his voice even as he replied, "Ellen, that's absurd and you know it. Melanie's nothing to me but a fine friend. As for the money, I've told you the truth. Things are tight . . . and they're going to get tighter. All we have to sell is cotton, and as you've probably heard, it's going to be impossible to sell cotton if Davis and the Congress go through with their plan to cut off sales to England."

She glared at him, then raged as he stood there regarding her. Finally he said, "Your hotel bill is paid. If you've spent the rest of your money, you'll have to stay here — or eat with your friends in Richmond."

Instantly she laughed, her lips contorted. "You'd like to know who takes me out to dinner, wouldn't you?"

"No, I wouldn't." Clay turned and walked

away, going out the front door, sickened by his brief interview with Ellen. He knew that she hated him. That had become clearer than ever after an incident that had occurred months earlier. When he had first returned, Ellen had slashed at him, warning him that he would never be a husband to her. Clay had expected that, and it relieved him greatly. He did not want anything from his wife, especially physical intimacy. But when Ellen saw that he seemed uninterested, she paradoxically began to try to gain his attention. Finally she had come to the summerhouse late one night to see him alone. When Clay had rejected her, she had cursed him like a madwoman. From that time, she had made little or no effort to hide her hatred, and Clay had been forced to endure her tirades as best he could.

Clay headed for the summerhouse. It was a small structure, only two rooms, but Clay had made himself a cozy bachelor's quarters out of it. Decay had been at it, but he had taken pleasure in working hard with the help of Highboy and a few others to make it into a very attractive place. Now as he walked down the narrow lane that led to it and entered the sequestered area under tall pines where the house rested on a slight rise, he felt a sense of despair.

Entering the house, he sat down and stared blankly at the floor for a long time. Thinking of the problems that loomed ahead for him, he felt drained and tired. He thought of the war that was on the horizon. No battles had been fought since Fort Sumter had fallen, but they would come. There were too many fire-eaters in the Southern camp, and the people of the North were bound and determined to keep the Union intact. He saw nothing but ruin down that road, for he had been in the North and knew that it was a sleeping giant, with factories, coal, steel mills, and industrial might as yet unrealized. His own life, too, was a shambles. His marriage was a farce, and Denton, he well understood, resented him for his long absence. The other children had forgiven him as best they could, but he had robbed them of a father, and that he could never restore.

"Daddy?"

Clay gave a start, then smiled as Rena opened the door and peered in tentatively. "Daddy, can I come in?"

"Come in, Rena," Clay said, and his mood lightened as the girl came to stand before him. She had been withdrawn and hostile when he'd first returned to Gracefield, but he'd found out that she was really starved for affection. It had gladdened his heart as she had slowly opened up to him, and now he smiled at her fondly. "What's on your schedule today? Finding more sick animals to take care of?"

Rena made a face at him, for it was something he teased her about often. She had something in her that made her want to help when sickness came to humans or animals. That desire most often found an outlet in taking care of any animal that became ill on the farm, or any injured or ailing wild animals that were brought to her. Not long ago Clay had brought her a small raccoon with a broken leg. "How's Bandit?" he asked.

Her expressive face brightened as she replied, "Oh, Daddy, he's almost well!"

As she went on to tell about her care for the wounded animal, Clay thought, *If everyone were as sweet and gentle as this child, it'd be a good world.* Finally he said, "That's good, Rena, but don't get too close to Bandit."

"Why not, Daddy?"

"Because you'll have to part with him sooner or later."

"Can't we keep him as a pet?"

"No, he's not a tame animal. He's wild, and sooner or later he'll have to go back to his own."

"But — I don't want him to go," Rena protested. "I love him!"

Clay reached out and drew the girl closer, his arm around her. She did not hold back as she once would have done. "I know," he said gently, "but it wouldn't be best for Bandit. Wild things aren't happy in cages, and that's what you'd have to keep him in." He hesitated, then added, "You have to learn to let things go, Rena. We all do."

She was very still in his embrace, her features troubled. She was the most sensitive thing Clay had ever known, and his love for her was beyond measure. Finally she whispered, "I won't have to let you go, will I, Daddy?"

His grip on her tightened, and he realized suddenly that Rena was more deeply scarred than he had guessed. The shame of abandoning her cut into him like a razor. She was afraid he would leave again. More than anything he wanted to give her security, but he knew better than to make any promises that went beyond his power to keep.

He drew her closer and kissed her cheek. "You'll never lose me if I can help it, sweetheart," he said huskily. "Lots of things are happening, but I'll do my best to stay close to you always."

"Will you really, Daddy?"

"Really!"

She lay against him, seeming to soak up the love that she sensed in him, but finally she asked tentatively, "Daddy, will we ever . . . be a family again?" It was not quite what she wanted to ask, and she pulled back to look into his face. "I mean, will you and Mother ever be together?"

Clay wanted to assure her but knew that he could not. "I don't know what's going to happen, Rena. But one thing I do know — I love you, and I won't ever leave you if I can help it. And I'll always help your mother as much as I can."

Clay had no idea how much Rena understood about him and Ellen — probably more than he had thought — but he could say no more.

She seemed content to stand there with him, not replying. Finally she looked up at him and smiled. "I'm glad you're here, Daddy. I was so lonesome for you while you were gone!" Then she seemed to feel uncomfortable, or at least her mood passed. "Daddy, can I go to the ball in Richmond next week?"

"You're too young for balls," he told her with a smile, relieved at the change of topic. "Besides, you're getting too pretty. Some young fellow might try to steal you."

"Oh, Daddy!" Rena flushed with pleasure, then began to beg him to let her go. Clay had already decided that he would take her, but he let her wheedle him, taking pleasure in her bright eyes and eager voice.

Finally he said, "All right, but you can only dance with me or your brothers."

"Oh, thank you, Daddy!" She kissed him with a loud smack, then ran off, saying, "I've got to get Grandmother to help me with a dress!"

Clay stood there watching her fly up the path to the Big House; then he moved back inside. If only he could win the hearts of others as easily as he'd won Rena's.

CHAPTER 8
THE YANCYS

The Reverend Jeremiah Irons had some of the quality of his name in his character. Not that he was a weeping prophet like his namesake in the Old Testament, but there was something of a stubborn streak in him. In fact, so strong was this streak that some of his parishioners called him "Old Ironsides" — the nickname given to Oliver Cromwell, who had ruled England with an iron fist.

Despite the shared nickname, Jeremiah Irons was nothing like the dour Cromwell. Rather, the pastor of Grace Congregational Church fully appreciated a good joke. This fact and his renown as a crack shot made Irons a popular man with the hunters of the county. He was always welcome on a hunt — though he steadfastly refused to join them in a drink of the fiery liquor that usually accompanied them on such expeditions. But there was no sign of humor on the minister's broad lips as he drove his buggy along the road leading to Gracefield on Friday afternoon. His fifteen-year-old daughter, Ann, sat beside him, chattering away about things that mattered to her. From time to time he would put in a question, but his mind was elsewhere. A man of no more than medium height, Irons was still as wiry at the age of forty-one as he had been when he had left the hills of Arkansas at the age of sixteen. He was not a particularly handsome man, though he had neat features and agreeable brown eyes. He was the despair of a large segment of his congregation — that segment made up of single young women, women with marriageable daughters, and widows looking for a second go at marital bliss.

When his wife, Lorraine, had died, he had stubbornly insisted on rearing their two children alone. It had been a difficult time for him, as well as for the children, Asa and Ann. They had, he had always known, missed their mother and had fully expected him to remarry. Now Asa at the age of sixteen and Ann at fifteen were still showing signs of resentment over his refusal to marry. Asa had said nothing, but Ann had more than once questioned him closely about his singleness. Looking at her now, her face illuminated by the afternoon sun, he felt guilty over his failure.

His elders at the church had often expressed their displeasure over his single state. When he had quoted St. Paul's maxim from scripture, "I say therefore to the unmarried and widows, it is good for them if they abide as I," they had frowned, indicating that that was very well during biblical times, but the pastor of Grace Church needed to set an example for his congregation. Irons's refusal to marry had been a touchy subject, and at the last meeting Elder Rufus Matlock had said bluntly, "Rev. Irons, if you can't see your way clear to marry, it would be best if you found another congregation."

Irons had stared at the elder with a pair of direct brown eyes, knowing that this was a final warning; the two had clashed over this matter many times. As the pastor drove along the dusty road, then turned into the oyster-shell drive of Gracefield, he knew that in a power struggle against Elder Matlock, he would lose. Irons had no patience with political maneuvering, and his direct preaching had not been calculated to make him popular. He had offended many with his direct bombshell hits on sin, and if the matter came to a vote, he knew that he would be without a congregation.

He glanced at the Rocklin mansion as he drove closer. As always, he admired the lines of the house and the way it overlooked the expanse of green, but his mind was on things other than architectural beauty. He was a man who never flinched from a hard task, but the occasion of his visit to Clay Rocklin was especially difficult. He and Clay had been friends for years; there was no man who admired Rocklin's determined efforts to rebuild a shattered life more than the pastor of Grace Church. Irons was closer to Clay than any other man, and the pastor knew that hard times lay ahead for Clay Rocklin because of his stand against the war.

Now he was coming to add to the big man's burden.

Irons pulled the buggy up to the front porch and handed the lines to Moses, then moved with Ann up the steps. They were met by the mistress of Gracefield, Susanna Rocklin. "Come in, Brother Irons, and you, too, Ann. My, what a pretty dress!"

"Thank you," Ann said with a nod. Then she asked at once, "Is Rena here, Mrs. Rocklin?"

"She's down at the summerhouse, Ann. Why don't you run on down, and you two can have some time together. You're staying for supper, I trust, Reverend?"

There was no table that Irons enjoyed more than the one set by Susanna Rocklin, but an uncertainty moved in him. When he hesitated, Susanna was surprised. It was so unlike Irons to show any sort of doubt that she knew at once he was struggling with a problem. "Of course you will!" she said quickly, taking the struggle out of his hands. "You've been neglecting me lately, so tonight you've got to give me some of your time."

"All right, Susanna." Irons smiled, knowing that she had noted his uncertainty. He turned to his daughter. "You run on to see Rena, Ann. Have a good time." As she ran down the steps, Irons followed Susanna into the house.

She led him into the small parlor she used for sewing and said, "You sit right down. I'll have Dorrie make us some fresh tea — no, you like coffee better — and Dorrie made a cake this afternoon. It won't spoil your supper to sample it."

As she moved away, Irons relaxed on the horsehair sofa and looked out through the mullioned windows. A small crew of slaves were barbering the green lawn just outside. They moved slowly, clipping the grass carefully, and the sound of their lazy laughter floated on the air.

Why didn't Harriet Beecher Stowe put that in her book? he thought with a stab of irritation. He himself hated slavery and made no bones about it, but he knew full well that the North deceived itself, believing that freeing the slaves would bring them into an Edenic state. He had no answers to offer for the nation's conflict — but thought of the words of the fanatic John Brown, who had said before being hanged, "This thing called slavery can only be washed away by blood."

The pastor sat there in the quietness of the room, trying to find some way to avoid talking to Clay. But he was grimly aware that there was none. He was trapped by his position as minister, and Clay was bound by other forces. Now he could do no less than meet the thing head on.

"Now you eat this, Brother Irons," Susanna said, returning with a silver tray filled with coffee, tea, and cake. "I can bake a better cake than Dorrie, but she refuses to admit it. I'm sure you'll agree." She smiled at him, pouring his coffee into a fragile china cup that looked small in the pastor's hand. "Remember that chocolate cake I sent to you last month?"

Irons smiled at her but said, "Susanna,

I'm bound not to say who's the best cook. An old bachelor like me can't afford to offend anybody who can cook." His lips parted in a smile, and humor lit his brown eyes. "Now between ourselves, I'll admit you're the best cook in Virginia, but I'll never repeat that in front of Dorrie."

"You're a fine minister!" Susanna cried out in mock horror. "Dorrie just told me you said she was the best cook in the whole state!"

"I'm just a poor sinner," Irons said mournfully, shoving a huge bite of the cake into his mouth. "Especially where cake is concerned, Susanna. Got no character at all."

She smiled at him, and he was touched by her warmth. Their close friendship had begun almost as soon as he had come to Grace Church as pastor. He had made enough mistakes to get ten preachers run off, and it had been Susanna Rocklin who had brought him through the difficult years. She had smoothed ruffled feelings among the congregation while she taught Irons that a pastor could be strong and tactful at the same time. He had discovered in the woman a strength that was lacking in her husband, Thomas. It was to her that he often came with his problems.

Finally, after they had talked quietly,

enjoying each other's company, Susanna asked, "What's troubling you, Jeremiah?"

He looked at her with a smile. "I never could hide anything from you, could I?"

"You can't hide much from anyone," she said. "You're a direct man. It's hard for you to cover things up." Susanna sipped her tea, then asked quietly, "I suppose it has something to do with the Rocklin family?"

"Well, yes —" Dissatisfaction stirred the shoulders of Irons, and he gripped his hands together, which Susanna recognized as a sign of agitation. "I'd rather be whipped than come here with this, Susanna."

"What is it?"

"It's about Clay," he said evenly. "And Melora Yancy."

Susanna did not speak but let her eyes remain on the preacher's face. She had been expecting something unpleasant, and now it was here. The silence ran on, and finally she said, "It's especially hard for you, Jeremiah."

In that one phrase she said a great deal. In it, she indicated that she was aware that Jeremiah Irons was in love with Melora Yancy, which was no secret, since most people suspected it. Susanna had known for a long time of the minister's love for Melora, though he had never spoken to her of it. Still, Susanna had seen it in his attitude

180

toward the woman, in his eyes when he looked at her, and in the gentleness he always manifested toward her.

Susanna knew, perhaps better than anyone else, the loneliness in Irons. She was lonely in much the same way. His wife was dead; her husband was removed and weak in many ways. She could no more get close to Thomas than Irons could get close to his dead wife.

"The elders . . . they insist that I speak to both of them." Irons rose, walked to the windows, and peered out, seeing nothing. After a moment, he came back to stand and look down on her. "I ought to resign from the church, Susanna."

"What would that accomplish? Whoever came to follow you wouldn't be God's man for Grace Church."

"He wouldn't be all tangled up in his own harness, either!" Irons said almost bitterly. "How can I talk to Clay about this? Or Melora?"

Susanna rose and took his hands. "You'll talk to them as you talk to everybody, Jeremiah. Honestly and without guile. Do you think they don't know there's been talk about them?"

The preacher's face flushed, and he shook his head. "I nearly punched the jaw of Elder

Matlock when he came to me and said Clay and Melora were too close."

"He's only repeating what others have said," Susanna said gently. "You can't go around punching the jaw of every gossiper in the community, can you?" Then she said, "Sit down. We must pray about this."

Irons sat down and said quietly, "Yes, we'd better pray, Susanna. Because only God can do anything about this thing. It's beyond me — beyond anybody!"

Rena Rocklin and Ann Irons were best friends. They seldom had much time together, so the afternoon was a pleasure for them both. At fifteen, both girls were filled with the fears and anticipations of that particular age. They had grown up together, sharing the same tutors who had come to Gracefield and attending the same church all their lives. Often they had spent the night together, alternating between Gracefield and the parsonage, where the Irons family lived.

All afternoon they talked eagerly as they roamed the fields together and retired into the summerhouse. Rena found plenty of snacks, and as the two ate cookies and drank fresh milk, they giggled and laughed outright. Rena showed Ann the new drawings she had made, brought her up to date on her "hospital" of sick and wounded animals, and listened in turn as Ann talked about the Jennings family, a new family that had moved into the community and joined the church. She said so much about one family member, a boy named James, that Rena finally grinned, saying, "I think you've got a case on him, this James Jennings."

Ann stared at her, then cried out, "Oh, Rena, I like him so much — but Papa goes into a fit if I even eat a bowl of ice cream with him at a sociable! I wish I were dead!"

Rena, well accustomed to the overreactions of her friend, comforted her as well as she could. "Tell me about him, Ann. Is he tall? How old is he?" When she had absorbed all the details, she nodded, saying, "Listen, my birthday is in two weeks. I'll make Daddy ask him to my party. Then you can eat all the ice cream you want with James Jennings."

Ann was ecstatic. She hugged Rena and walked around the room making plans for the unknowing young man. Rena was glad she could do so much for Ann, for she was fond of her. But unfortunately, she blundered into the one topic that brought Ann's joy to a halt. Forgetting that Ann was the daughter of a minister and therefore was unable to attend dances, she mentioned that her father had just told her that she could attend the Officers' Ball in Richmond the following week. She was so excited at the prospect that it escaped her notice that the more she spoke of the ball, the more Ann Irons turned gloomy.

Finally Ann cried out, "It's not fair! You have all the good times, Rena! I never get to have any fun!"

Rena was caught off guard, but when she saw the resentment on Ann's brow, she grew a little angry. "What do you mean I have all the good times? I've just told you how I'm going to get that old boy to my party, and just for you!"

"Who cares about your old party?" Ann snapped back, not meaning a word of it but mortified and stung by Rena's attack. "What's a silly old party next to the Officers' Ball in Richmond?"

"Well, if you feel like that, you don't have to come to my party yourself!" Rena regretted the words the moment they left her lips. She was a gentle girl and hated to hurt anyone. She was about to apologize and put her arms around Ann, but she was too late.

One thing that Ann Irons had inherited from her mother was a quick temper, and it rose up in her at once. "I wouldn't come to

184

your old party!" she cried out. "My father wouldn't let me. He doesn't want me having anything to do with the daughter of an adulterer!"

The words hung in the air, both girls shocked into silence.

"Oh, Rena — !" Ann exclaimed, horrified at what she had said, but at that moment the door opened and her father walked in, along with Clay Rocklin.

The two men had been walking slowly down the path from the house. They had had their talk, and it had been very painful for both of them. Irons had put the matter simply: "Clay, I know you and Melora are innocent, but people are talking. They're saying that you spend too much time with an unmarried young woman. The elders asked me to speak to you about it, and they'd like you to meet with them. I've done that now, so I'll say no more."

Clay had flushed, an angry retort rising to his lips, but when he saw the pain in his friend's face, he swallowed the words. "It's hard on you, Jerry," he had said. "I'll pray about it."

That had been the extent of their conversation, and both of them were saddened by it. Clay had known for a long time that Irons had refused to marry because he was in love with Melora. More than once he had urged the minister to press his case. But Irons had said evenly, "In Melora's eyes you're the only man in the world, Clay." Since then, the two had steered clear of talk about the situation. The fact that they remained close friends despite all this was evidence of the depth and strength of their bond.

Now as they entered the summerhouse, they looked at the girls. Both men had heard Ann's angry cry, and Irons said firmly, "Ann, you will apologize for your remark. It's not true, and you certainly never heard me say any such thing."

Clay saw the humiliation on Ann's youthful face. At once, he went to her and put his arm around her, saying gently, "Don't make her do that, Reverend. Ann didn't mean it."

Ann looked up at him, tears running down her cheeks. She threw her arms around Clay and whispered, "No! I never did!"

Catching Irons's glance, Clay shook his head slightly, and the other man understood. "Well, sometimes we all say things we don't mean. Don't cry, Ann."

Ann left Clay's embrace and flew to Rena. The two girls were weeping, and Rena said, "It's all right, Ann. You mustn't feel bad!"

It was a tense time, and Irons made his

departure as soon as possible. Rena called out as they were well away from the house, "Don't forget my birthday party, Ann!" Then she turned to her father, who was watching her strangely. Rena felt awkward, and there was a heaviness in the room, but she looked up and said, "I'm sorry you had to hear what Ann said, Daddy."

"I'm sorry you had to hear it," Clay said. He gave her a careful look, then asked, "You've heard it before — talk about me and Melora Yancy — haven't you, Rena?"

Rena flushed and wished she'd never listened to the gossip. She had heard it from one of the girls at church, a daughter of Elder Swinson, and it had angered her. Then she had heard some of the slaves talking about it, but they had not known she was listening. She had wept herself to sleep over it more nights than one but had never mentioned it to a living soul. Now she lifted her head, her youthful innocence plain to see. "Is — is it so, Daddy?"

Clay shook his head instantly, more glad than he could say to be able to look his daughter in the eye. "No, Rena. It's not so. You know Miss Melora. There's no finer woman on earth than her, and she'd never do what people are saying."

"Oh, Daddy! I'm so glad!" Rena went to

her father, and he held her closely. The strength of his arms comforted her, and finally she drew back with a frown on her face. "You ought to shoot whoever starts those old stories, Daddy!"

Clay smiled in spite of himself. "Hey, that's no way to talk! In the first place, I'd run out of ammunition," he said, making a joke out of it. Then he paused, his lips growing firm as he said, "It hurts me that I've been the cause of harm to Melora. I don't think we'll be able to see her much anymore." He had taken Rena with him to the Yancy place more than once, and the girl had taken to Melora instantly. The two of them had become fast friends.

Clay looked down at his daughter. "Don't let this make you hate anyone, Rena. Never let anything do that." He kissed her, then looked into her clear eyes and said quietly, "I let hate and bitterness get into me once. And it cost me the dearest thing in the world."

Rena understood instantly that her father was speaking about whatever it was that had taken him away from Gracefield for so many years. She nodded, her eyes suddenly filled with love for her father. "I promise, Daddy!"

That was all. Except that when Rena left to go back to the Big House, she asked,

"Daddy, when you see Miss Melora, will you tell her why I won't be coming to see her?"

"I'll tell her. She'll understand."

Clay stood at the head of the path that led through the trees, watching his daughter make her way between the huge trunks. The scene had torn at his insides, but now he faced something even worse.

Tomorrow I'll go tell Melora.

The thought was painful, and that night he slept little, knowing that it must be done yet dreading it with all his heart.

Clay Rocklin was no man to put off an unpleasant chore, so he saddled King and left Gracefield early the next morning, just after dawn. The distance was not far and he walked the horse most of the way, but it seemed when he came in sight of the Yancy house that the ride had been very brief. Buford Yancy was working in his barn, shoeing a nervous mare, and he called out as Clay dismounted, "Come in here and help me with this animal, Clay! She's more likely to shoe me than t'other way around!"

"Fine mare, Buford," Clay said, taking the horse's head and holding her firmly. "Out of Thunderhead, if I remember?"

The two men talked as they worked, but

Clay was thinking back over the years. Buford Yancy was one of the innumerable poor white farmers who filled the South. He was, at the age of fifty-four, stronger and more active than most men half his age. He was six feet tall and lean as a lath, with a pair of quick, greenish eyes and a head of tow hair that he hacked off with a knife when it got in his way. He was as independent as a lion — and proud as one, too.

Clay thought back to how the two of them had become friends. Clay had been a young fool, filled with pride and arrogance. Then a hunting accident had felled him when he was hunting with Jeremiah Irons, and he had been brought to the Yancy cabin while the minister went for help. Clay smiled as he thought of how he'd learned that it was not the aristocrats who had real pride, but men like Buford Yancy!

He thought, too, of the small girl who'd taken care of him, how womanlike she had been though she was just a child. Melora . . . he'd been taken with her childish ways and the wisdom she often displayed that seemed so far beyond her years. The days he'd spent there had taught him much about children — at least about one of them. Melora was bright as a newly minted coin, and when he'd asked her what she wanted for taking care of him, she'd told him she wanted a book.

That had been the beginning. It had gone on like that, and his delight in bringing her books and reading the difficult ones to her was the chief solace in his troubled life. Her favorite had been *Pilgrim's Progress,* and when he'd left to go to the Mexican War, seeking glory to equal that of his cousin who'd married the girl Clay loved, he'd said on his last visit with the child, "I'll slay a dragon for you, Melora!"

But he had slain no dragons in Mexico. He had disgraced himself by getting drunk and allowing the men of his company to be butchered by the enemy. He was dishonorably discharged. No sooner had he gotten home than he disgraced himself further by forcing his attentions on Melanie, Gideon's wife. That had been the end of it. His father had driven him from Gracefield, and he'd wandered the world, a drunken derelict. Finally a ship's captain had seen something in him, taken him aboard, and trained him. Clay had risen in that business — the slave running business — until he grew sick of heart and soul at what he was doing and came back to Virginia.

Now, looking down at Buford as the man worked, Clay felt a quick flash of affection.

No matter how many of his old friends — or his family — had shunned him, Buford Yancy had not. He had watched Clay carefully for a time; then one day he said easily, "Glad you come back, Clay." That had been all, but to Clay Rocklin it had been the equivalent of a brass band and a dozen speeches. Since then he and Yancy had grown close. Clay had found great solace in the friendship he shared with Buford. And with Melora.

If Buford was one of his closest friends, Melora was . . . well, she was probably the one person who really knew Clay, really understood him. It had been she, with her quiet ways and solid faith, who had finally lifted Clay out of the blackness that he had thought would destroy him — by leading him to the Lord.

As Buford's long figure rose from his work, Clay watched him, then said, "Buford, have you thought about what we talked about last time?"

"Shore. It's okay with me, Clay."

Rocklin was surprised. He had come a week earlier to convince Buford that he should plant corn and raise hogs instead of raising cotton. Clay had been expecting to have to overcome the tall man's objections. "You made up your mind already?"

"Makes sense to me. Cotton ain't gonna feed nobody this fall. Can't eat the blamed stuff." Yancy's green eyes gleamed with humor as he added, "To tell the truth, Clay, I've always hated cotton — blasted stuff!"

Clay laughed but warned at once, "People will say you're a fool. They've already said as much about me. They say it's not patriotic to raise anything else."

"I never thought it made a man a patriot to raise cotton. Now let's figure some on this corn business. And how we gonna hold them hogs? Take a heap of fencing, won't it?"

The two men went out and sat under a spreading ash as they talked, and it was a pleasure for Clay. He'd been called a fool and a traitor by so many for wanting to break with cotton. Now he knew that he was right. There was an inborn shrewdness in Buford Yancy, and Clay had grown to trust his judgment on anything concerning farming.

Finally Clay paused, looked at Buford, and said flatly, "Rev. Irons came to see me yesterday."

"Thought he might," was Yancy's comment. "About you and Melora, I expect."

His quickness stopped Clay for a moment, but he nodded. "People are talking. I've got to do something about it."

"You do whut's right, Clay. And in my mind they ain't nothin' right about lettin' a bunch of long-tongued busybodies run your life."

Clay said soberly, "Not worried about myself, Buford. It's Melora who's getting the worst of it."

"Wal, here she comes. Tell her about it; then you do whut you got to do." He got up and went across the yard, disappearing behind the house.

Clay stood up and turned to Melora, who had left the cabin and was walking across the yard. "Come for breakfast, Clay?" She laughed, a tinkling sound on the morning air. "You always manage to show up here at mealtime. You're bad as a preacher about that. Breakfast is almost ready. We'll have to wait for the biscuits."

Clay smiled slightly. "You're as bossy as you were the first time I ever saw you." His eyes crinkled with humor as he added, "You weren't more than six or seven, and you bossed me around like you were a sergeant in the army." He paused, then added thoughtfully, "I think of those days often, Melora. More than you'd know."

He watched her smile answer him. The morning air had roughed her cheeks and put sparkles in her eyes. She had a beautifully fashioned face, all of its features graceful yet generous and capable of robust emotion. She was a girl with a great degree of vitality and imagination, which she held under careful restraint. He saw the hint of her will — or of her pride — in the corners of her eyes and lips.

She looked at him now, her green eyes shining. "I think of them, too, Clay."

They stood there, and finally he took a deep breath. "Melora, I need to stop coming here." He watched for her reaction and was astonished when she showed little emotion. "I said —"

"I heard what you said."

He stood motionless in the bright sunshine, her presence hitting him with a jolt. She saw what was happening to him, but she stood still. Within her own chest she felt a sudden heavy undertow of feeling starting to unsettle her resolution and turn her reckless. She made a sharp movement to break that moment and wheeled away. Clay stood still, and presently she turned back to face him, her face almost severe. For a moment they watched each other, completely still. Then she lifted her chin and took his arm.

"The biscuits will be ready. Come to breakfast."

He held her back for one moment. "But what about the talk, Melora?"

"If you stop coming to see me, you'll be saying that they're right. I don't like to see you run from anything, Clay."

He shook his head slowly. "It's you I'm worried about."

There was pride in the woman's eyes, and her lips were firm as she answered him. "Before God, we have done nothing wrong. You can run if you like, but I won't do it!"

Admiration ran through Clay, and he said, "By heaven, Melora, you're right! Come on, let's eat breakfast!" She smiled at him, and the two of them entered the cabin.

CHAPTER 9
THE OFFICERS' BALL

The war fever that struck Richmond following the fall of Fort Sumter was, in many
respects, like an epidemic. It reached into
every home, from the palatial mansions of
the wealthy planters to the unpainted shacks
of the poor whites scattered in the deep
woods. The young men flocked to Richmond to enlist, their greatest fear being that
the great battle would be over before they
could become a part of it. The term *war
fever* was not inaccurate, for the populace
behaved as though they were infected, rushing around from rally to rally, faces flushed,
shouting war slogans.

Volunteer companies sprang up like mush-
rooms, most of which bore names reflecting
their patriotism and the terror they sought
to inspire: Baker Fire-Eaters, Southern
Avengers, Bartow Yankee Killers, Cherokee
Lincoln Killers, and Hornet's Nest Rifle-
men. A few titles even had an occupational

flavor, such as the Cumberland Ploughboys or the Cow Hunters.

Almost constantly the city held ceremonies full of staging and flourish designed to thrill the hearts of the home folk. The speeches became almost as stereotyped and platitudinous as the high school valedictories of later years.

When Clay brought his family to Richmond on Friday morning, he found such a celebration going on. The main streets were so packed with wagons and buggies that he had to hitch his own rig several blocks from the center of town. "I'd better keep an eye on you two," he said to David and Lowell as he handed Ellen down from the rig and they all made their way through the shouting throng. "You might get carried away with all the excitement and join up."

Rena glanced at her brothers, wondering if they might do just that. David merely grinned and shook his head, but Lowell was looking at the crowds, taking in the spectacle. He was seventeen years old, and several of his close friends, no older than he, had already signed up and were urging him to join their outfits. Lowell was a throwback to Noah Rocklin, the founder of the family. He was thickset and stubborn — and it was that which made Clay keep his eye on the boy.

Got to watch him, he thought as he led the way to the raised platform where the speakers were already winding up. *He's too much like Grandfather — and like me, I guess,* he thought wryly.

Clay and his family found a good spot close to the platform and watched as a battle flag made by the ladies of Richmond was presented with great ceremony to the new company, which had the rather ferocious name of Southern Yankee Killers. The volunteers stood in ranks, their eyes fixed on the speakers, who gave them a flowery tribute. Then the color sergeant advanced with his corporals to receive the flag, rising to the occasion with an impressive response:

"Ladies, with high-beating hearts and pulses throbbing with emotion, we receive from your hands this beautiful flag, the proud emblem of our young republic. To those who will return from the field of battle bearing this flag — though it may be tattered and torn — in triumph, this incident will always prove a cheering recollection. And to him whose fate it may be to die a soldier's death, this moment brought before his fading view will recall your kind and sympathetic words; he will bless you as his spirit takes its aerial flight."

On and on went the speech, and others much like it. Finally, though, the oratory stopped long enough for the soldiers to receive liberal offerings of cake, cookies, punch, and coffee from the young ladies, all of whom were adorned in their best dresses. Along with the refreshments, kisses were sometimes added, and David nudged Clay with an elbow, whispering, "Makes me want to sign up, Father. Let's both of us join the company!"

Clay grinned rashly at him, but Lowell said soberly, "Joke all you want, David, but those fellows are doing something."

David snorted impatiently. "Yes, swilling down lemonade and eating cake and kissing girls. As soon as the train leaves to take them to camp, that'll be over."

Clay nodded his agreement but saw that the two of them were in the minority. He had made his own position on the war clear, but only David agreed with him. The carnival atmosphere that so effectively whipped up the spirits of the crowd did nothing but depress him. Finally he said, "Dent's company is giving a drill exhibition on the green. Let's go watch."

Making their way to the large area adjacent to the courthouse, they arrived just as the Richmond Grays were beginning their drill. The square was packed, and as the Grays went through their paces, there were cheers of admiration.

"They are pretty good, aren't they, Daddy?" Rena said, her eyes bright with excitement. "And Dent is the most handsome of all the officers."

Ellen was standing close to Clay, wearing a bright yellow dress and a broad-brimmed white hat adorned with blue flowers. She liked the excitement, for she was a woman who could not be happy in solitude. Now she pressed against Clay as she said, "It's so exciting! I never saw such handsome young men!" Then she pulled away and gave Clay a critical look, whispering, "You should be proud of your son! He's a patriot, serving his country. Why don't you at least try to look like all this is important?"

Clay shrugged his shoulders, saying, "Sorry, Ellen. I'll try to do better." And he did try. All afternoon he took his family to the drills and ceremonies, even taking time to visit the officers of the Grays. Colonel James Benton greeted him effusively. "Clay, glad to see you! Isn't this a fine group!" Benton was Melanie Rocklin's father, Gid's father-in-law, but the man never mentioned either his relationship to the woman Clay had once loved so foolishly or Clay's past conflicts. Now he seemed almost majestic, albeit overweight, in his new uniform. He had no military experience at all, but he had raised the regiment at his own expense, and now his life was nothing but the military. He spent all his time making speeches, studying strategy from officers of the Regular Army, and talking about the war.

Clay spoke with Taylor Dewitt, captain of the Grays and one of his oldest friends. "You look great in your uniform, Captain Dewitt," Clay said with a grin, then added a barbed comment. "Now if you drop dead of excitement over being an officer, we won't have to do a thing to you except put a lily in your hand."

Taylor flushed, then laughed loudly. "You could always puncture any kind of pride I had, Clay!" Taylor was a tall, erect man of thirty-eight, aristocratic to the bone. "You son of a gun!" he said, thumping Clay's shoulder, "I wish you were in this thing gate of his enemies with me. I don't know any more about soldiering than I know about Chinese painting. None of us do."

As he spoke, the pair of them were joined by Bushrod Aimes, another old crony of Clay's. He wore the insignia of a second lieutenant and looked sheepishly at Clay, saying, "Taylor's right about that, Clay. We none of us know a thing. Talk about shoving off to sea in a sieve!"

"You'll do fine, both of you," Clay said, nodding and looking fondly on the pair. The three of them shared some very fine memories of their youth, when all had been golden and there had been nothing but fun on the horizon. Clay spoke what the three of them were feeling. "Maybe I never said so, but you two have always been pretty special to me. We've had some good times."

Dewitt gave him a rash grin, saying, "That sounds like an epitaph, Clay. Don't be so confounded sentimental!" Then his thin face grew sober, and he looked at the milling figures of the company surrounding them. "Well, all kidding aside, I've thought of those days myself. They were fine, weren't they?" A shadow crossed his face, making him look tired and older. "They go pretty quick, the good days. Now we're walking into a rough time. Not all these boys will be here when the shooting's over."

Bushrod Aimes shook his head, for he was a careless fellow who had always refused to think of unpleasant things. "My gosh, Dewitt, you're worse than Rocklin here! We're going to do fine!"

Dent chose that moment to step up to the trio. "Like to speak to you, sir, when you've finished," he said to Clay.

"Why, now's fine, Dent," Clay said. He nodded at his two old friends, saying, "I'll be careful to pray for you fellas." Then he followed Dent, who was making his way through the crowd.

Bushrod stared at the two, then shook his head. "Pray for us! Boy, that sure don't sound like the Clay Rocklin we grew up with, does it, Captain Dewitt?"

"No, but I think it's the real thing." Taylor's face was thoughtful as his eyes followed Clay. "Guess he'll need all the religion he can get, Bushrod. Right now, it takes a lot less courage to be a soldier and take a chance on a bullet than it does to stay out of the army. Clay's taking a lot of abuse over his stand — and it'll get worse, I reckon."

Clay shouldered his way through the crowd, following Dent off the green. There had been a tense look on Dent's youthful face, and when he reached a relatively uncrowded spot near the firehouse, there was an edge of temper in his voice as he spoke. "I've been talking to Mother. She's very upset."

"About what, Dent?"

"About the miserably small allowance you dole out to her. You've got to give her more money!"

Clay clamped his lips firmly together, choking back the hot retort that leaped to them. He drew a steadying sigh. "I've talked to her about that, son. She can't seem to understand that things are very tight right now — and likely to get worse."

"Things aren't that bad," Dent said, a stubborn air in the jut of his chin. "Isn't it bad enough that she had to survive all the years you weren't around? Do you have to punish her now that you've got control of all the money?"

Clay wanted to remind Dent that Ellen had lived very well during the years he was gone and, in fact, that the bills she had run up then were a large factor in the financial ruin he had found when he had come back. But Dent was in no mood to hear the truth. Besides, Clay felt the old streak of guilt over his past, so he merely said, "Dent, if you'd like to go over the books with me, I'd be happy to have you find some extra money. But I'm telling you now, there isn't any. As a matter of fact, I may as well tell you — the way this war is shaping up, we're going to have to cut back even more. The first thing to go will be the personal expenses of all of us. That means the room your mother keeps rented here in Richmond will have to go, I'm afraid."

What followed was as unpleasant as anything Clay had endured since his return. His son had a fiery temper, and for the next five minutes, Clay had to endure the worst of it. While Dent stood there, pale with anger and resentment, speaking bitterly about what a pitiful excuse for a husband and a father he had been, Clay could only stand and hold his tongue.

More than once he'd had to fight down the impulse to strike out or to turn and walk away from his son's invectives, which burned as they fell on him. There had been a time when he would not have been able to endure such things, for his pride had been every bit as high as his son's. Now as he stood there enduring Dent's torrent, he took some small comfort in the fact that he was able to hang on to his temper — he knew it was not in him to endure such a thing, and that, as much as anything that had happened, convinced him that his life had been touched by God.

Angrily Dent clamped his lips together. There was a wild look in his eyes, as well as exhaustion. He was like a man who'd run himself out and was now at the end of his resources. Since the day his father had come home to take over Gracefield, a bitter streak of resentment had galled Dent. Now, here in the bright sunlight, he had let all that lay within him spill out. Yet it had not brought relief. It would have been better if his father had struck out at him; nothing would have pleased him better than a rousing battle with blows and shouts. But his father did no more than stand there quietly, looking at him with pain in his eyes, making no defense.

Finally, drained and bitter, Dent said, "I'll never ask you for anything again!" then turned and stalked away. He didn't look back, but if he had, he would have seen the anguish on Clay Rocklin's face that he had so longed to put there. He had not really expected that his father would do anything for his mother. In fact, down deep he was ashamed of his tirade, for he had already spoken to his grandmother, who had told him the same thing he had just heard from his father. Even so, something in him had driven him to seek the confrontation — some demon that seemed to eat away at him.

Now he moved away, stiff with anger and bitterness, and went into a saloon and ordered a bottle. For the rest of the afternoon he sat there, ignoring those who came to clap him on the shoulder and acclaim him as a patriot. The darkness that was in him seemed to deepen, and as he slumped in his chair, sullen in the midst of the laughing crowd, he wondered why he could not forget his father and get on with his life.

Colonel Benton had rented the ballroom of the Capitol Hotel for the Officers' Ball, and when Dent arrived, the floor was already filled with couples spinning around the room. The amber light from the glass chandeliers picked up the brilliant colors of the women's dresses, and the brass buttons on the gray uniforms of the officers winked merrily as the music beat out a steady tune.

Bushrod Aimes had found Dent drinking alone and had practically hauled him bodily to the affair. "What's wrong with you, Dent?" Aimes had demanded. "No sense paying for your own liquor. It'll be free at the ball. I hear Colonel Benton bought out the bar for tonight. Come on, let's go let the ladies make a fuss over us!"

Dent had decided not to go to the ball, for he was still filled with anger, having spent hours brooding over the scene with his father. But the liquor he had consumed had dulled the edge of his anger, so he allowed himself to be bullied by Aimes. When the pair arrived, he suddenly became the center of attention for several lovely young ladies. Some of them he knew well, and for the next hour he was able to thrust the memory of the quarrel with his father from his mind.

One newcomer was a beautiful girl named Leona Reed. Mrs. Mary Boykin Chesnut, the leader of society in Richmond, had led the young woman up, saying, "Lieutenant, you must meet one of our distinguished guests. You've heard of her father, Samuel Reed, I'm sure. Miss Reed, I present to you Lieutenant Denton Rocklin, one of our fine officers from the Richmond Grays."

"Thank you, Mrs. Chesnut," Dent said instantly. "May I have this dance, Miss Reed?"

"Of course, Lieutenant."

She stepped into his embrace, and as they spun around the floor, he was captivated by her beauty. She was not tall, but her bright orchid dress set off a trim figure. Her blond hair was done up in a coronet around her shapely head, and the sweep of her cheeks was intensely feminine. A pair of large blue eyes and beautifully formed lips made her an attractive girl. But as taken as he was with her beauty, he was aware almost at once that she was a fiery patriot, for she spoke of "the Cause" in a fervent tone.

That was natural enough, for her father,

Samuel Reed, was one of the Southern senators who had led the South down the pathway to secession. Reed was a wealthy man who had gone into politics in his forties and had been as successful there as he had been in the field of business.

When the dance was over, Taylor came over to say, "You're starting at the top, Dent, old boy! Brains, beauty, and money! But you'll have to edge out half the officers in the regiment to get her."

Dent grinned rashly. "She's a woman, isn't she? I'll turn my fatal charm on, Captain." And at once he went away to demand another dance, noting that Miss Reed was not disappointed when he came.

As he spun her out on the floor, Mary Chesnut said to Colonel Chesnut, her husband, "They make a beautiful couple, don't they?"

Colonel Chesnut cast his look on the pair, then shook his head. "Mary, will you give up this eternal matchmaking?" But he added later, "They do look well. But a soldier's got no business thinking of women before he goes to battle."

Mary Chesnut moved her shoulders angrily. "You have no more romance in you than a cabbage, James!"

As the night wore on, Dent Rocklin maneuvered himself into every dance he could with Leona Reed. It was a matter of guile, for she was highly sought after. When he wasn't actually dancing with her, he was at the refreshment table imbibing the liquor that flowed quite freely. By ten o'clock, he was beginning to feel the effects of the liquor. When he danced he was not nearly so smooth as he thought, and he laughed more loudly at things that were not really funny.

The colors of the dresses swirled in front of his eyes in a kaleidoscopic fashion — reds, yellows, and greens. His dances with Leona Reed were as intoxicating as the liquor he consumed, for she spoke of his company urgently and with pride. When she praised him for throwing himself into the glorious struggle to preserve the South they all loved, he felt a glowing sense of exaltation that blotted out all else.

After eleven o'clock, he was unable to get another dance with Leona. He was on the verge of leaving when Mrs. Chesnut appeared and asked, "Lieutenant, you see that young woman sitting alone? Would you talk to her for a few minutes?"

"Of course, Mrs. Chesnut," he said. He moved toward the girl. When he reached her, he bowed and asked, "May I have this dance, miss?" He was surprised when the young woman hesitated. She seemed preoccupied, and he thought that she had not heard him. "My name is Denton Rocklin," he said in a louder tone. "I'd like to dance with you."

The girl looked up with a faraway look in her eyes. "I — I don't dance very well, Mr. Rocklin," she said in a small voice.

"Oh, that's all right," Dent said at once. "I'm not any prizewinner myself. But that's a good band." He put out his arm, but she seemed to ignore it, so he simply put his arm around her and swept her out on the floor.

It was a slow waltz, and Dent was aware that the girl was not a good dancer. She did not move easily with him, seemed not able to anticipate his movements. At first it was a matter of steering her around on the floor, and she whispered, "I don't think I can do it, Mr. Denton."

"Oh, sure you can! Be a good time for you to practice." He looked down at her curiously, for all the girls he knew were accomplished dancers. It was the one skill they made certain to attain! She was, he saw, not over average height, no more than five feet four. Her head was down so he could not see her face plainly, but she looked lovely in her pale blue dress. When she did look up slightly, he saw that she had an attractive heart-shaped face and that her eyes were dark blue. She was not, he decided, a raving beauty, but she was pretty enough. "I didn't hear your name," he said when she had begun to dance with more assurance.

"Raimey Reed," she said quietly. She kept her head down, seeming to concentrate on her feet. Her hair was long, auburn, with a glint of gold where the light from the chandeliers touched it, and he could smell a hint of lilac scent. She had a beautiful complexion, rich and smooth as a child's.

"Raimey? Never heard of a girl named that," Dent muttered. "Or a boy, for that matter."

"It's my mother's maiden name."

Dent blinked as a thought came to him. "You said Reed? I just met a girl named Leona Reed."

"My sister."

Her answers were brief, which was somehow disturbing to Dent. He was accustomed to girls who talked much. He began speaking of the war and how glad he was to serve in the Richmond Grays. When she said nothing, he added, "Your sister is a great patriot. I suppose you are, too?"

Raimey Reed hesitated somewhat awkwardly, then shook her head, the motion sending the mass of auburn hair shimmering over her shoulders. "No, I'm afraid not, Mr. Rocklin."

At first Dent thought he had misunderstood her. Looking down he said, "I beg your pardon?"

"I said I'm not a patriot. I think this war is a terrible blunder."

Her words came to Dent clearly, and his reaction was anger. He stopped dead still, leaned back, and snapped, "A blunder! You think it's a blunder for a man to fight for his country?"

A flush came to the girl's face. She looked up at his harsh tone but said only, "I don't think this is the proper place to discuss it, Mr. Rocklin."

Dent stood there, trying to sort it all out. His thoughts came slowly, and all he could do was say angrily, "Miss Reed, you're a disgrace to Southern womanhood! I think you should listen to your sister. She's the kind of woman a soldier can be proud of!"

At that moment, a wave of dizziness caught up with Dent, and he was afraid he was going to be sick. "I'll just leave you here, Miss Reed. I don't think you'd care to dance with a simple soldier who's about to offer his life for his country!"

The speech sounded pompous and stilted even to his own ears, but Dent wheeled around and walked away, leaving the girl standing alone in the center of the floor. Anger boiled up in him, and he muttered, "Little snob! Let her dance with some Yankee!"

He reached the edge of the dance floor and started for the door, but he was halted when Mrs. Chesnut barred his way, her face stern.

"What are you doing, Lieutenant?" she demanded. "You've left Miss Reed alone!"

Dent stared at her, standing very straight, and said, "Miss Reed is not sympathetic to the cause —," he began, but he was cut off by an angry gesture from the woman.

"Go back and get her at once!"

"I won't dance with a — a —"

"You fool!" Mary Chesnut said, her usually gentle dark eyes sharp with anger. "Go at once and get her!" She leaned forward and whispered in a tight voice, "She's blind!"

Dent blinked and turned his head as if the woman had slapped him. He turned and saw that the girl was trying to make her way through the throng of dancers. Her hands were held before her, and her eyes were staring straight ahead.

"My God!" Dent groaned and at once plunged into the crowd. He upset several couples as he shoved his way toward her, getting rough looks from some of his fellow officers. His legs were unsteady and a cold sweat broke out on his brow, but he did not stop until he got to where the girl was struggling to find her way off the floor.

He took her arm, saying, "Miss Reed — !"

"Leave me alone, Mr. Rocklin!"

He noted that she turned her face to him as she attempted to pull away. He held her firmly. "I've got to talk to you!" he muttered, and ignoring her attempts to pull away, he moved her across the floor, sheltering her from the dancers. He was aware that people were looking at them strangely, but it was too late to remedy the thing. He didn't stop when he got her to the side of the floor, but continued to pull her along. He had been outside earlier and knew that a small balcony lay to the side of the ballroom. He pulled the door open and led her out into the open air, then closed the door.

"Where is this?" Raimey asked at once. "Please, take me back!"

"In a few moments, I will." Dent stood beside her, taking deep breaths of the air. The music came to them, muted by the door, and he could smell the aroma of the firs that flanked the building. A large magnolia tree grew twenty feet from the balcony, and one of the branches dipped so low that he could smell the sweet richness of the blossoms.

Finally he released her arm and, turning to face her, said, "This is a small balcony just outside the ballroom."

"I want to go back inside."

"All right, but first you have to let me say something."

Raimey Reed cocked her head very slightly. In the relative silence of the secluded balcony, she heard Denton Rocklin's voice clearly for the first time. She had known from the first that he was drunk, or almost so. Now she seemed to grow calm. She turned and faced the open lawn, saying nothing. Dent waited, trying to frame some sort of apology, but everything he thought of seemed stupid.

Suddenly she said, "I've never danced before. Not at a real dance."

Dent stared at her, not knowing how to answer. Finally he said carefully, "You did very well for your first time. With a little practice, you could be very good."

The air caressed her cheeks as she turned slightly and said evenly, "I'm not likely to get much practice. I should have warned you. It wasn't fair to you."

Dent said stiffly, "Miss Reed, anything I say will sound downright dumb, but I am sorry."

He stood there, knowing that he had treated her abominably, almost wishing she would turn and rail on him. But she did no such thing. She suddenly lifted her face and smiled. A deep dimple appeared in her left cheek, and it was impossible to tell from her eyes that she was blind. "Let that be a lesson to you, Mr. Rocklin, against taking up with strange women." Then she said, "Don't let it upset you. I'm not hurt — and I did get to dance, didn't I? That's something, isn't it?"

He blew his breath out, saying, "I feel rotten!"

"That's because I'm blind," Raimey said with no particular note in her voice. "You've probably treated girls much worse than you treated me, haven't you?"

"Why — !" Dent was absolutely floored at her matter-of-fact question. Then he laughed shortly, nodding. "Yes, I have."

"Well, you don't have to add your impoliteness to me to your list of sins. I forgive you."

Dent was feeling very strange. "I'll accept

that on one condition."

"What condition, Mr. Rocklin?"

"That you dance with me again."

His request disturbed her. Her full lips tightened, and a shadow fell across her cheeks. "You say that because you feel sorry for me," she said in a voice that was not quite steady. "I'm used to it. People often don't know that I can't see, and they make mistakes. Like yesterday a woman came up and asked me to read an address for her. She couldn't read herself, and when I told her I was blind, she acted as though she'd done something horrible. You don't have to dance with me. That's just something you want to do because you feel guilty."

Dent said patiently, "You can argue all you want, Miss Reed, but when you run out of argument, I'm going to be standing here waiting for you to dance. Maybe you're right — that I just want to wash out my guilt. Well, give me a chance to do it, then, will you?"

Raimey stood there, uncertain for the first time. She had thought that her words would drive Rocklin away, but now she felt his sincerity. She was adept in dealing with people who were awkward about her handicap, but now she felt awkward. Finally she laughed. "All right, just one dance to show that I'm not angry."

"Fine!"

He led her to the floor, and she came into his arms readily. She was not afraid now, and by the end of the dance, she was moving around in his arms with confidence. "Now this next one will be a little faster," he said. "We'll see how you do with it."

"You said one dance," she rebuked him with a smile.

"I lied," he announced calmly. For the next three dances they moved around the floor.

Then she said, "I think four dances ought to blot out your guilt, Mr. Rocklin."

"I do feel much better," Dent said and escorted her to the seats. He found Leona waiting for him.

"Well, I see you've met my sister," she said, looking at him strangely.

"Yes, Miss Reed." Dent nodded. He guided Raimey to her chair, then bowed. "I must be off, I'm afraid. Drill begins early. Thank you both for the dances."

He moved away, and Leona asked, "How in the world did that happen? You've always refused to learn how to dance."

"I don't know. He just asked me and I said yes." She lifted her face to her sister. "What does he look like, Leona?"

Leona sat down and took her sister's hand. "He's the best-looking man I've ever seen. Black hair and dark, soulful eyes." She smiled, a dimple exactly like Raimey's peeking out of her cheek, then added, "And he's got a body like mortal sin!" She laughed when Raimey rebuked her, then grew serious. "I'd think you two would have little to talk about. He's going off to fight for a cause you think is dead wrong."

Raimey said, "It scares me, Leona. To think that he might be killed, along with thousands of others like him. And it can't make any difference! So many dead, for nothing!"

Leona had argued with Raimey too many times over this, so she simply said, "Let's go home, Raimey. It's late."

"All right." Raimey allowed Leona to lead her to the carriage. As she passed across the lawn, she caught the rich smell of magnolia, and she knew that whenever she smelled one of those blossoms, she'd think of her first dance and the man with whom she had shared it.

CHAPTER 10
"BECAUSE I'M DIFFERENT!"

Dulcie was an excellent reader. She had a smooth, clear voice and had been trained by a noted teacher of diction, but she could not disguise her disgust with what she read. The mulatto slave girl loved romances with knights in armor and maidens who were rescued from fire-breathing dragons. She could not understand why her mistress had her read a dull poem again and again. She held the old copy of *Graham's Magazine* and stared at the top of the page at the title, "The Arsenal at Springfield." Noting that it was written by some man named Henry Wadsworth Longfellow, she began reading:

"This is the Arsenal. From floor to ceiling,
Like a huge organ, rise the burnished arms;
But from their silent pipes no anthem
    pealing
Startles the villages with strange alarms."

She waded through several stanzas, all dealing with war and battle, then lowered the magazine and protested, "Miss Raimey, do I have to read this old poem again? I don't see no sense in it!"

But her mistress, lying on the floor, said, "Read it." So Dulcie, giving her head a disgusted shake, went back to the poem. When she finished and was about to close the book, she heard a muffled voice. "Read the last two stanzas again, Dulcie." Knowing that argument was useless, she read the words:

"Down the dark future, through long
    generations,
The echoing sounds grow fainter and then
    cease;
And like a bell, with solemn, sweet
    vibrations,
I hear once more the voice of Christ say,
    'Peace!'
Peace! and no longer from its brazen
    portals
The blast of War's great organ shakes the
    skies!
But beautiful as songs of the immortals,
The holy melodies of love arise."

Raimey gave a slight shiver as the last line

223

fell across the quiet of the room. She had been lying flat on her stomach, her face buried in a pillow, listening to the slave girl read. Now she sat up abruptly, exclaiming, "Isn't that a marvelous phrase, Dulcie? 'The holy melodies of love arise.' " Her rich auburn hair fell down her back in masses of curls, and there was a look of pleasure on her wide mouth as she repeated the phrase.

"I don't see what's so great about it," Dulcie snapped. "I don't see why people can't say what they mean instead of usin' this poetry! I don't think it means anything!" A sudden irritation brought creases between her brows, for she took more liberties than any other Reed slave. This stemmed partly from the fact that she had been taught to read as a child, but it came even more from the fact that her duty went far beyond that of the ordinary lady's maid.

When Raimey Reed had become blind at the age of seven, Samuel Reed had spent a fortune on doctors, attempting to find a cure for his daughter. When he finally resigned himself that a cure would not be found, he turned his energies to making Raimey as able as she could be to live in the world. Dulcie had been his most successful move. Dulcie had learned to read by "accident." She had merely sat with the girls while their tutor went over the letters and, to the shock of everyone, learned much faster than Leona. This shook the bottom out of Sam Reed's theory about black people, which was that they had no soul and were incapable of learning anything except to pick cotton and perform other menial tasks. Reed was, however, a flexible man. When he had Dulcie tested and found out that she was extremely intelligent, he'd made her Raimey's maid at once.

The choice had been wise, for Dulcie had become everything to the blind girl. Not only did she function as Raimey's maid, keeping track of her clothes and fixing her hair, but she served as the girl's eyes. The two were inseparable, and as Dulcie saw, she spoke. It was through her that Raimey received much of her impression of the world. She could not have had a better guide, for Dulcie was alert and had a natural flow of rather poetic language, enabling her to make anything she saw come alive for her mistress. She could describe things — such as the sweeping flight of a kingfisher swooping down to scoop a minnow from a pond — so graphically that Sam Reed once said, "Blast my eyes! That Dulcie can see more and say more in less time than any human on God's green earth!"

Dulcie loved to read. She did it well, and Samuel Reed had filled his home with books of all kinds to feed Raimey's voracious hunger for knowledge. Every day the smooth, beautifully cadenced voice of the maid could be heard in the Reed house, and Raimey's mother had said more than once, "Sam, what would we have done without that girl Dulcie?"

"I don't know, but she's got enough gall for ten Caesars!" her husband often replied ruefully. "She's got us, Ellie! She knows we can't do without her and she does as she pleases. And there's not a blessed thing we can do about it!"

Dulcie continued to argue about the poem and finally threw the magazine down with disgust, just as the door opened and Miss Leona Reed dashed into the room.

"Raimey, you're not even dressed yet! Dulcie, why haven't you helped your mistress!"

Now as Leona stood looking at the pair, Dulcie showed no fear. "I told her to get ready, but you know how she is. I had to read this old poem to her ten times!"

"Well, it's nearly time to go," Leona snapped; then she shrugged. "Come on, I'll help you, Dulcie. We have to be at the Chesnuts' in an hour." The two girls began at once, and together they were able to get Raimey into her dress and her rebellious curls in some sort of order by the time they heard their father roaring outside the door, "Come on or get left, you two!"

The sisters scurried down the stairs and were handed into the carriage by their father, who complained, "You two girls will be late for the Resurrection!" as he climbed in and settled himself heavily next to his wife. "Whip up those horses, Job!" he called to the driver, and the matched grays leaped at the touch of the whip. Reed settled down, pulled a cigar from his inner pocket, lit it expertly, then leaned back and looked at his daughters. He was a tall, corpulent man of forty, success written in his every inch. "You look very well. How much did I pay for those dresses?"

"Oh, Father, they're old as the hills!" Leona said. "All my good dresses are at home. Mother, we've got to go shopping tomorrow. I'm ashamed to wear this old thing to meet the president!"

Ellie Reed, a calm woman of thirty-three who had smooth brown hair and large eyes, said, "I think President Davis will be thinking of more important things than your dress, Leona." Then she glanced out the window, took in a troop of soldiers drilling on a field, and began to describe them. "What funny uniforms!" she exclaimed. "They're wearing some sort of puffy scarlet trousers. What are they, Sam?"

Reed took a look, then said, "They're Colonel Field's Louisiana Fire Zouaves. A bad outfit, or so I hear. The sweepings of the worst of New Orleans riffraff." He took up the description from his wife without thinking, describing the lean, evil faces under the tasseled hats, which were much like the Persian fez, and the garish colors of the uniforms. It had become second nature to all the family to speak what they saw, creating the world in words for Raimey's sake.

Raimey sat upright beside Leona, listening carefully as her father described the troop. She was as aware of sound as a fox, her ears recording the creaking of the carriage, the shout of some man yelling, "Stop that, Craig, or I'll bust you!" and the slap of the hands of a group of drilling soldiers on their muskets as their drill sergeant called out sharply, "Present — arms!" Deprived of sight, Raimey had developed her other senses to extraordinary degrees. She smelled the acrid odor of tar as the carriage wheeled by a barrel that was smoldering slightly. Instantly she recognized the sharp smell of a blacksmith shop, smoky and vaguely metallic, and over the open carriage came the scent of magnolia — bringing instantly the thought of her encounter with Denton Rocklin.

Listening to her family describe the bustle of Richmond's streets with one ear, she allowed the memory of that evening to flow through the other part of her mind. She was gifted with a keen imagination, and her blindness had sharpened even that so that she could recall an event clearly, recreating it quite vividly. As the carriage turned and her father said, "There's the Chesnut house, Job, the white one with the green shutters," she had the strongest possible memory of Rocklin's every word, of the touch of his hand on her waist as they had gone around the floor. She had thought of it constantly since that night, for there had been something in his touch and in his presence that had been different from that of any other young man.

Now the carriage pulled up, and Leona moved close to her so that as they moved down a brick walk and up three steps, Raimey did not need to take her arm at all. By merely brushing her sister's gown, she was able to walk into the house, for Leona was able — as were the other members of the family, and Dulcie most of all — to measure distances so that Raimey would not bump into objects or doorjambs. So well did they do this that strangers meeting the family for the first time often had to be told that Raimey was blind.

"Mr. Reed, Mrs. Reed, come in with your girls." Raimey recognized the voice of Mrs. Chesnut instantly. The sound of a voice to her was like the sight of a face to others; once she heard the voice of man, woman, or child, she recognized it instantly, no matter how faint it was or how long it had been since she had heard it last. Now she stood there listening as Mrs. Chesnut and her parents exchanged greetings, smelling the fresh wax, listening to half a dozen conversations going on inside a large room off to her left, and sensing the bustle of servants moving busily over the smooth wooden floors.

"You young ladies come with me," Mrs. Chesnut said, and Raimey knew by her tone she was smiling. "The officers are waiting for you. I've told them that the two most handsome young ladies in Richmond are to be here. Now be on your guard, both of you. You know how these soldiers are!"

Leona laughed, and as they moved from the foyer into the large drawing room,

Raimey sensed the size of the room. She had been told that James Chesnut was a very wealthy planter from South Carolina who had recently moved to Richmond because he was a member of the brand-new Confederate Congress. He was an amiable man, but it was his wife, Mary Boykin Chesnut, who was the magnet that drew the cream of Southern society to her house — even the president of the Confederacy, Jefferson Davis.

Mrs. Chesnut was not a raving beauty, as several had told Raimey, but she was one of those women whom men liked. She was thirty-eight years old, a small woman with black hair and lustrous dark eyes. Now she said, "Mr. President, may I present our two young guests, the daughters of Mr. Samuel Reed. This is Leona and her sister, Raimey."

Feeling a touch on her arm by Leona, Raimey put out her hand, which was taken instantly. Davis's hand was thin but strong, and he said in a pleasant high-pitched voice, "Where do you find all these beautiful young ladies, Mrs. Chesnut? Your house is filled with them."

Raimey felt the touch of a light kiss on her hand; then a woman's voice said, "Now, sir, be careful! You know I only allow you to kiss one fair hand in the evening."

"Oh, Varina!" Davis said to his wife, humor in his voice — an unusual thing, for this new president had little of that quality. "You mustn't be jealous of two staunch supporters of our cause."

Sam Reed spoke up very quickly and rather nervously, for he had a sudden fear that Raimey might speak her convictions against the war on the spot. "Is General Johnson here this evening, Mr. President?"

"No, but General Lee is here. You ladies will excuse me? I'm sure the gallant officers of our fine troops will entertain you."

Raimey and Leona were surrounded at once by several officers, all trying to gain their attention. Leona spoke lightly, laughing at their eagerness, and Raimey spoke with one or two of them. She recognized the instant that one of them became aware that she was blind. He broke off suddenly, his speech faltering, and then he picked up the threads of his thought, speaking more loudly.

This was something that Raimey had experienced many times, and it no longer troubled her. On the contrary, it made her conversation much easier. But she had never learned quite how to handle the matter of letting strangers know she could not see. She had once said plainly, "I'm blind," but that had so embarrassed the man she was speaking to that she never repeated that tactic.

For the next hour, Raimey spoke with several of the officers, mostly of things other than the war itself. But the war was the center of all things now, she realized, and the light voices and the warm ease of the men were somehow an omen to her. For each one who stood beside her, pressing refreshments on her and laughing at the frivolous jokes that ran around the room, was on his way to something dark and grim — something more ominous than any of them seemed to realize.

Then as she was speaking with a youthful captain, she heard the door to the foyer open and close. A man's voice, low as it was, came to her, and she recognized it at once as Dent Rocklin. She didn't move and continued to speak with the captain, but she was acutely aware of Rocklin's presence in the room. She heard him speak to Colonel Chesnut, and as the two of them spoke, she wondered if he would come to her.

He did come, almost at once. She heard the sound of his boots on the pine floor; then he said, "Miss Reed — ?"

She turned to face him quickly, saying with a smile, "Hello, Lieutenant Rocklin.

How are you this afternoon?"

Her instant recognition of his voice caught Rocklin off guard. He had gone over the strange experience of their meeting again and again. She had gotten into his thoughts, and now he said, "I didn't know you'd be here this afternoon. It's good to see you."

She nodded, and they stood there talking of unimportant things. As they spoke, he studied her carefully. He realized that though she was not beautiful, she was most decidedly pretty. There was a freshness in her youthful skin, which glowed like translucent pearl. Her eyes were blue, large, and well shaped. There was, he noted instantly, no sign of damage to them. On the contrary, they were quite beautiful, marred only by the fact that they did not focus. Her lips were wide and well shaped, mobile, and firm. The heavy mane of auburn ringlets that hung down her back was beautiful indeed, and the white dress with yellow lace at the throat set off her trim figure.

There was an innocence about this girl that Dent had never seen before. And Rocklin knew women very well. They had provided a game for him, one that he had learned how to play well. Most women played the game as well as he, but what had worked with other young women seemed wrong and out of place with Raimey Reed.

For the next thirty minutes he stayed close beside her, sharply observed by Mary Chesnut, who whispered to Raimey's mother, "Better be careful, Ellie. Denton Rocklin is quite a ladies' man."

The room buzzed with talk and laughter; then Raimey heard the president say, "And this is the daughter of Mr. Reed. Miss Raimey, may I present General Robert E. Lee."

"I'm happy to know you, General," Raimey said and put out her hand, which was taken at once. Lee's hand was square and very firm. "Only last week I read your account of the action at Cerro Gordo in Mexico."

Lee was amused, they all saw. His deep-set eyes gleamed with humor, and he said, "I wish I could have gotten the cadets at West Point to read as easily, Miss Reed. But that must have been dreary reading for a young lady!"

"Not at all." Raimey smiled then, the dimple in her left cheek appearing. "But I must confess my maid got very tired of it. I made her read it twice, and she went to sleep the last time."

Something changed in Lee's eyes. He had just realized, Dent noted instantly, that the girl was blind, and Dent spoke up quickly to cover the moment. "My uncle didn't grow tired of it, General Lee. He was with you when you found the way through the mountains." Catching Lee's attention, he said, "That was Lieutenant Gideon Rocklin, General."

Lee nodded at once. "A fine officer. Very dedicated." Then he asked with a slight hesitation, "Will he stay with the Union, Lieutenant?"

"Yes, I'm afraid so, General Lee."

"Well, each of us must decide about that. It's not an easy choice. Give your uncle my best regards when you write him."

Lee and Davis passed on, and Rocklin told Raimey, "My uncle says Lee is the finest soldier on the planet. It almost broke my uncle's heart when Lee chose to stay with Virginia. It hurt Lincoln, too." Then he said, "I've got to get back to camp."

"We'd love to see the camp, Lieutenant Rocklin!" Leona had come up while Lee was speaking, and now her eyes were alert. "Father would like to go, too."

"All of you are welcome," Dent said but added, "There's not much to see, I'm afraid. Just dull duty and drill."

But Leona insisted, and Dent asked, "Would you like to go, Miss Raimey?"

"Yes."

"Very well. I'll invite your father."

Samuel Reed declined the invitation but offered the use of his carriage and driver to bring the girls home. They left at once, and as soon as they got to the camp, Dent took the young women to meet his staff. Almost at once, Leona was invited to watch target practice, and she left with Second Lieutenant Bushrod Aimes and Third Lieutenant Tug Ramsey. Dent put his hand on Raimey's arm, saying, "You might be more interested in watching some close-order drill, Miss Raimey."

Raimey said, "Of course," and the two of them walked along the dusty lanes between the rows of Sibley tents. Dent put himself close to her, and she put her hand on his arm at once. The air was still hot, and when they had come to the drill field, Rocklin explained what was happening, watching the movements of the men carefully. Raimey faced the field, the sun making a golden candescent gleam on her smooth cheeks. Listening to the shouted commands, some of them profane when the men faltered, she asked, "Is this important? I mean, when men go into a battle, they don't keep step, do they?"

"Not as they do in Europe," Dent said.

"But it's important for the men to learn to obey quickly." He saw that she was really interested and said, "Let's get under those trees, Miss Raimey. This sun is too hot for you." Fifty yards past the field was a grove of tall pecans, and as soon as they moved under their shade, Raimey asked, "Where's the brook?"

"The brook?" Dent had not known there was a brook. Looking around, he said, "No brook, I'm afraid."

"Yes, it's over here." Raimey moved toward the deeper part of the woods, and soon Dent heard it too. "That's such a nice sound!" Raimey said. "Is it deep?"

"No, I don't think so." Dent led her to it, saying, "It's a pretty little creek. Full of small fish, I'd guess. I used to catch redear perch from one just like it when I was a boy."

Raimey said, "I'd love to wade in it!"

Denton was amused. "Why don't you? It's not deep, and it looks cool."

"Turn around while I take my stockings off." He turned at once, a grin on his face. Soon she said, "Now you can turn around." She was moving, even as he turned, toward the creek, and he stepped forward, afraid she would fall. But she guided herself using the feel of the moist earth and the sound of the gurgling water. Lifting her skirts above her calves, she began to wade back and forth. She made a pretty picture standing there, with the sun coming through the tops of the high trees, flecked and barred on her face as she laughed softly.

I wish I were a portrait painter, Dent reflected. *I'd like to keep this forever.* But he realized at once that no painter on earth could do more than suggest the beauty of the scene.

For ten minutes Raimey walked on the rounded stones of the brook, delighting in the cool water and the smell of old moss. She grew bolder, going down the creek in search of deeper water. Dent followed along the bank and, noting an ebullience in the stream, warned, "Better be careful, Miss Raimey — that looks like a pretty deep pool there."

But he was too late, for Raimey stepped into a sudden drop-off, threw her hands wildly around in a vain attempt to gain her balance, then plunged headlong into the pool. Dent cried out and went splashing into the creek in waist-deep water. Raimey came to the surface, her hair plastered to her head, her hat floating downstream, and he caught her by the arm. Then as she gasped for breath, he swept her up into his arms and waded out.

When they got to the shore, she sputtered and wiped her face with her hands. Then she began to laugh. It was a delightful sound, completely natural and without inhibition. Dent suddenly grinned, then chuckled. He knew that any other young woman of his acquaintance would have been horrified at her appearance, but this one didn't seem to care.

He stood, holding her for a moment and watching her, when suddenly she realized that she was in his arms. She caught her breath, waiting for him to put her down. When he made no move to do so, she asked with a smile tugging at the corners of her mouth, "Are you trying to guess my weight, Lieutenant?"

A redness touched Dent's cheeks, and hastily he let her down. "Are you all right?"

"Oh yes. It caught me off guard. I swim in the river near our house every day in warm weather." She plucked at her wet blouse, saying, "But I'll look like a fool going back to camp."

"I'll bring the carriage around here with some blankets. No one will see you, Raimey."

"Thank you." Raimey had noticed his unconscious use of her first name and smiled. "Let's just sit in the sun for a little while. Leona won't want to leave so soon. Is there a sunny spot where we can't be seen?"

"Sure. Right over here."

Again she took his arm, saying, "Let's get my stockings. At least I'll have dry feet on the way home." Her hand rested on his arm, and when Dent had retrieved the stockings, he led her to a sunny spot at the edge of the field, cut off from the camp by a low rise covered with second-growth timber. "Here, sit on my coat," he said, stripping off his jacket and placing it on the grass. She sat down and he joined her, facing her two feet away.

"The sun is nice," she said, holding her face up, and he noticed that she closed her eyes as she faced the sun. He wondered why and reclined on his elbow to watch her. She was in a good humor, made so, he realized, by the fall into the creek. It had been an adventure, one that took no vision to enjoy, and she was excited and pleased with it.

They sat there, and the event seemed to have freed some constraint that he had always been aware of. She asked about his duties, then about his home and his family. As he spoke, slowly and casually, her hair began to dry, curling rebelliously so that it became a mass of curls, with red and golden tints in the red rays of the late afternoon sun.

He thought he spoke guardedly, but he soon realized that this girl heard more than words. When he had traced his family for her, mentioning all of them briefly, he paused and saw that she was thinking hard. A single line appeared between her brows, and she asked quietly, "You don't get along with your father?"

Dent stared at her, for he had said nothing to indicate the conflicts he had had with his father. Then he realized that it had not been the words, but something else. She could not see his face, but she must have had heard some bitterness in his voice. It could be nothing else, and it troubled him.

"You're very quick," he murmured. "No, my father and I don't agree." He intended to say no more, but somehow he began to speak, diffidently at first, tracing his father's history. He mentioned how Clay had abandoned his family. As he finally came to the present, he said, "You and Father would get along. He thinks the war is wrong just as you do." Then he shook himself and tried to laugh. "Good grief! I've talked you to death, Raimey! Sorry about that. I'm not usually such a chatterbox."

"It's all right."

As he looked at her, he saw the sweetness on her lips and the goodness in her face. Her skin glowed in the sun with a diaphanous quality, fine and clear. "I've never talked with a girl like this."

"It's because I'm different, Dent," she said with no trace at all of pity. "You're always on your guard with other girls, because they're out to get you to marry them."

He stared at her with amazement. "Why, not all of them!"

"Pretty much so," she said with a nod. "It's the only way for a young woman to live, doing all she can to find a good husband. It's what all women study and train for."

"Good night! I can't believe you're saying these things!"

Raimey smiled and picked a blade of grass. She tasted it, then turned her head to one side. "That's sour," she commented, then added, "Even if a young woman isn't out to catch you, you think she is. I suspect all handsome young men feel that way."

"How do you know I'm handsome?" Dent was amazed at the play of their words and asked the question without awkwardness.

"Leona said so." Then she paused, a

thought coming to her. "May I touch your face?"

"Why — I guess so." Dent sat still as Raimey leaned forward and touched his chest, then let her hand rise to his face. Her hand was soft — and her touch was the softest thing he could imagine.

"You have a wide mouth," Raimey murmured. "And a strong jaw." As her hands moved over his features, she cataloged them all. "Broad forehead, deep-set eyes — very black, Leona said — high cheekbones, small ears. Very thick hair — black as night, she said." Then she removed her hand and sat back.

"Yes, you're very attractive, Dent." He was so speechless that she laughed at him. "Never had your face pushed and probed by any of your young ladies, did you? I'm sorry. But it helps. I know what you look like now." Then she added, "But you've been so free with me because you feel none of that pressure with me that you feel with other girls. You're safe."

Dent stared at her. "Maybe you're right."

"I am right," she announced with a brisk nod. Then she said in a different tone, "I wish you'd make it up with your father. Even if he's wrong, you'll be sorry if you don't." A breeze lifted a lock of her hair, and she pushed it back with a quick gesture. "There are only two things on this earth that really matter, and your family is one of them."

"What's the other?"

"Why, God, of course!"

Dent nodded. "I know you're right about that, Raimey, but I just don't have it in me to forgive him. He's hurt us all too much." He expected her to preach at him, but she sat there quietly. She seemed to be listening to something he could not hear, and finally he grew nervous. "I guess that sounds pretty feeble to you. But I'm just a weak character, Raimey. You strong Christians can turn the other cheek, but fellows like me, why, we just can't manage things like that." A strong memory of his last argument with his father came to him, turning him sour. "I'll go get the carriage," he said. "Just stay here. Nobody will trouble you."

He left abruptly, and she stood up as he left her. She wanted to cry out to him, to warn him of the peril of hating his father — but it was too late.

She waited until the carriage came back. Leona was put out with her, but Dent had calmed down. As he held Raimey's hand and put her into the carriage, he said, "I'll stop by tomorrow to apologize for letting you fall in the creek."

"Come for supper, Lieutenant, six o'clock sharp," Leona said instantly. "And bring that handsome Captain Forbes of D Company with you." Without waiting for his answer, she said, "Let's go, Job!" and the carriage leaped ahead. Denton stood there, staring after it, then went over and picked up his jacket. As he put it on, he suddenly shook his head, a look of admiration in his dark eyes. "She's some girl. I couldn't handle a thing like that!"

He returned to the camp, found Forbes, and the two of them made their plans to go into Richmond. When Dent asked Captain Taylor for permission, the captain gave him a careful look. "Better get your running around done quick, Dent. And get the men ready. Something's happening. When orders come, we'll have to move fast." He drummed on the table with his fingers, then remarked, "Fine-looking girls, the Reed women. Too bad about the younger one."

"Yes," Dent said, then left the tent.

CHAPTER 11
A HOUSE DIVIDED

As May gave way to June, summer fell across the land, wrapping it with a mantle of blistering heat. The field hands at Gracefield endured the white-hot sun patiently, larding the fields with their sweat; but for Clay Rocklin the sultry heat was one more irritating factor he didn't need. By nature he was a hard-driving man in the physical sense, and he had always been able to override any sort of trouble in his mind by hard work or play. Now, however, no matter how many hard, long hours he labored in the fields, when night came he tossed restlessly on his bed, getting up hollow-eyed and tired.

"You don't look well, Clay," his mother said as he came to the big house late one night. It was after eleven, and she had found him in the kitchen eating a piece of cold chicken from the cellar. "You're working too hard."

"I'm all right," he said briefly, but his face

was slack with fatigue as he chewed listlessly on the cold meat. "The black mare had her foal tonight, but she had a hard time. I thought Fox and I were going to lose them both for a while, but she had a fine colt. What are you doing up so late?"

"Oh, I just couldn't sleep."

Clay glanced at her sharply. "Father's not doing well?"

"No. I'm worried about him, Clay. He's been poorly all winter and spring, and this heat seems to make him even worse."

"What does Dr. Medlin say?"

"He doesn't know." Susanna brushed her hair back from her forehead with a weary gesture. The pressure of running Gracefield was heavy, and Clay noted that new lines had come to her face. "Those terrible stomach pains frighten me — him, too, though he won't say anything. I guess we both are thinking of Noah, your grandfather. He had the same kind of trouble before he died."

They sat at the table, talking slowly, letting the time run on. The grandfather clock in the hall ticked on with a stately cadence and loudly struck one reverberating, brassy note to mark the half hour. Susanna felt close to this tall, sunburned son of hers, perhaps because — of all of her children —

he was the one closest to God. Or perhaps it was because he had been lost for so many years, and when he had come back, she had received him as a gift from God. He was, she thought as she studied his aquiline features, a strong man — stronger than his father or any of the other Rocklin men. The genes of Noah Rocklin, her husband's father, ran strong in Clay and were evident in the same streak of stubborn individualism that Susanna had so much admired in Noah.

The sound of a horse coming down the drive at a trot broke through to them, sharp and clear. "That's Denton, I expect," Susanna said.

"What's he doing away from his company?"

"He took those Reed girls over to Brad's to visit with Amy." Brad Franklin was married to Amy, Clay's sister. They lived twenty miles away on Franklin's large plantation, and the two families were very close. Their sons had grown up together, even though Brad's son Grant was older than Clay's twins.

"I wish Brad had stayed out of this war," Clay said, frowning. "He's not cut out to be a soldier — and he's got plenty to do on that place of his."

"I know, but he's caught up in it," Susanna agreed. Then as footsteps sounded on the side walkway, she lowered her voice to say, "Dent's getting pretty thick with those Reed girls. He's been to their house two or three times, and now he's taken them to Brad's."

"Maybe he's getting over Deborah," Clay said, but then steps sounded on the porch and he fell silent until the door opened. "Hello, Dent."

Dent stopped at the sight of Clay at the table, but nodded at him briefly, then said, "Hello. You two are up late."

"How are Amy and her brood?" Susanna asked, listening as Dent gave a brief report. Dent was wearing his uniform, and he looked very dashing in the yellow lamplight. He was, Susanna saw, uncomfortable with his father. That grieved her, but there was nothing she could do about the situation. Finally when he paused, she asked, "When are you going to bring those young women by for me to meet, Denton?"

"Oh, maybe day after tomorrow. That's what Aunt Amy said, I think." He hesitated, then walked over and got a drink of water from the pitcher. There was a restlessness about him that kept him in motion, and he said briefly, "I have to be back for drill.

Good night, Grandmother . . . sir." He left without a pause, and the echo of his horse's hoofbeats came to Clay and his mother on the night air.

"I'm sorry he feels as he does, Clay, about you."

"He thinks I'm unfair to Ellen. And he's never really forgiven me for leaving you all in the lurch." Clay's expression turned heavy, and he got to his feet. "Better get to bed, I guess." He moved over to Susanna, leaned down, and kissed her cheek. "Good night, Mother."

"Good night, Clay." Reaching up, she patted his cheek. "It'll all come out. God is still with us."

"Yes, He is." Clay turned to go, then hesitated. "I'm worried about Lowell. He's restless."

"Most of his friends have joined the army. He feels left out."

"I know. Do what you can to keep him out of it."

"You know how stubborn he is, Clay."

The corners of his mouth twitched. "Like me? Well, I'm going to spend more time with him. Maybe if he stays busy, he'll be content. We've got up a hunting trip tomorrow. We'll leave before dawn, so you'll be asleep. May stay two or three days, but things are in pretty good shape here now. Good night."

He left the house and went at once to his own place, slept poorly until four in the morning, then rose and dressed. He walked to the Big House, entered the kitchen, and started coffee. Lowell was a heavy sleeper, so Clay had to go into his room and shake him thoroughly before the boy got out of bed.

"I'll fix some breakfast," Clay said when he was sure that Lowell was really awake, then went downstairs. Ten minutes later Lowell stumbled into the kitchen, bleary-eyed with sleep, and the two of them sat down and ate the bacon and eggs. The food brought Lowell out of it, and when they finished, they cleaned up the kitchen and left for the stables. Soon they were on their way down the road, leading two mules that would pack the meat back. The cool air lay across the earth, and fragments of gossamer clouds drifted across the pale moon. By the time they had reached Wilson's Creek, the sun was up.

As they moved westward, the flatland began to break up into small rises covered with scrub pine. By midmorning they were in the foothills and stopped long enough to eat some sandwiches and make coffee. The sun was hot, but Clay was glad to see that Lowell was enjoying himself.

Should have done more of this with all my boys, he thought. *If I had, maybe Dent and I wouldn't be so cut off from each other.* He resolved to throw himself into his family, and as they moved on toward the higher ranges, he drew Lowell out, trying to understand what was going on in his mind.

Lowell was quite different from the twins, in both appearance and manner. He was shorter, more muscular, and had little of the darkness of the other men — the Black Rocklins — of his immediate family. His hair, darker in his youth, was now light brown, thick and full, and he had a set of clear hazel eyes. His complexion was fair, like his mother's, and while he was no scholar like David and had little of Dent's impulsiveness, he had a quick mind and always finished what he started. That had been clearly evident even when the boys were young. Clay had noted that when David and Dent gave up on a project, it was Lowell who forged ahead with a dogged patience until the thing was completed.

As they rode through large stands of virgin pine, Lowell began to speak freely. At first he talked about his horses, for he was the best horseman of them all and had shown great perception in breeding good stock. But inevitably he spoke of the war. It came out as he spoke of his cousin Grant. "Grant's going into the cavalry — did you know?"

"No, I didn't."

"Well, he is. Uncle Brad tried to get him to join the Richmond Grays, but Grant says he'd rather ride than walk." A smile touched Lowell's lips, and he shrugged. "Guess he's right about that, but the Grays are a good outfit. Dent's been telling me about how good they are." When his father said nothing, Lowell gave him a quick glance. "I guess you know I've been thinking about it a lot."

Clay nodded slowly, thinking of the best way to respond. If he turned the boy off with a curt refusal, he knew he would be closing a door that he'd not likely open again. Still, he yearned to keep Lowell out of the army. Finally he said, "Sure, I know. All your close friends are signing up, and you feel left out."

Lowell nodded quickly, a little surprised at his father's understanding. "Yes, sir, they are. And I feel like a quitter — like I'm letting them down and letting my country down, too." He hesitated, then added, "I know how you feel about the war, but what's going to happen to us if the Yankees take over our place? We'll lose everything!"

Clay let Lowell talk, aware that the boy's head had been filled with war talk and propaganda of all sorts. Some of it was true, much of it was not, but at the age of seventeen, Lowell was not going to be able to sort it all out. If men such as Robert E. Lee had trouble, how could a mere boy do better? Clay had had second thoughts himself — many times. He believed the war was an invitation to tragedy for the South. Still, he was a Virginian, and the idea of failing his own was a bitter one to him.

"Nothing's much worse than being left out, Lowell," Clay answered thoughtfully. "And when you're seventeen, to be on the outside is just about unbearable. I was a lot older than you are now when the Mexican War started, but I was itching to join. Gideon was in the army getting ready to go, and lots of my friends were rushing to sign up." As he spoke of those days, the memories came back to him, and Lowell listened avidly, for his father never spoke of that time. "I couldn't stand it, Lowell, so I signed up, too. And for me it was a bad decision."

Lowell listened as his father told of his time in the army. It was not a pleasant story, and Clay Rocklin did not spare himself. He spoke of how he had been weak and unsteady and far more interested in personal glory than in serving his country. Bitterness scored his lips as he related how he'd failed his unit at the most critical hour. He didn't add that it was not altogether his fault, but shouldered the entire blame for the loss of life that had come when he failed his duty.

Finally he stopped, and after a moment of silence, Lowell said, "Thanks for telling me, sir. I — I know it wasn't easy."

"Never easy for a man to talk about his failures," Clay said evenly, then added, "I've not been a good father to you, Lowell. I wish I had been, but I've made many mistakes."

Lowell recognized instantly that his father was referring to his relationship to his mother and looked at him quickly. It had been difficult for him to accept his father when he had returned, but he had come to have hopes that his father and mother would be happy together. Lowell knew more about his mother than he would ever voice, for her reputation in Richmond was unsavory, and there was no way he could have failed to hear of her affairs. He loved his mother but was keenly aware of her shortcomings. Glancing at his father, he had a sudden insight into what a travesty his parents' marriage had been.

"We all make mistakes, sir," he said quietly and was glad to see that his remark had pleased his father. "And maybe it would be a mistake for me to go into the army — but how's a man to know what to do? Everybody is saying that it's right, that we've got to defend the South. And you know better than most what happens when a man refuses to go along. You've taken a lot of abuse because of your views on this war. How do you know you're right? Can you tell me?"

"I wish I could give you a formula," Clay said slowly. "It would be nice if everything were clear-cut, but most things aren't that way. The North has been wrong for years, burdening the South with unfair economic policies, but the South is wrong, too. At least, I think so. Slavery has to go, Lowell. Men like Lee know that, but they're part of the system the North has saddled us with. As for states' rights, well, I don't know. Most of us in the South say that if a state agrees to join the Union, it can decide to withdraw. But Lincoln and others like him feel that if that happens, this country will die; break us up into a lot of tiny nations and America will cease to be."

Lowell listened carefully, then sighed. "I

don't know what to do, sir." Then he asked, "Would you agree to let me enlist, if that's what I decide is right?"

"If you decide it's the right thing, Lowell," Clay said, "I guess I wouldn't stand in your way. But lots of men are signing up just for the thrill of it, some to get out of boring work, others because they've been shamed into it. I wouldn't want to see you go unless you knew it was for a better reason than some we've seen."

Lowell was thoughtful as they went deeper into the woods, but said no more. Clay didn't know if what he had said was a help to his son, but he had done his best. They made camp, hobbled the animals, then went hunting. The woods were stiff with game, and Lowell brought down a fat buck with one shot. Lowell's youthful face was aglow with pleasure, and Clay enjoyed the kill as much as the boy. They dressed the deer, cooked up huge steaks over the fire, then sat back and enjoyed the night, talking until the stars glittered overhead. When they finally rolled into their blankets, Lowell went to sleep at once. Clay lay on his back, watching the opalescent gleam of the stars as they wheeled around in their old dance. Then, after saying a brief prayer, he dropped off to sleep.

The next day they hunted the ridges all morning, taking small game, but at three o'clock, Clay said, "Let's go over to Blackwell Peak. Your grandfather might like some fresh bear meat. He was always partial to it." Lowell had never shot a bear, so he was eager to go. They broke camp, moved across the upper reaches of the Mogolla Mountains, and came to the foot of the Blackwell range late that afternoon. Clay knew the country well, and as they came into a small valley, he said, "Looks like somebody beat us to it, Lowell. But we can move on around to the other side of this ridge."

But as they drew near the camp, where a fire was sending a thin line of white smoke almost straight up in the still air, Clay smiled, saying, "Guess we won't have to move on. It's Buford Yancy." As they rode in, he called out, "Don't shoot, Buford! We're friendly."

Yancy had been squatting at the fire, cooking a chunk of meat in a blackened skillet, and he rose at once, calling out, "Well, dang me, if it ain't Clay Rocklin! Come and eat, you fellers! How are you, Lowell?" Without waiting for an answer, he commanded,

"You, Bobby! Git them animals tied up, will you? Come and set, both of you."

Clay and Lowell dismounted at once and went to greet Yancy. "You located some bear sign, Buford?" Clay asked, then looked at the meat. "I see you have."

"They're plum thick this year, Clay." Yancy grinned. "And bold, too. Won't even run from you. Feller could hunt 'em with a good-sized stick." He looked over his shoulder toward the tent. "Melora! Come outta there and wait on these fellers!"

Clay looked startled as Melora stepped out of the tent. She emerged with a pleased look on her face. "How are you, Clay? And you, Lowell?"

She was wearing a pair of worn jeans that had belonged to one of her brothers, a faded blue shirt of Buford's, and a pair of low, worn boots. She looked trim, her full figure set off to good advantage by the rough clothing. Clay noticed that Lowell spoke briefly, and he felt a pang of regret.

He's heard the talk about Melora and me, Clay thought, but said only, "Came to load up on bear meat. Mother says bear fat makes the best soap, and Father likes a bear steak real well."

"Too late to go after bear today," Buford announced. "Bob wants to go for coon after

260

dark. That's for young folks, fallin' all over your feet in the dark."

"Come along with me, Lowell. We got some good dogs — a new one that can track a coon over runnin' water." Bob Yancy, at the age of seventeen, was a carbon copy of his father. He knew Lowell fairly well, though they came from different backgrounds. They'd met at church, and several times Lowell had gone hunting with the Yancys.

"Sure, Bob," Lowell agreed. "I promised Dorrie I'd bring her some fresh coon. She can sure cook it good, too. Let's see that new dog."

The young men went off, talking dogs and guns, and Clay sat down, leaning against a tree. He watched as Melora moved around, putting a meal together. The two men spoke quietly, mostly of farming and horses. Finally the meal was ready, and Melora called the younger men to the fire. She served them all fresh bear steaks, sweet potatoes cooked in hot ashes, and black coffee. When the men were served, she fixed a plate for herself and sat on a blanket with her father. As they ate with gusto, Buford asked, "Why does grub taste so much better outdoors than in a house?"

"Must be fresher, I guess," Clay ventured.

"If this meat was any fresher, it'd still be on that ol' bear!" Bob Yancy said with a grin and spun out the story of how he'd tracked the bear and shot it. When he was finished with that tale, Buford told about a mountain lion he'd shot the previous week. For a long time they sat around the fire, drinking the strong black coffee and listening to the stories. Finally Bob said, "Let's go for them coons, Lowell," and the two young men got their guns, whistled up the dogs, then plunged off into the growing darkness.

Melora cleaned the dishes as Clay and her father spoke of their venture with corn and hogs; then she came back to sit on the blanket again. They talked intermittently, pausing to listen to the dogs, whose howls scored the night with sharp crescendos. Buford nodded when one long, drawn-out note floated to them on the night air. "That's Bess," he said. "That dog is death on a cold trail!" Finally he asked, "Whut about this war, Clay? You still agin it?"

Clay leaned back against the tree, and for some time they talked about the war. Both of them had sons who were vulnerable; in fact, one of the Yancy boys, Lonnie, had already enlisted in the Richmond Grays.

Melora saw that Clay was weary over it all. She spoke little herself but listened carefully, as always treasuring any time in his presence. She was now twenty-six, ready for marriage and feeling a strong desire for children of her own. But she knew that her love for this tall man sitting across the fire would spoil her for any other man. She had often thought of marrying and had not lacked for suitors. Rev. Jeremiah Irons had long waited for her to turn to him, but Melora knew that she could never bring what she felt for Clay Rocklin to another man. And the thought of concealing her feelings for a lifetime from a husband she could never fully love was repugnant to her. She had called herself a romantic fool often enough, but still, there it was. She could not shake off what she felt for Clay as she would shake off an old garment. She could only choose not to act on her feelings — and this she had done.

The night wore on, and finally the hounds' clarion cries grew nearer. Buford, always the hunter, could stand it no longer. Rising and picking up his rifle, he grinned. "Them young fellers don't know much about coons. I better go give 'em a hand."

He disappeared into the dark shadows, and Melora laughed. "Pa's never satisfied with anyone's hunting but his."

"Best man in the woods I ever saw," Clay

said. Then he looked across the fire at her. "How have you been, Melora?"

"All right," she said, smiling. Drawing up her feet, she rested her chin on her knees and regarded him. "Tell me about everything, Clay."

"Big order — everything."

"Tell me about what you've been doing."

"Working, mostly." He sat there, the firelight playing on his face, speaking slowly of himself. The peacefulness of the night was on him, and in Melora's presence he relaxed — as he always did. He dropped his head, thinking of all the problems that loomed ahead of them, and then looked up. "Sometimes I wish life were as simple as the stories you used to love, about knights and maidens — where there's always a happy ending. Seems like in real life, things usually go wrong."

"Don't give up, Clay," she said instantly. Her eyes were bright as she added, "Think how God has brought you home from all sorts of dangers. He's given you so much!"

"You still believe, Melora? With everything coming down around our heads, you still believe that things will work out right?"

"I think God knows we're trusting Him, Clay." Then she murmured, "I love you, Clay. That's enough for me. You've been faithful to Ellen and to God. That's what's important."

They sat there in silence for a few moments; then a sound made Clay turn. He saw that Lowell had stepped out of the brush and was standing absolutely still, his rifle in his hands. His eyes were filled with hurt, and at once Clay knew that he was thinking of his mother.

"Lowell —," he said, but even as he spoke, he saw the hardness form in the boy's face, so Clay said no more.

"I came back for more ammunition," Lowell said, and walking stiff-legged, he moved to his pack, filled his pockets with shells, then gave them one look before half running out of the camp.

"I'm sorry, Clay," Melora said.

"I'll talk to him," Clay said, but he knew it would not solve anything. "Better go to bed, Melora."

"All right, Clay."

The next day Lowell got his bear, two of them just for good measure. But on the way home, there was a wall between the father and son, and nothing Clay could say could break it down.

Finally they reached the drive to the house, and Clay abruptly pulled his horse to a halt. "Lowell, you're wrong about

Melora and me." He hesitated, pain on his face, then explained, "Your mother and I — don't get along. I can't explain it or defend myself. I wish it were different. But before God, I have never been unfaithful to her with any woman."

Lowell sat on his horse, his face frozen. He wanted desperately to believe what he was hearing; he had always liked and respected Melora Yancy. But the sight of his father sitting cozily with the woman by the campfire, looking at her fondly, had pulled down the younger Rocklin's defenses. He said in a tight voice, "I wish I could believe you. I'd like to. But I can't." He clenched his fists over the reins until his fingers were white. "I can't believe anything anymore, not even what you say about the war. Maybe you're just a coward! I'm joining up tomorrow, no matter what you say!"

Clay sat stiffly in the saddle, longing to find some way to convince this boy that he was telling the truth. He loved Lowell, and it seemed as though the boy was about to step off his road into a deep and dangerous chasm.

A thought came to Clay, which he rejected at first. Then it came back, so strong that he sat there considering it. Lowell, seeing his strange expression, asked, "What is it?"

"Lowell," Clay said, speaking slowly as the idea formed within him, "maybe there's a way."

"A way to what?"

"To show you you're wrong about me."

"It's too late." Lowell spurred his horse forward, leaving Clay to look after him. Time ran on, and still he sat there until finally he slapped his thigh, his mouth drawn into a tight line.

"It's the only way!" he said aloud; then he touched King with his heels and rode toward the house, wondering if he was right in his intention. But right or wrong, he had decided that it was best to try anything to save this youngest son of his.

CHAPTER 12
THE LAST RECRUIT

Dulcie glared with exasperation at Raimey. "You ain't going to the ball like that, I hope!"

Raimey was wearing a new dress of pale blue with a billowing hoop skirt that swept the floor. Graceful swirls of indigo velvet traced their way around the skirt, the dark blue almost an exact match for Raimey's eyes. The bodice was trimmed with fine lace interwoven with a delicate ribbon that framed the girl's graceful shoulders.

"What's wrong with this dress?" Raimey demanded. She had bought it on a shopping trip with her mother and had put it on by herself while Dulcie was helping Leona dress.

"What's wrong is that you ain't got on your corset!" Dulcie shook her head with disgust and marched over to pick up the garment stiff with whalebone stays. "Now you come out of that dress and put this on right now."

"I won't! I hate that thing, Dulcie." Raimey shoved the maid's hands away, stating flatly, "The dress fits me. I don't need to be squeezed by that stupid thing."

Dulcie had to admit that the girl was right, for the dress lay smoothly on Raimey without straining at the seams, but she was adamant. "I don't care. You've got to wear a corset. It ain't decent to go to a party without one. What will your mama say?"

"I won't tell her until we get there, and don't you tell either."

"I will, too!"

Raimey knew Dulcie very well. "If you don't tell, you can have my red dress and the petticoat that goes with it."

Greed struggled with indignation on Dulcie's face, for she had long coveted that dress. Finally she said piously, "Well, if you want to go to that party looking like a hussy and if you want to deceive your poor mama, I guess I can't stop you."

"I knew all the time you'd say that, Dulcie." A smile came to Raimey's face, and she said, "Now do my hair — and get some of that perfume that Leona uses."

Grumbling under her breath, Dulcie picked up a comb and began to coax Raimey's thick curls into order. As she worked

269

on the lustrous hair, she talked constantly. "What about that young Rhett boy? Is he going to marry with Miss Leona? That other man, the tall captain who's been chasing after her, he's better looking, but he ain't got no money. Now I think Miss Leona better . . ."

As Dulcie rattled on, Raimey sat impatiently, anxious to be gone. It was the Presidential Ball, in honor of the Davises, and she and Leona had talked of little else for a week. After their visit with the Franklins, the two sisters had come back to Richmond and found that everyone was certain the army would be called to march into battle at any moment. The ball had been scheduled for the middle of July, but Varina Davis had persuaded her husband to set the time for the twelfth so that the officers would be sure to be in the city.

The visit with the Franklins had been, for Raimey, a splendid time. She had liked the Franklins, especially Amy, who was a cheerful woman, always happy to spend time with her young guests. She liked their daughter, Rachel, too, who was a beauty according to all she heard. The boys, Grant and Les, as expected, fell half in love with Leona — but then, all the men did.

But it was her visit to Dent's home, Gracefield, that had been the high point of the week's visit. Dent's mother, Ellen, had not been there, but his grandmother, Susanna Rocklin, had been delightful. Raimey had liked Clay Rocklin, Dent's father, very much. He had been careful to spend time with her, and even from that brief visit, Raimey could sense the goodness of the man.

Dent was there, of course, and he took the two girls all over the plantation. More often than not, however, Leona preferred to stay in the house, so Raimey went alone with Dent. He took her to the slave quarters and to the blacksmith's shop, where an elderly slave named Box made her a ring out of a nail. She had rubbed the velvet noses of the horses in the pasture, sat beside the duck pond listening to the endless gabble of the ducks, and run her hands over the glossy sides of the wild-eyed new colt.

Once she said to Dent, "I'm taking too much of your time," but he had said, "Raimey, I'm the most selfish fellow you ever met. If I'm spending a lot of time with you, it's because I want to."

They had been sitting in a sequestered nook set off by grapevines now thick with leaves, underneath a huge oak that dipped low over the pond. The afternoon sun had dropped halfway behind the distant hills, shedding golden rays that turned the pond crimson. Dent described some ducks that were making their way across the pond, saying, "They look like a small armada with feathers!" and the description had delighted Raimey.

The two young people were drinking tea and resting after a brisk walk to the pond. Raimey turned her face to the man at her side and asked suddenly, "Why aren't you chasing after Leona, Dent? She's the most beautiful girl in the world, and the two of you surely agree about the war. I believe you could make her fall in love with you if you tried."

"Too much competition," Dent said with a smile. He sat there, sipping from his tall glass, studying Raimey. Indeed, he was puzzled at his own behavior, for he himself had thought how strange it was that he was not drawn to Leona Reed. Always he had been drawn to the most beautiful girl at hand, but he found that he merely liked Leona in a cheerful way.

"No, that's not so," Raimey said. "You're the sort of man who likes competition." Her lips were pursed in a delightful way, and he had become accustomed to the fact that the blue eyes never focused on him. "I think you're still in love with that cousin of yours, Deborah Steele."

A frown touched Dent's brow, and he demanded, "Who told you about her?" Then he shook his head, half angry at her. "This whole county's a gossip mill!"

"You were in love with her, weren't you? Everybody says so."

"I don't want to talk about it." The coldness of his tone made him ashamed, so after a moment he added, "I don't know, Raimey. Deborah's a fine girl, but she's for the Union. Why, she's a rabid abolitionist! The two of us would eat each other alive!"

Raimey, he saw, was considering his words, which made him rather nervous, for she had an uncanny ability to sift through what he said and arrive at the thoughts his words covered. Now she said slowly, "I'm sorry, Dent. It must be hard to lose someone you care for."

Dent stared at her with a mixture of exasperation and amazement. "You know too much, Raimey," he said with a wry smile. "The man you marry won't have a secret in the world!"

"I'll never marry."

Her statement brought Dent's head up sharply. "Of course you will!"

"No." Her voice was inexorable as she

added, "A blind wife would be too much to put on any man."

She had spoken quietly, and he had found no answer.

Dent never knew how to speak of Raimey's infirmity. She was matter-of-fact about it, but he could not be. It made him feel awkward.

He had gotten to his feet, saying, "I guess we'd better go in. It's getting dark."

A smile had tugged at her lips as she turned to face him and said, "That's your problem."

He admired courage greatly and knew suddenly that was why he was drawn to her. He did not fear death, but he knew deep within that he could not have handled blindness, that he would have ended his life if such a thing had ever come to him. Now as she stood there, her lips parted with humor at her own remark, he felt strangely protective, so much so that he put his hands on her shoulders. "Raimey, you're a wonder!" When she did not answer but tilted her face up to listen to his words, it seemed natural enough to lower his head and kiss her.

She did not pull away, and there was such innocence in her that instead of a light caress, he drew her closer. If she had resisted in the least, he would have released her, but she did not. When she drew away, she was in some way still with him. She was smiling, but he could not read the expression that lay on her lips, on her face.

"That was nice, Dent," she had said quietly; then they had turned and gone to the house, not mentioning the kiss again.

But now as Dulcie brushed her hair, Raimey thought of it. And not for the first time, for she had thought of it often. She was a young woman of no experience with men, having missed the usual girlhood experiences because of her blindness. When boys were around, Dulcie or someone else was there, as well. Even when she came into her teens and was taken to parties, nothing had occurred. One boy, a fat young fellow named Len Sykes, had kissed her once when she was fifteen, but it had been an awkward affair, leaving her untouched inside. Many of the books she had devoured spoke of love, but those were things in books, not life. She had tried to get Leona to tell her about such things, but Leona was embarrassed and kept herself back, saying, "It will come to you, Raimey."

But it had not come, and even as she sat feeling the comb go through her hair, hearing Leona getting ready in the next room and the clatter of hooves on the street outside, Raimey felt again the touch of Dent Rocklin's lips on hers — and was stirred.

Then it was time to leave, and she joined Leona in the carriage. Leona was excited and chattered all the way to the Masonic Hall, where the ball was to be held. All her talk was of the officers — how dull it would be when they left, but how proud they all were of them. Mr. Reed said little, and Raimey knew he was troubled. She didn't know the source of his discontent and could only think it was something to do with business. Her mother reached over to push away a curl that had fallen over her brow, saying, "You girls will probably have sore feet tomorrow. All the officers will want to dance with you."

But it wasn't like that, at least not for Raimey. The officers came to her, of course, greeting her, and were amazed that she knew them at the first word they spoke. But they did not ask her to dance. It was not their fault, for they assumed she could not dance because of her affliction. The dance went on for an hour, and Leona, of course, danced every dance. Raimey's mother was asked to help with the refreshments, which left Raimey alone, sitting in a chair, trying not to show how lonely she felt.

"I believe this is our dance, Miss Reed?"

"Oh, Mr. Rocklin!" She turned to face the voice with a smile, glad to meet Dent's father again. "How nice that you're here."

"It's good to see you, Raimey. Now how about that dance? But I'll have to warn you, I'm not much of a dancer."

Raimey rose and timidly put out her hand. "I'm no dancer at all. I never danced at a ball in my life — except with Dent at the Officers' Ball."

"Well, don't expect an old man to be as light on his feet as that young fellow, but I think we'll do all right." He took her in his arms and carefully moved out on the floor. He was, in fact, an excellent dancer, and he enjoyed watching the girl's features glow with pleasure as they moved across the floor. "You're not telling the truth, I think," he said easily. "You've danced more than once."

"Oh, we had lessons when I was fifteen, but I didn't try very hard. It didn't seem as though I'd ever need them." The tune was a fast one, but she followed him smoothly around the room and finally asked, "How's the new colt? The black one?" She listened as he spoke of the colt, then of other things she'd heard about on her visit. When the dance was over, she applauded with the others, and he took her to the refreshment table. She took the glass he handed her, and the two of them stood there talking over the sound of the music.

She wanted to say something about Dent but could not find the words. It was he who brought up the subject. "You and Dent have become good friends, haven't you, Raimey? I'm glad to see it." He hesitated, then added, "He was hit pretty hard over Deborah Steele."

"He was very much in love with her, I think."

"Well, she's a beautiful young woman — but it would have been bad if they had married. They don't agree on some important things, and they're both very stubborn. It would have been painful for both of them."

"I wonder how she feels about him now."

"My mother got a letter from her this week. It seems that Deborah is very involved with a young man. A strange sort of thing! He's from a very poor family, not really of her station. She got him to enlist; then his whole family got sick and she went to take over their care. Deborah found out her friend has a real gift for writing, and the two of them are thick. Of course, he'll be leaving any day with his unit."

"And Dent will be leaving to face him," Raimey said thoughtfully, her face suddenly losing its lightness. "Dent loved her, and she's interested in another man — and now this Northern boy and Dent may kill each other. What a terrible waste!"

"Yes, it is." Clay dropped his eyes, then lifted them. "I know you feel the war is wrong. So do I. But it's hard for a man to know what to do —" He was about to say more but broke off when he saw an officer coming across the crowded floor. "Here comes Dent, Raimey," he said quietly.

Dent had seen them and came right to where they stood. "Hello. Have you two been having a good time?"

Something in his voice caught at Raimey. "Is something wrong, Dent?"

He glanced at her, then shrugged at his father. "Can't hide a thing from this woman! Well, not wrong — but we'll be moving out right away. Not tomorrow, but the day after."

"The Federals are on the move?" Clay asked.

"Yes, so the scouts say." Dent looked serious, but there was a light of anticipation in his eyes. "Word is that McDowell has left Washington with several divisions and is moving west. It's the real thing this time.

Colonel Benton just got the word this afternoon, and he called all of us in for a staff meeting."

"I suppose this is all highly secret?" Clay said.

Dent looked around and saw his fellow officers who had been at the meeting moving about the room, talking with animation. "Supposed to be, but we've been waiting too long for this." He gave his father a calculated look, saying, "I don't think you'll enjoy the rest of the ball, Father. It'll probably be pretty much a celebration of the battle to come. I know you won't like that."

Clay said only, "Did you know your brother enlisted in the Grays this morning?"

Dent stared at him, shock pulling his mouth open. "David?" he asked incredulously.

"No, Lowell."

"But — he's only seventeen years old!"

"How many of your men are seventeen, Dent? Quite a few, and some of them even younger, I'd venture."

Dent was disturbed by the news. "He can't enlist without your permission, sir."

"I've given it."

Dent stared at his father, but no words came from his lips. Lowell had mentioned wanting to enlist, but all the young fellows wanted that. It had never come into Dent's head that his father would let him do it. It upset him, and he said angrily, "If you're so set against this war, why did you let him do it?"

Clay shook his head. "If I'd said no, he'd have run away and enlisted in another state, Dent. His mind's made up, and you know how stubborn he is. Nothing I could say made any difference." He shrugged his shoulders, then said, "Good night, Miss Reed," and left the floor.

Dent was shaken by the news. It made things different somehow, in a way that he could not quite explain. He had no fear for himself, yet the thought of his brother being killed brought a strong reaction.

The music started, and he pulled himself together. "Will you dance with me?"

Raimey said, "Yes, Dent," and the two of them joined the other couples out on the floor. She moved easily in his embrace, and when she realized that he was still thinking of the scene with his father, she said, "Are you so worried about Lowell?"

"Yes. He's too young."

"Two years younger than you and David."

He glared at her, then laughed. "You have a fiendish way of bringing a fellow down, Raimey! Yes, that's right, but he's —"

When Dent broke off, unable to find the word he sought, Raimey said, "He's young, Dent. But so are you, most of you. And so are the men who are coming to meet you."

"I know, Raimey." Dent seemed subdued, and they moved around the floor without speaking for a time. Then he said, "Blast his eyes! Why did he have to do it? Now I'll be worrying about him all the time, afraid he'll get himself shot!"

"That's exactly the way your father feels about you, Dent!" Raimey said gently. "Can't you see that?"

Dent stared at her, unable to answer. "No, he doesn't care about me."

"Don't be foolish," Raimey chided him. "If you don't sense his affection, you're a very dull man. Dent, don't you see that the things you hate about your father, they're not in him — they're in you."

Her statement hit Dent hard. "You can't know that, Raimey," he said. "You don't know what he's done to all of us, his family. He's ruined our lives!"

"Dent, being blind is pretty bad, but it has one advantage. A blind person, in some ways, is outside of things — standing off and watching, not really a part of what's happening. So he or she can be pretty objective. I've learned to get to know people better than most. What do you think about your grandmother?"

"Why, she's the best there is!"

"And does she think your father is a fool? Does she hate him?"

"Well, he's her son, Raimey."

"You know that's no answer. What about the slaves — do they hate him? No, they all respect your father. What about Rev. Irons? He's a fine man. Does he hate Clay Rocklin?" She paused, and sensing he could not answer, she grew gentle. "Is it possible that you've built up this bitterness for him and just can't let it go?"

She said no more, but her words had burned into him. When the dance was over, he took her back to her seat. "I'll be back soon. I have to talk to Major Radcliff."

He left, and the dance went on, but the officers had seen Raimey dancing and came boldly to claim her. She didn't know that several times Dent was on his way to her but stepped back when other officers came to dance with her. She sensed that she had hurt him and wished she had not spoken so bluntly.

Then, late in the evening, he came to her. Just as the music ended for one of the waltzes, he was at her side. "My dance, isn't it?" When she turned to him with a smile, he said, "I know a balcony around at the rear. Care to see it?"

"We always end up on balconies, don't we?" she said with a smile, and soon they were outside. "This is nice," she said. "The smoke gets very bad inside." Then she turned to him, her face luminous in the moonlight. "I spoke too harshly to you, Dent. I'm sorry."

He stood there studying her features. "Well, it came as quite a shock, Lowell enlisting. I wasn't ready for it."

"Do you think your brother David will enlist?"

"Not right away. David's a heavy thinker. It'll take him a year to sort the thing out. But my cousin Grant, he's in the cavalry. We grew up together. Hate to see anything happen to old Grant!" He fell silent, then said, "Up until now, it was all sort of a game, like chess. But now that it's come, I see it's not like chess at all. You can lose a pawn at chess and it's no matter. But if something happens to Lowell or Grant, it's final."

Raimey nodded. "Yes." Then she lifted her hand to his chest, wanting to touch him. "Oh, Dent, be careful!" she whispered. "Be very careful!"

He took her hand, moved by her concern,

and lifted it to his lips and kissed it. "I will, Raimey."

They stood in the moonlight for a long time, saying little. He was troubled as he never had been before, and Raimey was moved by the emotions she sensed in him. Finally a cloud covered the moon, and he said heavily, "Almost time to go. We'd better get back." Impulsively he reached out and touched her face. "Remember when you touched my face — so you could remember? Well, it's my turn."

Raimey stood still as his hand moved over her cheek. It was a hard, rough hand, but it felt strong on her face. Finally he withdrew it and said with regret, "Time to go."

They left the balcony, and shortly afterward the ball broke up. In the coach on the way home, Raimey's mother said, "You'll miss the young men, won't you, girls?"

"Oh yes!" Leona said — but Raimey kept her silence, still feeling the roughness of Dent's palm on her cheek.

"Sir, a recruit to see you. Says he wants to sign up."

Taylor Dewitt looked up from the map he was bending over. "Tell him to see the recruiting officer in Richmond. I don't have time for him now."

"I did tell him that, sir," Sergeant Huger insisted. He was a tall man with thick auburn hair and gray eyes. A graduate of the Virginia Military Institute, he would be an officer at some point. He had learned to read men pretty well, and he suggested, "Captain, I'd see this fellow if I were you. He looks pretty seasoned to me."

Taylor threw down his pen and made a helpless gesture toward Dent, who had been examining the map. "Well, bring him in, Sergeant."

"It's pretty late to enlist any new men, Captain," Dent commented.

"Lieutenant, I've learned to trust my sergeant. I don't know what the blazes I'm doing — but Sergeant Huger does. I feel like a child around him!"

"You'll learn. We all will," Dent said. Then he turned to face the two men who entered Captain Dewitt's tent, and shock caused his eyes to spring open.

"This is Clay Rocklin, Captain Dewitt," Sergeant Huger announced, then left the tent.

"Hello, Taylor. Good morning, Dent," Clay said. He saw that both men were staring at him in amazement. "Don't blame you for looking so shocked. I feel that way my-self."

"What's this all about, Clay?" Taylor asked at once. He liked Clay, but he could not believe what Huger had said.

But Clay responded at once, "I want to enlist, Dewitt." He shrugged his heavy shoulders, adding, "I know everything you're going to say. You'll say I'm too old, that I've been against the war from the start, that I've got a bad record. Well, it's all true enough, but I'm asking you to give me a chance."

Taylor shook his head. "I don't want to do it, Clay. Blast your eyes! It's not right, somehow."

Dent asked suddenly, "Does this have anything to do with Lowell?"

Clay turned to him. "Yes, it does. I've disappointed Lowell. He thinks I've let him down. I tried to get him to stay out of the army, but he's joined up to spite me — at least that's part of it."

"Well, Clay, that's bad, but how do you think enlisting will help that situation?" Taylor asked bluntly.

"Right now, I have no idea," Clay admitted. "I guess I got the idea that if I was in his unit, I might be able to look out for him a little. Probably that's crazy. I don't know, really, but the other part is — I've got to show him that I care about him. The only

287

way I can think of to do that is to enlist. So I'll begin the worst way in the world, Dewitt. I'll presume on our friendship. A favor. Take me into your company. Put me close to Lowell."

Taylor Dewitt stared at the man in front of him. "I thought I knew you pretty well, Clay, but I don't understand this at all."

Clay smiled without humor. "Makes two of us, Dewitt. Will you do it?"

Taylor turned to face Dent. "What do you think, Lieutenant?"

Dent realized that Captain Dewitt was leaving the decision up to him. If he said no, he knew that Taylor would turn down his father's request. And that was exactly what he wanted to do! The thought of his father serving under him seemed ridiculous. He knew it would spread throughout the regiment, and even higher, for many officers knew of his father's shameful record in the Mexican War.

And, too, he did not want to believe that his father was honest in what he was saying. If Clay Rocklin were doing this — giving up everything for a cause he didn't believe in out of love for his son — that would mean that he, Denton Rocklin, would have to admit that he was totally wrong in his bitter judgment of his father.

The silence ran on, and Clay understood what was happening. He had no idea what Dent's decision would be, but he did not beg.

Finally Dent's lips tightened. He said in a sparse tone, "Captain, you know the potential for trouble in this thing, how the men will talk. But I'm willing to let him try."

"All right, then, get him sworn in. Put him in Waco's Platoon with your brother." He turned to Clay, saying, "Another old friend of yours is the lieutenant. Bushrod Aimes. Now that's the last favor you get from me, Private Rocklin — and don't even ask one from Lieutenant Aimes!"

"Of course not, Captain Dewitt," Clay said, realizing that the close relationship with Taylor was over, at least for a time, for there was a great gap between officers and enlisted men. "Thank you, sir."

He turned and followed Dent out of the tent. "This way to the commissary," Dent said in a clipped tone.

When they had gone past several tents, Clay said, "Sorry to put this burden on you, Dent. I know you don't like it, and I know you don't trust me. I'll do my best to make no trouble for you."

"All right, we'll leave it like that," Dent said. He was silent for six more paces, then added, "It's going to be an awkward business."

"You'll have to be harder on me than on any of the other men," Clay said flatly. "If you don't, you'll get criticized for showing favoritism. That goes for me and Lowell, as well. You know that, but I want you to pour it on, Lieutenant."

"I'll just do that, Private Rocklin!"

Two days after Clay signed up with the Richmond Grays, the regiment pulled out, heading for Manassas, Virginia. Dent had been true to his word, and Clay had taken quite a bit of hazing when it was discovered that he was a wealthy aristocrat and the father of the lieutenant — and an old friend of the captain's. But the men had been convinced there would be no favoritism when Dent had assigned the worst work details in the company to his father and his younger brother.

Lowell had been almost as shocked as Dent when his father appeared in uniform. "Well, Lowell, here I am," Clay had said evenly. "Looks like we've got a war to fight."

He was a very quick young man, Lowell Rocklin. Instantly he knew exactly why his father had enlisted. He said huskily, "You didn't have to do this, Father."

"Yes, son, I guess I did," Clay answered — and right then he knew that if he got killed with the first shot, he would at least have done one thing right with his family, with this son whom he loved so much.

The regiment marched to the train, flags flying and the band playing. When they got to the station, they were primed by refreshments and sent off with a fiery speech by the secretary of war. Then they moved to the flatcars and seated themselves, and with a blast of the whistle, the train gave a lurch and they moved out of the yard.

"There's Mother," Lowell said, waving to Ellen. "And there's Grandfather and Grandmother! Look, sir, Grandfather — he's smiling!"

So he was, Clay saw. Thomas Rocklin at last had found cause to smile at his son. Clay waved to his parents — then he saw Melora. She was alone, away from the crowd. He had seen her once before they boarded, but Ellen was there, and they had not spoken. Even now she didn't wave, but their eyes leaped the distance and something passed between them.

Lieutenant Rocklin had stood beside the Reeds for one brief moment. When the warning whistle blew, he hesitated. Mrs. Reed glanced at Raimey, aware of the agitation in this daughter's heart. She loved Raimey desperately, as a woman will love an afflicted child, and she knew — without Raimey's awareness — how the girl felt about the tall soldier standing there. At once she made a decision. "I'm sorry to inform you, Lieutenant, but you'll have to give this old woman a kiss."

Dent grinned at her, understanding at once what she was up to. He glanced at Sam Reed, who was smiling, and said, "Well, I guess you don't get to kiss a good-looking man very often, Ellie." He kissed her soundly, then moved to Leona and gave her a kiss. Then he stepped in front of Raimey, saying, "Don't try to get away, Miss Raimey. It wouldn't be patriotic." He put his arms around her, and she lifted her face. Her lips were soft, and her hands tightened on his arms as he held her.

"Good-bye," he said abruptly and left to step aboard the train, which was moving out of the station. The men of his company had seen him kissing the women and gave him a rousing cheer, which brought a flush to his face, but he knew it was in fun.

The crowd stood cheering until the train was out of sight. Then the silence that fell was heavy and oppressive. It was similar to that moment after a graveside service when the mourners don't know what to do. Raimey felt the gloom and, as they walked away, heard one firecracker explode.

It was only a tiny popping sound, but she thought at once of the sound of cannons that would soon roar over the men who had just left. Then another firecracker made its miniature explosion, and Raimey was glad to move away from the station.

■ ■ ■ ■

PART THREE:
BULL RUN

■ ■ ■ ■

CHAPTER 13
PRELUDE TO BATTLE

The appearance of a great comet in the sky on June 30, 1861, seemed to many to be a sign. The tail was in the form of a bright streamer with sides nearly straight and parallel. The *New York Herald* wrote solemnly about the "celestial visitor that has sprung upon us with such unexampled brilliancy and magnitude. . . . Many regard it with fear, looking upon it as something terrible, bringing in its train wars and desolation."

It was rumored that an elderly slave named Oola, who belonged to the Baynes family — close friends of Mary Todd Lincoln and her husband — had an evil eye and could "conjure spells." The slave woman was tall and large of frame, with eyes like gimlets and gray-black skin drawn tightly over her forehead and cheekbones. She said of the great comet, "Ye see dat great fire sword, 'blaze in de sky? Dat's a great war comin', and de handle's to'rd de Norf and de point to'rd de Souf, and de Norf's gwine take dat sword and cut de Souf's heart out. But dat Linkum man, chilluns, if he takes de sword, he's gwine perish by it!"

When Mrs. Baynes told the Lincoln boys about Oola's prophecy of war, carefully omitting the dire prediction regarding their father, Tad was greatly impressed and carried the story to his father. Mrs. Lincoln laughed, but the president seemed strangely interested.

"What was that, Tad, that she said about the comet?" he asked.

"She said," Tad answered, "that the handle was toward the North and the point toward the South and that meant the North was to cut the South's heart out. Do you think that's what it means, Pa?"

"I hope not, Tad," answered his father gravely. "I hope it won't come to that." But Mrs. Baynes reported that the president often looked intently at the comet, a forlorn look in his deep eyes.

Comet or no comet, everyone knew there would be a battle — the president, the army, the people, and certainly the press. There had to be a war! Hadn't the Rebels threatened the very substance of the nation? Horace Greeley thumped the patriotic drum daily in his newspaper with headlines that shouted, "ON TO RICHMOND!"

The young men of the North flocked to enlist by the thousands. Lincoln had called for seventy-five thousand volunteers after the fall of Sumter, but he could have trebled that number and not been disappointed. At times the whole thing looked like a big picnic. One Ohio boy wrote home about "the happy, golden days of camp life, where our only worry was that the war might end before our regiment had a chance to prove itself under fire." An Illinois soldier wrote to his people back home of "the shrill notes of the fifes and the martial beat and roll of the drums as they play in unison at early twilight." It was the sweetest of all music to him.

It did beat clerking. Boys whose recruit roster was not full rode about the country in wagons, drummer and fifer to play them along, seeking recruits. The cavalcade rode into towns with all hands, yelling, "Fourth of July every day of the year!" The training the recruits received once they reached camp was very sketchy. Almost all of them, including many of the officers, were amateurs, and it was not uncommon to see a captain on the parade ground consulting a book as he drilled his company. Most of the privates had been recruited by one of their acquaintances and, having been on a first-name basis with their officers all of their lives, could see no point whatever in military formalities. Gideon Rocklin heard one private of the Washington Blues call out after a prolonged drill to his lieutenant, "Hey, Jim, let's quit this fooling around and go over to the sutler's." These civilian-operated shops, which were located on army posts, were a favorite gathering place for the troops.

Professional soldier that he was, Rocklin had turned to rebuke the soldier, but his commanding officer, Colonel Bradford, had only laughed, saying, "You can't do anything about that, Major. These boys aren't professionals and don't intend to be. After we put the run on the Rebels, they'll take off their uniforms and go home again."

"Colonel, if we can't get the men to obey orders on a drill field, how can we expect them to obey when the bullets are flying?"

It was not a new argument, and a line of irritation creased the colonel's brow. He had raised this regiment with his own money. At first he had listened to advice from his adjutant, Major Rocklin. But as the war fever had risen in Washington, Bradford was more and more convinced that the war would be one quick battle and the Rebels would scatter. Now he turned to the major with a superior air. "Gid, you're a good soldier, but you don't know politics. The South has some great orators, and they've convinced themselves that they can pull out of the Union, but they don't have a chance!"

Gideon knew argument was hopeless, so he clamped his jaw shut. The two of them were on their way to a meeting with General Scott, and afterwards to a flag raising in front of the Capitol. There had been several of these, but this time, Rocklin realized, there would be action. He listened to Colonel Bradford speaking cheerfully as they drove to the War Department, but his mind was on the problems looming ahead — problems to which men like Bradford and some of Lincoln's cabinet seemed blind.

General Scott shared the major's concerns. He'd said to Gideon, "Blast it, Rocklin! I feel like a man on lookout up on the mast with icebergs dead ahead! And no matter how loud I shout, the politicians and the newspapers seem deaf! Do we have to rip the bottom from the ship before they'll wake up?"

When Bradford and Rocklin arrived at the large room where the president met with his cabinet, they found Scott already under fire. The old general, dropsical and infirm, a swollen and grotesque caricature of the brilliant soldier who had won the Mexican War, was flushed with anger. As the two officers entered and moved to stand along the wall, he was almost shouting, "You think the Confederates are paper men? No, sir! They are men who will fight — and we are not ready to engage the enemy at this time!"

Edwin Stanton stared across the room with hostility in his cold blue eyes. "General, we've been over this time and time again. I concede that we are not as well prepared as we would like to be, but neither are the Rebels. And I must insist that we have here more than a military problem. Surely we all realize that our people must have a victory now. If you do not know how transient and changeable men are, I do! If we do not act at once, the issue will grow stale. Already the antiwar party is shouting for peace — and many are listening. We must strike while the iron is hot!"

The argument raged back and forth for the best part of an hour, but Gideon noticed that the president was taking no part. He was sitting with his long body slumped in his chair, fatigue scoring his homely face. *He's got an impossible load to carry,* Gideon thought.

But suddenly the president stood up, his action cutting all talk short. Every man in the room was alert, waiting for his word. When it came, it was given softly, without special emphasis.

"Gentlemen, I have listened to you all — and I have prayed for wisdom. I presume that Jefferson Davis is praying for that same quality," he added with a faint glow of humor in his dark eyes, but at once he shook his head. "We have little choice. I feel that from the military point of view, General Scott is absolutely correct, but as Mr. Stanton has pointed out, there is the matter of the people. They must agree to this war, and they must have something immediately. Therefore . . . the army will move at once. General McDowell will be in command. He has his orders to march as soon as possible and engage the enemy. Some of you disagree with this decision. I can only ask you to put aside your objections — and join with me in prayer for our Union."

That ended the meeting, but General Scott grunted to Gideon, "Come along to the flag ceremony. I want some uniforms surrounding the president."

Gideon and Bradford followed the president and the cabinet to the front of the White House, where a large crowd had gathered to witness the raising of the flag. The platform was crowded, and the president took his place by his wife. Gideon looked over the brilliant groups of officers and their aides, the cabinet, and the cluster of ladies in hoop skirts and blossoming bonnets, then centered his gaze on the tall spare form of the president.

After the inevitable speeches, the moment came for the flag to be raised. The Marine Band played the national anthem, and all rose, officers at salute, civilians with their heads uncovered. Lincoln moved forward, took the cord, and gave a pull —

And the cord stuck. He pulled at it harder, and suddenly the Union flag tore, the upper corner coming off and hanging down. Those close enough to see the sinister omen gasped with surprise and horror, and when no one moved, Gideon leaped forward to where the ladies sat, extended his hands, and hissed, "Pins! Pins!"

Several were placed in his hands almost at once, women taking them out of their lace collars and dresses. Swiftly and efficiently, Gideon pinned the corner and nodded at the president.

With a look of gratitude at Gideon, Lincoln pulled the cord, and the flag rose to the top of the pole. The band had continued to play, and the people standing at attention below did not notice anything unusual except that there was a slight delay.

When the ceremony ended, the president extended his hand to Gideon, saying, "Major, you have my thanks." His hand was hard and gave the impression of tremendous physical strength. Lincoln apparently forgot that he was gripping the officer's hand. The Union's chief defender was staring at the nine stars torn from the flag by his hand. He finally released Gideon's hand, saying again, "Thank you, Major."

Gideon was not a superstitious man, but in the long days of war that followed, he often thought of that torn flag — and of the strange look in the eyes of Abraham Lincoln.

Amos Steele looked at the dress his daughter had donned for his approval. As Deborah whirled around, he noted the flush on her cheeks and the sparkle in her eyes and said, "Looks like you've succumbed to the allure of foppish attire, daughter." He added solemnly, "I saw some mission lassies on my way home. Now there are ladies who know how to wear modest attire!"

"Oh, Daddy, don't be silly!" Deborah lifted the skirt, curtsied deeply, then came to hug him. "You'd be shocked if I went to the reception wearing a dowdy old black dress." Then she laughed, adding, "Of course, I could go with a tambourine. The lasses like to shake those."

Her mother came in and caught the last of the sentence. "You young women will do anything to catch the attention of a soldier, but I forbid you to take a tambourine tonight." She was smiling, but then she frowned slightly. "A letter just came for you, Deborah. It's from Richmond."

Deborah took it at once, stared at the writing on the envelope, then said as she tore it open, "It's from Aunt Susanna." She scanned the lines and then became aware that her parents were watching her closely. They had said little about her attachment to Denton Rocklin, but she knew they were both concerned.

"She says that the world's upside down there, every man going for a soldier." She read a few more lines, then looked up with surprise. "Dent is a lieutenant now — and he's seeing a young woman quite a bit." Reading on, she seemed to stop and reread the lines; then she lowered the letter. "Her name is Raimey Reed. She's the daughter of a wealthy planter from Alabama — and she's blind."

The Steeles exchanged looks; then Amos said, "That's a strange one. Is he serious, does she say?"

"No. Just that he's seen her fairly often." Quickly she read the short letter, giving them the essence of it. "Uncle Thomas isn't well. Susanna's afraid he's going down, and the doctors can't seem to do anything." She hesitated, then added, "She gave me an invitation — more or less. But I don't think I'd want to go back, much as I'd like to see her."

Laura Steele nodded. "It might be difficult with the war hanging over us. Not very pleasant for anyone from our world to be in Richmond."

Amos pulled out his watch, squinted at it, and said, "Deborah, I'm going to see Colonel Bradford this morning. Any message for him?"

"No. He's taking me to the reception tonight. I'll see him then." There was no excitement in her face, but she brightened when she said, "I'm meeting Pat and Noel downtown at noon. We're going out to eat, and then I've got a surprise for Noel."

She turned and ran away to change, and Amos gave his wife a baffled look. "Do you think she's serious about this man Bradford?"

"I don't think so, but he's serious enough about her," Laura said. "He's taken her out three times. I don't care much for him, Amos. He's wealthy and fine looking, but a very worldly man."

"Well, he'll be gone with the regiment soon. Now I must go."

"Amos, are you sure this war is of God?"

"As sure as I've ever been of anything in my life!" He turned and left, whistling off-key as he went.

Noel Kojak stood somewhat in awe of Pat Steele. The tall brother of Deborah Steele was handsome and well educated, and at first Noel had hung back. But the two of them, being in the same platoon, soon came to be fast friends. Pat, of course, had been coaxed by Deborah to show attention to Kojak, and he did so, out of curiosity, wondering what his sister could see in a lowly workingman. He was prepared to be condescending to the young fellow but discovered to his dismay that young Kojak was a better soldier than he was.

Some of the companies got easy duty, but Lieutenant Boone Monroe of the Second Platoon, A Company, Washington Blues, had other ideas. He was a tall, raw-boned Tennessean who had come up through the ranks and was hard as nails. He worked his men hard, and Pat was soft. His first contact with Noel came when the two of them were assigned to dig a ditch. By ten o'clock Pat was gasping for breath and his palms were covered with blisters.

Noel had been watching Steele, and since they were the only two on this duty, he said, "Pat, you're going to ruin your hands. Take it easy and let me dig this old ditch."

"I can't do that!"

Noel had reached out and turned Pat's hand over. Shaking his head, he said, "You've got to toughen up. This won't hurt me, but you won't be able to hold your musket tomorrow if you keep on. Here, wrap my handkerchief around one hand and use yours for the other. Just sort of make the motions. Sergeant Gordon doesn't care who does it, as long as the ditch gets dug."

Pat had stared at his bleeding hands, then surrendered. He had wrapped his hands and watched as Noel made the dirt fly. They had talked all morning while Noel dug the ditch, and Pat discovered how mistaken he had been to assume Noel wasn't intelligent. Noel was quiet, but he had read a great deal, just as Deborah had said.

They didn't see Corporal Buck Riley, but the stocky Riley had sharp eyes. He'd seen what was going on and reported to the lieutenant. "Maybe I ought to eat them both out, Lieutenant. Can't let them get by with that."

"Let it go, Corporal," Monroe said in his twangy voice. "Anything them boys do for each other will pull 'em together. That Kojak, he ain't afraid of work, is he? And the best shot in the platoon." He thought about it, then shook his head. "I know Zale's been giving Kojak a hard time."

"Yes, sir. Mostly on account of Kojak's religion — but he's jealous, too, 'cause the boy's a better soldier than he is. I expect he'll pick a fight sooner or later." Riley shrugged, making his evaluation. "Zale's a tough one. Kojak would take a pretty stiff beating. But there's nothing we can do about that."

The trouble Corporal Riley had seen coming between Zale and Noel Kojak erupted not an hour after he had mentioned it to Lieutenant Monroe. It came when Noel and Pat returned to their tent. Most of the squad was there, having come in from drill, and Manny Zale was seething with anger over a tongue-lashing he'd taken from Sergeant Gordon for falling over his feet in drill.

When Noel and Pat came in, Zale scowled at them. He was a quarrelsome man, requiring a fight from time to time as other men require food. He had decided days earlier that he would establish his place by giving Kojak a sound thrashing. He sat there, watching as the two cleaned up, and when Kojak started outside, he made his move. Rising to his feet, Zale made for the entrance of the Sibley tent, reaching it at the same time Kojak did.

"Who you think you're shovin' around?" Zale said loudly and, with a curse, gave Noel a hard push that sent the young man sprawling in the dirt just outside the tent. Zale followed at once, and as Noel got to his feet, he yelled, "You've been bragging about what a fine Christian you are — now you go shovin' a fellow around! Well, I ain't no Christian, and you ain't either!"

Jim Freeman, a happy-go-lucky young fellow of eighteen, said, "Aw, back off, Manny!"

"Keep your trap shut, Freeman!" Zale scowled. "You're another of these imitation Christians. I'll fix you when I finish with the preacher here." He stuck his face close to Noel's, saying, "Now it says in the Bible, don't it, Preacher, that a Christian's got to turn the other cheek when somebody takes a poke at him. That right or not?"

Noel saw what was coming but could not

think of any way to avoid Zale. "That's right, Manny."

Zale looked around, a grin on his wide face; then without warning his fist shot out, catching Noel high on the temple. Noel fell to the ground, the world spinning. He heard Zale say, "Well, c'mon, Preacher! Get up and turn me that other cheek!"

Noel got to his feet unsteadily, knowing that Zale would keep it up, but suddenly Pat Steele came to stand beside Noel, his eyes gleaming, and said, "Hey, Zale, I'm a Christian."

Manny Zale had no use for Pat Steele and shouted, "Well, take this, then —"

But when Zale threw a hard punch at Steele, Pat moved his head to one side, and as the burly soldier was off balance, Steele clipped him on the chin with a powerful right cross that dumped Zale on his back. A shout went up, and Zale made two tries before he got up. He was an old hand at brawls, however, and waited until his eyes cleared. Glaring at Steele, he demanded, "If you're a Christian, how come you busted me?"

Pat Steele smiled at him, then winked at Freeman and Tate Armstrong, who had come to watch. "I'm a backslider, Manny. That means that I'll beat your brains out if you don't stop throwing your weight around." Then Steele shrugged. "I'm just not as good a Christian as Noel, Manny, so come on and I'll give you the best we've got in the house."

With a snarl Manny threw himself forward, and as the two men slugged it out, a crowd gathered. Manny was tough, but so was Pat Steele. He had taken up boxing at college and had had a fine instructor. Now he stood off and with his long arms hammered at Zale's lantern-shaped jaw. Both men were bloodied when Lieutenant Monroe came strolling in. He'd been alerted but had let the two fight for a while before he came in to say, "All right, you two, break it up."

Zale and Steele stood there, gasping for breath, expecting to be punished for brawling, but Boone Monroe liked to see a tough streak in his men. "Better save some of that fer the Rebs," was all he said; then he strolled off.

Manny glared at Steele, cursed, and walked off to wash his bleeding face. Pat laughed, saying, "Come on, Noel. We've got a date with a lady. Let's see if we can get me patched up."

Noel tried to thank Steele, but the tall young man only laughed. The two of them dressed and caught a ride into town. When they got out of the wagon, Noel said, "Pat, you don't need me around. You'll want to spend the time with your sister alone."

"Nope. Deborah said to bring you along, and I always try to mind her. She's a pest when she doesn't get her own way. Come along now. We're supposed to meet her at the Baxter House."

If he could have thought of a way, Noel would have fled, but Steele had a hold on his arm, and soon they were in front of the large white building with the imposing sign saying BAXTER HOUSE in front. Pat walked jauntily into the lobby, then took Noel's arm again. "She's probably already in the restaurant." The two of them entered the huge double doors, and when a white-coated waiter came to them, Pat inquired about his sister. The waiter said, "Yes, sir. Miss Steele is already seated. If you'll come this way, sir."

Noel followed Pat, more terrified by the elegant setting around him than he had been by anything he'd seen in the army. The enormous room was flanked with high windows admitting bars of sunlight, which caught the gleaming silverware resting on a hundred white tablecloths and glittered and refracted through the crystal chandeliers.

314

The men and women were richly dressed: the women with jewels gleaming, the men with gold watch chains and heavy gold rings.

Then he heard Pat saying, "Well, Deborah, here we are."

Noel looked up and saw Deborah smiling at him. She said, "Come and sit down. We've been waiting for you. This is Mr. Langdon Devoe. My brother, Pat, and this is Private Noel Kojak."

Noel took the man's hand, mumbled something, and fell into his seat with relief. A waiter came, and the other three talked about food, but Noel was speechless. It came as a welcome relief when Pat said, "Noel, I've eaten here before. Would you trust me to order your dinner?" Noel nodded, never suspecting that his friend had eased the thing after getting a nod from Deborah.

The meal was fine, but Noel was so tense he could not have said later what he ate, except for the dessert, which was ice cream in a frothy crust, browned in an oven. He had relaxed a little during the meal, for the others carried the talk without demanding anything from him. Finally Pat said, getting up to leave, "Well, I've got important business. Strictly a military secret. See you back in camp, Noel."

"I'll bet that 'military secret' is a beautiful blond with blue eyes," Mr. Devoe said, smiling. He was a small man of thirty-five, with reddish hair that was receding rapidly and a full mustache that covered his lips. He wiped it now with his napkin, leaned back, and examined Noel. "Now then," he said with a gleam in his eye, "so this is your discovery, is it, Deborah?"

"Now you be nice, Mr. Devoe," Deborah said sharply. She was wearing a silk dress of green and white, and a hat covered her hair. "You can be very sharp when you want to."

"Why, I meant no harm," Devoe said in surprise. Deborah had warned him that young Kojak was terribly shy, and he saw that she had not exaggerated. He asked, "You're from Washington, Private Kojak?" and slowly he drew a response from Noel. But Devoe was a man who knew how to talk and how to make others talk, and soon he had put Noel at ease.

"Noel — if I may call you that? — I've read some of your stories. Did you ever hear of the *New Review*? No? Well, I'm the editor of the thing. Miss Steele has worked with me often, and she brought me some of your work." He put his sharp, dark eyes on Noel, saying, "I think it has potential."

"Well, it's just things I saw, Mr. Devoe. I

— I don't really know much about writing."

Devoe laughed; then when Noel looked at him with alarm, he waved his hand. "Sorry. It's just that most writers have an ego bigger than the Rock of Gibraltar! Comes as quite a shock to find a young fellow who still has modesty." Then he said, "I want to print one of your stories, 'No Hope for Emily.' It's a good piece of work, though you'll need a little help in putting the finishing touches on it. I think Deborah will help you with that."

"Yes! I will, Noel — and there's more!" Deborah had gone to see Devoe with Noel's work and had practically forced him to read the stories. Now she said, "Tell him the rest, Mr. Devoe."

"Well, I'd like you to write about the war, Noel. You'll be moving out soon, I hear. You'll be very busy, but as soon as you can, write down what you've seen. It doesn't have to be about battle. Write about the marches, about the food you eat, about what the men are saying. I want to give people the real thing!"

Devoe spoke with excitement, then finally asked, "Well, will you do it? Oh yes, I forgot, you'll be paid for this, of course."

"Paid for writing?" Noel said with such amazement that the other two smiled at him. "Well, I — I don't know, Mr. Devoe —"

"Oh, Noel, you must!" Deborah cried out. "God has put this talent in you. You mustn't bury it!" Her eyes were wide, and Noel thought he'd never seen her looking so beautiful. "Please, Noel!" she begged.

Devoe looked at the two shrewdly, then rose. "You two settle it — and I hope it works out, my boy. You do have an exceptional talent, as Deborah says. I'll expect to hear from you."

After Devoe left, the two of them sat there for an hour. Noel could not believe what had transpired, and it took much persuasion on Deborah's part to bring him to agree.

Finally he said, "If you think I can do it, Deborah, I'll try."

Delighted at this, Deborah put her hand over his, smiled at him, and said, "Oh, Noel, it's going to be wonderful! You're going to be a fine writer!"

Finally she said, "Oh, pooh! It's time to go. I have to go to a reception tonight." They rose and walked out of the hotel, and she left, saying, "I'll bring your writing kit to the camp tomorrow, Noel. You can get started right away."

Noel took her hand, said good-bye, and

then she was gone. He wandered the streets for several hours, then went back to camp. Pat came in later and asked, "You going to do it, Noel — be a writer?"

"I guess so."

Pat laughed. "Sure. I knew you would. Watch out for that sister of mine, Noel! She thinks she can boss every man she sees! She'll be running your life just like she does mine if you let her."

CHAPTER 14
ROAD TO MANASSAS

Captain Hiram Frost was standing outside the large tent that served both as his private quarters and as headquarters for A Company. He looked up as a soldier came on a half run from the drill field where Lieutenant Boone Monroe was putting his platoon through close-order drill.

A little earlier, Frost had been thinking about his three children and his wife, Kate, in Maine, when a message from regimental headquarters had been handed to him by one of Colonel Bradford's sergeants. He had read it and sent at once for Private Kojak. While waiting for the private to report, he resolutely put his family out of his mind and ran over the multitude of details that were his responsibility. The Blues would move out at dawn the next day, assigned to Sherman's division, and all of the details had to be complete before then. And now this message from Colonel Bradford!

Frost watched the young private approach, thinking of the sort of man he was, and it struck him that an infantry company was not too different from a large family. As the captain, he was the father, who supervised the daily routine; saw that the men were equipped, fed, clothed, and sheltered; heard their complaints; administered punishment for minor offenses; looked after their health; provided for their general welfare; and led them into battle.

Frost knew every man by name and was fairly well acquainted with his circumstances and even individual members of his family. The lieutenants, sergeants, and corporals were his helpers, their position comparable to that of older children in a family — but the welfare of A Company lay on the shoulders of Captain Hiram Frost. As Kojak entered the room and Frost returned the private's salute, he mentally listed what he knew about him.

A workingman and a good one. Poor family and a large one. Dedicated Christian. Was having trouble over that with some of the tougher men in his platoon. A good soldier whose equipment is taken care of. Best shot in the company. Wish I had more like him.

He drew a breath, then plunged in. "Kojak, you've got a brother named Bing. Well,

I've got some bad news for you." Frost paused, calculating the sudden expression on the young soldier's face, then said quickly, "He's in trouble with the law. I don't know the circumstances, but he's headed for jail."

Noel bit his lip, then said, "He's been running with a bad crowd, Captain Frost. I've been afraid something like this would happen."

"No question of his guilt, but I think it's not as serious as it might have been. The judge has given him a choice: go to jail or join the army. And he's asked to join this company."

Noel looked relieved. "That's good news, sir! Bing wouldn't be able to stand being locked up."

"I'm not sure I want him in the company, Private. He's a troublemaker, and we've got enough of those." Frost caught the disappointed look on Kojak's face, then added, "If I agree to let him join, I'll expect you to keep an eye on him. Keep him out of trouble. Be your responsibility. What about it?"

"I'll do my best, Captain. He's — pretty wild, but we've got good sergeants and a corporal who'll bear down on him. It's what he needs most and never got. One good thing is that he's fit enough, real strong."

"All right." Frost nodded. "I'll send word to have him transferred at once. And I'll advise Lieutenant Monroe to keep an eye on him. That's all, Private."

"Thank you, sir!"

Noel went through the rest of the morning automatically, worried about Bing. At noon in the chow line, Pat asked, "What's wrong with you? Your mind is someplace else, Noel." When Noel told him about Bing, revealing some of his problems, Pat shrugged and grinned. "Don't worry about it. Lieutenant Monroe will take the starch out of him!"

In fact, that was what happened. Bing arrived at camp late that afternoon, and his first interview was with First Lieutenant Boone Monroe. The camp was in a furor with men getting equipment together, ammunition being issued, and the cooks preparing rations for a three-day march. Bing Kojak stood in front of the lean officer, rebellion in his eyes, saying nothing. At first he had been relieved to escape a prison sentence, but now he was sullen and resentful.

Boone Monroe was a tough man, hardened by years in the Regular Army. He knew men, and he was an expert on the hard ones

— those who fancied themselves tough. See-ing the anger burning in Kojak's eyes, he let the hammer down. "Kojak, you're no good! It ain't for me to question my commanding officer's choice, but it's me who's gotta make this platoon run. You think you're a tough pumpkin? That's fine! We'll see how tough. I reckon in a couple of days you'll be begging for a prison cell!" Boone came to stand before Bing, his eyes hard as agates. "You're a fighter, I hear tell, a pug. Right now, you're thinking you can whup me. Go ahead, take a swing — then you can see if you're tougher than a firing squad, which is what you'll get if you ever lay your hands on me or any other officer! And I'll tell you this, you use your fists on any feller in this squad, and on every march you'll carry sixty pounds of bricks in addition to your regular pack. And you'll do it on bread and water! Any questions, Private Kojak?"

"No," Bing growled through clenched teeth.

" 'No, *sir*!' Kojak! You forget that one more time and you'll dig more latrines than you can think of. Come with me!" Boone walked out of his tent and when he found his sergeant, Jay Gordon, said, "Sergeant, this here is Bing Kojak. See that he gets equipped at once."

Gordon was a smallish man but tough. He resented big men and had just lost his two children in the epidemic. Now he stared at the tall, strong figure of Kojak and asked, "You a relation of Noel?"

"My brother."

"All right. You do as well as he does and we'll have no trouble. Get out of line one time and I'll make you miserable. We're pulling out in the morning, so I don't have time to teach you anything. You stay with your brother; do what he says."

Noel was getting his gear in shape when Bing walked in, his arms piled high with his uniform and gear. Sergeant Gordon said, "Here's your brother, Noel. Get him as ready as you can. We'll pull out at dawn, and I don't want him getting lost."

"Hello, Bing," Noel said. The other members of the squad were there, so he said nothing of the trouble that had brought Bing here. Instead he said, "This is my brother, Bing, you fellows."

"Hope you don't snore as loud as Noel," Amos Wilson quipped with a grin. He was a tall, thin young man from Illinois, a big talker who bragged about how many Rebels he would kill, but Noel felt that the talk was to cover up something.

"This is Tate Armstrong, Bing," Noel said,

at the same time indicating a spot where his brother could pile his load. "He thinks he's going to be a doctor. Might as well, because he can't hit the side of a barn with his musket."

Armstrong nodded. "I'm too good a man to waste in the infantry." At twenty-two, he was short and trim and a very fast runner. He had spent much time trying to get transferred to the medical branch of the army, with no success. "Glad to see you, Bing. Hope you can shoot as good as Noel. Make up for how sorry I am."

Bing dropped his uniform and gear and turned to face the squad. "I guess I can do anything my brother can do," he said, a sour expression on his wide mouth. He was a rather formidable figure, six feet tall and powerful. His black hair was wavy and hung over his brow.

Manny Zale studied the new arrival, then asked, "You another psalm singer like your brother? If you are, I'm moving to another squad."

"Not hardly," Bing said quickly, sizing Zale up as one of his own kind. "I got no time for such stuff."

Noel said quickly, "This is Fritz Horst; that's Emmett Grant; and this is Caleb Church." Horst nodded briefly. He was

German and still spoke with a strong accent. He'd joined the army because he'd been unable to find work. He was a good soldier, having served in the German army and grown accustomed to taking orders. Grant was a good-looking man of twenty-one, who was a good hand at card playing, so much so that he kept the others in the squad broke. He was terrified at the very thought of battle, though, and tried hard to cover his fear.

Caleb Church was the oldest man in the regiment. Though he was sixty, he was one of those men who had not lost any physical strength with age. He was a farmer from Ohio, and now he said, "Glad to see you, young feller. I wuz in the Mexican War, and it was the best time of my life. You come at a good time, I tell you, 'cause we're going to have some fun with those Rebels, by gum!"

Bing gave the old man a grin, for there was something comical about Church — or perhaps it was the reckless, happy-go-lucky spirit in Church that he liked. "All right, Grandpa. Maybe you're right." Then he looked at Noel, saying, "Big brother, any way I can get some grub?"

"Sure, Bing," Noel said instantly. "Let's go down to the mess hall and we'll see what we can promote."

As they left the tent and walked toward the mess hall, Bing said, "Noel, don't give me no sermons, you hear? This ain't my choice, but I'm stuck with it for three months. All I want to do is keep from getting shot, so don't try to make a soldier out of me, get it?"

"All right." Noel said no more, but he knew that sooner or later his brother would bring trouble to him. Bing always did.

At dawn the first platoon of A Company was on the way to Manassas Junction. The Washington Blues were almost lost in the host of other units headed for that small town. The first day's march allowed the men to get adjusted, and the camping out had the flavor of a boys' camp, with the men singing and playing tricks on one another. But the next two days wore them down so that there was little horseplay, and many of them had shed their heavy coats, tossing them in the supply wagons.

Watching them on the morning of July 18, Gideon said to Hiram Frost, "They look tired, Captain, but you've done a good job."

"Well, I've got some good lieutenants." Frost lifted his eyes to the distance. "Think we'll lock horns with the Rebs at Centreville, Major?"

"General McDowell thinks so," Gideon said. "He doesn't have any grandiose ideas about taking Richmond. All he wants to do is take Manassas Junction. That's a critical spot. The Manassas Gap Railroad runs through there straight to the Shenandoah Valley. As long as the Confederates hold that, they can move their troops by train to meet any attack we make. As a matter of fact, that's what I'm worried about."

"I understand General Patterson is supposed to hold the Rebel force being led by Joe Johnston in the Shenandoah. If he does, we shouldn't have any trouble whipping Beauregard at Manassas," Frost said. He had a keen grasp of military strategy and added, "We've got five divisions, which means we outnumber them greatly."

Gideon looked troubled. "If we go straight in, that's right. But if General McDowell hesitates, Joe Johnston will have time to move his army from the Shenandoah to Manassas. Then we'll be in real trouble, Hiram! I wish we had a general with more push." Then he shook his head and came up with a smile. "I'll keep my eyes open for your company. Best in the regiment, I do think!"

But there was no battle at Centreville, for the Confederates pulled back. Instead of plunging ahead against the thin ranks that had drawn up behind a small stream called Bull Run, McDowell waited. And this delay, as Gideon had predicted, gave General Joe Johnston time to move his men by train from the Shenandoah to reinforce General Beauregard — it was the first use of railroads to move masses of men to battle, and it changed the course of the battle of Bull Run.

When A Company marched across Bull Run into battle on July 21, 1861, they met not a skeleton crew, but thick ranks of tough Confederates reinforced by the likes of Thomas Jackson and his Virginians, who arrived in time to throw a blistering sheet of fire into the very face of Noel Kojak and his platoon as they advanced into their first battle.

Captain Taylor Dewitt drew a rough sketch on a sheet of paper of Manassas Junction and the small stream called Bull Run. He'd just come from a staff meeting where General Beauregard had delivered a fiery speech and given his plan of action. "Here's what we've got," Taylor said, pointing at the map with his pencil.

The officers were all tired, exhausted by the rough train ride from Shenandoah to Manassas. Captain Dewitt scratched his itchy three-day growth of whiskers, noting that his three lieutenants — Dent Rocklin, Bushrod Aimes, and Tug Ramsey — looked as rough as he did. What they needed was a good rest, but he knew there was none coming. He had gotten off the train long enough to meet with General Beauregard's staff, and now he wanted his lieutenants to know what was likely to happen in the morning.

"Our army is here along Bull Run. The Yankees are on the other side. This stream doesn't look deep, but it can only be crossed at a few fords or over the Stone Bridge. We've got those places heavily enforced. We're here on our right flank, because that's where General Beauregard thinks the attack will come. But what we're going to do is attack before the Yankees are ready. We can hit them hard and roll them up, then drive them before us all the way to Washington."

Dent stared at the map, then asked, "What if they go around our flanks?"

"We'll be in trouble, Lieutenant," Taylor said roughly, then added, "That's why we must attack. We're still outnumbered, even with Johnston's army from the Shenandoah to reinforce us. I think we'll go at that about dawn, so have your men ready. The well will run dry soon enough, so fill every canteen with water. Take fifty additional rounds of ammunition." It was already dusk as he added, "When we attack, be sure there are no stragglers. I'll be in front, but you two follow the company. Be sure your sergeants keep an eye out for men holding back."

Bushrod looked at Dewitt quizzically. "What'll we do, Captain, shoot 'em?"

"Make them think you're going to," Taylor snapped. The four officers lingered over the map, trying to convince themselves that the next day would be easy, but with no success.

Farther down the line, Waco Smith's squad was gathered around a fire where Corporal Ralph Purtle was roasting a couple of plump chickens on his bayonet. Smith sat back watching the juices drip from the birds, saying in a satisfied tone, "Purtle, if you could shoot as good as you can rustle up grub, we'd win this heah war tomorrow." Smith was a lean Texan who stood just under six feet. He had light green eyes and aquiline features and had been a buffalo hunter, a cowboy, and a Texas Ranger. He ran his squad with an iron hand, still carried a .44 in a holster tied to his thigh, and could pull and shoot the weapon in one unbelievably fast movement.

Corporal Ralph Purtle was a pudgy man

of twenty-five who spent most of his waking hours either eating or thinking about eating. Waco had already decided that when the regiment outran its supply lines, Purtle was the man to do the foraging. "Hurry up with that chicken. We've got a busy day tomorrow," Waco said.

"You really think the Yankees will come at us, Sarge?" The speaker was the youngest of Waco's squad, Leo Deforest. Leo was only sixteen and had had to find a drunken recruiter in order to get accepted. He had a boyish freckled face and was eager for the fight to begin.

Private Con Ellis sat across the fire from Leo. He lifted his head, revealing battered features, the marks of his years in the ring. His eyes were hazel, almost yellow, and hard drinking had put blue veins in his nose and cheeks. "Don't be asking for that in your prayers, sonny," Con rumbled. "Army life is fine — until somebody starts shootin' at you." That summed up Ellis's philosophy. He was one of those men who was happy to let someone make his decisions for him in exchange for a few dollars a month. He had a cruel streak in him and leaned over to pick up his bayonet. He gave Homer Willis a hard rap on the soles of his boots and laughed roughly as the boy let out a yelp and drew his feet back. "That hurt, Homer? Wait till the Bluebellies put a minié ball in your guts!"

Willis bit his lip but said nothing. He was seventeen and even more immature than Deforest. He had enlisted because a girl had egged him into it, and now every night he cried into his pillow, longing to be anywhere but in this army that was marching straight into destruction.

Waco said, "Cut it out, Ellis, or I'll bat your ears down."

"Just kidding, Sarge," Ellis said. He was a rough man in a fight, but he knew that Waco was too tough a man to bluff. "What's goin' on out there?" he asked, waving toward the small stream that lay ahead of them.

"Yankees are coming, Con." Ira Sampson was a teacher of Latin and was never called anything but Professor by the men. He had fair hair and blue eyes and wore a pair of steel-rimmed spectacles. "They'll be coming for breakfast early in the morning." A wry smile came to his thin lips, and looking across the stream to where faint campfires of the Federals made flickering lights in the darkness, he said softly, *Omni a mutantur, nos et muta murinillis."*

The strange sounds and cadence of Sampson's words caught at Lowell Rocklin, who sat back from the small fire. "What the blazes does that mean, Professor?"

"All things are changing, and we are changing with them."

"Sounds pretty confusin' to me," Buck Sergeant Holt Mattson remarked. A lean, clear-eyed man from Georgia, Mattson was Waco's right-hand man.

Clay Rocklin had been looking at the fires as they burned like small golden ingots across Bull Run. Now he turned his head swiftly toward the slight form of Sampson. "That's about right," he said softly, and his comment brought the attention of most of the squad. Clay had been the most silent member of the small group, speaking pleasantly enough but not joining in the frolic in which some of the men had engaged. He had been a rock, however, to Waco Smith, who longed to see him made a corporal. Waco had seen that the older Rocklin had whatever quality it is that commands other men. But Clay Rocklin had shown no inclination to move up, and Waco knew better than to push it.

A terrifyingly deep bass voice shattered the silence. "Well, what's that mean? I don't get it!"

Clay turned to see Jock Longley staring at him. Longley was the smallest man of the squad. He was twenty-six and had been a jockey. Now he complained constantly about having to walk, lamenting the fact that he had not joined the cavalry. "Just what it says, Jock," Clay murmured. He made a strong shape in the darkness, the high planes of his cheekbones and his deep-set eyes giving him a masklike appearance. The men around him, and men in other companies, had discussed him endlessly. They all knew he'd been a deserter or something equally rank in the Mexican War, that he was opposed to this present conflict, and that he was the owner of a huge plantation — but nothing seemed to fit. He was by far the most able man in the squad; he could outmarch the best of them, and he was a deadly shot with his musket.

Now Clay saw that they were all watching him, and he said, "Well, things are changing, aren't they, Jock? Our world's not the same."

"Yes, but it will be when we put the run on the Bluebellies, Clay." Bob Yancy sat close to Clay, for he knew the man and trusted his wisdom.

"That may not be as easy as you think, Bob," Waco interjected. "Some pretty tough boys on the other side of that creek."

"Aw, one Confederate can whip five Yankees anytime, Sarge!" Ralph Purtle said. He pushed his knife into one of the roasting birds, grinned, and said, "Suppertime!" He stripped the chickens expertly, giving each man a portion, then sat back and began to munch one of the drumsticks. "Ain't that right, Sarge?" he finally asked Waco. "What I said about us and the Bluebellies?"

"Ralph," Waco said as he chewed a chunk of white breast, "if we meet up with a bunch of Phil Kearney's division tomorrow, you'll run backwards so fast you'll lose some of that hog fat under your belt."

Lowell said quietly, "I've been wondering about that, Sarge. Will I run when the bullets start flying?"

Waco Smith said, "No man knows that until he's seen the elephant, Lowell. We can train you to drill, but when your friends start dropping around you, nobody knows if you'll keep going or not. Guess we'll find out tomorrow."

Waco's words brought a silence around the fire, and the men sat chewing on their chicken, all of them thinking of the next day. Finally Clay got to his feet, saying, "Guess I'll go listen to the chaplain."

His words stirred the group oddly. Some of the men got up at once, but Con Ellis jeered, "Got to have some religion to git you through the night, Rocklin? Not me. I'll take a good jolt of this whiskey!"

Clay made no answer, but when he arrived at the open spot where a large group of men had gathered, he was pleased to see that at least half of the squad was with him. Lowell said, "Look, there's Rev. Irons, Pa."

Large fires had been built to give light, and Jeremiah Irons had already gotten up on a small rise. He saw Clay and Lowell, nodded cheerfully, and said, "Well, I thought I could do as I pleased when I left home. But I see some of my congregation is here — so I'll have to behave myself." The men laughed, and one of them called out, "Don't worry, Preacher, we won't tell on you!"

Irons stood there smiling as the men settled down. He had volunteered for the army after a long struggle with his soul, but from his first day as chaplain of the Richmond Grays, it was obvious that he was going to be a success with the men. He was not a hellfire-and-damnation preacher but preferred to stress the grace of God and the love of Jesus for all men. He was physically a match for most of the men, and on the long marches he often dismounted and let one of the men ride while he walked.

Now he began to speak. "We had a barber in our town who got saved last year, a man named Claude Foote. He was anxious to share his faith with people, to see someone get converted — but he found it hard to be a witness. Being a barber, he was a great talker, but he just couldn't find any way to begin telling men about God's love. Well, he came to me one day and asked me if I could help him get started. I suggested that he memorize a verse of scripture and that he simply repeat it to people."

The men were quiet, listening carefully, and Clay smiled. He knew Irons so well! The preacher was a good fisherman and knew how to lure his hearers in close so he could set the hook.

"Well, sir, Claude thought that would work. He went home that night, searched his Bible, and found a verse he thought would be effective. The next morning the first man to get into his chair was Les Burns, and a more nervous man never lived! He would jump at the sight of his own shadow. Claude put the towel around Les's neck and lathered him up good. He took his razor, stropped it until it was keen enough to cut a feather, then laid the blade right on Les's neck and said, "Les Burns — 'Prepare to meet thy God'!"

The men roared, and Irons stood there smiling until they grew quiet. "Well, my verse for you men is the same as the one Claude gave to Les Burns. It's found in Amos, the fourth chapter, the twelfth verse: 'Prepare to meet thy God, O Israel.' "

Irons paused, letting the silence deepen. The sounds of men and horses stirring were on the night air, but within the grove the men felt the draw of the chaplain and strained to hear.

"Tomorrow, some of us may be in the presence of the Almighty," Irons said. "And then what will be important to you, should you be one of those who leave this earth to stand before God? Your money? What would you buy with it at God's bar of judgment throne? No, only one thing will have any importance at that awful time: Are you prepared to meet your God? And there is only one way to be prepared, men. Jesus said, 'I am the way,' and He is the only way. His blood is all that God can see. You may say, 'I was a Baptist,' but God will say, 'Where is the blood?' You may say, 'I led a good life!' But God will say, 'When I see the blood, I will pass over you and not destroy you!' "

For nearly an hour Jeremiah Irons spoke of Jesus Christ, surrounded by listening men who stood in the flickering firelight. He pointed the way to Jesus as the only hope, and when he came to an end, he said, "I feel that some of you fellows would like to prepare to meet God. But let me warn you that I am not selling fire insurance! You cannot come to God just to escape the dangers of battle, the death that may well be yours tomorrow. You must come with your life in your hands, and you must hold that life up to God, saying, 'God, I have sinned, but my hope is in the blood of Jesus. I give You my life, not just for a day — but forever!' If you're ready to follow Jesus, come and let me pray for you."

Clay watched as many men with tears on their faces, trembling in their limbs, stumbled toward the front of the clearing. Homer Willis had stood close to Clay during the sermon. Now he said, "I–I'd like to go . . . but I'm afraid."

Clay turned to the boy. "I know, Homer. We're all afraid to come to Jesus. It scared me to death. I cried like a baby!"

"Did you really?"

"Sure." Clay put his arm around the boy's thin shoulders. "Would you like for me to go with you while the chaplain prays for you?"

"Y–yes!"

Clay made his way forward, and when he got to where the chaplain stood, he met the man's eyes. "Chaplain, Homer is ready to give his life to Jesus. Will you pray for him now?"

Jeremiah Irons had left a comfortable life to join the army, giving up all security. But as he came and joined Clay Rocklin and the trembling boy, he knew it was worth it all!

CHAPTER 15
BATTLE MADNESS

Though Brigadier General Irvin McDowell, a graduate of West Point, had served with General Scott in Mexico, he had had only one battle in his military career. With a watermelon. McDowell, renowned for being a glutton of immense proportions, often became so absorbed in food that he had little time for conversation at the table. This, combined with the fact that he was short-tempered and socially inattentive, did not make him popular. Furthermore, he wore an absurd bowl-shaped straw hat, giving himself a ridiculous image that was far from what people desired for the general of the Union's first army. As for his military campaign, he once launched an attack on a watermelon, which he soundly defeated, consuming it single-handedly and giving it the epitaph of being "monstrous fine."

But on the morning of July 21, the general did not find the situation at Bull Run Creek "monstrous fine." Discovering that the Confederates were lined up across the small creek, he had determined to sweep to his left and cross with his forces at McLean's Ford, striking Brigadier General Beauregard's right flank. Then all he had to do was sweep forward, catching the Rebels from the rear.

But he soon found that Beauregard had amassed troops at that spot, including the brigade of Colonel Thomas Jackson. McDowell then thought to try the left flank of the Confederate Army, but he vacillated so long that more troops in gray had time to gather along the creek. Eventually thirty-five thousand Confederates had massed, which meant that while the Federals still had thirty-seven thousand men, the balance of power had been lost.

Finally at two o'clock in the morning, McDowell put his forces into motion. Brigadier General David Hunter, commander of the Second Division of McDowell's army, would move to the right, crossing Bull Run at Sudley's Ford. This night march proved to be dreadful, but finally the Federals came across, and at once sporadic rifle and artillery fire broke out from each side of the stream.

The battle would have been lost then

and there, a glorious victory for the Union — except for Shanks Evans! Colonel Nathan G. Evans of the Confederate Army — called "Shanks" because of his lean legs — was outflanked and outnumbered, but the crusty officer had all the instincts of a rough-and-tumble brawler. He was the most accomplished braggart on the Rebel side, as well as one of its most intemperate drinkers. He even kept a special orderly with him whose chief duty was to carry a small keg of whiskey and keep it at hand at all times. But for all his faults, Shanks Evans was not a man to be tangled with!

He met Hunter's division with the fierce anger of a tiger. For an hour, with fewer than four hundred men, he held Hunter's force of ten thousand. He had saved Beauregard and Johnston from disaster, and when the Creole general and Joe Johnston became aware that the Federal attack was on their left flank, they began rushing reinforcements toward Evans — the forces of Brigadier General Barnard Bee, Colonel Francis Bartow, and Colonel Thomas Jackson.

Even as these fresh Southern troops were on their way, General Hunter fell, severely wounded with a bullet in the neck, and General Ambrose Burnside took command of the Federal forces. He threw his command forward, but just as his troops were about to overrun the Confederate line, the men of Bee and Bartow arrived and halted their advance.

Clay Rocklin and the rest of his squad had been dug in with the rest of Jackson's brigade since dawn. The Confederate troops had suffered heavy losses, including Colonel Bartow, who was killed as he led an attack; and Brigadier General Bee would be severely wounded and would die the next day. Rocklin's squad had been sure an attack was imminent, but it didn't come — and when heavy firing came from their left, Clay commented to Waco, "The fight's over there, Waco."

"I hope it stays there!" Con Ellis grunted, but the firing grew louder, and the men saw a courier come dashing up on a wild-eyed horse. The rider reined the horse in, gave some sort of message to Colonel James Benton, then rode down the line again at full speed.

"That's business," Waco murmured. "We'll get pulled out of here pretty soon." He was correct, for Major Brad Franklin came at once to speak to the captain.

"The Yankees are rolling up our left flank," he said, and there was a wild look in his eyes. "Get the company moving, Captain Dewitt, and don't waste any time!" He moved hurriedly down the line, passing the message to H Company, who were dug in behind some logs, and soon the Richmond Grays were moving toward the sound of the firing.

The double-time march took the steam out of the men, and by the time Captain Dewitt halted them on a rise of ground, all of them were gasping for air. Clay had kept close to Lowell, and when they got to the hill, he saw that Bob Yancy was not out of breath. He grinned at the boy. "Wish I were your age, Bob!"

Then Lowell exclaimed in a shocked voice, "Look, they're running away!"

The sound was overwhelming, for Federal artillery was in action; the crackling sound of musket fire reminded Clay of corn popping over a fire or of dry wood snapping. Then they all saw the ragged line of figures in gray and butternut materializing from the smoke and coming toward them.

"They're falling back!" Clay said. "Looks like they've been cut to pieces!" The squad watched silently as the men of Bartow's command came stumbling by with ghastly faces, stunned and powder-blackened. Some of them were still firing; others had no weapons at all and were simply running.

Out of the rolling black smoke that concealed the enemy, an officer came dashing back. "That's General Bee," Dent said to Taylor Dewitt. Then he pointed, "Look, he's going to speak to Jackson." Jackson was on a slight hill next to a house called the Henry House. Dent and Taylor had moved close enough to hear Bee yell, "Jackson, they're beating us back!"

Jackson's eyes peering from under his shabby forage cap were a fierce light blue, hence his nickname "Old Blue Light."

"Well, sir," he said to Bee, "We'll give them the bayonet."

Bee nodded, turned, and rode back toward his command, yelling, "Look! There is Jackson standing like a stone wall! Rally behind the Virginians!"

C Company was in the second position of the regiment, and they crouched with their ears assaulted by the thunder of the Union guns. For two hours the battle raged as Beauregard extended his line of Confederate forces until it was fully eight miles long.

Dent moved up and down the lines, speaking to the men. "Looks like we'll get our chance pretty soon," he said, the light of battle in his dark eyes. There was no fear in him, and as the minié balls made their slipping, whining slash, he paid them no more attention than if they were butterflies. Once he came near where Lowell stood with Clay. His eyes came to rest on his younger brother, and he seemed to search for words. Finally he said, "Lowell, keep your head down when we charge."

"Sure, Dent — I mean, Lieutenant," Lowell agreed. His voice cracked, but he grinned, adding, "I'm scared spitless, to tell the truth — but I'm in good company." He glanced at his father, adding, "Lots of Rocklins here today. The Yankees can't handle us!"

Dent shifted his eyes to his father. "Watch out for him . . . and for yourself," he said.

Clay nodded. "You'll be the one up front, Lieutenant." He wanted to say something better, warmer, but knew that Dent would resent it.

"Get ready to charge!" The three men looked toward the front of the line to see the captain holding up his saber. "Come on!" Taylor Dewitt yelled over the sound of the exploding bursts of spherical shells. "Move out! Move out!"

Dent whirled and pulled his revolver from his holster, and the line moved forward. There was a house off to the left, scarred and pocked, flanked by a dense stand of timber. Nearby a Confederate artillery battery was engaged in a furious duel with the Federal gunners.

As they pressed forward, Lowell stumbled on something soft, and looking down, he saw a bleeding corpse. He didn't look down again but moved carefully to keep from stepping on any of the yielding forms that carpeted the field.

A high-pitched wailing rose above the other noises of battle, and Clay realized that he, too, was yelling with all the rest. Their cries made a weird incantation, shriller than the whining shells overhead. He lunged forward, aware that Waco Smith, a lupine expression on his long face, was moving to strike at some of the men in their platoon with the flat of his sword. Mattson was next to him, doing the same. One of the men who received a swat, Clay saw, was Leo Deforest. Leo yelped, then began to run with the rest of them.

Then Clay saw the blue forms through the smoke, undulating and weaving like dusky phantoms. The fire from the Federals rose to a crescendo, and he saw a man drop on his face down the line. Others were falling, too. Clay kept his eyes on Lowell, but there was nothing he could do — nothing any one man could do for another in that wild charge.

He felt the shock of his rifle butt against his shoulder and saw one of the blue figures driven backward. As he stopped to reload, Corporal Ralph Purtle came huffing up. The fat soldier had a scarlet face, for the charge had taken all his wind. Purtle stopped to look at Clay, his eyes white and rolling. "Clay!" he gasped. "I got to rest! I can't —"

A bullet struck Purtle in the temple, making a plunking sound, driving his head to one side. For one instant he stood there, dead on his feet; then his eyes rolled upward and he fell loosely.

"Ralph!" Homer Willis had been right behind Purtle. He fell on his face with fear, but Waco Smith yanked him up, put his revolver to the boy's ear, and said, "Willis, move out! The Bluebellies might shoot you — but I *will* shoot you here an' now if you don't get moving!"

Willis stood there, his face dissolving and his blue eyes filled with torment as he stared down at the body of Purtle. Clay had finished loading and said, "Come on, Homer. It's worse to stand here than it is to charge. Get moving." He pushed the boy forward and moved after him.

Waco panted, "Clay, these boys ain't goin' to stand much of this. You git on the other side of the line and hold 'em in place. I'll anchor this end."

"Sure, Waco!" He lifted his musket and waved his hand forward, saying, "Come on, you Richmond Grays! You volunteered to die for your country, so here's your chance!" The squad, which had been halted in the advance, looked at him . . . and something happened. The sight of Clay Rocklin's face, calm and without fear, gave them courage. Ira Sampson laughed wildly, crying out shrilly, *"Dulce et decorum est pro patria mori!"*

Holt Mattson, his lean face blackened by powder, stared at Sampson, then demanded, "What the blazes does that mean, Professor?"

Sampson grinned, his teeth white against the powder stains on his lips. "It means 'It is sweet and fitting to die for one's country.' "

Jock Longley had been listening to the exchange. Now his lips curled as he laughed harshly. "If that's whut education does for a man, I'm glad I never got any!"

Clay looked back and saw that the men would follow him. "Let's go!" he cried, and Waco's platoon swept up the hill into the blistering fire of the muskets that blinked like malevolent yellow eyes in the smoke.

■ ■ ■ ■

Major Gideon Rocklin had seen men die in action in many ways, none of them pretty. But as he watched Laurence Bradford lose his courage as the Confederates pressed their attack, it was somehow worse than any death by bullet or cannon.

The Blues had been part of Hunter's division and so were one of the first groups to cross Bull Run. Ever since Shanks Evans's men had shattered the first line of the brigade, Colonel Bradford had been out of control. His face was drained of all color, and he was incapable of thinking. He was not the first man to discover that the skills that bring a man to prominence in the world of business or politics often are of little help when death flies thick in the air.

All along the march to Sudley's Ford, Bradford had been in an exalted mood, stopping his horse to make short speeches to the men. He had been, so it appeared, happy and excited, but Gideon had watched him carefully, for he had seen such behavior before.

Even when the first shots were fired, Bradford seemed all right. "Don't mind those bullets, boys," he'd called out gaily, riding along the front of the regiment. "We've got the Rebels where we want 'em!"

But five minutes later, a Confederate shell had exploded just in front of the line of battle. It had turned men into chunks of red meat, and a part of an arm was thrown against Colonel Bradford's chest. He had looked down at the bloody stain on his chest, then at the arm lying at his feet, and had begun to make queer sounds in his throat.

"You all right, Colonel?" Gideon had gone to him at once and had been shocked at the vacant expression in Bradford's eyes.

"Are you hit, sir?" asked one of Bradford's aides who came running up.

Gideon added urgently, "Sir, they're going to enfilade us if we don't get over to that bluff." When Bradford only stared at him, Gideon made an instant decision. "Lieutenant, take the colonel to the rear. I'll take command until he's able to return."

He didn't wait to hear the aide's answer but began shouting orders at once. "Captain Frost! Get your men in position on the top of that bluff. The Rebs will be on top of us, and they've got to come up that hill. Hold 'em back as long as you can!"

"Yes, sir!" Captain Frost ran to where Lieutenant Boone Monroe was standing.

"Major Rocklin's in command, Boone — he says we've got to hold that bluff or the Rebels will break through."

"The colonel get hit?"

"No. Lost his nerve, I think. Wouldn't be good for the men to see him. Now get your platoon up!"

Frost moved quickly to the other platoons, and Boone yelled, "We'll form a line along the crest of that bluff!" Then he wheeled and shouted, "First Platoon! Let's move!"

Noel moved at once, running through the brambles that tore at his legs. Then when he got to the top of the ridge, he stopped dead still, staring through the amorphous forms of the Confederates as they appeared dimly through the smoke. As Pat came panting up to join him, Noel said, "There they come, Pat." He heard Monroe's shrill yelping command, "Shoot them down! Shoot them down!" and put his musket to his shoulder. The charging Confederates were dim figures, half hidden by the clouds of smoke. The air was filled with the shrill cries they made as they came on, and their bullets were whistling in the air around the platoon. Something clipped a branch from a sapling just to Noel's right.

Lifting his musket, Noel drew a bead on one of the gray-clad men, and for one brief moment, his finger seemed to freeze.

I'm about to kill a man! The thought flashed through his mind, and he couldn't pull the trigger. He, along with others in the company, had wondered how he would take a man's life — and fear had been in him that he would be unable to do it. But he had prayed long and, without coming to any firm theological answers, had resolved to do his duty as a soldier. He had spoken of this once to Pat, whose answer had been, "Noel, if you can't do it, get out of here. The man next to you is counting on you, just like you're counting on him. I hate it, too, but we're here, and we've got to do what we came for."

A faint cry came from Noel's left, and he shifted his glance to see Emmett Grant drop his musket and fall to the ground, clutching his stomach. His eyes were filled with terror as he looked at Noel, and he was making a mewing sound that rose above the crack of muskets.

Noel tore his glance from Emmett, took aim, and fired. His target threw up his hands in a wild helpless gesture, then fell motionless to the earth. Noel wanted to drop his musket and flee, but he clamped his lips tight, loaded his musket expertly, then fired again.

The Confederates came on, yelping like hunting dogs with their shrill, fierce cries, and Noel loaded and fired like an automaton. He was like a man building something, going through the motions of loading, then firing, then loading again.

But when the attack ran down and the Confederates melted back into the smoke, he looked around to see that men were down all along the line. He stared at Pat, who was looking across the ravine for a target, saying, "We've got some of our men down, Pat."

Pat's mouth was black from the powder of the paper cartridges, and his eyes were wide. Looking down the line, he seemed to be drugged. He drew a hand across his face, gave a ragged sigh, then said, "We made it, Noel." Then his glance shifted and he said, "Let's see about the boys."

They put their muskets down and joined Lieutenant Monroe, who was bending over Emmett Grant. Monroe's eyes were angry as he looked up. "Emmett's gone." He closed the dead soldier's eyes, and the three of them moved down the line, finding that one more of the squad had been killed — Corporal Silas Tarkington, a silent man of thirty-five from Ohio. He had taken a bullet in the throat, and the front of his uniform

357

was drenched with scarlet.

"He was a fine fellow," Pat whispered, his throat dry from the scorching heat. "Got a wife and baby boy back home. He was proud of that boy."

"I'll have to write her a letter," Monroe said. Looking down the line, he called out, "Anybody else hurt?"

"The dirty Rebs shot me in the rump!" Manny Zale called out. "I better get to the hospital!"

Monroe walked over, said, "Pull them pants down, Zale," and discovered a slight scratch on the soldier's hip. "I've had worse than that pickin' blackberries," he snapped, dismissing the complaint with an angry gesture.

He went back to stand by Sergeant Gordon, who said, "Think they'll be back, Lieutenant?"

"You kin bet on it!"

Noel walked over to where Bing was standing. "You all right, Bing?" he asked.

Bing gave him a tight look, his mouth drawn up into a pucker. He cursed, saying, "Be better off in jail than here!" Bing Kojak did not lack physical courage — he had plenty of that — but he was a man of totally selfish impulses, and the thought of having his life cut short for nothing angered him.

He had made up his mind while enduring the enemy charge that somehow he was not going to risk getting killed, but he was too crafty to say so to Noel. "You all right?" he asked finally.

"Yes. They'll be back, though." Noel hesitated, then said, "I'm glad you're all right, Bing." He got only a nod in response, then moved away. Sergeant Gordon called out, "Kojak, you and Steele take the canteens back to that creek and fill 'em up."

"Sure, Sergeant." The two men made their way to the sluggish stream, and as they were filling the canteens, Pat said, "It wasn't like I thought it would be, Noel." Holding the canteen under the surface, he thought about the action, then shook his head. "Maybe I heard too many speeches, all about how glorious the war was. But it's not, is it? It's filthy and mean."

"Always has been, Pat," Noel agreed. "Guess I'm like you. Read too many novels where the heroes went in with flags flying. But when I saw poor Emmett's eyes when he took that bullet in the stomach, I saw what it's going to be like. And it's going to get worse, Pat! I —"

He broke off, for the sound of musket fire crackled sharply. "That's our bunch, Pat!" he said, and the two scrambled back in time to join the platoon, which was under another heavy attack from the Confederates.

"Gordon's down," Corporal Buck Riley growled as the two men fell into line beside him. "And our lines are breaking. The Rebs have broke through to our left. They can come in behind us, so keep an eye out to the rear." A shell exploded down the line, scattering bodies, which flew like tattered dolls through the air. The men close to the explosion began to run for the rear but found Lieutenant Ben Finch there ready to beat them back into line.

"Can't stand too much of this, Noel!" Riley said, a bitter light in his eyes. "You two keep an eye on the boys. We gotta hold this ridge."

And hold it they did, though the battle raged on for hours. Noel lost track of the charges made by the enemy and knew that the Rebels were taking terrible losses, but so was A Company. All down the line bodies were slumped, and the survivors robbed their cartridge cases for ammunition.

Once Major Rocklin came by to encourage them. He spoke with Captain Frost, saying, "Your company has done fine work, Captain."

"What's happening, Major?"

Gideon pulled off his cap and looked

around at the thin lines. "It's not good, Hiram. We waited too long, and now the enemy's got plenty of firepower." The two men spoke quietly, and finally Gideon said, "If we get hit hard one more time, I don't think the men will be able to stand it. If we have to retreat, we have to do it in an orderly fashion."

"Hate to think of retreat!" Frost snapped, shaking his head angrily. His blood was up, and he asked, "Can we charge 'em? What about the colonel?"

Gideon gave him an oblique stare, then shook his head and said bitterly, "He's at the rear. And McDowell won't give the order for a general attack. It's all that'll save us, I think." He turned and walked down the line, speaking with the men. When he got to Pat, he grinned, saying, "Well, Private Steele, you're a soldier now."

"Yes, sir, I guess so." Pat nodded, then looked at Noel. "We did the best we could. Noel here, he's the steadiest one in the platoon."

Gideon said, "I remember the day you enlisted, Kojak. Guess you've been giving that some second thoughts? Like to be back in the factory?"

Noel flushed but said at once, "No, Major."

His brief answer pleased Gideon. "Good man! We'll come out of this. Keep your heads down." He smiled and said, "If I see Deborah, I'll tell her her recruit is doing a fine job — and her brother, as well."

Major Rocklin moved on, and Noel said, "He's a real fine man, Pat." He thought of Deborah, and as the firing began to pick up, he wondered when he'd see her again. But that seemed far off and remote, and the men rushing toward him through the smoke of battle were terribly real.

It was an hour after Rocklin left that the Confederates received fresh reinforcements. Another train had arrived at Manassas Junction, and Brigadier General E. Kirby Smith and Colonel Arnold Elzey arrived at Bull Run, throwing their forces into the battle. The turning point was a head-on cavalry charge led by Colonel Jeb Stuart. As the horses crashed into the infantry, the men in blue could not stand it. Throwing their guns down, they ran blindly, and their panic became epidemic. All up and down the line, the Federals, seeing the fleeing hordes, collapsed.

Beauregard, seeing the sudden shift, ordered a general charge of the whole line, and the gray-clad Confederates swarmed toward the thin blue line.

Captain Frost had seen other companies break and run, but he held A Company fast. "Stand still, men. We can hold 'em! Don't run!"

Noel saw the waves of Confederates sweeping across the terrain, yelling like fiends. He was aware that some of the platoon had thrown their muskets down and joined the rout — Bing among them — but he loaded his rifle, took aim, fired, then loaded again. He had no hope of survival but continued to fire until the wave broke and a lean Confederate lieutenant appeared right in front of him. His musket was not loaded, so he raised it like a club. He heard Pat yell wildly, "Noel — !" and he saw the flash of light on the revolver the Confederate officer lifted.

Then the explosion came, sending a long, cold sliver of pain through Noel's side. He tasted the dirt as his face hit the ground, and the earth seemed to swallow him as the din of battle faded into a mute silence.

CHAPTER 16
THE RESCUE

Waco's squad had fought their way halfway up the ridge, but a Federal cannon found its range, and Waco shouted, "Take cover!" He led them to a waist-deep ravine, and the men fell panting on the ground, trembling with shock. The struggle continued, making an angry clamor that drowned out everything else.

Waco's men were in the wake now, in one of those abrupt interstices of battle, and a fresh rank of butternut troops surged past them, then another, then another.

"Them's General Smith's boys," Waco said with a nod to Clay, who had plumped down near him. "Looks like we got the Yankees on the run!"

"We'd better pick up all the ammunition we can," Clay said. "And canteens, too." Waco called out an order, and soon the squad had scoured the field, bringing back all the water and cartridges they could find.

"Gives me the creeps, taking stuff from dead men," Lowell said with a shiver as he returned.

As he took a drink from a canteen, Clay looked at him quickly but said only, "They won't be needing it, Lowell, and we will."

"Think they'll come again, Clay?" Jock Longley asked, looking over the hill. "I've had plenty of what they offered us. Let them fresh boys handle it."

Waco, sitting with his head down, noticed how the men seemed to look up to Clay Rocklin. It was a thing that was in some men, he knew. If a man had it, it was there, but if he didn't, nothing could put it in him.

Clay looked at the sergeant. "I'd guess we'll do the charging from now on, don't you reckon, Waco?"

"I hope we chase the Bluebellies all the way back to Washington," Waco said. He tilted a canteen; then the sound of a beating drum rattled over the air. "Signal to form up," he said. "Let's go." He led the squad to where the regiment was being put in formation by Colonel Benton, and soon they caught up with some of the men who'd relieved them.

"What's going on, Lieutenant?" Benton demanded of one of the officers from Smith's division.

"Got a tough spot in the line up there, Colonel." The speaker was a short, red-haired lieutenant with a bristly beard. "We've hit that hill three times but can't make a dent in it. They got the whole division pinned down here."

James Benton had visions of a political future when the war was over, and he knew that a good war record would be necessary. Looking up the hill, he saw the flicker of small-arms fire, but there was no artillery. At once he said, "We'll take that piece of ground!" He wheeled his horse around and rode to where Major Brad Franklin stood waiting. "Brad, we've got to take that hill."

Franklin stared up the hill, then shook his head doubtfully. "We better wait for some artillery, Colonel. That's a long distance for the men to be under fire. They're shooting right down on us, and there's no place for a man to hide and reload."

"Have the men fix bayonets," Benton commanded. "We've got good men, and the Feds' ranks are pretty thin, I'd guess."

Franklin moved away and, passing down the line, gave the order. He stopped by C Company and spoke to Captain Taylor Dewitt and Lieutenant Dent Rocklin. "I'd just as soon wait for reinforcements, to tell the truth, but the colonel won't hear of it. Taylor, send half of your company up the hill and keep the other half in reserve."

When Franklin moved along, Dent said, "Brad's right about that hill. Why don't we go around and flank them, Captain?"

"Because that's not as glamorous as a bayonet charge," Taylor said bitterly. "Benton's got to have a headline, and I'm thinking some of us are going to pay a pretty high price for it."

Dent said abruptly, "Let me take the men up, Captain. Bushrod can stay here with the reserves."

"All right, Dent."

Half of C Company was chosen, and when Waco saw that his platoon was not going, he cursed. "We all should go up that hill," he said bitterly. But he was almost alone in his eagerness to make the charge.

Clay stood beside his son and Bob Yancy, watching the men form up, and Lowell said, "I wish Dent wasn't going up there."

"I'd guess he volunteered for it, Lowell," Clay said slowly. He didn't like the decision, believing that it was a useless charge. The Federal line was pulling back all along the stream, and the unit holding the hill would join them, given time. Benton was stubborn and proud — and he was going to put the lives of five hundred men on the line.

Benton rode out on his horse, waved his saber, and cried out, "Come on, you Richmond Grays!" As he turned and his horse moved up the hill, the company began to run.

"Benton's a fool!" Waco said, biting his words off. "He's the man on the horse. Every Yankee in that bunch will be trying to put him down!"

And he was correct, for before the men had gone fifty yards, a bullet struck Colonel Benton's horse. The animal went down, pinning Benton's leg, but he cried out to Dent Rocklin, who came running to help, "Never mind me, Rocklin! Take the men up!"

A fire was in Dent's blood, and he yelled, "Come on!" He ran up the hill shouting and was aware that the fire from the Yankees had slackened. Perhaps there were fewer of them; perhaps they were low on ammunition — whatever the reason, the lull allowed Dent and his men to push forward. Now they were halfway, then close enough to see the faces of the enemy. There were not as many as Dent had feared, but looking around, he saw that not many of his men had made it. Some were down on the ground, lying still; others were running back down the hill. Only a few men were with him, but Dent saw that if they tried to run back, they'd be shot down.

He leaped ahead, crying out, "Come on, Grays!"

His breath was ragged, and his chest felt as though it were on fire. Then, suddenly, a young Union soldier was in front of him, swinging a rifle. Dent lifted his pistol and pulled the trigger. The slug struck the soldier in the body, and he grunted, then fell to the ground. At once another soldier came at him from the right, his bayonet aimed at Dent's belly. Dent turned sideways, letting the blade go by, and shot the soldier in the chest. The man dropped his rifle, stared at Dent reproachfully as if he'd done something terribly wrong — then sat down, staring at the ground.

"Come on, men!" Dent yelled. "We can hold this spot!" It was bad, he saw, but they had broken the line in the right place. The gray line of Confederates was convoluted, twisted and strung out to his right and to his left, but if he could get them together, they could make a stand. Men began crowding in, and he screamed, "Reload! Reload!"

Back down the hill, Captain Dewitt saw what was happening. He had watched the charge fall to pieces and knew that there was nothing he could do. Colonel Benton had scurried back to safety and stood there now, shocked and horrified by the sight of his men being cut down as though by a giant scythe.

"We've got to go help them," Taylor said.

"No!" Benton cried out. "It'll be suicide! Look at how many men we've lost!"

They were standing not ten feet away from where Clay and Waco were waiting. Clay was sickened over the slaughter. Then Lowell, who had the best eyes in the company, said, "Look! Dent's making a stand!"

"Can you see that far?" Waco demanded. "What's happening?"

"Dent's got a few men together, but they're going to get swallowed! We've got to help!"

Clay looked around and saw that some of the officers' horses had been brought up from the rear. He whirled and ran for them. When he reached them, he discovered that Waco, Lowell, and Bob Yancy had followed. Bob grinned at him, his greenish eyes alive with excitement. "I do believe we're about to join the cavalry, Clay!" he yelped. He reached out for the reins of one of the mounts, and the horse-holder, a skinny young man with a sunburned face, cried out, "Hey! You can't take these horses!"

Clay brushed him aside and swung into the saddle. Lowell and Waco had each grabbed a horse and were waiting for him. "I'm going to get those boys!" Clay said, then drove his heels into the sides of the horse. The animal shot off like a rocket. The four of them hit the open, and Taylor Dewitt and Colonel Benton stared at them. Taylor said, "Colonel, if we don't support them, you'll never get a vote from me or my folks."

Benton glared at him, then shouted, "The devil with your votes, Taylor! Let's go, men!"

Dewitt's stubbornness and Benton's decision probably saved Clay and the others, for the brigade moved up the hill, firing as they ran, and the volley shook the defenders so badly that they dodged and were unable to hit the four horsemen.

Dent heard one of the Union soldiers scream, "Look out, you fellers! Them Rebels is coming! It's a cavalry charge!" Looking over his shoulder, Dent saw the movement of the gray line that had left the trees and was sweeping up the slope. He saw the horsemen, too, and could not understand who it could be. "Keep at 'em, boys!" he yelled and stopped to reload his revolver.

But even as he looked down, he heard one of his men scream, "Look out, Lieutenant!"

A shadow fell over him, and he saw the bulk of a horse that was headed for him. He saw the uplifted saber, too, and the grim face of the Yankee captain who held it. Frantically he threw himself to one side, throwing up his pistol to fire, but he was too late. The falling saber struck his forearm, slicing into the flesh, and the gun fell from his nerveless fingers. There was no pain, just a numbness, and he stepped back, but the sun blinded his eyes. He saw the flash of the sun on the saber and tried to duck, but the blade fell inexorably, catching him on the left side of his face. He felt the blade grate against bone, and the blood spurted into his eyes, blinding him. He fell to his knees, waiting for the next blow — the one that would kill him — and was filled with a great regret.

He felt no fear — rather, he thought of all he would lose. In that one moment he thought of Gracefield, of Deborah Steele, and most clearly of all, he saw the still features of Raimey Reed. *By the Lord!* he thought in anguish. *I hate to lose it all!*

But the blow never came. Instead there was a commotion over him, and he heard a voice cry out. Then hands were on him, holding him up, and a voice was crying out, "Dent! My boy! My boy!"

Clay had driven the horse at top speed, and when he crashed into the midst of the Yankee line, he instantly saw the Yankee captain charging down on Dent. Clay's musket was empty, but the bayonet was in place, and he drove the horse forward, thrusting the bayonet into the officer's side. The man cried out and fell to the ground, and Clay, heedless of the fierce fight going on all around him, fell to his knees beside his son, lifting his head. He was weeping, thinking he was holding a dead son — then Waco's voice broke through. "Clay, we got to get that arm tied up 'fore he bleeds to death!"

The Texan shouldered Clay to one side and in a moment had taken off his neckerchief and whipped it around Dent's arm. "That's a bad cut," Waco said, "but the face looks worse! Here, let's get some of this blood away so we can see what it looks like —"

The firing had died down, and Lowell came to stand over the wounded man. As Waco wiped the blood away, Lowell grew sick, for the saber had left an awful wound. It started at the skull over Dent's left temple, and Lowell could see the whiteness of bone in the gaping crevice of flesh.

"May have got his eye," Waco said doubtfully. "Let's put a bandage on this and get him to the surgeons. That's got to be sewed up fast!"

The four men improvised a stretcher out of saplings, used the coats from dead soldiers to form a base, then made their way back to the field hospital. It was over a mile, and they were all gasping when they got there. The ground was covered with wounded men, but Dr. Carter came to them. "What is it? Put him down over here."

Clay watched numbly as the doctor examined the wounds. He was praying silently and did not know that he was crying. Lowell, pale as a sheet, came to stand beside Clay while Waco and Bob stood slightly back. "Kind of a family affair," Waco murmured to Bob Yancy. "Sure hope that young fellow makes it."

After what seemed like a long time, Carter came to stand beside Clay and Lowell. "Two bad wounds," he said abruptly. "May lose that arm and may lose his eye."

"Don't take the arm!" Clay said instantly. "I'm believing God will heal it."

Dr. Carter knew the Rocklins well. He practiced in Richmond and knew the history of the trouble between Clay and his son. He had spoken harshly of Clay when he'd heard of the stand Clay had made against the war, but now he stood there, his eyes thoughtful. Finally he said, "I'll leave it on — but he may lose it later. I think the eye is all right if the muscles aren't cut."

"Do your best, Dr. Carter," Lowell pleaded.

"Certainly, but —"

Clay saw that something else was troubling Carter. "What is it?" he asked.

"Well, I sewed up his face, but it's a terrible wound, Clay. Going to leave a frightful scar. Nothing more to be done, though." He turned away, saying, "I'll do my best on the arm."

Waco came to Clay's side, stood there for a moment, then said, "I guess Bob and me better get back, Clay. You and Lowell stay here until you find out about the lieutenant."

"Thanks, Waco — for everything."

As Yancy and the sergeant moved away, the younger man said, "Shore hope he makes it, Waco. I've knowed the Rocklins since Hector was a pup." He chewed thoughtfully on his plug of tobacco, then added, "Mr. Dent, he was always the finest-looking feller in the county. Had his pick of all the good-looking girls. But I guess he won't be so free to pick anymore — not with a face like he's likely to wind up with."

Waco shook his head. "He's alive, Bob. That's more than some of the boys can say. I guess he'd rather be alive with his face cut up than still be handsome and dead."

Bob Yancy said only, "I dunno about that, Sarge. When a fellow's got something, he don't think about it much. But when he loses it, it can take the sap out of him. I seen that a lot, ain't you?" Waco disagreed, and the two of them argued about it as they made their way back to the company.

Clay and Lowell waited until Dr. Carter finished, then carried Dent's still form out of the tent. "I used a lot of chloroform on him," Carter said as they left. "Did the best I could with the arm. Keep it tied up tight; don't let him move it."

The day ran down, and at about eight o'clock Taylor Dewitt came to stand beside the Rocklin men. His face was gray with fatigue and strain as he asked, "How is he, Clay?" When he got the report, he nodded briefly. "We've got a lot of wounded men and plenty of prisoners. Take four men from the company and take charge of the detail."

"Ought to be Sergeant Mattson, I would think," Clay offered.

"He's dead," Taylor said briefly. Then he lifted his eyes and studied Clay. "You're a sergeant now. Need some kind of authority, and Waco says you're the man." He hesitated, then asked, "Will you do it?"

Clay nodded. "All right. I guess Lowell and Bob Yancy will do, and Leo Deforest."

"I'll send them here right away. Dr. Carter wants to get these wounded men to a hospital as quick as he can." He looked down at the still form of Dent Rocklin, then back to Clay. "That was pretty good, Clay, that ride up the hill. Colonel Benton said he was going to mention you in the report. You might even get a medal."

"I guess Dent deserves one more than I do, Captain." Clay stood there, his eyes thoughtful. "Like the men who died on that hill . . . but they won't get any medals."

"No, they won't." Taylor nodded. He saw that Clay knew the charge had been foolish, a waste of lives, but said only, "Take them to Richmond, Sergeant. Report to me when you get back."

Clay went back and sat down on the grass beside Lowell. The two of them had said little, but now Lowell began to talk. "I know you joined the army just to look out after me, sir." He broke off, unable to say what he felt. The night was dark, with few stars in the sky, but Lowell could see his brother's face swathed in white bandages and said, "I think it was for Dent's sake, too. If you hadn't led us up that hill, he'd probably be dead now. So it's a good thing we came, don't you think?"

Clay knew the boy had been scarred by the death and terror of the day, that he was looking for his father to give some kind of an answer that would put the puzzle together for him. He sat there, thinking of what had happened, and finally said, "We're sort of blind down here, Lowell. Most of the time we can't see where we are, we don't know why we've done what's in the past, and we can't even guess what's ahead. Lots of people take a look at life and give up. They just live and never ask why things are like they are. But I trust you're not one of that kind, for that's foolish."

The night air was hot, and Dent suddenly stirred, moving his legs and making a small sound. At once, Clay dipped a cloth into the pan of water beside him and bathed the fevered face. He waited silently until the wounded man lay quietly on the blanket, then sat back and looked across at his son.

"Lowell, God is in everything. We're looking at things from a pretty narrow point of view, but God knows all about us. Something happens that we think is bad, and we think God's gone to sleep or that He doesn't care. But He does care. That's why He made us, son, because He's a God of love. And even our pain, that's got something to do with God, with what He's trying to make of us." He took a sudden deep breath and added gently, "Guess you didn't ask for a sermon, but all I can say, Lowell, is that I believe that our God knows about me and you and Dent. He's working on us. And we're so blind and hard, sometimes He has to use some pretty tough means to get us straightened out. But I believe God will help us through all this. Do you believe that?"

Lowell nodded slowly, then said, "I do now. I guess I've been pretty careless with my life. But this war, it makes a man see things different — you know, what matters and what doesn't. Charging up that hill, I learned more about how good life is than I've ever learned up until then."

They sat there, speaking quietly, until Lowell finally lay back and went to sleep. Clay kept vigil all night, dozing off from time to time but coming awake instantly whenever the wounded man moaned.

Just before dawn, Dent awoke. He tried to cry out and ask for water. Clay held his head up and gave him sips of tepid water. It was hard, for Dent could not move his lips because of the stitches in his cheek.

Finally he peered at Clay through his right

eye and whispered, "What — what's wrong with me?"

"You took a couple of pretty bad wounds, son," Clay said. "Don't worry. You'll be all right."

Dent was still foggy from the chloroform and lay there trying to think. Finally he asked, "Where am I hurt? In the head?"

"Yes, and don't touch the bandage. A bad cut on the cheek, another on your arm."

Dent turned his head and considered the shadowy figure beside him. "Who is this?"

"Your father, son."

Dent grew still, then asked, "Was it you who came up the hill to help us?"

Clay said, "I'll tell you about it later. Take some more water and try to rest." He gave the thirsty man another drink, and almost at once Dent dropped off to sleep. Thirty minutes later, the sun shattered the ebony darkness, lighting up the east, and Clay Rocklin got up to meet the day, knowing that the way ahead was not going to be easy.

It's just starting, he thought as he watched Dent's face in the pale light. *But we'll make it, Lord. You've got to bring us through — because no man can win out in this thing if You don't stand beside him!*

CHAPTER 17
THE PRISONERS

"Who are those troops? They're going the wrong way; the battle is ahead, isn't it?"

Deborah Steele turned, pulled abruptly out of her thoughts by the words of Matthew Pillow. Pillow, a congressman from her district and a friend of the family, had pulled the buggy off the road with a jolt just in time to avoid a collision with a wagon-load of Federal soldiers. The driver was whipping the horses up, and soldiers were stumbling along in the wake of the wagon, trying to keep up. Many of them looked over their shoulders fearfully as they moved down the road toward Washington.

Pillow, a large man with a full beard and a foghorn voice, called out, "Here now, what's happening?"

The soldier sitting in the rear of the wagon lifted his head and called wildly, "Get back! The Rebs is coming — Black Horse Cavalry!"

Mrs. Pillow grabbed her husband's arm fearfully. "He can't be right, can he, Matthew?"

Pillow stared at the soldiers who came along the road in an ever-increasing stream, none of them carrying muskets, and shook his head. "I don't believe it! Let's go on a little and try to find an officer."

As he pulled the buggy back onto the road, Deborah sat up straighter. She'd been invited by Helen Pillow, the daughter of the congressman, to come and witness the battle. Helen, a tall, plain girl of twenty, had been excited. "You've just got to come with us, Deborah! We'll get to see a real battle — and after our men whip the Rebels, there's going to be a victory dance at Fairfax Courthouse! Isn't it exciting? You must come, Deborah. We've got the picnic lunch and plenty of room. Lots of the congressmen are going out to see the battle."

Deborah had agreed, but as they drove down the road — which was growing more and more filled with soldiers who were obviously fleeing — she knew that the easy victory the North had been expecting was not going to happen. Pillow was a stubborn man, however, and kept driving the buggy down the road, dodging to avoid wagons and even a twelve-pound Napoleon howitzer that rumbled along, pulled by heaving white-eyed horses.

An hour later Pillow pulled up, his face pale and perspiring. "I don't know about this, Helen," he gasped. "Something's gone wrong!"

At the moment he spoke, the bridge he'd just managed to get across, despite heavy traffic, was hit with a Confederate shell. It blew one side of the bridge to splinters, killing two horses that were pulling a wagon and blowing men into the creek below.

At the same time, a lone rider, an officer on a sweaty-flanked black horse, came around a bend. He pulled his mount up abruptly when he saw the confusion at the bridge.

"Captain!" Pillow shouted, waving his arms. "What's happening? Where's our army?"

The captain gave him a sour look. He was a short, muscular man with a pair of muddy brown eyes. His mouth twisted with rage as he shouted, "Our army? Probably either dead or on their way to Richmond. Get your women out of here, man! The whole Rebel army is on its way!" He drove his horse toward the creek, forded the swift stream, then rode off at full speed.

"Matthew!" Mrs. Pillow screamed, "We've

got to go back!"

Pillow nodded, his face ashen. Seeing that the bridge was going to be a bottleneck, he drove his team downstream and put them across, despite their reluctance. As the wagon bucked and plunged over the rough stones of the creek bottom, the lunch basket fell out, but no one noticed. It landed upside down, and the sandwiches came out and began to float downstream. A huge loggerhead snapping turtle, as big around as a washtub, rose slowly to the surface, opened his frightful jaws, and clamped down on a cucumber sandwich. Not forty feet away, men were raging and fighting to get over the ruined bridge, but the snapping turtle paid no heed. He closed his jaws, his wise old eyes yellow in the sun, then dropped back down to the ooze of the creek bottom.

When Congressman Pillow let Deborah out at her home, she went to her mother and told her what had happened. The two of them soon found that Washington was ablaze with rumors about the battle. All day long the stragglers of the army came stumbling back to Washington, and Abraham Lincoln and General Scott made plans for a last defense of the city — they even went so far as to order the state papers to be loaded so that the capitol might be moved to another city.

For two days the tension hung on, most citizens expecting the Rebel army to come charging into the city at any moment. Deborah and her family worried about Pat, and finally Gideon came to see them. Deborah and her father sat there wordlessly as he told of the defeat. "It could have gone the other way," Gideon said bitterly. "If we'd hit them hard the first day, we'd have sent them reeling, but McDowell's no fighter. He's finished as a general, and that's a good thing!"

"Do you think the Rebels will attack?" Amos asked.

"No, they took lots of punishment," Gideon said. "But they won the battle, Amos. Now maybe people will stop that silly talk about a short war. Maybe they will finally see that the Confederates are tough — they're fighting for their homes, and they're not going to quit."

"What about Pat, Uncle Gideon?" Deborah asked. "Is he all right?"

Gideon bit his lower lip. "I hope so, Deborah. I didn't see him after the Confederates made their big push and drove us back. But one of the men in his company, a man named Jim Freeman, knew Pat was my nephew, so he came to me and told me . . .

385

that Pat was captured."

"What exactly did he say?" Amos asked tightly.

"Pat's platoon was in a hot fight, and they got overrun by the Rebels' charge. Freeman was off to one side when they hit, so he ducked into a ditch and hid. He said that Pat took a bullet in the arm, but it wasn't a serious hit. His platoon was just overrun — and had to surrender."

"Did he mention Noel Kojak, Uncle Gideon?"

Gideon had been dreading the question. He faced Deborah, saying reluctantly, "It's bad news, Deborah. Freeman said that Kojak fought to the last, but he was shot down by one of the Confederate lieutenants. Freeman had to get away quick, so he didn't know how badly Noel was hit."

Deborah's face was pale. "It's my fault. I was the one who talked him into enlisting!"

Gideon shook his head, and his voice was kind as he answered, "You can't take the blame, Deborah. The boy was a good soldier — the best in his company, his captain said. And he may be all right. If he was wounded, he'll be taken to a hospital in Richmond. I'll find out about him and Pat as soon as I can."

"Thank you, Uncle Gideon," Deborah

said evenly. She sat there quietly while the two men talked, but a heaviness such as she'd never known had come to her. She had not known until this moment how fond of Noel Kojak she'd become, and her heart broke as she pictured him dead on the field of battle, buried in a shallow grave.

Noel Kojak was not, however, in a shallow grave. Even as Gideon Rocklin was telling Deborah and her father the bad news, Noel was being jolted along in a wagon, half conscious and racked with pain. But he was alive.

He had first been taken to the same field hospital where Dent Rocklin, the man who had put the bullet in his side, was lying. A rough surgeon had looked at the wound and shaken his head, saying, "Too close to the spine. Can't do anything for him." Noel had been put on the ground with other wounded Federal soldiers and passed the night in delirium. The next morning he had awakened and found Pat beside him, his arm in a sling.

"Hey, Noel!" Pat said when he saw the young man's eyes open. "How are you?"

Noel opened his mouth to answer, but as he shifted his body, an explosion of pain blossomed in his side, and he could only gasp. He lay there until the sheets of pain ebbed, then whispered, "Where are we, Pat?"

"Prisoners," Pat said, shrugging. He looked carefully at Noel's face, not liking what he saw. "There's some soup left. I'll get you some."

"Just — water," Noel croaked, suddenly aware of a raging thirst. He gulped frantically at the tepid water Pat gave him from a dipper, then lay back, the world spinning. He tried to speak, but he was slipping back into a deep, black hole with no bottom.

Pat covered him up, knowing Noel had a fever, then sat there despondently. The doctors had worked all night and were still working. They had no time for anyone except the worst cases, so there was nothing to do but wait. All morning he sat there, giving Noel a sip of water from time to time, keeping the blanket over him.

At noon several wagons pulled up and began loading the wounded. A strong-looking Confederate in his forties came down the line of wounded. The Confederate wounded had been taken earlier. Now, as the leader of the detail came down the line, Pat struggled to his feet. He saw that many of the wounded would have to be left and said, "Please, take my friend!"

The Confederate stopped and looked down at Noel. "He hit bad? Can't take any dying men, soldier. Only those with a chance."

Pat said quickly, "He's got a bullet in him, but if he can get to a hospital, they'll take it out and he'll be all right."

"Well . . ." The sergeant hesitated; then something in Noel's face seemed to touch him. "All right. But we can't take you in the wagon."

"I can walk," Pat said at once. "I'll take care of him." Then he said, "God bless you, sir!"

Clay Rocklin gave him a quick look. "You're a Christian?"

"Yes. Not much of one, I guess," Pat said. He watched as the Rebels loaded Noel into the wagon with the other wounded, then waited until the train pulled out.

All afternoon Pat trudged along, several times almost ready to faint, but the pace was slow and there were frequent breaks. When they pulled into a grove of trees near a creek to camp for the night, Pat almost collapsed. He lay on the ground while the guards cut wood for a fire, then went to sleep while supper was being cooked. He came awake when a hand touched his shoulder and a voice said, "Better come and get some of this grub, son."

Pat opened his eyes with a sense of alarm, not sure where he was. Then he glanced around and saw the ground covered with the wounded — and it all came back to him. The smell of bacon and coffee hit him like a blow and was followed quickly by sharp hunger pangs. He struggled to his feet. "Your friend is over here," Clay said, and he led Pat to where Noel lay. Pat knelt down and saw that Noel's fever was high.

"He's pretty sick," Clay said gently. "That's a bad wound. Bullet ought to come out, but no way to do it here." Then he said, "Get some grub inside you. We've got a ways to go."

He led Pat to the edge of the fire and got two plates, and then they sat down. Pat ate like a starved wolf and was sleepy as soon as he'd finished. His wound had sapped his strength more than he'd realized. "Can't stay awake," he mumbled. A thought came to him, and he stared at the figure of his captor. "I guess I can't do much but thank you, sir. Are all Rebels as thoughtful as you?"

Clay chuckled. "I guess we're just like you Bluebellies. Some good, some bad." Then he saw the boy's eyelids drooping. He got up and pulled a blanket out of one of the wagons, then came back to hand it to Pat. "Get all the rest you can."

"I should stay with Noel," Pat protested.

"I'll sit with the boy," Clay assured him. "Not much I can do for him except pray, and I'll be doing that. Now go to sleep."

Pat slept like a dead man and felt better the next morning. His arm was painful, but he made the day's march in better condition. They moved slowly once again, taking many rests. Pat knew that most of the enemy would not have been so careful of their "cargo" and would have driven straight on. That night he sat with Noel after supper but again grew sleepy.

Noel was awake, though, so Pat forced himself to stay awake, too. It was well after dark when Clay came over to the two, carrying two cups of coffee. "See if you can get some of this down," he said gently, helping Noel sit up and watching as the wounded boy took the cup with trembling hands. Pat took a cup and drank slowly, leaning back against a small tree. The keening of crickets made him sleepy, and he dozed off.

The stars were out in force, a sparkling canopy spread across the velvet blackness, and Clay admired them for a while in silence. "We may be in Richmond in a couple of days," he finally said quietly to the wounded man. "They'll take care of you boys there. What's your name?"

"Noel Kojak."

"I'm Clay Rocklin."

Noel blinked and said, "I worked for a man named Rocklin. At the foundry in Washington."

Clay stared at him, then smiled. "That's my kin, Noel. My father's brother." He studied the wan face of the boy, then said, "That's a strange one. Small world, isn't it?"

Noel nodded; then a thought came to him. He looked at Pat, trying to remember something, then licked his lips and said, "I guess Pat's some kin of yours, too. Pat — wake up!"

Clay stared at the boy as he roused, then said, "My name's Rocklin. Noel thinks we might be related. What's your name?"

"Why, I'm Pat Steele." He was confused, then said, "But my mother was a Rocklin."

Clay demanded, "Do you have a sister named Deborah?" When Pat said that he did, Clay said slowly, "It's a smaller world than I thought. I know your sister, Pat. She was at my plantation earlier in the summer. As a matter of fact, my son was quite taken with her."

Pat stared at him. This was the father of

Dent Rocklin, the man Deborah had fallen for in Virginia. "She's spoken of you," Pat said, then asked, "Do you know my uncle, Major Gideon Rocklin?"

Clay sat there, stunned by the chance that had brought the three of them together. Images of Gideon and Melanie — and of all the three of them had been through — raced through his mind, but he said only, "Yes, I know him. He's my cousin, Pat."

Pat Steele suddenly remembered the fragments of family history and said, "Oh, I know you now! You're the one who — !" He broke off in confusion and stared across at Clay with embarrassment.

Clay smiled at him. "You've heard about me, I see. The wolf with the long ears and the sharp white teeth? Well, it's all true, I guess — or it was." He sat there idly, thinking of the past, then said, "I'm sorry you boys had to get shot, but I'm glad to be around to give you a hand. All in the family, isn't it?" Then he got to his feet, saying, "Better rest, boys. Long road to Richmond."

It was not, in fact, all that far to Richmond, but by the time the wagon train pulled into the city, Noel was unconscious and Pat was exhausted. Clay found the hospital, helped get the prisoners inside, and said before he left, "Pat, I'll send a wire to your people telling them you're all right."

"Thank you, sir," Pat said, then asked, "Could you send word about Noel? To my sister, Deborah. She'll want to know about him."

"Sure, I'll do that." Clay left, then looked up the section of the hospital reserved for Confederate officers. He found Dent asleep and decided to come back later. On his way out, Clay spoke to the doctor, a thin, hard-faced man of fifty.

"The face is healing, but he's going to have a terrible scar," Dr. Amos Medlin said. He added at once, "The arm should be taken off. It's never going to be any good to him, and I'm afraid of gangrene. He fights it, though. Try to talk him into it. Better to go through life with one arm than to die with two."

Clay said, "I'll talk to him as soon as I can, Doctor." Then he asked, "You treat the Yankee prisoners, don't you?"

"Yes."

"I wish you'd go see one of them I've just brought in. Noel Kojak is his name. Got a bullet that should come out."

"What's your interest in him?"

"He works for my uncle," Clay said. "A good boy."

"All right," Medlin said with a shrug.

"Talk to your son. That arm's got to come off."

Clay nodded, then left the hospital, going at once to the telegraph office. He sent a wire to Gideon and included the news of Noel Kojak, asking Gid to pass the word to Deborah. He left the telegraph office, then obtained lodging for his men. Finally he got into one of the wagons and started for Gracefield, grateful for the short leave he'd been granted upon his arrival in Richmond.

The telegram reached Gideon the next day, and at once he went to the Steeles. "Just heard from Clay," he said. "Pat's all right. He'll be a prisoner, but I think we can get him exchanged."

"Thank God!" Laura Steele cried, embracing her husband.

Gideon turned to Deborah, saying, "Bad news about Noel, I'm afraid."

"Is he dead?"

"No, but he's badly wounded. Clay doesn't think he'll live."

He gave the details, and as soon as he finished, Deborah grew still, then said, "I'm going to Richmond."

The others stared at her, and her father exclaimed, "You can't do that, Deborah!"

But argument did nothing to shake her

resolve. Deborah listened to them all, then said calmly, "I can see that Pat has what he needs. And I won't have Noel alone in that place."

The next morning as the train pulled out of the Washington station, Deborah was aboard. Her face was set in an expression of iron determination, and as the train raced across the countryside headed for the South, she gave no thought to the difficulties that lay ahead. She only knew one thing: She was determined to see her brother safe and out of prison — and to see Noel Kojak live.

All else seemed to fade in importance.

■ ■ ■ ■ ■

PART FOUR:
CHIMBORAZO

■ ■ ■ ■ ■

Chapter 18
A Strange Volunteer

The battle of Manassas was won by the Confederates, but by a perverse development, it was the North who profited most from the battle — simply by seeing the results of it.

Washington saw the worst: the sorry picnic crowd that came back bedraggled and frightened; the broken troops who came shambling in, streaked with dirt and almost out of their heads with weariness. . . . These sights quenched the "On to Richmond" fever that had forced Lincoln to send the raw troops into battle. Some of the most rabid of the warmongers made a full circle, such as Horace Greeley, who wrote Lincoln a letter full of incoherent woe.

"On every brow," he wrote despondently, "sits sullen, scorching, black despair. . . . It is best for the country and for mankind that we make peace with the Rebels at once and on their own terms!"

Abraham Lincoln, however, had steeled himself for war. "The fat's in the fire now," he wrote to his wife two days after the defeat, "and we shall have to crow small until we can retrieve the disgrace somehow. The preparations for the war will be continued with increasing vigor by the Government."

Somehow he managed to communicate some of his iron will to the people of the North, and they bowed their heads and went to work. The beaten army was placed in the hands of General George McClellan, who began to put it back together — a task McClellan would do better than any other general during the entire war. The factories began to pour forth a stream of guns, cannons, small arms, uniforms, and the thousand other items required by a huge army.

The people of the North were humiliated by the loss at Bull Run, but they did not quit. The defeat merely hardened their purpose and, in effect, forced them to become an industrial nation.

In the South, the victory at Manassas was signaled by cheering crowds, clanging church bells, and thunderous salutes of cannon fire. Stonewall Jackson, though, was not celebrating. He was one of those who saw the dangers of the victory. "It would have been better if we had lost," he said to one of his aides, "for now the people will be overconfident, thinking the worst is over." He knew that was far from the case, as did other men with a clear vision.

Manassas was but the opening note of a symphony of suffering and death that would be played by both North and South — a symphony that would crescendo for the next four years.

When Deborah Steele stepped off the train at Richmond, she took a deep breath, then asked the station agent, her voice strong and determined, "How do I get to the military hospital?"

He directed her willingly enough, but she got no farther than the front gate of the hospital, where Noel Kojak lay on a bed of pain. She tried at once to see him but was stopped by a hard-eyed Confederate lieutenant named Josh Hanson. He met her with open suspicion and, upon finding out that she was from Washington, said at once, "I can't admit you to this hospital without a pass, lady."

"Where can I get a pass?"

"From the commanding officer, Colonel Prince."

But Colonel Prince was even more suspicious than Hanson. It took Deborah two days to get an audience with him, and when she stated her errand, he stared at her angrily, stating flatly, "You're in the wrong city, Miss Steele. I can't let one of the enemy have access to a Union prisoner." Donald Prince was not ordinarily a hard man, but his youngest son lay dead, shot down by a Union soldier at Bull Run. He had kept his bitterness and grief under control, but the sight of the Yankee woman caused it to spill over. "I'm giving an order that you be forbidden to enter any Confederate institution. Go back to your Yankee friends in Washington," he said bitterly and turned her out of his office harshly.

Deborah left the colonel's office and walked blindly down the street. A fine rain was falling, and she was soaked by the time she got back to her small hotel room. Stripping off her wet clothes, she dried off with the small towel provided, then wrapped up in a blanket while her dress dried. She had brought only one other dress and decided that she must save it. Going to the window, she looked down on the street below, watching it slowly turn to mud as the rain fell harder and harder. Her mind was busy, trying and rejecting plans, and finally she sat down on the bed, totally dejected.

She considered going to the Rocklins for help but rejected that idea at once. With the anti-Yankee atmosphere that was almost palpable in Richmond, she knew it would be dangerous for them to ask a favor on her behalf. Finally her mind was exhausted, and she sat there with tears running down her face. As they flowed, she began to pray. She firmly believed in prayer, but it had always been a thing of logic to her. God had made certain promises in the Bible concerning prayer, so all one had to do was memorize the promises, move forward boldly, and the thing would be done.

Well, that wasn't working. She had been praying from the time she had left Washington, yet the door was barred, and no human effort seemed likely to open it. As fatigue and frustration built up in her, Deborah did something she'd never done in her life, something that would have horrified and disgusted her if she'd seen someone else doing the same thing.

"God!" she cried aloud, coming off the bed and shaking her fists in a gesture of protest. "Don't You even care?" She was trembling, trying to hold back the tears, shocked at her own actions yet so angry that she began to walk the floor. Gripping her hands into fists, she cried out, "Where are

You? I've done everything, and You haven't done a thing!"

Her angry speech grew shriller, and she suddenly dropped to the floor, pressing her face into the carpet, lying there as a paroxysm of grief shook her. She had seldom wept as a girl and never as a grown woman. Now, though, the tears flowed freely, and great tearing sobs racked her body until her chest hurt. She began gasping, "Oh God! Oh God!" and could say no more. The words had been said. Now all that was left was a terrible emptiness that frightened her more than anything she had ever known. She was like a very small child who was lost in a frightful place and who sensed terrible things lurking close, watching her.

After a time, the wrenching sobs ceased to tear through her, and she lay there with her face pressed into the wet carpet. Her spirit seemed dead, beaten flat by the storm of grief that had passed over her. And then as she lay there, something began to happen. She was never able to explain it to anyone else, but somehow a strange sense of peace began to grow in her. At first she wasn't even aware of what was happening; she only knew that she was very tired and weary. Then she suddenly realized she wasn't weeping, and she had no desire or need to grieve.

What's happening to me? she wondered, bewildered by the feeling that was sweeping over her. She lifted her tearstained face, seeing only the pale blue wallpaper of the wall, and then she rose to stand in the center of the room.

Suddenly, as she waited, she was filled with a verse of scripture. She had heard the verse many times, for it was a favorite of her father's, but now it came into her mind with a force that caused her to gasp, and she sat down on the bed, her legs having grown weak.

"My peace I give unto you."

Deborah had known about God since she had been a small child. Her life had been spent in church services, and she had godly parents who had read the Bible to her from her infancy. But for the first time, sitting on the bed in a small hotel room in Richmond, Deborah Steele met God! The sense of His presence filled the room, and she grew weak as the peace of the Almighty filled her. She sat there for a long time, her spirit open. She could never fully express to anyone what that time meant to her, but as she sat there, she finally knew what to do. And as the answer came, she lifted her hands and began to praise God.

She had sung songs of praise often, but this time it was different. There was nothing of ritual as she prayed, no set phrases or stilted speech. Instead, joy and thanksgiving seemed to flow from her lips without effort, like a spring bubbling over. She didn't understand what had happened to her, nor did she understand the words that flowed from her lips with such ease, but when finally she rose from the bed, she knew that life for her would never be the same.

Slowly she dressed, her mind still and a smile of wonder on her face. She picked up her umbrella and left the room. She moved confidently out of the hotel, went to a store down the street, made several purchases, then returned to her room. It was growing dark — too late for her to do anything more that day — so she left her purchases, went to the dining room, ate a good supper, then sat at her table alone, thinking of the morning to come.

Finally she rose, paid her bill, and returned to her room. She undressed, put on a gown, and climbed into bed. Then as she lay there, a stab of fear came, followed by the thought, *What if I've made all this up? What if I lose this peace?*

But she rejected that thought and began

406

to pray. It was the same as before, and as she praised the name of her God, she realized that the Comforter had come — and that He would never go away!

"But we ain't got no more beds!"

Matron Agnes Huger lifted a pair of gunmetal gray eyes to the orderly who stood in front of her desk. The matron was a woman of thirty-five and stood only five inches over five feet tall, but she held herself so erect that she seemed taller. She had come to Chimborazo Hospital with a letter from Jefferson Davis, which had said, "Mrs. Agnes Huger will be in charge of Unit B. Medical personnel will give her full cooperation."

The physicians in charge of the overflowing hospital had resented her, and the orderlies had hated her. Since the battle, chaos had reigned in the hospital, and Mrs. Huger had done a strange thing: She had given the wounded men first priority, regardless of which uniform they wore. She started out by announcing that the distribution of all whiskey in the ward would come under her control. The surgeons and orderlies, both of whom had been imbibing freely of this commodity, raised a howl of protest. When Chief Surgeon Monroe Baskins had come raging into her office threatening to have her put out of the hospital, Mrs. Huger had listened to him rave, then asked, "Are you certain you want to offend President Davis, Dr. Baskins? Well, I'm certain he can find a place for a fine surgeon like you on the front line of battle, perhaps with General Jackson's regiment."

That had been the end of the revolt, and Matron Huger had ruled her ward firmly. Now she stared at Jesse Branch, the chief orderly, as he argued, "Ma'am, we jist ain't got no more room! Whut we ort to do is move them Bluebellies outside and let our boys have their beds!"

The hospital, a converted two-story factory, housed two hundred fifty Confederate soldiers on the first floor, while on the second floor, fifty of the wounded Federal soldiers were cared for.

"That'll be enough, Jesse," Matron Huger said sharply. "I'll have more cots brought in at once." Her eyes pinned him where he stood as she added, "The night cans in Ward B were not emptied this morning. Would you take care of that at once?"

Branch, a skinny man of thirty-five with a scraggly beard, nodded quickly. "I'll see to it, Matron." He had been insolent to Mrs. Huger when she first came, but when she mentioned that he was the proper age for enlisting in the army, he had suddenly become quite cooperative. Now he said, "Well, we got to have some more help, ma'am, especially with the Yankees. Most of the ladies who come to help won't have nothin' to do with them."

"I'll see what can be done." The matron dismissed the orderly abruptly and rose to go to the medicine chest. She was making a list of the contents, worrying over the scarcity of drugs, when a knock sounded.

"Yes?" she called, and Jesse Branch stuck his head inside.

"Old woman out here, Matron. Says she wants to help."

"Send her in, orderly." Closing the chest door and locking it with a brass key from the small bunch that hung around her waist, Mrs. Huger moved across the room to her desk. Any volunteers were welcome, for there were few funds to pay for help. The women of Richmond had volunteered eagerly enough for a few days after the battle, but time had put a stop to that. People got excited for a time when tragedy struck, but emptying bedpans or changing the dressing on raw stumps quickly dispelled most of the "glamour" of the work in a hospital.

A woman entered, and the matron allowed

a quick flash of disappointment to show in the pressure of her lips. She had been half hoping that the woman would be intelligent enough to carry some responsibility, but that did not seem to be the case. "Good morning. I'm Matron Huger," she said politely. "How may I help you?"

The woman who entered was not young, and she certainly did not look as though she had enough intelligence to do anything difficult. She was wearing a shapeless cotton dress, which was faded from countless washings and not particularly clean. A pair of rough man's brogans made a clumping on the floor as she walked, and her dirty hand held tightly to a burlap feed sack.

Lord knows how we'd ever get those nails clean enough to change a dressing, the matron thought. Brown stains spotted the front of the woman's dress — the residue of the snuff that made a pouch of the lower lip. A gum twig was stuck in the middle of the woman's mouth, and she shifted it enough to say in mushy tones, "Howdee. I come to hep with the sodjers."

"That's very good of you," Matron Huger said, nodding. "What's your name?"

A dry cackle escaped from the snuff-stained lips. "I'm Jemima," she said. Her face was difficult to see, for she wore a limp bonnet with a large hood pulled down over her eyes. She nodded vigorously, causing an iron gray lock of dirty hair to drop over her forehead. Shoving it back with a dirty forefinger, she added, "Everybody call me Jemmy."

I don't suppose she needs clean hands to empty bedpans, Matron Huger thought, and she said, "We can use help, Jemmy, but it's hard, dirty work, you understand?"

Jemmy looked around and, finding no spittoon, walked to the window and sent an amber stream onto the yellow roses outside. "Wal, missus, I ain't had nothin' but that since I wuz a younker," she said, moving back from the window in a strange sidling motion. "I reckon I better tell you, missus, I got a boy on t'other side."

"A Union soldier?"

"Aye, missus. Went off to fight with the Yankees." Jemmy nodded sadly, and her eyes seemed strangely bright to Matron Huger but were mostly hidden beneath the brim of the bonnet. "I got to thinkin' mebbe I ort to hep some of them Yankee fellers who got here. One of 'em might have heered of my Lonnie. He's the onliest chile I got left. Cholera took the rest of 'em."

Quickly Matron Huger seized the opportunity, saying, "We need help with the cleaning. Could you come in and help with that?"

"Yes, missus. I got me a job washing dishes at a big hotel, but I can come in when I ain't workin' at that."

"That's fine, Jemmy. Now let me fill out a form for you — or can you write?"

"No, missus."

"Well, I'll do it for you, Jemmy." Quickly she filled out the basics, then wrote something on a slip of paper. "This is your pass to get into the building, Jemmy. Just give it to the guard each time you come. Don't lose it. Now when do you want to start?"

"Now as good a time as any, missus."

"Good! Come along — and you should call me Matron, Jemmy."

The two of them left the office, Jemmy following the matron with her strange gait. "Are you crippled, Jemmy?" the matron inquired.

"Oh no, Matron! Got my foot gnawed by a hog when I wuz a creeper, but it don't hurt none."

The matron led the woman through a large open room filled with beds, all occupied by wounded men. There was a fetid odor, but not as bad as it had been when Matron Huger had arrived. "These are Southern men," she explained.

When they passed out of that room, there was a hallway crossing at right angles, and a guard with a musket sat in a chair beside a stairway. "Private, this is Jemmy. She'll be coming every day to help. Her pass will be checked at the front gate, but you check it, as well."

"Yes, ma'am, I'll do that."

The old woman had some difficulty climbing the stairs, Matron Huger noted, but when they reached the top, she did not seem out of breath. Another door opened off the end of a short hall, and when the two stepped inside, Jemmy looked around at the ward. It was one large room with a sloping ceiling, the bare rafters showing and dormer windows on one side admitting light and air. The cots, most of them occupied, were arranged in rows. "We have fifty-two men in this ward," the Matron said and nodded to a short woman dressed in white. "Mrs. Keller, this is Jemmy. She's going to help with the cleaning in your ward."

Mrs. Keller was a woman of fifty, and her small black eyes lit up at Matron Huger's words. "Well, thank God! We need all the help we can get." She peered at Jemmy over her steel-rimmed spectacles and looked doubtful, but only added, "I'm glad to have you, Jemmy. These poor boys need a lot of care. When will you start?"

"Oh, I'm ready now, missus!"

In a short time Jemmy was moving down between the lines of cots, mopping with an unexpected vigor. The two women watched her from the far side of the room, and Matron Huger shook her head. "I wish I could get you more nursing help, Mrs. Keller. I'll try."

"Well, if Jemmy can mop the floor and empty bedpans, maybe take water to the men, it'll free me for other things."

Matron Huger smiled with a gentleness that usually remained hidden. "Molly, I don't know what I'd do without you! You're the only one who's been faithful to stay with these men." Then she looked at Jemmy, who was chatting with a soldier who had lost an arm and had a bandage around his head. "She looks dreadful, doesn't she? Try to get her cleaned up. She's a country woman. I expect she's done a little primitive nursing. Maybe you can teach her to change bandages."

"I'll scrub her down myself, Matron!" Mrs. Keller exclaimed. The matron left, and Mrs. Keller kept an eye on the new volunteer for an hour. She was pleased to note that the woman did a good job on the floors, changing the water frequently, and also that she spoke to many of the men. When the job was finished, Jemmy came to ask, "Whut now, missus?"

"Call me Mrs. Keller, Jemmy. My, you did a good job on those floors!" She praised the woman carefully, then said, "Would you see that each man has fresh water? Here's the water barrel. Just fill this pitcher and fill each man's glass." She hesitated, then said carefully, "Maybe you'd like to wash your hands first. We keep a basin and soap for ourselves back in my office." She led Jemmy to the small room, which served as the supply room, as well.

Mrs. Keller watched as Jemmy washed, wanting to say something about the snuff but not daring to do so. *I'll work on it,* she thought as Jemmy took a pitcher and moved down the lines of cots. *Can't afford to offend her. She looks rough, but I don't think the boys will mind.* Mrs. Keller was a motherly woman who thought of the soldiers as boys, as in fact many of them were. She had never had children of her own, and the hospital ward had become an outlet for the very real mothering instinct that ran in her.

All morning she kept an eye on her new helper, and at noon, she said to Matron Huger, "Jemmy's going to be a great help. She's not feeble at all. These hill women are often deceptive. Some of them work until they're ninety. I know the hospital can't afford to pay her, but I'd like to give her a little something."

"A new dress or a good used one would help. Let's see if we can make her look a little less haglike."

But though they tried, Jemmy was firm in her refusal of new clothing. "I reckon these will do," she'd said so firmly that Mrs. Keller dared not insist. She had not, however, objected to soap and water, so that afternoon she got a basic lesson in changing bandages — and had been exceptionally deft at the business.

Mrs. Keller's gratitude was boundless, and she said, "Jemmy, you're an angel!"

Jemmy cackled and wiggled the gum snuff stick wickedly. "Never knowed no angels to dip snuff," she said. "Ain't no wings sproutin', neither."

By midafternoon, the work was so far ahead of schedule that Mrs. Keller asked, "Jemmy, would you give the boys fresh water? Then you should go home. I don't want to wear you out on your first day."

"Yes, missus." Jemmy filled the pitcher and made her way around the room. One of the soldiers, who had both legs amputated at the knee, looked at her out of a pair of hopeless black eyes. Jemmy poured his water, then said, "Now looky at this! You ain't et yore chicken!"

"Not hungry."

Jemmy picked up the chicken and thrust it at the young man. "I get ferlin' mad when I see food go to waste! Now you eat that, or I'll take a switch to you!"

Several of the men who were listening laughed, and a tall fellow in the next bed said, "Better eat it, Ned! You'd be shamed forever if it got back home about how you got a switching in the hospital."

The one named Ned glared at him but grabbed the piece of chicken and began gnawing at it.

"There's a good feller!" Jemmy said with a nod. She moved along, then refilled the pitcher and moved down the line of cots directly under the windows. "Well, you done woke up, I see." She stopped to fill the glass, then asked, "Whut's yore name, sodjer?"

"Noel."

"Noel? Now that's a right purty name." Jemmy picked up the glass and said, "Kin you set up and take a drink?"

Noel looked up at the woman, confused. "Who are you? I never saw you before."

"I'm Jemmy. Come to hep you Yankee fellers git well. Now lemme hep you set up.

You got a bad belly?"

"My — side!" Noel gasped, the pain shooting through him as he tried to sit up. "Had a bullet in me. . . . Doctor took it out, but —" He fell back, sweat on his forehead. "Can't do it."

"Wal, it don't matter." Jemmy moved across the room, pulled a chair beside the bed, and sat down. Picking up the water and a spoon from the table, she filled the spoon, then placed it on Noel's lips. He took the water thirstily, but after she had repeated the act several times, he said, "I'm taking too long."

"I ain't in no hurry," Jemmy said placidly.

She ladled the water carefully until he said, "That's fine. It was so good!"

"Water the best thing to drink they is." Jemmy nodded. She filled the glass again but did not rise. Her back was to the window, so all Noel could see was the outline of her face. When she didn't move, he felt uncomfortable, feeling that she was studying him. "I — I guess you must feel funny, taking care of an enemy soldier, don't you?"

"Not got much feelings about it, young feller. A sick man ain't a Yankee nor a Rebel, I don't reckon. Jus' a man." Suddenly she rose, went to the end of the room, then came back with a basin of water and a cloth. She dipped the cloth into the water, wrung it out, then began bathing Noel's face.

He lay there quietly — the cool water was the most delightful thing he'd ever felt. He'd had a fever for days, and his face seemed stretched tight. Now the coolness of the water seemed to soak into his body, and he dropped off to sleep. When he awoke, he looked around, finding Pat watching him. Pat's arm was in a sling, but he was able to sit up and even walk around. "Got yourself a nurse, didn't you?" He grinned.

Noel nodded. "I thought I dreamed it."

"She's a nice old lady." Pat nodded. "Dirty as a pig, but it'll be good to have somebody who cares in this place."

Deborah entered her room in the run-down boardinghouse, sighing wearily. She had left the hotel, taking the cheapest room she could find. She knew that if she went into a respectable hotel in her disguise, she'd become conspicuous. So she'd found a room that was just one step above staying on the streets, where nobody would notice her as she came in. All she would have to do was keep still and pay her rent.

She removed the shapeless dress and washed her mouth out, but she could not get rid of the terrible taste of snuff. *I think Jemmy's going to decide to give up snuff,* she thought, smiling grimly. She examined her hair, pleased to find that the dye had not run. Then she washed as well as she could, thinking of how her plan had gone. She had played an old crone once in a school play and now found she remembered the skill well.

Getting into bed, she pondered her plan, which was nothing less than to get Noel and Pat out of the hospital and back to the North. Ordinarily she would have been up all night worrying about it, but tonight she simply began praising God for who He was rather than for what He was going to do for her. As before, the Comforter was there, and the presence of Jesus was more real than she could ever have dreamed. The praises came to her lips freely, and she went to sleep with them in her heart.

CHAPTER 19
DEBORAH MAKES A CALL

When August came to scorch Richmond, the city was still tingling with the thrill of the victory at Manassas. For Dent Rocklin, however, as he lay on his cot in the hospital, there was nothing to cheer his spirit. His face was still puffed and swollen from the rough stitching at the field hospital; it was not healing as well as it should. Dr. Baskins had followed the customary practice of the day in keeping it bandaged. The dressing was changed, but on Thursday when he came by and examined Dent, he was not happy.

"Some infection in the face wound," he said, peering closely at Dent's cheek. "We'll keep the bandages on for another week or so." Then he unwound the bandages from Dent's arm, and when he had finished his examination, he shook his head. "Lieutenant, you've got to be reasonable. The cut destroyed too many muscles and ligaments.

Even if we got this infection cured — which I don't think is possible — you'd never have the use of your hand."

"No amputation." Dent lay back, his eyes bright with fever. He had gone over this with Baskins often, and there was an adamant set to his face as he lay there. "Either I'll have two arms or I'll be dead."

Baskins stared at him helplessly. He was a heavy drinker, and the veins on his nose were inflamed. However, he was a good doctor and had talked with both Dent's father and his grandfather, urging them to convince the patient that he must have the arm amputated. Neither of them had been of any help, and now he slapped his thigh angrily. "You Rocklins are as stubborn as mules! Well, I can't force you to be sensible. But I'm washing my hands of you!"

As the doctor moved away, muttering to himself about fools, Matron Huger came to replace the bandage on Dent's arm. She bound the wrapping expertly, then stood looking down at him. "The doctor is right, Lieutenant. Your arm is lost. I wish you'd reconsider." Her gray eyes could be hard as agates, but now they were soft. She tried to be objective, to keep herself at a distance from the men — it hurt too much when they died. But for some reason, she had let her emotions get in the way of her head where Dent Rocklin was concerned.

His eyes were sunk back in his head, and his lips were cracked, the result of the fever brought on by the infection of his wounds. His eyes were bright with fever, and there was a smoky anger in them, too. "If I don't make it, you'll have an extra bed for some fellow who can be of some use."

Matron Huger started to protest, but there was such a rebellious set to his lips that she knew persuasion was fruitless. "We've got some fish today. Try to eat all you can."

He said nothing and dropped off into a restless sleep. All afternoon he tossed on his cot, the pain from his arm not allowing him to sleep soundly. Finally he heard the clatter of dishes and opened his eyes, aware that the evening meal was being served. He had a raging thirst and struggled into a sitting position, then threw the cover back and sat up on the cot. His head reeled and he swayed uncertainly, closing his eyes until the weakness passed.

Four orderlies were moving down the rows serving the men, and the room was filled with the hum of talk. The cot next to Dent was empty, the captain from Tennessee having died the previous day. The man had been in a coma since being brought in and had died without ever speaking another word. The officer on Dent's right, a cheerful second lieutenant from the tidewater, glanced at Dent but continued to speak with the man across the aisle from him. His name was Simon Alcott, and he had tried to be friendly with Dent. But after getting practically no response, he had given up.

The smell of fish came to Dent, along with the sharp tang of fresh coffee. He sat there with his head bowed, staring at his wounded arm, so lost in thought that he started slightly when a voice said, "Here now, young feller." He glanced upward and was surprised at the sight of the old woman who stood there with a tin plate and a cup of steaming coffee. "Looky here, now," she said in a nasal voice, "nice catfish today."

"Not hungry."

"Why, 'course you air hungry! Now you jist set thar, and ol' Jemmy will cut this heah fish up." She put the tray down on the table and thrust the mug toward him. "You kin sip on that whilst I fix the fish."

Dent took the cup, sipped at it cautiously, then considered the woman. "You new? Never saw you before."

"Fust time in heah." Jemmy nodded as she broke the large chunk of fish apart with a fork. "I been takin' care of them Yankee fellers upstairs." The brim of a large sun-bonnet shaded her upper face, and several strands of iron gray hair slipped out from the edges. Finally she got the fish cut to her satisfaction and nodded firmly. "Now you git on the outside of this, young feller. Whut's yore name?"

"Rocklin. I don't want any fish. Just the coffee."

"Why, thet won't do! How you gonna git well if you don't eat? Now looky here, you jist hang on to that mug, and I'll shovel some o' this fish down yore gullet — there!"

Dent opened his mouth to object, but the woman pushed a morsel of the white flaky fish into it deftly, and he could only chew it. "Now thet's a good feller!" Jemmy nodded. "I fed my younguns like this, don't you see? Now you wash thet down with some cawfee, Mis' Rocker."

Dent sat there chewing slowly, finding his hunger rising, and finally he smiled at the old woman. "All right, you win. Just leave the plate. I'll promise to eat it."

"See you do!" The old woman nodded, then moved away to feed others. When she came back thirty minutes later, she looked at his plate and gave a high-pitched cackle of a laugh. "See, Colonel Rocker, you wuz plum hongry. Now you jist set. . . ." She moved away with a curious sideways gait and soon was back with a small bowl and a fresh cup of coffee. "Got some nice cherry cobbler," she announced and then hesitated. "I better hep you with this," she announced and, holding the cobbler in one hand, took a dollop on the spoon and pushed it toward him. "Now don't argify with me! Open yer mouth!"

Dent had eaten little up until now, but his fever seemed to be down, and the sharp smell of the cherries made his mouth water. He got back onto the cot, his back against the wall, and sat there munching the succulent berries. The old woman chattered on, ladling the dessert into his mouth from time to time, and he listened as she told about the parade she'd seen the previous afternoon.

Finally she put the spoon and saucer down and stared at him. "Lemme git a rag and wipe yore face, Major Rocker." She was gone, then was back with a damp cloth. Carefully she wiped his mouth, then his unbandaged cheek. "That's a pretty bad wound, ain't it? But I reckon the good Lord will git you all healed up."

"Don't talk to me about God!" Dent's mouth drew into a sharp line, and he would say no more. When Jemmy moved away, he was aware of Simon Alcott's eyes fixed on him with displeasure.

"Wouldn't kill you to say thank you to the old woman, Rocklin," he said evenly. "You think you're some kind of special case?"

"Shut up, Alcott!"

"Yeah, I'll shut up," Alcott snapped. "You just lie there feeling sorry for yourself, Lieutenant. Never mind that some fellows have lost both arms and some both eyes. You just lie there like a big baby cryin' because you lost your dolly in the dirt." He rolled over, careful not to damage the bandage on the stump of his right leg, and began speaking to the man next to him.

Jemmy returned to the second floor, meeting Matron Huger, who was just leaving after an inspection. "Matron, thet young feller named Rocklin, he pretty bad, is he?"

Matron Huger was not surprised at the question, for Jemmy seemed to be curious about all the men. Shaking her head, she answered, "His face isn't dangerous, but if he doesn't let them take his arm off, he'll die, Jemmy. Don't say anything to him, though."

"No, ma'am." Jemmy went about her work, saying little. She stopped once to speak to Pat Steele, who was trying to shave with one hand. "You're about to cut your nose off," she observed. "Set down and let me do that."

Steele laughed at her but surrendered the razor. "Don't cut my throat, Jemmy," he said. But she finished the job with a deft touch. "Where'd you learn to give a shave, Jemmy?"

"Used to shave my ol' man," she cackled, then whispered, "I got you and Mr. Noel a surprise. Some fresh cherry cobbler. Some lady brought a batch of it fer the fellers downstairs, but I saved enough of it fer you two. Wisht I had enough fer the hull bunch, but I couldn't make off with thet much. I'll sneak it to you at supper."

"Why, bless your heart, Jemmy!" He smiled and patted her shoulder. "Why are you so partial to Noel and me?"

"Shucks, you two air jist like my own younguns!" Jemmy looked down at Noel, who was asleep. "You take keer of the boy," she said.

Pat's face clouded. "We'll be leaving here soon. Hate to think of going to a prison camp. It'll be pretty bad."

"Better put yore trust in Jesus," Jemmy said and then left him to go down the line of cots.

"Funny old woman," Pat murmured. "Won't be any like her in the camp."

After Deborah left the hospital, she walked the streets of Richmond, thinking of Dent. She came to a park and sat down under a magnolia tree. The rich, heavy perfume of the blossoms filled the air, and pigeons came up to feed, cooing their liquid warble. Those who passed paid little heed to the old woman who seemed to be a little drunk or senile, for she was talking to herself.

There was a girl Dent was seeing — what was her name? Deborah thought, and then it came to her. *Raimey Reed, that's it! And she's a Christian girl, Aunt Susanna said.* A thought took root, growing in her, and she got up and moved down the street so quickly that it caused one man to say in surprise, "She moves fast for an old woman, don't she, now?"

"There's a woman to see you, Miss Raimey. Says her name is Deborah Steele."

Raimey looked up in surprise. The name sounded vaguely familiar, but she couldn't place it. "I don't know anyone by that name, Dulcie. What does she want?"

"Don't know." Dulcie shrugged. She and Raimey had been out in the garden, where Dulcie had been reading a crazy novel called *Tristram Shandy* to her mistress. The slave was glad enough to be interrupted by the sound of the brass knocker on the front door. "She's a mighty nice-looking woman. You want to see her?"

"Why, yes," Raimey said with a nod. "Bring her out here." She listened as Dulcie's footsteps tapped across the walk, then as she spoke to someone. Raimey got to her feet as the guest was brought outside. "I'm sorry to disturb you, Miss Reed. My name is Deborah Steele. Could I speak with you a few moments — alone?"

"Get us some tea, Dulcie," Raimey said. "Won't you sit down, Miss Steele?" She heard the sound of the woman sitting down, then asked, "Have we met before?"

"No, but we have a mutual friend — Dent Rocklin." Deborah was watching the young woman closely and didn't miss a movement of the girl's lips. "I think he's in a bad way, Miss Reed."

"He's in the hospital, isn't he?"

"Yes, with a bad wound. Very bad." She began to speak, watching the girl's face. When she had finished, she said, "I think you should go to him, Miss Reed."

"Me? Why — I couldn't do anything!" Raimey was troubled, for she had thought of little but Dent Rocklin since the news came that he'd been wounded. Once she had mentioned going to visit him, but her mother had said, "It's not a nice place, Raimey. Wait until he's released to his parents' home; then we'll go." It had not satisfied her, and she knew that her parents were overprotective where she was concerned. Now she thought of Dent, of how they had danced, and of his kiss. Then it came to her. "I remember where I've heard of you. Dent's in love with you."

Deborah said quickly, "We were interested in each other once, but I've told him it can never go any further. And it was never as deep an attraction as Dent thought." She paused, then asked, "I know it's rude of me to ask, but — do you care for Dent?"

Raimey flinched slightly, her face coloring. "Why, he was very nice to me. But as you can see, Miss Steele, I'm blind."

Deborah said quietly, "I see that you're a very lovely girl. Being blind doesn't mean you can't love a man, does it?"

"No! It doesn't!" Raimey's voice rose with a trace of anger, and then she stopped. "But nothing can come of it. I could never ask a man to bear my affliction."

Deborah sat there, thoughts rising within, and asked for guidance from God. It was very plain that Raimey Reed was in love with Dent Rocklin, but how could she speak of it without offending the girl? Finally she

431

decided to voice the simple truth. "May I call you Raimey? And you can call me Deborah. I've heard that you're a Christian, Raimey. Do you believe that God speaks to His people?"

"Why — certainly!" Raimey hardly knew what to make of this, but she sat there listening as Deborah told her how God had directed her to come see her.

Deborah carefully concealed any mention of Noel or Pat but said finally, "I think Dent's going to die if he doesn't get help, Raimey. There's a shadow on him. He's given up. I think he wants to die, and somehow I think that you're the one who can save him."

Raimey put her hands to her breast, shaken by what she had heard. But she felt a stirring of anger, too, which caused her to say, "It's very well for you to talk, Deborah Steele! You're beautiful, I've heard, and can have any man you want. And you can see! But it's unkind of you to come to me telling me that God wants me to do something about Dent. Why don't you save him? You're the one he loves, no matter what you say!"

Deborah sat still and, when the storm was past, said gently, "Raimey, all of us are in God's hands. I can't tell you what to do." She hesitated, then rose from her chair, noting that Raimey, catching the sound, rose at the same time. Deborah went to the girl, so innocent in the sunshine, and said, "I don't want to be unkind, but I know you love Dent, and he desperately needs someone who loves him. He won't listen to anyone in his family. But I think he may listen to you. Won't you try?"

Tears rose in Raimey's eyes, and she struggled vainly to speak. Finally she cried out, "I can't! I want to, but I don't know how to help!"

Deborah put her arm around Raimey's shoulders, saying, "I can't tell you how it will be, but I know the first thing you must do. Go to him! Go to Dent, Raimey! And then let God use you. Will you pray with me about that?"

Raimey nodded, and as Deborah prayed, she began to weep. Dulcie returned and stopped dead in her tracks with the tea tray in her hands. She had never heard anyone pray like this lady! There was something odd about it, and Dulcie was glad when she heard the visitor say, "God is with you, Raimey. Trust Him!"

"Yes, Deborah. I will!"

Dulcie stepped forward, saying, "Can I show you to the door, miss?" and Deborah left at once, aware that the maid was glaring at her with disapproval in her eyes.

"Now don't you cry, Miss Raimey!" Dulcie said protectively when she came back. "She's gone now. What was she saying to make you feel so bad? I won't let her in this house again, you can bet!"

"Dulcie," Raimey said in a tone that Dulcie had never heard. "Go get Leroy to bring the carriage around. And get ready yourself."

"Where do you think we're going?" Dulcie asked in alarm. Raimey's parents were both gone for the day, and something in the expression of her mistress frightened her.

"We're going to the hospital." When Dulcie began to protest, Raimey said, "Be quiet, Dulcie. Go to the kitchen and have Evangeline make up a big basket of sweets — everything she can find."

Dulcie blinked, but she turned and left at once. As soon as she was out of hearing distance, she muttered in disgusted tones, " 'Be quiet, Dulcie!' I wish I'd never let that woman in this house!" But complaining was no good, and one hour later she was sitting beside Raimey, headed for the hospital.

Chapter 20
Angel in the Ward

Sometime during the night Dent flung his arm upward, striking the wall. The pain that exploded made him cry out, and he slept no more until about an hour before dawn. When he began again to stir and opened his eyes, he saw that someone was sitting in the chair beside him. He blinked and wiped his eyes with his good hand, then, seeing more clearly, said, "Hello, Mother."

Ellen Rocklin, looking totally out of place in a bright green dress and too much makeup, started guiltily, then exclaimed, "Why, you're awake! I thought I'd better let you sleep, Denton." The light of early morning fell across Dent's face, and with his ragged beard and stained bandage, he was not a pretty sight. Ellen, however, was determined to cheer him up. She said brightly, "Well, look at you! I could just kill your father! Here he's been telling me how awful you look! Why, you look just fine,

Denton!"

"Sure. How've you been, Mother?"

"Oh, just terrible! I've been so worried about you! I wanted to come and see you, but your father wouldn't let me. Well, I just decided to come anyway, Denton!" The truth was that Clay had asked her to visit Dent many times, but she had resisted. Now she felt virtuous, going into her act of the Faithful Mother Visiting Her Wounded Son. Ellen always played a role; she had done so for so long that she no longer had any idea who she really was.

She babbled on, speaking of how wonderful Dent looked and how she was absolutely certain that he'd soon be home where she could take care of him properly. She stayed until breakfast was brought, insisting on waiting on him, putting sugar in his coffee (which he never took), and urging him to eat more.

After breakfast, she settled down, talking about how awful things were in Richmond — "Prices have literally gone out of sight, Denton!"; Gracefield — "Your grandfather, poor thing! I doubt if he'll live a month!"; her husband — "Clay absolutely refuses to give me what I need, Denton. You'll have to speak to him, I'm afraid. I've worn this old rag of a dress for a year or longer, and now with so many social events coming up, I simply must have some new things!"

Dent lay quietly, listening to her talk. She was a silly woman, and nothing would ever change for her. She was, he knew, an immoral woman, as well, though none of the family ever spoke of it. For years Dent had excused all of her flaws by blaming them on his father's act of desertion. Now, lying in the ward with dying men and with his arm throbbing, he suddenly understood that Ellen Rocklin had not been formed by his father's behavior. She was what she was, and the knowledge sank into him that nothing he could do — or that anyone could do — would bring sense and decency to his mother.

Ellen was talking about the party she had attended at the home of the Chesnuts when she was interrupted. " 'Scuse me, missus. I need to change this feller's bandages."

Ellen turned sharply to see an old woman in a shapeless dress standing at the foot of the bed, holding a tray with bandages and medicine. "Why — of course!"

She rose and made room for the old woman, wondering why they didn't get more attractive people to take care of the men. She had a sudden vision of herself, dressed in a beautiful white uniform, moving through the hospital, bringing cheer to the boys. She saw herself saying to President Davis, "Why, it's very hard, Mr. President, but we must all do our best for our glorious cause!" The thought pleased her, but she did not watch as the woman carefully removed the bandage that covered the side of Dent's face.

When the bandage was gone, Ellen did look. The sight of her son's ravaged face shocked her so badly that she cried out, "Oh no!" and put her hands over her face. Then she turned away, putting her back to the two. She didn't see the looks of disgust on the faces of the men close by . . . nor did she see the look on her son's face.

Jemmy saw it though — and wanted to cry. Dent sat there staring at his mother; then he suddenly turned to Simon Alcott. "Give me your shaving mirror, Alcott."

Alcott said quickly, "I think I let Sim borrow it."

"It's there on the table," Dent growled. "Let me have it, blast you!"

Reluctantly Alcott picked up the small mirror and handed it to Jemmy, who just as unwillingly put it into Dent's hand. He lifted the mirror and stared into it. It was the first time he'd seen the wound — and he sat there staring at his ruined face without a word.

The saber had raked down the side of his face, narrowly missing the eye, then had sliced through the flesh down to the cheekbone. The solid bone had turned the blade, forcing it forward so that it had narrowly missed cutting into the side of his mouth. Dr. Carter had done his best. He had pulled the flesh together as tightly as he could and put the stitches as close together as he could, but the damage was too great for his surgery to be more than a rough patch-up job.

Staring into the mirror, Dent saw a stranger, a gargoyle of a man. The eye was pulled downward at the outside edge, giving the face a sinister appearance, while the side of the mouth was pulled to the left, making it appear that a leer was fixed in place. The lips of the terrible wound were pulled together in some fashion, but the cheek was so distorted that the face staring back at him seemed to be the face of a monster.

He slowly handed the mirror back to Jemmy, saying, "Thanks for the mirror, Alcott."

A thick silence had fallen on them all, and it was Alcott who said, "Aw, it looks a little rough now, but when it heals, it'll be okay, Dent."

"It'll be worse," Dent said quietly. His voice was dead, and so were his eyes. He lay there staring at the ceiling as Jemmy finished putting on a fresh bandage, then moved away.

Ellen was trembling and tried to speak, but she could only say in a muffled tone, "I–I'll have to go now, Denton."

"Thanks for coming by, Mother."

She moved toward him as though to kiss him, then whirled and walked out of the room. Dent waited until she was gone, then looked at Alcott, saying evenly, "A mother's love is a wonderful thing, isn't it, Simon?"

"Aw, come on, Dent — !" But Alcott said no more, for Dent Rocklin had put up some sort of fence around himself, even higher and more impregnable than the one he'd already built.

Raimey could sense the reluctance in Matron Agnes Huger and didn't wonder at it. She had come prepared to force her way into the hospital and had started at the beginning of the interview by saying, "You won't agree with what I want to do, Mrs. Huger, but I'm a very stubborn young woman. I want to come every day and help

the men." Raimey had developed an uncanny discernment and knew at that instant
that the matron was searching for a way to
refuse her. "My father is Samuel Reed, Mrs.
Huger. He's a very important man. In fact,
he's a personal friend of President Davis."

Agnes Huger let a smile touch her lips.
"So am I, Miss Reed."

Raimey stopped, thought for a brief moment, then said simply, "Then I can't
threaten you with the president, can I?"

"I'm afraid not."

Raimey said quietly, "Please, Mrs. Huger,
let me do this thing. I want to help so much.
I'll do anything at all."

The matron was touched by the gentleness of the girl. "We need help, of course,
Miss Reed, but I don't see how —"

"I thought of it before I came. The men
must get lonely. Isn't that so? Well, I can
talk, Mrs. Huger — my father says I talk
too much! — and don't some of them need
to write letters?"

"Can you do that, Miss Reed, write letters?"

"My maid Dulcie can! She's an excellent
writer, so she could take the letters down,
and I could talk." Raimey leaned forward
and said, "There isn't much I can do. Please
let me do this."

The matron made up her mind. "We'll be glad to have you, Miss Reed. When would you like to begin?"

"Now! We've brought an absolutely huge basket of cakes and pies for the men."

Her face glowed, and Matron Huger felt a pang of sorrow for the girl but said only, "They'll love that. Now let me make out passes for yourself and your servant; then I'll show you around."

Thirty minutes later Matron Huger had led the two women into the ward and was saying, "Gentlemen, this is Miss Raimey Reed and her servant Dulcie. Miss Reed wasn't certain that any of you liked cake, so you'll have to let her know if you do." She waited until the calls came from all over the room, then nodded. "If any of you need a letter written, Miss Reed's maid will be happy to write it for you. Now behave yourselves." She turned to Raimey a little uncertainly. "Would you like for me to take you around, Miss Reed?"

"Oh no," Raimey said quickly. "Dulcie and I will do very well, Matron." When the matron left, she said, "Tell me about the room, Dulcie."

The maid began describing the room, knowing exactly how to present the details. "There's five rows of beds with aisles between them —" She rattled off the details, then said, "Where you want to start?"

"At the first row of beds." She followed Dulcie as she usually did, almost by instinct, and when the maid stopped, she said, "Hello, would you like some cake?"

"Yes, miss." The soldier was smiling and added, "Sure is nice of you . . . to do this."

The break in his words had come when he had discovered she was blind, Raimey knew, but she gave no sign. "How about chocolate?"

"It's my favorite, ma'am," the soldier said.

"Let me have the basket, Dulcie. You go find somebody who wants a letter written."

Even as she spoke, a voice to her left said, "Right here, I reckon," and Dulcie moved to his side, saying, "You just tell me who it's to and what to write."

The man began dictating a letter, and Raimey opened the lid of the basket, picking out the chocolate cake. Expertly she lifted the cover, then asked, "Is there a table here?"

"Yes, miss, right here by the bed." The soldier watched, fascinated, as Raimey moved to the table, put the cake down, then sliced a piece off. As she handed it to the soldier, she asked him, "What's your name?"

"Lieutenant Hankins. I'm from Arkansas."

Hankins took the cake and began to eat it. He found himself telling her about his farm — and his new bride — that he'd had to leave behind. He was lonesome and finally said, "I don't know about goin' home. I mean — well, when I left Irene I had two arms, and now I've only got one."

At once Raimey knew he was worried about how his new wife would take his injury. "Your wife will be so glad to have you back." She smiled, then began to encourage him. Finally she put her hand out, and he took it. "God bless you, Lieutenant. I'll pray that you'll soon be back on your farm with Irene."

She moved to the next bed, saying, "Hello? Do you want pie or cake?" The soldier, a tall, thin young fellow with both feet heavily bandaged, said shyly, "Pie, please." Soon Raimey had heard about his injury and knew his parents' names and promised that Dulcie would write to them for him.

After the first awkwardness, Raimey found it easy. *They're all like hurt little boys,* she thought as she moved down the line. Most of them were young and away from home for the first time, and though they would die before admitting it, they were afraid. There was an eagerness in the voices of most of them, and Raimey made slow progress. When she got to the last bed, Matron Huger approached and said, "Well, Miss Reed, you've made some of our men very happy. But you're about out of cake, I see."

"I'll bring more tomorrow," Raimey promised. She moved from the bed of the man in the last bunk, saying, "I'll bring a copy of that book tomorrow. Maybe you'll read some of it to me."

"I'll do that, Miss Reed," the soldier replied, nodding, and the matron saw his eyes follow the blind girl as she moved away.

"You did fine. Tomorrow you'll remember some of them, I'm sure."

Raimey smiled. "Give me the number of one of the beds, Matron."

"Why — number sixteen."

"That's Charlie Linkous. He's from Winchester. He's got a pretty serious wound in his thigh, but he's not going to lose the leg."

Matron Huger stopped dead still. "Can you name all the men like that, Miss Reed?"

"Yes. I have a very good memory." She changed the subject suddenly. "Mrs. Huger, is Denton Rocklin in this ward?"

"Why, yes. Are you acquainted with him?"

"Oh yes. Could I speak to him before we leave?"

"Right over here." The matron had observed that Raimey hated to be taken by the arm, so she tactfully moved closer, and the girl's hand went at once to her arm. She led the way to one end of the cots under the windows and then paused. "Here's a friend of yours, Lieutenant Rocklin."

"How are you, Dent?" Raimey asked uncertainly. He did not speak, but the matron said, "Take this chair while you visit, Miss Reed. I'll leave you now."

Raimey felt the chair, then sat down with her back stiff. Now that she was here, it all seemed crazy. Maybe he wouldn't even want to see her. She heard a slight sound, bed-covers rustling; then his voice came — "Hello, Raimey." He grunted with pain as he came to a sitting position, then added, "Nice of you to come."

His voice was different, she decided at once. He'd always had such excitement in his voice, and now that was all gone. *Deborah was right! He's lost all his hope.*

"It's very bad, the pain?"

"No worse than lots of others."

She hardly knew what to say, so heavy was the impression she got from him. "I have a little cake left, if you'd like some."

"No thanks, but you might give it to Simon. He's got a sweet tooth —" Then he realized she could not see his gesture toward

Alcott. "Just leave it here, Raimey. I'll give it to him."

She put the cake down, then suddenly held out her hand on an impulse. She felt his hand close around hers and said quietly, "I'm so sorry, Dent."

He looked at her closely. Her skin was so fine it was almost translucent, and her lips were soft and vulnerable, almost maternal. He was still filled with bitterness over his mother's reaction, but now as she sat there quietly, her hand resting in his trustfully, he knew that she was grieving over him. He held her hand, marveling at the fragile bones, the softness of it, then released it. "It happens in a war, Raimey."

"I know." She sat there quietly, saying nothing. He was glad she didn't overwhelm him with assurances that he was going to be all right, glad that she just sat there. It helped, in some strange way that he couldn't understand. Finally she said, "I've thought so often of how we danced at the ball. I'll never forget it." When he didn't speak, she said, "You can't know, Dent, but you did something for me that nobody has ever done."

"A dance? That wasn't much."

"You made me feel like a woman," Raimey said, so softly that he had to lean forward.

"You danced with me and then you — kissed me. It made me feel like a woman for the first time. Thank you for that, Dent."

He didn't know what to say. It had been such a small thing to him, but he saw now that it had been very important to her. "I've thought of it, too, Raimey. Just before we went in after the Yankees, I thought of that night out on the balcony with you." He let a smile come to him, thinking of it. "It was sure funny. The bullets were flying, and the shells were bursting — and there I was thinking about that night with you on the balcony. Sure was funny."

They sat there, each thinking their own thoughts; then Raimey said, "I'll be back tomorrow. Can I bring you something?"

"A new arm — and a new face," he said, and the moment was broken. "Good-bye, Raimey," he said and turned his face to the wall.

It took Raimey only four days to learn the names of every man in the ward, and the men could talk of little else. "Why, she knows who a fellow is as soon as he opens his mouth!" a short captain from Georgia said, marveling. "Never saw anything like it!"

Boredom was one of the worst aspects of confinement. There was nothing to do except talk, and that grew stale. But as Raimey came, day after day, she always had something for the men to do. On her second day, she brought four checkerboards and astounded the officers by winning a game against Simon Alcott. He was a good player and was prepared to let her win, but found himself badly beaten. He had taken a lot of ribbing about the loss but proved himself one of the best players. Raimey organized a checker tournament, and the finals had the men making so much noise that Matron had to come in to see what was happening and quiet the group down. Then she saw Raimey's small form in the center of a group of the walking wounded, and all the men cheering lustily, and she changed her mind and went back to her office, a smile on her lips.

Still, though Raimey was a success with most of the other men, Dent remained taciturn. Raimey tried everything, but nothing worked. Finally, one day she was sitting with Dent, both of them silent, when she heard the voice of Jemmy saying, "Now, Major Rocker, the doctor says you gotta be shaved."

"What for?" Dent asked roughly. "I'm not going anywhere."

Jemmy said, "Them whiskers gotta come

off. Now you set there and I'll rake 'em off."

"Blasted foolishness!"

"Never mind all that fussin'," Jemmy said. "Sit up thar and lemme do something 'bout them whiskers." Dent had seen her shave Buck Libby, who had lost both hands, and Libby had testified that the old woman had good hands. He sighed and moved to the chair.

She worked up a lather, then carefully pulled the bandage away from the wounded cheek. "I'll do this hurt side fust," she announced and, moving carefully around the stitches, shaved that side of Dent's face. A thought came to her, and she said, "You ever do any barbering, missus?"

"Me?" Raimey asked in a startled tone, then smiled. "Why, no, except for cutting my sister's hair. I've done that often enough."

"Wal, you ain't too old to learn," Jemmy announced. "Come here and I'll show you how. Major Rocker, here, he'll be a good one to practice on."

Dent suddenly laughed for the first time in days. "Jemmy means, I think, if you slice my right cheek, it'll be a match for the left one." He saw that Raimey was tempted by the idea and urged her on. "Have a try, Raimey. You can't do any damage."

Raimey hesitated; then she had a thought that made her cheek flush. *If I could just touch him, maybe somehow he'd know how I feel! Maybe he wouldn't be so far away.*

"Show me, Jemmy!" she said, moving to where Dent was sitting.

"Ain't nothing to it," Jemmy said. "You jist use yore fingers 'sted of yore eyes. Here, the razor — hold it like that. Now gimme yore hand. . . ."

Dent found the sight of Raimey standing there with a straight razor in her hands amusing. He sat very still as her fingers cautiously moved across his face, tracing his cheek and jawline. Jemmy stood there instructing her, and at first Raimey was frightened. But after she moved the razor down Dent's cheek, Jemmy said, "See thar! I tole you hit wasn't nothin' to barbering. Now the hard part is the lip, so you jist hold his nose with one hand to keep from slicin' it off —"

When the job was done, Jemmy said, "Feel how smooth his cheek is, jist like a baby's bottom, ain't it now?"

Dent felt the featherlight touch of Raimey's hand and was stirred by an old memory. "You did that once before, remember?" he said, his voice soft.

"I remember."

Dent said, "The other side's changed a lot."

Jemmy said, "It's a bit harder, dodgin' all them stitches. But I'm givin' this job to you, missus. I got plenty of Yankee boys upstairs to barber. Now looky here, gimme yore hand —"

Dent stiffened as he felt Raimey's fingers trace the scar on his cheek. He wanted to pull away, to shout angrily for her to leave him alone, but there was something in her touch that kept him still. Then the hand was gone, and Raimey said, "I'll do the best I can, Jemmy. Will you show me how to put the bandage back on? Then let me have some scissors and I'll cut his hair."

Jemmy showed the girl how to apply the bandage, then produced a pair of shears. Soon Raimey was working skillfully on Dent's shaggy hair. "I'm a little better at this," she said, smoothing his black hair and shaping it carefully. She had found that she could cut hair well. "Cutting your hair is easy," she commented. "You've got such a well-shaped head."

Finally she was satisfied. She ran her hand over his hair, saying, "How much do you usually pay to get your hair cut, Dent?"

"A quarter."

"You owe me, then," Raimey said. She

stood before him, a smile on her lips, pleased and excited that she had done something for him. "I'll bring one of my father's razors tomorrow. He has one for every day, with the day of the week on the handle."

"Get the one marked Friday," Dent said. He rubbed his cheek, saying, "Feels good. I always hated not shaving."

"I'll shave you every day. You'll owe me a lot of money after a week or so."

Dent's mood shifted suddenly, and she noticed it. He said nothing, so she asked quietly, "You just thought you might not be here in a week, didn't you?"

He stared at her, shocked that she should know his thoughts. "Don't think I like you knowing me so well — but yes, it did occur to me."

"Would it be so bad, Dent? Losing your arm?"

"Raimey, I can't say how I feel to you, not about that. I mean, you've lost so much more! But somehow I can't face it. I know there are men here who'd be happy to change places with me, but it's just the way I am. I'd get by, but it's not worth it. Besides —"

He cut his words off and then laughed.

"You know what I was going to say, don't you?"

"I think you were going to say something about being scarred."

He made a grimace, then said, "It's women who are supposed to be vain. But my own mother couldn't stand to look at me. I can't stand the thought of people recoiling from the sight of my face, Raimey."

He waited for her to argue, but she did no such thing. "I know, Dent. Do you think I haven't thought of ending it all?" His face registered shock, and she sensed it. "But God's given me some good things. And you have so much to give, Dent."

"It's — too hard for me, Raimey!"

She seemed to be listening to something far off. She finally whispered, "I believe God is going to give you your arm, Dent."

"I don't believe in miracles, Raimey."

She moved to the foot of his bed, her face composed. "I do," she said firmly and left the room.

Men said, "Good night," and she called each name — "Good night, Bax. Don't forget you promised to write to your cousin Donna."

After Raimey left with Dulcie, Dent struggled to his feet and moved to the window. He watched her get into the car-

454

riage, then kept his eyes on it until it passed from view. Then he turned to go back to his cot. When he sat down, he looked up to find Simon watching him with a peculiar look in his blue eyes.

"You know, Dent," he said conversationally, "you're a pretty stupid fellow."

Dent stared at him but found no anger in the man. "Stupid? I guess so, Simon. In what specific way?"

Alcott shook his head, and there was a vague disgust in his expression. "You're too dumb to understand how you're stupid," he remarked. Then with a shake of his head, he picked up his book and continued to read.

Dent lay down, and his arm began to send daggers of pain that scraped at his nerves. *It's getting worse,* he thought as he turned over, cradling the arm. He tried to sleep but could not. It was three in the morning when he was awakened by Sanders, one of the orderlies. "What are you doing?" Dent gasped.

"You're screamin' so loud you're keeping the men awake. This is just some morphine to help you make it."

Dent tried to protest but could not. The drug took effect quickly, but he knew that he'd come to the end of something. He'd never before let them give him drugs, but now he'd stepped over some sort of line. He had hoped to die, but somehow as he drifted into sleep, he resisted that.

As sleep took Dent Rocklin over, Alcott said, "He's had it, hasn't he, Sanders?"

"Gangrene." The orderly uttered that one word, then moved away, fading into the darkness.

CHAPTER 21
DEBORAH FINDS A MAN

"Your father wanted to see you, Clay, but he's been feeling so weak I hated for him to make the trip."

Susanna had met Clay at the front door, kissed him, then led him into the house. "He was taken bad last week but wouldn't let me send for the doctor."

Clay said, "I'll go right up, Mother. I've got two days' leave, so we'll have lots of time to talk." He turned and mounted the large stairway that divided in the middle, took the right section, then walked quickly to the door of his parents' room. When he knocked on the door, his father's voice came at once. Entering the room, Clay found Thomas sitting in a horsehide chair, a letter in his hand.

"Come in, Clay," Thomas said. Letting the letter drop, he put his hand out, and Clay moved to take it. "Glad to see you, son."

"I'd have come earlier, but I couldn't get

leave." Clay was shocked by the fragile touch of his father's hand but allowed nothing to show on his face. *Every time I see him, he's gone down,* Clay thought as he pulled a chair close and sat down. "You've been feeling a mite low, Mother says."

"Getting old, I guess."

"Not so old as all that." As a matter of fact, Thomas was only sixty-one, but he looked older. He had always been a handsome man, far better looking than his brother Stephen, but poor health had drained him of color and stripped away the flesh. There was an almost cadaverous look about him now, his eyes sunken and his lips seamed in the manner of the very old. He had the look in his eyes, Clay saw, of a sick person who is exhausted from fighting pain.

But he was glad to see Clay, and he smiled as he picked up the letter. "I got this letter from Colonel Benton three days ago," he said. "Can you guess what's in it?"

"No, not really. Is it about the regiment?"

"No, it's about you, Clay. Let me read it to you." He began reading, and Clay shifted uneasily as he went on. It was a letter of praise for Clay's action in charging up the hill in the face of intense fire. It ended with, "I think I know how proud you must be of Clay, Thomas. It will please you to know that I have mentioned the matter to General Jackson, with a recommendation for an appropriate decoration. You have a nephew who has been decorated for valor, and now I trust that you will have a son, also."

Thomas lowered the letter, and his lips trembled as he said, "I'm very much afraid I'm going to have to tell you what a good son you are to me, Clay."

Clay's face flushed, and for an instant he could think of no reply. He thought of all the grief and pain he'd brought to his parents, then shook his head. "Others did so much more, Father. And I don't know if I'd have gone up that hill if it hadn't been my own son who was in danger."

Thomas studied him carefully, thinking of how different this man was from the younger Clay Rocklin. "I think you would. You're like your uncle Stephen, Clay. More like him than you are like me, for which I'm thankful!"

Clay said at once, "I'm a Rocklin, sir, like you and Uncle Stephen both." He changed the subject, for he saw again what he had always known, that his father felt inferior to his uncle. The two of them were very different, and Clay didn't want his father to dwell on the matter. "Lowell is doing very well," he said, and for some time he spoke of his son's accomplishments in glowing terms. "He'll be a general before he's through, I'd venture."

Thomas sat there listening carefully, then asked, "Is Dent improved at all? What about his arm?"

"No better, I'm afraid. I wish he'd let them take that arm off. It's worse every day, and it could kill him."

"Your mother thinks he's afraid to face the world with such a terrible scar on his face. He's always been such a handsome boy, Clay. Do you think he might be wanting to die so he won't have to face the world?"

"It's — possible, sir," Clay agreed. "Dent's in a deep valley now. He's always had everything, and now he's thinking he'll only be an ugly cripple. He's a man without any props, and my hope is that he'll see how helpless he is without God — and that he'll turn to Him."

"I hope so." Thomas thought about it, then asked, "What about Sam Reed's daughter? Susanna tells me she visited Dent."

"She's a fine girl," Clay said at once. "I never saw a finer. She's a good Christian, and if anyone can touch Dent, I think she's the one."

For the rest of the day, Clay moved around Gracefield, accompanied by his daughter, Rena. She was delighted to have him there, and it was a keen pleasure for him to watch her riding beside him. Clay wished that her mother was more attentive to her, though he said nothing to Rena about that.

At supper that night, Thomas felt well enough to come down, though he ate little. David, Dent's twin brother, was anxious for details about the battle. They all listened as Clay told about it, making much of the efforts of Lowell and the others and minimizing his own part.

The next morning, he mounted his horse and rode to see Buford Yancy and, in effect, was forced to tell the story again. Buford and Melora met him as he rode up, and when they all sat down to an early dinner, Melora said, "Tell us about the battle, Mister Clay." She often called him that, for it had been her first name for him when she had been a child.

"Yeah, tell us about Bob," Josh insisted. He was fourteen and frantic with excitement about the war. So Clay went over the story again, this time making Bob Yancy the hero of the piece. Finally he held up his hand. "You've done all the eating, and I've done all the talking."

"Let him eat, you chirrun," Buford said. "After you rest a bit, Clay, I'll show you whut I done about the new pens." He drove his brood outside, and Melora came over to pour fresh coffee into his cup, then got a cup for herself and sat down beside him.

"Tell me about Dent," she said. The light came through the glass window, highlighting the planes of her face. She sat there, her head turned to one side, listening to him.

"Dent's in bad shape, Melora. I'm praying for him." He laughed ruefully as a thought struck him, adding, "I'm in pretty bad shape myself, come to think of it."

"What's wrong, Clay?" she asked. "Is it the war? I know you don't believe in it."

"I don't for a fact, but that's not why I'm in bad shape." He looked at her and smiled crookedly.

She knew him so well that he didn't need to say more. She was always happy to be with him but saddened by the way things were. She knew that Clay would be faithful to his marriage and that she would never be more than a good friend to him. Many had suspected that there was more to their relationship than just friendship, but they didn't know Clay. He had emerged from his prodigal youth as a man with a sense of honor so strong that he could not even think of breaking it with a low deed.

The solemn ticking of the clock on the mantel counted out the time, and each of them thought long thoughts. Finally Clay looked at her, saying, "It's hard, Melora."

"Yes, it's hard. But we have this much."

"Not much. Seeing each other and talking once every three months. You ought to marry, Melora."

"No, that's not for me." There was no sorrow or grief in her eyes. He knew she was not a grieving woman, but he wondered at the happiness in her clear eyes. "If I reached out and tried to grab happiness with you, Clay, it wouldn't bring me anything. I think we have to take every little good thing God gives us — no matter how small — and treasure it. But if we try to grab for more than He intends, it goes bad, just like the manna the disobedient Israelites tried to hoard. God told them to gather only enough for one day, to go back for more the next day. Remember what happened to the manna some of them tried to hoard? It went rotten and was filled with worms."

Clay was always impressed with the way Melora used the scripture to live by. "Never thought of that," he said. He sat there, holding on to the moment, for he knew that one like it would not come again soon. He spoke of it finally, saying, "I'll be gone a long time, Melora. This isn't going to be an easy war. And the South is going to be in a trial of fire."

"I'll be here when you get back, Clay," she said softly, and then he rose and took her hands in his. She held to him tightly, murmuring, "We'll be faithful to God's law, Clay. This love I have for you, it's from Him, and I will never dishonor Him with it. Don't ever worry about me, and don't ever doubt about us. God is going to bless us, even if we can never be together. He always honors those that honor Him."

They stood there, knowing that the world was falling down around them but aware that somehow the fiery trial would be endured and they would not be lost in it. When Clay left that afternoon, Buford said quietly, "Might be a spell before we see Clay again, daughter."

"He'll come back, Pa," she said firmly, and he saw that there was no doubt in her as she turned to her work.

Chief Surgeon Baskins studied the wound almost carelessly. He had seen so many wounds that a callousness had come over him — especially when the patient was a Yankee. He straightened up and said shortly,

"Looks a little better. Keep the bandages changed, Branch," then moved on down the line.

Pat Steele watched the surgeon leave. There was a sultry anger in his eyes. "He doesn't care if we live or die!"

Jesse Branch finished slapping a bandage on Noel's side, got up, and gathered his supplies. "He's better than some, Blue-belly," he said as he left. "But you won't have to put up with him long."

Pat stared at him. "He's leaving the hospital?"

"Nope." Branch gave him a sly look. "He ain't — you are." Branch loved to gossip and lowered his voice to add, "You'll be leaving in a couple of days for a prison camp. And from what I hear, it won't be no picnic. I 'spec you'll be crying for this hospital and this good grub in a few days!"

"Noel, too?"

"Nope. You and five more, I hear."

Branch left, and Noel said, "I ought to go with you, Pat."

"No, you need to be here. I'll be all right."

But either Branch had been wrong in his information or there was a change of plans. That same day after Jemmy had helped distribute the evening meal and while she sat beside Noel, talking with the two men, a

Confederate lieutenant accompanied by two privates carrying muskets came into the room. "Price, Duggins, Steele, Anderson, Lyons, and Ochner," he read from a list, then said, "Get your stuff and come with me. You're being transferred."

Pat began to gather his meager belongings. His arm was not healed completely, and Jemmy moved to help him. She caught at his arm, and in the shadow of the brim of her ever-present sunbonnet, he saw that her eyes were damp with tears. "I wisht you didn't have to go," she whispered.

"Me, too, Jemmy." Pat summoned up a smile. "You've been mighty good to all of us. Going to miss you."

Suddenly Jemmy threw her arms around him, gave him a hard squeeze, then turned and stumbled away. Pat watched her go, surprise in his eyes. "Why, that's funny!" he said. "The old lady's really got a heart for us, Noel." Then he turned and put his hand out. "So long, Noel. Hope this thing is over soon. Would you write to my people? Might not be a very good delivery service in the camp."

"Sure, Pat," Noel said. He came to his feet, grunting with the pain. "Guess I'll be seeing you pretty soon."

The two of them stood there, bound by

the code that said men shouldn't show any emotion. They had grown close during the past few weeks, and finally Noel leaned forward and put his arms around Pat, whispering, "By heaven! I'm going to miss you, Pat!"

Pat Steele was suddenly choked with emotion and could only say huskily, "Me, too, Noel!"

Then the lieutenant said impatiently, "All right, you men, let's go!"

Noel moved to the window and watched as the prisoners were marched out and placed in an open wagon. Pat looked up, saw him at the window, and gave a cheerful wave. Noel returned the salute and watched until the wagon, accompanied by two armed guards on horseback, disappeared down the road. Then he moved to sit down on his cot, filled with apprehension.

Finally Noel was aware that someone had come to stand beside him, and he looked up to find Jemmy watching him. "Well, Jemmy, I'm going to miss him," he said simply.

"He's a nice young feller," Jemmy said. "I'll miss him, too."

Noel examined her more carefully. It was hard to tell her age, for the bonnet she wore concealed the upper half of her face. She had iron-gray hair, but her hands were firm and strong, not wrinkled with age, and he asked curiously, "Why did you hug him, Jemmy? Did he remind you of your son?"

She hesitated, then shrugged. "Oh, I reckon I jist got fond of the scamp."

"How old is your boy, Jemmy? You never talk about him."

"Wal, he's about yore age, I reckon." She seemed uncomfortable and shifted the subject. "Whut about you now? You got a heap of purty gals back home, ain't you now?"

Noel shook his head, smiling at her. "No, Jemmy, I guess not."

"A fine-lookin' young feller like you? Come on, now, you kin tell ol' Jemmy!" When he continued to deny that he had a string of pretty girls waiting for him, she asked curiously, "Mebbe you ain't got no bunch of gals, but I'll bet my bonnet you got *one,* ain't that so?"

Noel flushed slightly, then laughed self-consciously. "Well, in a way maybe I have, Jemmy. There is a girl back home — but it's all one-sided. I think of her all the time, but she's not for me."

"And why not?" Jemmy demanded sharply.

"Oh, she's out of my reach." Noel

shrugged. "She comes from a good family. Her father's a wealthy man."

"I don't reckon she'd be marryin' yore family, would she?"

Noel said soberly, "In a way she would be. When people get married, their families are part of it. That's the way it is. And my family —"

"Well, whut about yore family?"

He hesitated but began to talk. Jemmy sat down on the chair, and after a while Noel forgot himself and told her the whole story of how he had met the young woman. Jemmy sat there silently, listening and watching him. Finally he gave a start, then smiled sheepishly. "Gosh, Jemmy, I didn't mean to tell you all that."

Jemmy's voice was usually high-pitched. As she spoke now, though, it was lower and smoother. "This heah gal, this Deb'rah? Whut you thinking 'bout her, Noel?"

Noel sat there, his face serious in the darkening room. He was not a man to say much about what he felt. His feelings were stronger than anyone had ever suspected, but he had kept them bottled up for the most part. But now he was far from home, and the wound had weakened him so that he said to Jemmy what he would not have let escape under ordinary circumstances.

"I love her, Jemmy," he said simply. "It won't ever come to anything. I sure won't ever tell her. She'd be kind enough to me because that's the way she is." His face had thinned during his illness, but there was still a stubbornness in his strong chin as he spoke. "She's a wonderful girl, Jemmy, but she's not for me."

He glanced at Jemmy, who sat so still that she seemed to have gone to sleep. Her upper face was hidden by the shadow of her bonnet, but Noel thought he saw her lips tremble. Finally she cleared her throat and said, "I reckon she's got a right to know how you feel about her." Then she rose, picked up his dishes, and left without another word.

Noel stared after her until she disappeared through the door that led to the stairway, then said slowly, "Now that's a funny one!" Then he lay down on his cot.

Jemmy left the hospital without saying good-bye to Matron Huger. Neither did she speak to the guard at the gate as was her custom. Turning to go down the road that led to her boardinghouse, she noticed a man standing beside a large oak. He was a large man and seemed to be watching the iron gate that she had just passed through. The darkness was falling fast, so she could not see his features clearly, and the slouch hat he wore was pulled down over his eyes.

Yet there was something vaguely familiar about the man, and Jemmy suddenly crossed the road. As she passed the man, he lifted his head and gave her a suspicious look. He was tall, about six feet, and had wavy dark hair that escaped the confines of the cap, and a pair of bold brown eyes. There was something about his stare, a wildness that flashed out at her, that almost frightened her. She walked by, her mind racing.

Then when she was six paces down the lane, it came to her. She stopped, turned, and moved back to the man who had been watching her. He turned his whole body to face her, alert and ready for trouble.

"What are you doing here, Bing?" Deborah asked.

Alarm leaped to Bing Kojak's eyes, and he took a step toward her, moving on his toes, ready to leap as he said, "Who the devil are you? My name's Jim!"

"The guard is watching us, Bing," Deborah said calmly. "He'll be suspicious, so come with me. Take my arm and lead me down the street."

Bing stared at her, but a glance toward the guard revealed that she was telling the truth. He took her arm in a paralyzing grip and moved away. When they were out of sight of the guard, he growled, "Now who are you?"

Deborah had been thinking rapidly and knew that Noel's brother could have only one motive in being outside the gates of Chimborazo. "I'm Deborah Steele, Bing. You've come to help Noel escape, haven't you?"

Bing was so taken aback that he could only stare at her for a long moment; then he slowly nodded. "That's it."

"Come to my room," Deborah said quickly. "We can't be seen together. I wish that guard hadn't seen us!" She led the way toward her boardinghouse but, when it was in sight, changed her mind. "No, this won't do. I don't want anyone there to see you. We'll have to talk here." She turned to face him, asking, "What brought you here, Bing? You never cared that much about your brother — or anyone else."

Bing glared at her, then suddenly nodded. "Right you are! You've got my number," he said angrily. Then he grew uncomfortable, shifting his feet and looking down at the ground. "Well, that's right enough, Miss Steele. I've been a hard one. Had to be, I guess."

"I know it's been hard on you, Bing — on all of you."

Her admission seemed to encourage the big man. Lifting his head, he said, "Well, I ain't done much to be proud of, but nobody ever accused me of being a coward. I thought — I thought I could take anything, no matter how tough it was. But then . . . when the battle started . . ." Bing gave her an anguished look and bit his lip. He had trouble speaking, then blurted out, "I run like a yellow dog, that's what I done! Noel and some of the others stayed and fought, but I run." He got control of himself, shrugged, then went on. "I didn't care at first. Just glad to be out of the thing. But it kept eatin' on me, you see? Me, Bing Kojak, runnin' away from a fight, like a spineless worm!"

"Lots of men ran away, Bing."

"Well, that's their problem! But I ain't no coward!" Bing glared at her as if challenging her to deny it, but found understanding in her eyes. "Well, I tried getting drunk, but that didn't help. Finally I knew I'd never have no rest until I showed I wasn't no coward. I could have gone back to the army, but I wanted to show Noel. I come to get him out of that hospital and back home — and I'm gonna do it, too!"

"I think that's fine, Bing," Deborah said quietly. "Do you have any ideas about how to go about it?"

"Naw, I can't figure nothing," he said, shaking his head gloomily. "Guards at all the gates and inside, too. All I know is to wait until the middle of the night, take one guard out, then go in and try to find Noel."

"He's on the second floor, Bing," Deborah said.

He stared at her, asking abruptly, "What are you doing here, all disguised?"

"The same as you, Bing," Deborah said and told him swiftly how she'd felt guilty over encouraging Noel to enlist and had come to try to do something.

"You got any ideas on how to bust him out?" Bing asked.

Deborah thought for a moment, then said, "If we get him out, Bing, it'll have to be at once. My brother Pat was with him until today. They took him to a prison camp, and I think they'll transfer Noel soon, maybe in a few days."

"We got to get him out! There must be some way!" Bing said savagely.

Deborah said, "We'll do it, Bing. If we do get him out, can we get him out of Richmond?"

"I'll handle that, right enough," he said

with a nod. "There's wagons and boats and trains, and they can't watch them all. Just let me get him out of that place, and the rest will go all right!"

Deborah said at once, "Bing, you start looking for a way to get him out of Richmond. Do you have any money?"

"Not a lot," he admitted.

"I've got enough. Find a way and meet me here tomorrow about this same time."

"All right." Bing hesitated, then asked, "You got an idea how to get him out?"

Deborah said, a peculiar look in her eyes, "The Bible says that God sets the prisoners free. All I have to do is ask Him how to go about it."

Bing stared at her, then shook his head. "You talk to God, then. I'll be here tomorrow." He wheeled and disappeared into the darkness.

Deborah went to her room, but she didn't sleep that night. By the time dawn came through the grimy window of her tiny room, she still didn't have an answer.

CHAPTER 22
THE MIRACLE

"You want my advice," Chief Surgeon Baskins said, "I think we ought to put some drugs in his food, then take him down to surgery and take that arm off. When he wakes up he can rave all he wants to, but he'll still be alive." He looked across Matron Huger's office to the medicine cabinet. "Give me some whiskey."

Matron Huger frowned but didn't argue. She got the whiskey from the cabinet and put the bottle and a glass before him. Baskins sloshed the liquor into the glass and drank it down.

"We can't do that, Doctor," she said as he sat there frowning at the table. "It's his life — and besides, he has a family. If anyone makes a decision like that, it'd have to be them. And they're not going to do it."

"Blast the man!" Baskins growled, slamming the table with his fist. "Why's he making such a fuss? He ought to be thankful it's not worse."

Matron Huger didn't argue, but she thought she knew why Dent Rocklin refused surgery. She had talked with the man's grandmother, a sensible woman, and had discovered that her own guess about the man was correct.

"He's got too much pride," Susanna Rocklin had said, sorrow in her fine eyes. "He's had everything, and now he can't face up to the loss. He'll have to be broken before he'll agree to the operation — and I think he'll choose to die."

It looked as though the old woman had been correct. Matron Huger hated to lose patients, hated it with all the vigor of her soul and spirit. She rose suddenly, left the office, and went into the ward room. Raimey Reed was sitting beside Denny Gipson, a seventeen-year-old from Texas. Matron Huger waited until the boy finished telling the girl about his home along the Rio Grande, then said, "Miss Reed, may I speak with you when you're finished with Denny?"

"I think Lieutenant Gipson's told me all the tall tales about Texas that I can take for one day, Matron." She reached out, and the soldier took her hand eagerly. "I'll bring the book with me tomorrow."

Matron Huger said, "Come to my office.

We'll have some tea." The two women left the room and soon were drinking tea and talking about the men in the ward. "We lost Major Glover last night," the matron said. "I've been so upset over it."

"He was a fine Christian man." Raimey nodded. "He was a widower. I don't think he's been happy since his wife died."

"I didn't know that," the older woman said in surprise. "When did she die?"

"Two years ago. He talked about her a great deal, especially the last few days." She sipped the tea, a thoughtful expression on her face. There was an inner quietness in Raimey Reed such as Matron Huger had never seen in one of Raimey's age. Usually such peace and serenity were seen only in the very old or in small children. "I was with him just before they came to get him for the surgery. He knew he was going to die, but he wasn't afraid. The last thing he said was, 'Thank God, I'll be with Doris now!' "

Tears rose to the matron's eyes, though she was not a woman who usually allowed such a thing. "Well, he's with Doris now," she murmured.

Raimey lifted her head. "Don't cry for him, Matron," she said with a fine smile. "He's happier there than he could ever have been here."

Matron Huger was taken aback. "How did you know I was crying, Raimey?" she asked.

"Your voice had tears."

Matron Huger shook her head. "You have more sensitivity than any young woman I've ever known, Raimey," she murmured. The two of them sat there drinking tea, and finally the matron said, "We're going to lose Lieutenant Rocklin, I'm afraid." She saw a break in the girl's smooth countenance, which confirmed a conviction she had formed. "Even if he agreed to the surgery, it may be too late," she went on, then leaned forward. "Why don't you talk to him, Raimey? You love him, don't you?"

Raimey nodded slightly but said, "I've begged him to have the operation."

"Have you told him you love him, that it doesn't make any difference to you that he's scarred?"

"No!" Raimey said, her lips suddenly trembling. "I — I can't do that!"

"Why can't you? Or maybe it does matter to you? Some women can't abide such things."

"You know that's not true! But . . . I can't tell him that I . . . love him!"

Matron Huger paused, then knew she had to be cruel. "Oh, I see," she said quietly. "It's your pride, then. You can't afford to risk a refusal. Well, I suppose your pride is more important than Denton Rocklin's life."

"That's not fair!" Raimey rose with an angry gesture that sent the cup in her hands to the floor. It broke into pieces, but neither woman paid any heed. "I'd do anything to save his life!"

"I think you're his last hope, Raimey," Matron Huger said, her voice insistent. "He's a strong, stubborn man, and I think he's made up his mind that there's nothing for him to live for. He's proud, too, and it comes down to this — which of you is going to have your pride broken? I think he may care for you, Raimey. I've seen him when you were with him, and he watches you with the kind of look a man has when he loves a woman. He's gotten to be good friends with Simon Alcott. Simon is a pretty sharp fellow. We talk quite a bit, and he says that Rocklin is in love with you."

"Did he say so, that he loved me?"

"Of course not! He'd never admit it to anyone. That's his pride, and it's killing him. He's been a man who could attract women with no trouble, and now his own mother flinches at the sight of him — I could murder that woman! Now he's afraid that no woman could love him, so he wants to die. But if he knew it wasn't so, he'd want to live."

Raimey stood there, trembling and clasping her hands in an effort to conceal it. Finally she whispered, "All right, I'll do it."

"Fine! Fine!" Matron Huger cried and moved to put her arms around the girl. "Do it now, Raimey. He needs you."

Raimey left the matron's office, and Dulcie was waiting for her. She began complaining at once. "I don't know how I got any fingers left on my hand! If I have to write one more letter for one of them soldiers, it'll drive me crazy, Miss Raimey!"

"You've done so much for these men, Dulcie," Raimey said gently, her thoughts elsewhere. "They all love you for it, too."

"Hmmm! I don't know about that, but they sure can eat! Susie told me she was not going to keep making a hundred pies every day!" There was a pause, and Dulcie said, "We got to get home. Your daddy said for you to be home before dark."

"I want to talk to Lieutenant Rocklin, Dulcie. Then we'll go."

Dulcie stared at her mistress, a suspicion in her bright eyes. "You talking too much to that man. He's too sick to do much talking, anyway." But she had learned that a new authority had come into her mistress, so, grumbling under her breath, she led Raimey to Dent Rocklin's cot. Then she left, saying, "We have to leave before it gets dark, you hear me?"

"All right, Dulcie." Raimey touched the chair and moved to sit down, asking, "Lieutenant Alcott?"

"Simon's down at the end playing poker." Dent's voice was ragged with exhaustion, she noted, and she thought she could smell the infected wound. He went on, "Want me to call him for you?"

"No, Dent. I'd like to talk to you."

Dent looked at her, his face hollow with the fever that had raged for several days. His eyes were dull and his speech was slow. "Guess I'm not much to talk to, Raimey." He fell silent, the pain in his arm sapping his energy. He had eaten little, and there was no hope in him.

"I don't want you to talk to me, Dent. Not now. I — I've got something to say to you."

"All right, Raimey."

He could see the pulse beating rapidly in the blue vein in Raimey's throat and wondered what had upset her. She looked frightened — and fear was something he'd never seen on her face before. She drew a deep breath, then began speaking.

"Dent, I'm not like other girls. I've missed out on so many things that are natural with them. For a long time I was angry with God for letting me be blind. It didn't seem fair somehow. But when I was thirteen, a very wonderful thing happened to me. I was in a revival meeting with my parents, and for the first time I really heard the gospel with my heart. I guess I'd heard a thousand sermons on how people need to be saved from their sins — but I was too mad at God to believe anything. But that morning, the sermon was on the death of Jesus, and for the first time I understood what real suffering was — *His* suffering, when they nailed Him to the cross. . . ."

Dent lay there listening, half out of his head. If he had been himself, he would have refused to listen, for he had been angry at God since the battle. But his weakness kept him still, and he listened as Raimey told how she'd felt the weight of her sins and how she'd begun to grieve, finally calling on the name of Jesus.

"He saved me, Dent," she said simply, tears in her eyes. "Since that moment I've been happy."

"You're still blind," Dent said roughly. He had been touched by her story, but the bitterness in him was strong. "Why doesn't He heal your eyes?"

"I don't know why, Dent," Raimey said quietly. "But I know one thing, and that is that God loves me. And anything that comes to me — including blindness — comes through His hands. I know that, Dent, and I know that as long as I live He'll be there. There are worse things than being blind, Dent." She leaned forward, reaching out her hand, and he took it. Holding on to it as hard as she could, Raimey whispered, "Being bitter and unhappy is worse, being the way I used to be — and the way you are now!"

Dent held on to her hand, stung by her words but knowing that the ring of truth was in them. He couldn't answer, but simply lay there. As he did so, he began to feel peculiar. A strange sense of shame came to him, and myriad thoughts flowed across his mind in a montage of scenes — and in all of them he saw himself as a small man, petty and unkind. He thought of his father and how he'd spurned the advances the older man had made. These thoughts, and many more, coursed through his mind.

Finally Raimey said, "Dent?" And when he spoke, she said, "You know you're going to die if something doesn't happen?"

"Yes, I know that. Won't be much of a loss."

"It will be a great loss!" Raimey cried, clinging to his hand. Her voice wasn't loud, but it was strong. "What about your family? Your grandparents and your brothers and Rena? And your father? He loves you, Dent. They all do!"

And then when Dent made no answer, Raimey took a deep breath and went on, her voice unsteady. "What about me, Dent? Don't you know that I love you?"

Dent blinked and stared at her. His mind was working so slowly that he thought he had mistaken her words. "What did you say?"

"I — I love you, Dent," Raimey said, her head held up proudly. "I know a woman's not supposed to say things like that, and I know you don't love me — but I won't have you say that it makes no difference whether you live or die!"

Dent had been aware that Raimey Reed was a girl of powerful emotions, but he had never seen them evidenced. Now as she sat there, her chin lifted, her lips trembling, she was beautiful. Her glossy hair gleamed faintly, and there was strength in her firm jawline and beauty in the curve of her smooth cheek. Slowly Dent reached out and put his hand on that cheek — and felt the dampness of a tear.

"Don't cry, Raimey," he whispered. "There's nothing to cry about."

"There is!" she insisted with a sob and put her hands over his. "Dent, I've never loved a man before and I'll never love another. If you die, it will be death for me!" She moved from the chair and fell on her knees, putting her face against his chest. Her hair was fragrant and soft against his face, and he held her as her slim body was wracked with sobs. "I love you, Dent, as much as any woman ever loved any man!" she sobbed. "Please live, Dent! You don't have to love me — you can marry another woman, and I'll be happy just knowing you're alive!"

Dent had known many women, but none had affected him like this one. He had been dazzled by the beauty and charm of Deborah Steele, even ready to fight for her. But now . . . now the gentleness of the woman who knelt beside him and the declaration of her love hit him hard. His mind was cloudy with fever, but he knew what it had cost her to come to him. He held her until the sobs ceased; then when she lifted her head and started to move away, he whispered, "Raimey, I'm all mixed up. I don't know

486

what to do."

She sensed the confusion in his mind, and then something came to her. She knelt there, not moving, and the thought came back even stronger. She thought, *I can't say that! It would be cruel!* But as the doubt came to her, there was something else — a sense of the presence of God. She had felt such a thing three times in her life, and each time there had been in her spirit an absolute certainty that God was speaking to her. It was there now. Her lips parted, and she grew still as the impression became even stronger.

"What is it, Raimey?" Dent asked, noting her expression.

"Dent, will you let me pray for you?"

"Why — I guess so." The request made Dent feel uncomfortable. Others had asked the same thing, and he'd curtly refused, but now he felt strange. "I don't believe in God very much," he said finally.

"I believe that God is going to do something for you, Dent," Raimey said. She hesitated, then added, "I think He wants to heal your arm."

Dent looked down at the arm, aware that the doctors had given up, saying the infection had gone into gangrene. He was too weary now to be angry about it. So though the girl's faith seemed strange and unreal, he said, "Well, Raimey, if anyone does anything with my arm, it'll have to be God."

Raimey put her hands out, touching the ruined arm, and prayed a very simple prayer: "Oh God, my Father, in the name of Jesus Christ, I ask You to heal this infection in Dent's arm. I believe that You can do all things, that nothing is impossible for You. Give us this sign of Your power and Your love, for I ask it in the name of Jesus."

Dent lay there, then asked, "Is that all?"

"Yes." Tears flowed freely down Raimey's face, for she had been given an assurance that her prayer had been heard. "I must go." She got to her feet and called out, "Dulcie — I'm ready." Then as the maid came to get her, she turned to face Dent. Her face was luminous in the light that flowed through the window, and she whispered, "I love you, Dent!"

Dent watched her leave, then looked down at his arm. When Simon Alcott came back from his poker game, he looked at his friend. "How's it going, Dent? Any better?"

Dent looked up at him, his face sober and his lips tight. "I don't know, Simon." He looked at his arm and then back to Alcott. "I'm going to find out pretty soon if God is real or not."

His words made Alcott blink, and he thought at once, *He's getting delirious.* But he said only, "Take it easy, Dent. You'll be all right."

It was the longest and worst night of Denton Rocklin's life. He moved from a state of half-consciousness to a coma, then came back to reality, drenched with sweat. Fragments of nightmares came, leaving him shaking with fear, and the pain in his arm grew unbearable. When morning broke, he came out of his delirium to find Mrs. Wright, a nurse, standing over him, her face filled with fear and concern.

He croaked from a dry throat, "My arm — is it well?"

Mrs. Wright saw that he was beside himself. "No, Lieutenant, it's not well. You must let them amputate!"

"No!" he said, pulling away from her. "God's going to heal it!"

Mrs. Wright glanced at Simon Alcott with frightened eyes. "I'm going to get some morphine, Simon. Don't let him get up!"

She ran to the cabinet, then came back to give Rocklin the shot. When he grew still, she asked, "What's all this about his arm being healed?"

Alcott shrugged. "Miss Reed was talking to him. She's real religious. I guess she might have got him started."

"Well, she's got to stop!" Mrs. Wright left the room and soon was giving Matron Huger her views. "You've got to speak to Miss Reed! She's got Dent Rocklin's hopes up, says that God's going to heal his arm! You know that's impossible!"

"I asked her to speak to him, but I didn't think this was what she was going to say."

"Well, what are you going to do about it? We can't have the girl upsetting him."

Matron Huger was silent. The pressures of the job were severe, and she still was not able to accept death in a calm, logical manner. Finally she said, "He's not going to listen to anyone else, Mrs. Wright. He'll probably die, but let him die believing in God."

Dent was aware that everyone thought he was crazy. *I think so, too,* he thought wryly when he saw, the morning after Raimey prayed for him, that his arm was worse than it had been. But Raimey had come to visit that day, and when he told her that he hadn't been healed, she had said, "God is never late."

Somehow her serene spirit had touched Dent, and all that day and the next he had lain in a stupor on the bed, thinking of her prayer. His father came, and his grandmother, but neither of them had urged him to have the operation.

The administration had given up, especially Dr. Baskins. The rough surgeon had said profanely, "If he's fool enough to believe in that religious nonsense, let him die! We can use his bed!"

Dent himself, by the end of the second day, was so racked with fever and pain that he was not aware of the talk. That afternoon, Raimey came and sat beside him. She said little, and Dent was beyond speech. But there was a comfort in her presence. Finally when it was time for her to go, he whispered, "I — remember what you said." He had to labor to get the words out, his lips cracked with fever. "Tell me again!"

Raimey bent over him and whispered, "I love you, Dent, and God loves you."

All night Dent lay there, hearing those words over and over: "I love you, Dent, and God loves you."

Sometime during the night, he struggled out of the black pit of unconsciousness that drew him. The moon was out and the stars glittered brightly in the sky. The room was quiet, save for the moanings and mutterings of his fellow patients. Far down the room an orderly sat at a desk, reading a book by the pale yellow light of a lamp.

And as he lay there, only half conscious, Dent became aware that there was something growing in his mind. It was like a tiny light, from somewhere far down a dark road, so dim that it could barely be seen. It grew larger and brighter. It was not, he knew, a physical light or any light at all, but his spirit seemed to glow — there was no other way he could think of it. As the sensation grew within him, he relaxed and let his body go limp. He had kept himself so tense waiting for the next jolt of pain that he ached, and now a sense of security came to him. There was nothing else, just the sense of being cared for, of being loved.

Then he knew that he was not alone, that there was someone in the room other than the two hundred fifty wounded men. Fear came to him and he drew his legs up, sending pain through his arm. But nothing happened, except that the same sense of peace washed back, driving away the fear.

There was never any sort of voice, but he kept feeling that someone was reaching out to him, that he was being loved in a way he had never known. He did something then that he'd not done for years — he began to pray. And even that was strange, for he didn't ask for anything. That was what prayer had always been to him, asking for things.

He knew he was dying, yet he did not ask to be healed. Instead he asked that he might know peace. The longing for it was a sharp pain. Then, suddenly, he began to weep for the first time since he was a child. That was when he prayed for help, that whatever was in him, destroying him, would be taken away.

Then he prayed, "I want to know what love is, God! Take anything you see in me. I don't know what it is or how, but give me whatever I need to be the man you want me to be."

He dropped off to sleep then and didn't wake up until he heard Mrs. Wright saying, "All right, Lieutenant. Let's change this bandage and then you can have some breakfast."

Dent awoke instantly, his head clear. "All right, Mrs. Wright." He sat up, and though he was weak, there was none of the thick fogginess in his mind, and his speech was clear.

Mrs. Wright stared at him strangely, then put her hand on his forehead. "Why, your fever's gone!"

"I feel a lot better," Dent said. He looked down at his arm and slowly bent it. "Arm feels lots better, too."

Mrs. Wright removed the bandages, which were thick with dried pus and blood. She took a damp cloth and began to dab carefully at the wound, then stopped. Dent saw her staring at his arm. "What is it?" he asked.

"Your arm!" she cried out. "It's clear!" Dent looked down to see the raw edges of the wound. It was still an ugly gash, but he saw that the infection was gone, as was the swelling. All the flesh was ruddy and healthy. Mrs. Wright's hands were trembling, but she cleaned the wound, then sat there staring at it. Suddenly she put Dent's arm back across his chest. "Don't move! I'm going to get Dr. Baskins!"

She went out of the room almost at a run, and Simon Alcott woke up. He sat up on his cot, rubbed his eyes, then asked, "What's wrong with her?"

"My arm," Dent said slowly. "It's not infected."

Alcott shut his mouth with a distinct click, then stood up to look at Dent's arm. He said nothing for a moment, then slowly straightened up and said in a strange, thick voice, "It's clean!"

He stood there, and soon the space around Dent's cot was crowded. Dr. Baskins and

Matron Huger were there and two of the orderlies — not to mention several of the patients.

Baskins was staring at Dent's arm, his mouth in a thin line. "See if you can bend it," he commanded and watched as Dent obeyed. "That hurt?"

"A little," Dent answered, nodding.

The surgeon pinched the flesh around the lips of the wound, and Dent flinched. Baskins stood up and stared down, his red-rimmed eyes dark with some sort of doubt. "That flesh was dead yesterday. I pinched it then, and you didn't even know it."

"I feel it now," Dent said. He looked up at the crowd and then back at his arm. "It hurts, but it's a different kind of hurt."

Matron Huger stood there, lips trembling. "What do you think, Doctor?" she asked.

The surgeon was in some sort of struggle. He knew this man should be dying — he'd seen that type of wound with that sort of infection too many times. His reputation was on the line, for he'd proclaimed vehemently that Dent Rocklin couldn't live unless that arm came off. Now what he saw was a wound that was serious but that was healing well. Moreover, the moribund fever that had threatened Rocklin's life was gone.

Baskins stood there silently, then said, "I

have no explanation. This man ought to be dead." Then he walked away with his head down, shoving his way past the patients. He went to his office and drank half a bottle of whiskey, his mind rebelling.

As soon as the doctor left, the officers began to shout and cheer, and nothing Matron Huger did could quiet them down. Finally Simon Alcott said to her, quietly so that the others could not hear, "I guess this knocks the bottom out of what I've thought of religion, Matron. What do you think?"

Matron Huger smiled at him, her eyes misty. "Simon, there are more things in heaven than you've ever dreamed of!"

When Raimey came to the hospital, she was met by the matron, who said, "He's healed, Raimey!"

Raimey stopped dead still, and her face went white. She bit hard on her lips to stop them from trembling. "I want to see him. Take me to him, Dulcie."

Dent saw her as soon as she entered. "You fellows give me a minute, will you?"

The soldiers winked at each other slyly but moved away to create some sort of privacy. Dulcie brought her mistress to him; then she, too, moved across the room away from the couple.

"Come here, Raimey," Dent said and

struggled to throw his legs over the cot. She came close, and he reached up and pulled her down beside him with his good arm. "Did they tell you?"

"Yes! Oh, Dent, I'm so happy!" Her face was radiant, and she leaned against him. "Tell me everything!"

He did tell her, holding her with one arm. Finally he said, "I think I hit bottom, Raimey, and I guess that's what God was waiting for. My arm is healed, but more than that happened." He sat there, aware of her soft warmth. "I've made some kind of a new beginning, Raimey. I guess I'll fall on my face a thousand times, but last night I gave myself to God." He hesitated, then said, "I'm going to need lots of help."

"Your family will help you, Dent," Raimey answered. "They'll be so happy!"

"Sure, I know that, but I'm going to need more help than they can give. I need someone who's around all the time. It's going to be a long-term thing, Raimey. I think it's going to take a lifetime." He paused, and his arm grew tighter around her. "Tell me again, Raimey?"

"Tell you what?" she asked nervously. His arm was tight, and she was aware without seeing that every man in the room must be watching.

"Tell me that you love me," Dent said.

"Oh, I — I can't!"

"You said you did, Raimey, and I don't care if you say it again or not. I love you and I've got to have you! Will you marry me?"

Raimey could not speak, so great was the joy that welled up in her. She turned her face to him, and a smile lifted her lips. She knew that the patients were watching and listening, but she put her arms up and offered her lips. Then she drew back and said quite loudly, "Yes, I do love you, Lieutenant Rocklin — and I will marry you!" She turned to face the men gathered around them, men with missing limbs and bandages on their heads, and said sweetly, "I hope you all heard that! He's got to marry me now, with all of you as witnesses!"

A cheer such as had not been heard in Chimborazo Hospital broke out, and Dent Rocklin and his bride-to-be were swarmed by the Confederate Army of the Potomac.

CHAPTER 23
ANOTHER MIRACLE

Dent Rocklin's recovery sent reverberations throughout the hospital, and his family came almost shouting into the ward. Clay's visit was unforgettable. When he entered the room, Dent got to his feet, saying at once, "Sir, I've been wrong. Forgive me."

Clay blinked back tears, saying, "Dent, I think you must know nothing could give me more joy than to see you well!" The two tall men hesitated, then embraced — it was the first time Clay had held his son in his arms in almost fifteen years.

Clay sat down, and they talked about the war and the future. Then Raimey came in. She was wearing a pink dress trimmed in blue, and her hair fell down her back in gleaming waves. "Here's your new daughter-in-law, sir," Dent said, rising to put his good arm around her. "I hope you approve."

"She's got a job in front of her, getting you raised," Clay said, grinning. Then he stepped to the girl. "I'll have to welcome you with a kiss, Raimey." He kissed her cheek, then stepped back. "When's the wedding?"

Dent said, "I haven't asked her father yet. He may run me off with a gun. We may have to run away!"

"He's very happy, Dent," Raimey said quickly, "and so is Mother. I've already told him to see Rev. Irons and reserve the church. It'll be soon. You'll be going back with the Grays, won't you, Dent?"

"Yes, when I'm able."

"Take plenty of time, son," Clay said quickly. "I don't think we are going to see much action from the Federals for months. Lincoln's given the army to McClellan. He's slow, I hear. Won't move until everything suits him. Why don't you take your bride on a long honeymoon — maybe even an ocean voyage."

"Oh, that would be wonderful!" Raimey exclaimed. "Could we, Dent?"

"Well, it would be expensive —"

"Daddy's already said he'd give us whatever we wanted for a wedding present."

Clay grinned. "Well, I'm glad you're marrying into a wealthy family, son. Money comes in handy." He picked up his hat, then left, saying, "I'll leave you two alone. The doctor tells me you'll be coming home in a few days, Dent. I'll have your grandmother get your room ready."

When he left, Raimey said, "Now I'm going to give you a shave. Your face is like sandpaper!" They spent an hour together, making plans, and Dent said finally, "You know, Raimey, I can't get over how things look so different. Why, I've been thinking about that young Yankee I shot. He's here, you know, just upstairs." He rubbed his chin, saying slowly, "I've been thinking maybe I'd go visit him. Jemmy tells me he is getting better . . . but, well, I don't know, maybe he wouldn't like me to come."

"I think he might," Raimey said. "Jemmy talks about him a lot. Let me get permission from the matron, and we'll both go." It took only a few minutes, and she was back with Dulcie. "Come along," she said. "The matron said it would be fine." Then she said, "Dulcie, Lieutenant Rocklin can go with me. You write some more letters."

Dent saw the expression on Dulcie's face, and when they were on the stairs out of hearing, he said, "Dulcie doesn't like me much."

"Oh, she's just jealous," Raimey said. "But she'll love you soon enough." She squeezed his arm possessively, adding with a smile,

"After all, who wouldn't love you?"

"I can give you a long list," Dent said with a grimace. He reached up to touch the wound on his face. At Raimey's insistence he had left off the bandage, and he felt vulnerable. "I'll probably scare the poor fellow to death with this mug of mine," he said. Putting his hand over the wound, he added, "Maybe I ought to wear some kind of a cover."

"No! And don't put your hand over it," Raimey said. "It's a wound of honor, received in the service of your country."

Dent looked at her strangely. "You don't even believe in the war, Raimey."

"Neither does your father," she said at once. "But both of us love you, and we love the South. When it's all over, we'll still be here. Now don't ever try to hide your face, you hear me, Dent?"

"Yes, sir!" he said, grinning. "You sound like a tough sergeant." Then he said, "Here we are. There's Jemmy." He caught the woman's eye, and she came over to them at once. "Jemmy, do you think it would be all right if we visited with the young fellow I put in here?"

Jemmy was wearing the same shapeless dress and floppy bonnet that she wore every day. "Why, he'll be plum proud to see both of you, Major Rocker." She insisted on calling him "Rocker" and changed his rank anywhere from lieutenant to general from day to day. She turned, and the pair followed her to where a young man sat in a chair, talking with several other patients.

"This here is General Rocker, Noel," Jemmy said. "And this is his lady, Missus Reed. This here is Noel Kojak."

"Not quite a general, Private," Dent said. He was ill at ease and added, "If you don't want any company —"

"Oh no, sir!" Noel exclaimed. He got to his feet painfully and put his hand out. "I'm glad to meet you. Everyone's talking about how God healed you. Please sit down, sir — and you, Miss Reed."

When they were seated, Dent said, "A little different from our last meeting."

Noel smiled, saying, "Yes, sir. I don't remember too much about it, except that you fellows sure did make pests of yourselves, coming up that hill!"

They talked about the battle; then Raimey asked, "How are you, Noel? Jemmy says you're much better."

"Oh yes, Miss Reed," Noel said, nodding. "I expect I'll be transferred pretty soon, maybe even this week. They need the bed, you see."

Jemmy had hovered close, but when she heard this, she turned and moved away. She didn't notice when the pair left Noel, but came back just before noon to bring Noel's dinner — a plate of cabbage with a piece of pork and a slice of corn bread.

"Sure was nice of Lieutenant Rocklin to come and visit me," he said as he ate. "Did you know, Jemmy, it was Miss Reed that prayed for him to get well? Isn't that great!"

"Shore is," Jemmy said. She studied Noel, noting how his color was coming back. "Guess she's learned how to trust in the Lord."

"Yes." Noel grew thoughtful and finally said, "I wish I had that kind of faith, don't you, Jemmy? I know God is able to do anything, but somehow I can't seem to believe in asking for miracles." He suddenly lost his appetite and put the corn bread down. "I wasn't afraid of getting killed, but I'm afraid of going to a prison. Why is that, I wonder?"

Jemmy had no answer. She watched Noel's face, then said, "Don't guess you're the fust to git a mite skeered of a jail, Noel." She hesitated, then added, "Don't never let yore fears git the best of you. I been a'prayin' and I'm thinkin' the good Lord is gonna take keer of you."

She rose and left abruptly, leaving him to stare after her. She moved about mechanically, then left the hospital before long. The air was still and hot, but she didn't notice. For a time, she walked the streets, then went to a small stand of oaks that overshadowed the river. It was cooler under the trees, and all afternoon she prayed desperately. She had, in fact, prayed almost constantly since God had first spoken to her, but had felt nothing. Doggedly she kept praying, though more than once she was ready to give up. Finally it grew darker, and she moved away from the river.

For the next two days she struggled, but no plan came to her. Finally on Friday, as she walked wearily toward the spot where she met Bing, bitterness swept over her.

Why did You bring me here, Lord, if I can't do anything? her heart cried out. She was tired of her masquerade, and doubt had eaten away at her. She knew that at any time Noel could be transferred — that he might even be gone now.

When she met Bing, he saw at once that she was unhappy. "It don't look too good, does it, Deborah?" he said quietly. "I guess it's not going to work."

Deborah shook her head, saying wearily,

"I don't know what to do, Bing. I've done all —"

Suddenly she broke off, and Bing asked sharply, "What is it? You think of something?"

Deborah said slowly, "Bing, I don't know if it's of God or just an idea of my own, but something just came to me." He listened as she told him, then nodded.

"It's the only shot, Deborah! Let's do it!"

"If we get caught, Bing, we could be executed for being spies."

"Can't hang us but once, can they?" Bing's eyes glowed, and he said, "How'll we work it?"

The two of them talked for half an hour; then he left, saying, "I'll meet you here at three tomorrow." He was not a man of much patience, and the waiting had worn him thin. Now with action in the making, he was excited, his eyes glittering. "If this nutty thing works, maybe I'll want to know a little more about this religion stuff." Then he was gone, and Deborah went to her room. The hard part would be the waiting, but to her surprise, after saying a short prayer, she went to bed and slept like a baby.

"Matron, Jemmy wants to see you."

Jesse Branch found Matron Huger taking

a cup of tea in her office. "Well, send her in, Jesse." Then she looked up with surprise, for Branch came into the office pushing a wheelchair containing Jemmy.

"Why — what's wrong, Jemmy?" she exclaimed, getting to her feet. "Did you have an accident?"

Jemmy had a pair of crutches and several packages over her lap. Her left ankle was heavily bandaged, and disgust was in her tone as she answered, "Slipped on the dratted steps! Can't put no weight on the fool leg."

"You ought to stay in bed for a few days," Matron Huger said.

"Mebbe I will iffen it don't git no better. But I done promised that young feller with both his hands gone I'd bring him some of my plum cake. He's lookin' for'ard to it, so I brung it. Long as I'm here, I might as well set and visit with the pore child."

"That's sweet of you, Jemmy, but how can you get up the stairs?"

"Oh, that's took keer of." Jemmy nodded. "I brung my nephew to haul me around. I brung my crutches, and he kin haul me up them stairs. He a triflin' young buck. Not too bright, but he's stout. The guard, he wouldn't let him in the gate without you give him a permit."

"Well, I think you should stay off that leg, Jemmy. As a matter of fact, that's an order." The matron's face broke into a fond smile. "You can take the cake up, but I insist you stay in bed for a day or two."

"Yes'um, I reckon as how I will." She waited until Matron Huger wrote out a pass and handed it to Branch.

"Take that to the gate, Jesse," Matron said, then added, "It's just a permit for this one night, Jemmy. Now you take care of yourself. We couldn't do without you around here."

"Shore, and thank ye, Matron."

Branch took the pass to the gate and soon returned, saying as Bing took his place behind the wheelchair, "Now hang on to that pass. All the guards change at seven o'clock, and you'll need it to get out of the gates."

"Thanks."

Bing stuck the slip into his pocket, and Jemmy demanded, "Well, what are you waiting for, you big ox? Git me up them stairs!"

"Aw, don't be hollering at me, Auntie," Bing whined. But he wheeled her to the stairs, where a guard asked, "What's wrong, Jemmy?"

"Sprainged my dratted ankle, George," Jemmy said.

"Too bad. Better stay off it for a few days."

Bing pushed the chair through the door, then picked it up and walked up the stairs with no effort. "You're very strong," she said. When they got to the top of the stairs, she cautioned him, "Stay away from Noel. He might give us away if he sees you."

"Sure." He pushed her into the ward, and she got onto the crutches, then swung herself inside as Bing sat down to wait, well out of Noel's view. Most of the men she passed greeted her, asking about her leg, and she spoke to them cheerfully.

Noel got to his feet, concern on his face. She told her story, then said, "I got a plum cake for pore Andy. Come on, let's you and me try to cheer him up."

It was a long visit, and Bing sat alone, his nerves on edge, watching as Deborah moved about the ward speaking to the men. The time ran slowly, and he wished he could pull the sun down by brute force to bring on the night.

Finally the room grew dark, and most of the men started going to bed. A few of those with less serious injuries gathered to a section at one end of the room, where a card game took shape.

For another hour Deborah waited, until it was six thirty. She pushed the chair to where she could catch Bing's eye. He saw her and nodded slightly. She moved then to where Noel was sitting on his cot. He looked up at her with a smile, saying, "You're staying late tonight, Jemmy."

Deborah moved her chair as close as she could, noting that one cot next to Noel was occupied, but it was a young soldier who was in such poor condition that he seldom regained consciousness. The other bunk belonged to one of the men who was playing cards. She put out her hand, and when Noel took it in surprise, she said quietly, "Noel, you're leaving this place."

Noel's head moved sharply, and he leaned forward. "What's that you say, Jemmy?"

"Don't say anything, and don't make any sudden moves. As soon as I leave, I want you to go to the bathroom."

Noel stood absolutely still. His voice low, he asked suddenly, "Who are you?"

For one moment Deborah paused, then said, "It's Deborah, Noel. Now take this package." Deborah took the paper sack she'd kept close beside her, and he took it at once, staring at her with shock in his eyes. "Now go to the bathroom. If no one is there, put those clothes on. If someone is there, wait until they leave. When you come out, I'll be right outside."

"I'll never get down the stairs — or out the gate!"

"Noel, the clothes are like the ones I wear, a dress and a bonnet and a pair of shoes. There's a bandage, too. Put it on your ankle. Now listen. When you come out of the bathroom, take these crutches and go straight to the stairs. There's a man there. You know him, but don't say anything to him." She hesitated, then added, "It's your brother Bing." Noel's head snapped back and he opened his mouth, but Deborah said sharply, "Don't say anything! Pull the bonnet over your eyes and keep your head down. Pretend to be sick. Bing will take you past the guards and out the gate."

"But — what about you?"

"Don't worry about me! Now are you ready?"

"Yes!"

"Do it, then!"

Noel got up and walked to the bathroom, keeping the sack close to his body. He found nobody inside and did as the woman had said. It took only a few seconds, and he stepped outside to find her waiting. She handed him the crutches, whispering, "Now go to Bing!"

Noel awkwardly swung himself down the aisle. One of the men said, "Good night,

Jemmy," and he nodded, saying in a muffled voice, "Good night." Then he was past the beds. When he looked up, he saw Bing standing there with the chair. He leaned the crutches against the wall and fell into the wheelchair.

Bing stepped behind the chair and shoved it through the door. He reversed the chair and began backing down the stairs. When Noel said, "Bing — !" he said in a tense voice, "No time for talk. Keep your head down. You're sick. I'll do all the talkin'!"

They reached the bottom of the stairs. Bing paused, took a deep breath, then opened the door and shoved the chair out. The guard named George looked at them, then said, "Long visit, Jemmy." Then he looked closer. "Something wrong?"

Bing said quickly, "She's poorly. I think this trip was too much for her."

The guard stood there, looking down at the form in the wheelchair. He waited so long that Bing let his hand drop to his waist, where he had a .44 beneath his coat.

"Better get her home," George finally said. "Hope you feel better tomorrow, Jemmy."

"I'll see to her," Bing said quickly and moved down the hall. There was a guard at the outside door, but he only nodded at the two and continued his argument with one of the orderlies. As they moved outside, Bing said, "Good enough. Now the gate."

The guard at the gate was perched on a chair, leaning back against the fence. He got up and took the passes that Bing handed him. It was dark, with only the pale glow of a single lantern, and he peered at them for a long time. Then he stuck one in his pocket, saying, "Have to take yours up, fellow." He looked down, then handed the other pass toward the still form. "Here you go, Jemmy. How's the leg?"

"All right," Noel mumbled.

"How's that?" The guard frowned and leaned down. "You all right?"

"She's had a bad spell," Bing said. "I've got to get her home. She shouldn't have came in the first place!"

The guard still kept his position, bending over the wheelchair. "My wife, she's had some bad spells. Lemme write you a formula for a toddy she makes up."

Bing said, "I don't think —," but the guard insisted. He fumbled in his vest pocket, found a stub of a pencil, then searched for a piece of paper. He finally used the page of a book he kept beside him, writing slowly and giving advice constantly.

Bing's nerves were screaming and he longed to dash away, but he knew he had to wait. The next shift of guards came on at seven, and the whole plan centered on that. "You'll take Noel out in the wheelchair in my place just before seven," Deborah had said. "Then the new guard will come on, and I'll walk out like I always do."

But if the new guard came along and saw what he thought was Jemmy in the wheelchair, he'd know something was wrong when Deborah came out later.

". . . so you mix all this, add a jigger of whiskey, and heat it up," the guard said and, to Bing's relief, handed over the slip of paper.

"That ort to help. Thanks a lot!" Bing nodded and had to restrain himself from going too fast as he passed through the gates. Forcing himself to walk until they were out of the guard's line of vision, he wheeled Noel behind a line of bushes, then jerked to a stop.

"Bing! What's happening?" Noel asked as he got out of the chair. He looked ridiculous in the shapeless dress and floppy bonnet, but he didn't care. He stood there as Bing explained rapidly, and when he was finished, both of them stared down the lane anxiously, waiting for a glimpse of an old woman.

■ ■ ■ ■

As soon as Bing had disappeared through the door with Noel, Deborah walked slowly to Noel's bed and lay down on it, pulling the covers over her head. She had to stay out of sight until seven fifteen, and it was a long wait for her. Once a man came by, paused, and whispered, "Noel? You okay?" She had grunted and he had passed on. Finally she was satisfied that the time was right and lowered the edge of the blanket over her head cautiously. The card game was still going on as she slipped out of the cot. There was no way to conceal herself. If one of the men in the game spotted her, or if one of the men in the cots saw her, the game was up. She walked down the aisle, thankful that the card game was at the far end of the room. The rest of the room was dim, lit only by a single lamp that gave enough light to the orderlies and so the men could find their way to the bathroom.

Once a man snorted and gave a lurch on his cot as Deborah passed, and she stopped dead still, certain she was discovered. But there was no alarm, and she continued. With a sigh of relief, she moved down the stairs, then got the crutches under her arms and struggled down to the main floor. The guard, a private named Lew who knew her well, exclaimed, "Why, Jemmy, I thought you was gone! George told me you left in a wheelchair!"

"I did, Lew, but I come back. Didn't he tell you? Guess he forgot — no, come to think of it, he wuz talking to Leon when I come back. Guess he didn't see me. Good night, Lew."

"Good night, Jemmy."

She passed through the next gate, receiving about the same response, then swung on the crutches to the main gate. "Hello, Pete," she said. "Lemme out, will you? I'm plum tard to death!"

Pete Riley got up and came over to her. "Thought you was sick, Jemmy. They said you left."

"Did, Pete, but had to go back. I forgot my purse. Didn't need that ol' wheelchair noways, 'cept to get up the stairs."

"Yeah? Well, lemme see your pass, Jemmy."

Deborah made a business of looking through the old purse, then said, "Oh, rats! I left the blamed thing upstairs, Pete." She turned painfully and started back, but he stopped her.

"Oh, never mind, Jemmy. I guess you ain't dangerous, are you?"

"Plum dangerous, Pete," she said and cackled as she passed on through the gate.

When he called out, "See you tomorrow, Jemmy," she made no answer. "Pore ol'thing's going batty, I reckon," Pete muttered, then leaned against the fence trying to get comfortable.

Deborah swung down the lane, and when she turned the corner, two shapes rose in the darkness. "Deborah!" She found herself being embraced. Noel grasped her so hard that he hurt his wound, as well as her. "Deborah! I don't believe it!"

Deborah stood there, a warm sensation flooding through her, but Bing said, "You two can do your lovin' later! We ain't out of this thing yet!"

Deborah drew back, nodding. "We'll find someplace to keep out of sight, Bing. We can't be out in the open until dawn. We'll be at the dock at six."

"All right. Remember, it's the *Loretta,* a steam packet. Shouldn't be no one stirring at that hour, so I'll take you to the cabin. We'll be clear of Richmond by seven o'clock. Then for home! Don't be late."

"Bing — !" Noel caught at his brother's thick arm. "Bing . . . well, thanks!"

Bing paused, gave a sheepish grin, then reached out and pulled the bonnet down over Noel's eyes. "You sure look dumb in that outfit, brother," he said. Then he looked straight at Noel. "I hope this kind of makes up for runnin' away?"

"More than makes up for it, Bing!" Noel's eyes were happy and he would have said more, but Bing whirled and ran down the lane. Noel turned to say, "Deborah —"

"What do you think about prayer now?" she interrupted him. She pulled the bonnet from her head, and then the two of them stared at one another. She faltered, remembering how she had tricked him, and she saw that he was remembering it, too.

"Deborah," he said quietly. "I learned a lot out of this."

"Did you, Noel?"

"Yes. I learned to trust God more."

"Anything else?"

He swayed toward her, and she tried to draw back. "I learned that a man's got to let a woman know how he feels. So that's what I'm doing." He pulled her forward and kissed her. She clung to him, and when he released her, he said, "When we get back home, I've got something to talk to you about."

Deborah stared at him, then flushed. "Well, I guess we'd better get away from here. If people see two old ladies kissing

each other, it won't be so good, will it?" But
then as they left the shelter, she paused to
say, "Noel? You said you loved me."

"Yes!"

"Well, I'm expecting a little more courting
than that when there's time!"

CHAPTER 24
ENCOUNTER ON THE *LORETTA*

A carriage rattled down the cobblestone street, stopping at the wharf. The darkness still enveloped the waterfront, and a fine mist threw a corona around the lantern hanging beside the gangplank. Dent got out of the carriage stiffly, walked closer to peer at the side of the ship, then came back to the carriage. "This is the *Loretta*," he said.

Raimey got out, followed by Dulcie. Dent said, "Chester, put the baggage on board; then you can go home."

"Yas, suh, Marse Dent." The slave moved from the seat, and Dent walked to the gangplank with him and Dulcie. A sailor appeared almost mystically, and Dent said, "We've got two cabins reserved under the name of Rocklin." The man gave a jerk of his head, and the two slaves followed him, all three disappearing into the misty dark.

"I still think we should have put this trip off, Dent," Raimey said as they walked up the gangplank. "There's plenty of time before our wedding, and you're not strong enough."

"Listen, woman, I may not be as bright as you are, but I never turn down anything free. If your father wants to throw his money away on all kinds of fancy dresses for our wedding, that's his business. It's mine to take what he offers. Besides," he added as they stepped on deck, "it'll give us some time alone. Sort of a prehoneymoon honeymoon."

She smiled at that. *As much of a prehoneymoon as it can be with Dulcie at our side, anyway.*

Mr. Reed, Raimey's father, had insisted on sending them to Williamsburg to the best dressmaker in the South. Dent had not argued, for he wanted the time away from the family with Raimey. Mrs. Reed had wanted the two of them to get their photographs made there, as well, so he had gotten up and dressed in full uniform, including pistol and saber.

"I feel foolish in this rig," he said as the two of them stood leaning on the rail. He was still wearing a sling, but his arm was mending and the doctors were confident that he'd have full use of it — with perhaps some rheumatism when he grew older, just as a reminder.

They stood there, Dent's arm around Raimey's waist, talking quietly. He had never found anyone he could talk to as he could to this woman who had appeared so suddenly in his life. She knew him better than he knew himself, and her handicap had come to mean very little to him. Dulcie was like Raimey's eyes, and she would stay with her always.

As for Raimey, her heart was full. She had fully expected that she would never marry — and now she had a man who fit her like a glove. She loved him freely, openly, without limits, and she knew that time would only increase what she felt for him.

Dent was speaking about the plans for their stay in Williamsburg when he broke off suddenly. "What is it?" Raimey asked quickly, always sensitive to his mood.

"Somebody coming down the quay," he said. He studied the two figures who were moving slowly toward the *Loretta* and said, "Two people, but they're acting very strange. Something's wrong with them." He watched as they approached; then when they turned to climb the gangplank, he said, "Doesn't look right, Raimey. Stand back against the bulkhead. I think I'd better challenge them."

He waited until Raimey was back, then pulled his Colt free as the pair stepped on deck. He saw that one was a man, who was apparently sick, for the woman with him was holding him as though to support him. When Dent spoke, they both froze. "Hold it!" Dent said sharply. He half expected one of them to pull a gun, so careful had been their approach. "Who are you? Why are you sneaking onto this boat?"

The woman said quickly, "We have a cabin reserved."

As she spoke, Dent blinked, for she had stepped into the feeble yellow light of the lantern. "Deborah!" he said incredulously. "What are you doing here?"

Deborah and Noel had started walking much earlier, but it had proved too much for Noel. He had begun to lag, and by the time they reached the ship, he was able to do no more than stumble along with Deborah's help. Now he saw Dent standing before him, gun aimed, and he gasped, "Don't shoot! I'll go back, but let her go!"

It all was clear then, both to Dent and to Raimey. They had heard of Noel's escape, and the alarm was out to watch for a Federal soldier and an old woman. Dent looked at Deborah, and some of the old bitterness welled up in him. Deborah saw it rise in his eyes but could say nothing. She stood there, knowing that Dent had been a possessive man and was now seeing her as a woman who had been taken from him. And the man who had done the taking was in his power.

Raimey came forward and touched Dent's arm. She had known of Dent's obsession with this girl and had even been jealous of it for a time. Now she said quietly, "Dent, what are you going to do?"

Dent stood there uncertainly. He had been haunted for so long by thoughts of Deborah Steele, and now here she stood, looking as lovely as ever. Even in the pale yellow light of the lantern, her face was beautiful.

All you have to do is turn them in.

The thought pushed at his mind, and he stood there almost ready to call for the officers of the ship.

He stood there weighing the options in his mind — and suddenly he realized that to turn them in would be to become the man he had once been! There was still something of the old Dent Rocklin in him, something that he thought had been erased, buried forever when he became a Christian. Now Dent realized that the battle for a man's soul didn't end with becoming a Christian — rather, that was when it began in earnest. If he were to give in to this base impulse to get some sort of petty revenge on Deborah because she had rejected him, he would be taking the first step back to being the man he was before God had done such wonderful miracles in his life.

Deborah was watching him, waiting for his decision — as was the soldier. Dent felt Raimey's presence, too, even more strongly than he felt the presence of the two who stood before him. He waited for his impulse to weaken, to fade — and was appalled at how it only grew fiercer! But that very fact was his salvation, for he suddenly understood that it was not Deborah and Noel who were on trial. . . . No, *he* was the one being tested!

And he knew then the power of darkness and how it could destroy a man.

He looked at Deborah and saw the honesty on her face . . . and knew he couldn't do it. He lowered the Colt, holstered it, then said quietly, "You'd better get to your cabin. The whole city's looking for you."

At that moment steps sounded on the stones, and Bing came stumbling up the gangplank. He halted abruptly at the sight of a Confederate officer blocking the way. His face went tight and he reached under his coat, but he stopped when Deborah said, "Bing! It's all right. Let's get to the cabin."

Dent stepped back, and as Deborah passed she gave him a beautiful smile, saying, "Thank you, Lieutenant." Then the three of them disappeared into the corridor.

Raimey pulled at Dent's arm, and he turned to her. "Dent, I'm so proud of you!" She reached up and pulled his head down. Her lips were soft and gentle, yet strangely possessive. When she pulled away, she said, "Now you're really all mine, Dent. Until this moment, part of you belonged to Deborah. But no more, isn't that right?"

"No more," he whispered, and they stood there watching the sun peep over the eastern rim.

"What's going to happen to them, I wonder?" Dent mused.

"They'll be fine," Raimey said. "They're like us, Dent. They love each other, and when two people love each other, not even a war can take that away."

He held her close and said quietly, "I almost missed you, Raimey, but now I'll never let you go."

The boilers under their feet began to hiss, and the ship gave a slight shudder. An hour later the *Loretta* cleared Richmond, and as it moved down the river, there were those aboard who knew that life was good. The sun was up, bathing the ship in golden rays, and the white wake of the *Loretta* threw off golden flakes as the vessel moved toward the sea.

ABOUT THE AUTHOR

Award-winning, bestselling author, **Gilbert Morris** is well known for penning numerous Christian novels for adults and children since 1984 with 6.5 million books in print. He is probably best known for the forty-book House of Winslow series, and his *Edge of Honor* was a 2001 Christy Award winner. He lives with his wife in Gulf Shores, Alabama.